One Bright Christmas

Thomas Kinkade's Cape Light

One Bright
Christmas

KATHERINE SPENCER

BERKLEY
NEW YORK

BERKLEY
An imprint of Penguin Random House LLC
penguinrandomhouse.com

Copyright © 2020 by The Thomas Kinkade Estate and Parachute Publishing, LLC
Penguin Random House supports copyright. Copyright fuels creativity, encourages diverse
voices, promotes free speech, and creates a vibrant culture. Thank you for buying an authorized
edition of this book and for complying with copyright laws by not reproducing, scanning, or
distributing any part of it in any form without permission. You are supporting writers and
allowing Penguin Random House to continue to publish books for every reader.

BERKLEY and the BERKLEY & B colophon are registered trademarks of
Penguin Random House LLC.

Library of Congress Cataloging-in-Publication Data

Names: Spencer, Katherine, 1955– author.
Title: One bright Christmas / Katherine Spencer.
Description: First edition. | New York: Berkley, 2020. | Series: Thomas Kinkade's Cape Light
Identifiers: LCCN 2020011979 (print) | LCCN 2020011980 (ebook) |
ISBN 9780593198919 (hardcover) | ISBN 9780593198926 (ebook)
Subjects: LCSH: Cape Light (Imaginary place)—Fiction. | Christmas stories. |
GSAFD: Christian fiction. | Love stories.
Classification: LCC PS3553.A489115 O53 2020 (print) |
LCC PS3553.A489115 (ebook) | DDC 813/.54—dc23
LC record available at https://lccn.loc.gov/2020011979
LC ebook record available at https://lccn.loc.gov/2020011980

Printed in the United States of America
1   3   5   7   9   10   8   6   4   2

Cover art: **Victorian Family Christmas** © 2010 Thomas Kinkade Studios
Cover series design by Lesley Worrell

To my dear family and all the families that
have been touched this year by uncertainty and loss.
May we cherish and grow the love that remains,
which makes life truly worth living.

DEAR READER

As most of you know, a book is written far in advance of that happy day when the shiny, colorful cover appears on a bookstore shelf. As I write this note, we're in the midst of a crisis that has taken the entire world by surprise, and at this point, taken more than 375,000 precious lives. Sadly, by the time you read this note, that number will be even greater.

There's no doubt that we will all be touched in some way by the COVID-19 crisis and its aftermath. My own family and many close to me have already lost loved ones and look toward a financial future, once stable and sure, now clouded by uncertainty.

As I send this manuscript off to be printed, this story, intended to entertain, comfort, and inspire, seems as insignificant as a single teardrop falling on a firestorm of confusion and pain. But, as a friend pointed out, "When so much is uncertain and even torn away, much is possible."

We are now tasked to take a deep breath and give thanks for what remains. Especially the well-being and safety of those we hold dear. And tasked to look beyond the rubble and imagine how we can repair and restore, or build something entirely new. With patience, courage, and faith. As we warily move forward, we can find comfort and reassurance in the simple blessings, untouched by change and still easily discovered when our hearts are open.

In *One Bright Christmas*, three characters are surprised by challenges that upend their plans and expectations. Their difficulties are hardly as sweeping and complex as those we presently face. But I hope these stories offer ideas that are encouraging and even useful in your own life.

Lucy Bates has carried a secret in her heart for more than thirty years, the pain of a wrong that she vows will never be forgotten, or forgiven. As Christmas approaches, she struggles to find mercy in her heart and discovers that the gift of forgiveness is, most of all, a gift to herself.

After her high-powered career and romance crash and burn, Lauren Willoughby returns home from New York City to fit the pieces of her shattered life back together. Determined to batter down the door that's been slammed in her face, Lauren can neither see nor appreciate the window God has opened for her—one that frames the view of an even richer and more satisfying future.

Then there's Lillian Warwick, who must learn to bend and even toss aside long-held standards and directives for the sake of her beloved husband, Ezra.

As I write this note, the holiday season is six months away. Who can say what the world will look like by then? But if you have this book in hand, I hope that you return from your visit to Cape Light feeling refreshed and renewed, and just a bit more hopeful about your own future.

In the words of Reverend Ben, "May this Christmas mark a fresh start for all of humanity, leading us in a new and better direction."

With gratitude and love—

Katherine Spencer

CHAPTER ONE

*I*T WON'T BE LONG, TUCKER. THIS TOWN IS HEADED FOR THE big time," Charlie said. Lucy watched her husband toss a copy of the *Cape Light Messenger* onto the diner's counter. It landed right next to the plate of his favorite customer.

Officer Tucker Tulley sat on his usual stool, a fork in hand aimed at a plate of eggs over easy, bacon, and rye toast. He paused to scan the front page. "Oh, that movie business. Is that what got you wound up this morning?"

"I'll say I'm wound up. This village is going to be famous. And the diner, too, if I have anything to do about it."

Tucker managed a bite before he answered. "So you say, Charlie. Some folks don't agree. They don't want a film crew taking over the place. There's bound to be inconvenience, not to mention gawking fans rushing in for miles around. In the middle of Christmastime."

Tucker had patrolled the streets of Cape Light for nearly forty years. He spoke little but listened a lot. He knew, probably better than anyone, how his fellow citizens felt about important matters. He had an even keener sense of popular opinion than Charlie, who'd been

1

mayor for the past four years. Charlie sometimes thought of Tucker as his automatic polling center.

The debate had begun months ago, when the film production company scouted the area as a possible location. When the group contacted village hall, Charlie persuaded the village board of trustees to grant the permits and permissions over many objections. He was sure the visit would benefit the town.

Lucy sided with Tucker, but not because of parking problems or an invasion of onlookers. She had her own reasons—private reasons she would never admit to anyone. Certainly not to her husband and his pal. She didn't offer her opinion on the question and had no wish to take part in the debate. With any luck, she would be out of the diner and on the way to her first patient appointment in a minute or two.

She had only stopped by to pick up a binder she needed for work. She was practically positive that she'd left it at the diner on Saturday, when she had squeezed in a waitressing shift around the schedule of her real job as a visiting nurse. She did not miss her former career at the diner one bit, but she sometimes returned when Charlie was shorthanded.

She recalled flipping through the schedules and forms, in between orders, and was pretty sure it had ended up somewhere behind the counter. Keeping her head down—literally and figuratively—Lucy searched the low shelves below the countertop where glasses and dishes were stored. Flying under the radar made it easy to avoid the conversation between Charlie and Tucker.

Charlie took the newspaper back, his expression delighted as he read aloud, "'Lights, camera, action! Hollywood is coming to Cape Light!'

"People always say they don't want this sort of thing," he told Tucker. "But when it happens, they love it."

Tucker slapped a butter pat on a slice of toast and took a bite. "What do you think, Lucy?"

Lucy had just spotted her quarry under a pile of menus and grabbed it. She popped up from behind the counter like a meerkat. "Isn't this weather crazy?" she said, deliberately changing the subject. "I'm glad I grabbed my light jacket. I heard it might hit fifty this afternoon."

New Englanders never tired of talking about the weather, and Lucy thought the ploy worth a try. Especially with Tucker, who was outdoors walking his beat most of the day.

"It's that global warming." Tucker chewed with a thoughtful expression. "Skipped the thermals this morning—good thing."

Charlie looked baffled, then annoyed. "Do we really need to talk about your underwear issues, Tucker? With all this excitement going on?"

He glanced at his wife and waved his hand. "Lucy isn't interested in the movie crew coming. She's told me a few times. Right, honey?" He turned back to Tucker before Lucy could answer. "That's fine. Everyone's entitled to their opinion. But it doesn't change the facts. This movie will put our little village on the map. Right up there with those posh zip codes on Cape Cod and the Vineyard."

"We're already on the map, Charlie. A big red dot, right between Essex and Newburyport." Another voice joined the debate. Lucy turned to see Tucker's wife—and her best friend—Fran, stroll up to the counter.

"Hey, you." Fran greeted her with a familiar smile. "I thought you had an early patient today?"

"I just swung by to pick something up." Lucy waved her prize. "Maybe we can catch up tonight. I'll call you."

Fran looked confused by Lucy's rush. "Sure. I'll be home."

Lucy could tell Fran's radar was up, and she knew why, too. Their friendship went back to high school—though not quite as far back as Charlie and Tucker's, who had bonded over building blocks on the first day of kindergarten, so the story went. With Tucker doing the heavy lifting and Charlie directing, Lucy had no doubt.

She and Fran had a different sort of friendship. Fran knew her and loved her, just as she was, and Lucy felt the same about Fran.

"We were talking about the movie crew that's coming soon," Charlie said, sliding the newspaper toward Fran.

"Charlie can hardly wait," Tucker added.

Fran's eyes grew wide and she nodded. "Neither can I. Especially for the celebrity spotting. Craig Hamilton, for instance?" She caught Lucy's gaze as she was trying to maneuver her way past Charlie.

Charlie had fixed Fran her usual coffee-to-go without being asked. He tapped the lid on the cup and set it in front of her.

"Hamilton is a little past the heartthrob stage, don't you think?" Tucker said. "I hear he's playing a father role."

Fran laughed. "You forget, Tucker—his fans have gotten older, too. I think he looks better than ever." She gazed at the photo in the paper and then at Lucy again. But she didn't ask her opinion. *Thank goodness*, Lucy thought.

Tucker studied the photo. "Those can't be his real teeth. And you know that's a toupee, or a weave?"

Charlie waved a hand, dismissing the critique. "Fake teeth, bald as an egg, doesn't matter. He's a hometown hero. That counts for a lot."

Tucker was still not convinced. "Not exactly *our* hometown. He grew up in Newburyport."

"Close enough," Charlie insisted. "The article says he got his start right here in the Cape Light Community Theater." Charlie peered down at the newspaper again. "He had the lead in *Oklahoma!*—right before he left to make his mark."

Tucker squinted. "Must have missed that one. I don't remember our little theater doing *Oklahoma!*"

Lucy did, all too clearly. Way back when she aspired to be an actress. A silly, immature ambition, a fever that had taken over for a short time, like a twenty-four-hour bug—but one that had burned brightly. She had joined the amateur theater group after high school and taken part in a few shows, including a role in the chorus of *Oklahoma!* Farm Girl Number Three?

She had been one among many in the cast and on the stage. Craig Hamilton was the romantic lead, and even at that phase of his career, whenever he stepped into the spotlight, his presence was electric and commanding. Everyone said he could make it in Hollywood. And so he had.

"It must have been over thirty years ago," Charlie replied. "Who cares? The point is, we can definitely claim him as a favorite son. Let's tack this page on the bulletin board. I'll ask him to autograph it when he comes in."

"Assuming he does come in," Tucker added.

Charlie didn't seem to hear him. He turned to Lucy, who felt trapped. No matter which direction she moved, Charlie blocked her path from behind the counter.

"Hey, hon. Mind taking care of that? I got my hands full here."

Lucy nearly laughed. So far, he'd only served one order, and that was to Tucker. Trudy, the regular waitress, had been handling all the rest.

"I have to get to work, Charlie. If you could get out of the way and let me pass?"

Charlie's brow furrowed, surprised by her reaction. Lucy was always so easygoing and rarely objected to any request. "Sure, sure. Let me squeeze by before you run me over." He scuttled to the far end of the counter and headed for the big swinging doors that opened to the kitchen.

Lucy grabbed her cup of take-out coffee, the binder tucked under her arm, and headed for the door. Fran had also picked up her coffee, and now she swiped a slice of Tucker's toast. She hurried after Lucy. "Wait up, Lu. I'll walk you out."

Lucy glanced over her shoulder as Fran followed. She held open the door, and they stepped out onto Main Street. Lucy knew Fran wanted to talk—and what she wanted to talk about. But she wasn't in the mood, and she wasn't ready for this conversation.

Luckily, her car was parked in the opposite direction from Fran's office at Bowman Realty.

"My car's just up the street, near Pet Port. You have a good day. I'll call you later," she promised.

Fran shook her head. "You're not getting away that easily. Not from me, my dear. Charlie and Tucker might be oblivious. But I know you, Lucy. I know what's up."

"Nothing is up." Lucy shrugged. "I wish you'd believe me."

"Is that why you jumped out of your skin when I mentioned his name? Don't you want to get some closure, finally? Don't you want to talk to him? Just once?"

"Talk to him? That's the last thing I want to do. I don't even watch his movies. You know that."

Fran shook her head, her gaze full of understanding, even sympathy, though Lucy could tell she was still not convinced.

"I've said this before, but I'll say it again: The odds of Craig Hamilton returning to Cape Light must be one in ten million. Maybe even higher. But it's happening. You need to face it, Lucy. You need to reconnect and talk things out. You'll regret it forever if you don't."

Lucy bit her lip to hold back a sharp reply that had sprung up from somewhere deep inside, some painful place that had never quite healed. She wasn't mad at Fran. Her dear friend had good intentions. Lucy just didn't agree, and Fran couldn't seem to understand why.

"I know you mean well, and I love you for it. You're the only person in the entire world who knows the whole story. And you helped me so much when it happened. I'll always be grateful for that," she said sincerely. "But I'm over it, and I have no intention of going back there. No way, no how." Lucy paused and looked into her friend's dark eyes. "I hope we can drop it now once and for all. I don't want to talk about this again."

Fran's eyes flickered with disbelief. "All right. I'll leave it for today. Let's see how you feel once you see him face-to-face. If you're really as unfazed as you claim, not another word. I promise."

"You drive a hard bargain, lady." Lucy had to smile. "A good thing in the real estate business, I bet." *Though sometimes a sticky point in our friendship*, she didn't add. "If that's what it takes to convince you, all I can say is 'You'll see.' Now give me a hug, old thing. I'm sorry I got cross."

The women hugged and said goodbye. Lucy quickly walked the rest of the way to her car and headed to her first patient of the day. Rosemary Holmes, a seventy-year-old retired teacher, who was recovering from hip surgery. She lived alone on Ivy Street, a short distance from the heart of the village. Lucy had been visiting her every day since she had come home from the hospital last week.

Rosemary was an easy client who required little more than a check of her vital signs and blood sugar, plus a bandage change. But Lucy always spent time with her to provide a bit of companionship.

Strictly speaking, she wasn't required or even supposed to do that. She had a schedule to keep and other patients waiting. But a big reason she had switched from working in a hospital to working for a visiting nurse service was the one-on-one relationships with the patients. It was the facet of her profession she enjoyed most, and she truly believed her concern and attention contributed as much to the patients' healing as any of their medications.

Maybe she spent too much time with her patients. But many, like Rosemary, lived alone and had only a thin safety net of social connections. Lucy couldn't stop herself from trying to cheer them up a bit and to reassure them someone was thinking of them and cared about their recovery.

She knew many of her colleagues kept a tight lid on that side of nursing. Some boasted they flew through five, six, or even eight patient visits a day, all in time to pick up their children after school. Lucy knew she would never work that way. She was often in the field until after seven and then worked at home, completing reports for each case. She had never been a clock watcher, which had been a good thing while working at the diner as a waitress for all those years. It was a good thing now, too.

Lucy valued the years she'd spent at Southport Hospital and had gained a deep knowledge of nursing there, working mainly on the general surgery floor. But last summer she decided to switch tracks and move out into the field. She still did the occasional shift at the hospital if they were short on staff, but she was glad she had made the change. Working one-on-one with a patient in their own home was much more personal and rewarding than hospital nursing, which was so often a hurried business, with her patients coming and going in the blink of an eye.

She loved to take care of people and to help make them healthy.

It was the reason she had been drawn to nursing in the first place. How many years had she fantasized about becoming a nurse? From the time she was a little girl, playing with her dolls and stuffed animals. When she got older, there had been that brief detour into acting. But her first dream, her real calling, had never faded, though she'd dismissed it as too far out of reach—the years of school and training. The expense of it all. One summer, already well into her thirties, married with two little boys and only two years of college to her credit, Lucy had been encouraged by a younger waitress to go for her dream. If she didn't make it, at least she would have tried.

Silencing the voice of self-doubt inside had been a challenge. But the biggest hurdle had been Charlie's objections. He had some very practical reasons. They were already saving for their boys to go to college. Could they really afford to send Lucy, too? *And* lose her help at the diner? And what about childcare?

Lucy had to admit that it had all seemed a lot to ask. But still, she persisted, and finally, Charlie came to understand what it meant to her and agreed they would try to make it work. She loved him for that and for how, after making that commitment, he'd stepped up around the house and helped take care of the boys and rarely complained.

It hadn't been easy. Far from it. In the end, though, getting her nursing degree had turned out to be not just the hardest won but the most rewarding achievement of her life, aside from raising her children, Charlie Junior—C.J. for short—and Jamie and Zoey, whom she adored. Her husband had been bursting with pride when she'd graduated. Lucy felt the achievement was partly Charlie's, too. That's what it meant to be married. They shared in both the challenges and the triumphs and grew ever closer because of it.

As Lucy considered her patient roster and the day ahead, she knew that all the homes she visited took the *Cape Light Messenger*. Many if not most of her patients would talk about the movie crew coming to town. Some would even mention Craig Hamilton. He was the most famous star in the cast, and he was a local boy of sorts.

Lucy readied herself to listen and nod, to offer a smile and the most banal comments on the subject. The movie people would come and go, and no one would ever know what it meant to her. Not Charlie . . . Not even Fran. Who could ever guess how she truly felt about seeing Craig Hamilton again? Despite what she'd told her friend, Lucy knew that even she herself was not sure.

LAUREN WILLOUGHBY RELAXED HER SHOULDERS AND TOOK A SLOW, deep breath. She stared down at the golf ball and blocked everything else from her mind. Or at least tried to.

Joe Wagner stood a polite distance away, perfectly in keeping with golf etiquette. But she could still feel his gaze following her every move as she swung her hips to the right and pulled the club back over her head.

It was a bit unnerving, but as the club swung forward smoothly and struck the ball, she knew in her bones it was a sweet shot—a long drive straight down the middle of the fairway, easily clearing the sand trap and dropping a few yards from the green, an easy chip up toward the hole.

"Excellent shot, Lauren. Are you going to birdie this one, too? You're leaving me in the dust."

Lauren smiled at his good-natured compliments. "It's not over till it's over, Joe. Give yourself a chance."

She nearly added, *It was just a lucky swing*, or some other polite excuse to discount her skill. A female thing to do, especially when competing with a man. But a good shot was a good shot, and it was not only polite but honest of another player to acknowledge that. She was sure he would have said as much if he were playing with a man, and the man in question would not have apologized just to make Joe feel good. So she wouldn't either.

Lauren couldn't recall the last time she had been on a golf course. But her old clubs were still in her mom's garage, and she'd found a pair of golf shoes there, too. She had still hesitated to accept Joe's invitation, fearing she wouldn't play well. But after a hole or two, it had all come back, like riding a bike. It felt good to know she hadn't lost her touch.

Joe belonged to the club more for business and social reasons than for golf, he'd explained. He enjoyed the game, but as he struggled with his form and focus, his equipment and outfit fresh from a sports store, it was obvious he was still a newbie.

She actually liked the way he didn't take the game so seriously, unlike most players she knew, who often seemed tempted to throw their clubs—or themselves—into the water hazards after bad shots.

Joe hacked away, happy to trade his stuffy office for the fresh air and lush, peaceful surroundings. They had picked the right day for it, too. The weather was perfect, more like early spring than mid-November.

As Joe stepped up to address the ball on the fifth tee, she could see he wasn't shifting his weight correctly. The ball would hook to the right or left and land in the trees. Then he'd stare at it, totally baffled. But he hadn't asked for help, and she knew it wasn't her place to correct him.

She watched the club draw back, then arc forward. His timing was fine, and the head hit the ball with a loud *thwack!*

It flew a good distance down the fairway but finally veered into the wooded fringe, as she had expected. Luckily, it struck the trunk of a thick birch and settled in the high grass that bordered the fairway, about two-thirds of the distance to the pin.

He laughed at his good fortune. "I couldn't have hit that tree if I'd been trying. At least I won't be tramping through the woods for an hour looking for the ball." He stopped and glanced at her. "Or should we call that interference? It must be against the rules, right? We're not shooting pool."

Lauren smiled and shook her head. "You're in luck. Bouncing it off a tree is perfectly fine."

Lauren was hardly a rule freak, though having played competitive golf in high school and college, she certainly knew the book backward and forward.

"Play it as it lays," she said, hoping to strike an encouraging note. He answered with a thumbs-up but still had a hard time chipping out of the thick grass and then maneuvering the ball all the way to the putting green. They finished the hole with Lauren scoring one under par and Joe three over.

He marked his scorecard and tucked it in his pocket. Lauren avoided his gaze, wondering if his ego felt more battered right now than the golf ball. Most men hated it when a "girl" won.

But when he looked up, he offered a genuinely cheerful smile. "Onward. Ladies first." He extended his hand with a gallant flourish; the gesture made her laugh.

Lauren grabbed her golf carrier and tugged it up the path as Joe followed close behind. "I thought you said you haven't played for years," he reminded her.

"I haven't. I actually can't remember the last time I set foot on a course. A few summers ago, maybe? On a visit up here."

"I should have known I wouldn't beat the team captain. Undefeated in our senior year," he recalled.

"Nice of you to remember." Lauren glanced at him over her shoulder and smiled. "The basketball team was pretty good that year, too," she said, returning the compliment.

"We were. And I was captain of the benchwarmers. I must have clocked a whole . . . three minutes on the court that season?"

Lauren had to laugh. Joe's self-deprecating humor had always put her at ease when they were teenagers. She still found it charming.

"You were a good sport for getting out there. You had plenty of other accomplishments. Class president? Yearbook editor? Captain of the debate team?"

"The debate team—how could I forget? A hint of triumphs to come," he joked. "Though the cases we handle rarely get to court. It's a lot of negotiating—offers and counteroffers. A lot of letter writing and meetings. And I'm mostly managing the other attorneys."

Joe's firm was tiny, with only three other lawyers on board, compared to the huge firm in New York where Lauren had been working, which had over a hundred on the payroll. But in the local area, Wagner & Associates had a solid profile and was still growing.

"Do you miss the hands-on stuff?" she asked. They were almost at the tee for the seventh hole but had to wait for a foursome ahead to finish on the putting green.

"I do, a bit. Maybe I'll jump back in soon, with Caitlin out on maternity leave. Sorry to seem like I'm nagging you, Lauren. But have you thought any more about helping out while you're visiting?"

"Seventh hole. Not bad, Joe. I expected that question by five, or even four."

He laughed. Her blunt manner—which put a lot of people off—always amused him. "I was too busy fretting over my hook—and facing the fact that you're beating the stuffing out of me."

Now it was Lauren's turn to laugh. She knew a large part of this invitation was Joe's hope to persuade her to work at his firm as a hired hand while one of his key attorneys was on maternity leave. Lauren had come home a couple of weeks ago, in early November. "Just for a visit over the holidays," she told anyone who asked. "I'm starting a new job soon."

Which was actually a massive exaggeration, since it would be a new job she hadn't found yet. She had been more or less shamed out of her last position after working her heart out at a big, prestigious law firm for years in the hopes of being promoted to partner someday. All of her reviews had been stellar—until the most recent, when she'd been told she was no longer on that track.

There was no recourse but to resign, and without ever really knowing why or where she'd made a misstep. Had she left a poor impression on a client or some higher-up? Did she not seem sharp enough or tough enough? Or had one of her peers seeded doubt with the senior partners who decided these things?

Lauren blamed no one. She knew the game was cruel and the competition played rough. She had known the rules going in. No one had forced her to pursue corporate law. The competitive spirit was in her blood. She wanted to play at the highest level. She had believed with her whole heart that she would measure up, that she'd rise to the top of the pile and make the cut. She had won before at every game she had ever pursued. If not at the first try, then eventually. She would go to some other firm and try again. She was only twenty-nine. Most people didn't make partner until well into their thirties, or even older. The inning had ended, but there was plenty of ball game left for her.

Persistence was in her nature. On those rare but eye-opening moments when she fell short of a goal, she would brush herself off and tackle it again, twice as hard and twice as determined. This time, though, she'd walked off the field stunned and brokenhearted. Just thinking of the last few weeks of her life in New York still stole Lauren's breath away.

"So I guess that means that you've been thinking about my offer? You might have an answer soon?" Joe artfully circled back to his objective—pinning down a reply—as a skilled attorney should.

"Yes, counselor. I will admit to thinking it over."

"I'll take that as a good sign." He looked encouraged. "We don't have to talk about it here. That's not why I asked you to play today, Lauren. Not the only reason."

His dark eyes caught hers, and Lauren realized that his looks had improved over the years. Tall and gawky in high school, he'd filled out just the right amount, the rough edges smoothed over by time and maturity, and by fine clothes that fit his position as a young, successful attorney. She knew that most women would find him very attractive. But to her, he was still just her old pal Joe.

Ever since they had met up in the village soon after she arrived and Joe had found out she wasn't dating anyone, Lauren had sensed he wanted her to think of him differently—as a romantic possibility. It was certainly flattering that he still felt that way after all this time.

She also worried about the invitation to play golf and even about the employment offer. Not worried, exactly. More like wondering what she was getting into by rekindling their old friendship, which went all the way back to middle school. Back then, she had always known that Joe Wagner had a crush on her but was happy to settle for friendship.

He'd been a good friend, too, all through high school, dragging her through trig and physics. He had even asked her to the senior prom, making sure she knew that he knew she only thought of him as a friend. With the ground rules clearly marked and no one else vying for her hand, Lauren had accepted his invitation. She didn't have romantic feelings for Joe, but their relationship meant a lot to her, and going to prom together "as friends" seemed a fitting way to close their shared chapter before heading off on their new paths.

But the moment she appeared in her living room in her long dress and fancy hairstyle, she wondered if it had been a good idea after all. Dressed in a black tux, his hair smoothed back, he looked awestruck as he watched her walk down the stairs, his hands shaking as he offered a flowery wristband.

Lauren knew it was more than her glamorous transformation. As they posed for photos and then walked to Joe's car, she felt the night was doomed to end in disaster.

And she had been right. The evening went downhill from there, ending with a confession of adoration that made Lauren cringe and run. Recalling the memory as an adult touched her heart. More recently, it reminded her that at least at one moment in her life, there had been a guy who truly did adore her and had offered his heart and soul.

Joe never referred to that night. Either he'd buried it in his subconscious or he was still so embarrassed that he preferred to pretend it never happened.

He only talked about their friendship, then and now. But she wondered what he was really thinking. She would be leaving town in January; she had made that clear. Perhaps there was no reason at all for her to be concerned about their personal relationship wandering out of the friendship lane, or even about working for him for a few weeks.

The foursome in front of them had finished on the putting green and replaced the flag in the hole. One of the men in the group waved, signaling the coast was clear. Joe stood with his gaze fixed on her, waiting for an answer.

"I'm thinking about it, Joe. I really am. But I won't be here past Christmas. Maybe you should find someone with a longer shelf life."

"I choose quality over quantity every time. New York experience counts for a lot around here, Lauren. You could write your own ticket to any firm on the North Shore, or even in Boston. But here you can have it all—a good career *and* a life. Are you really sure you need to go back to New York?"

Lauren knew what he said was true. But she had her own compelling reasons to stick with her plan. "I've been thrown off a New York horse, Joe. I have to get back on that one. Not a pony in Boston, or even a donkey in . . . Peabody."

"A pony and a donkey, huh? What does that make my firm—a Chihuahua?"

Lauren felt her cheeks flush. *Good work. The guy goes out of his way to make you feel valuable, and even offers you a job, and you insult him.* The problem was genetic; her mind worked faster than her mouth. Her mother was the same way. But Lauren also knew she had to try harder to control it.

Suddenly he laughed and shook his head. "Lauren Willoughby cuts to the chase. No soft soap, no sugarcoating. That's your *brand.*" He pulled a three wood from his bag and pointed it at her. "That's why I want you to work for me."

Without waiting for her reply, he stepped up to the tee and prepared to take a shot.

Lauren felt relieved. Not everyone saw her blunt style as an asset. Her former boyfriend, Greg, had found it amusing at first, then irritating. Each time her inner filter slipped, he quietly simmered, and she felt punished by his disapproval and the tension between them.

It was hard if not impossible to keep a muzzle on her mouth and a lid on her authentic personality. It was bound to pop out from time to time, like a jack-in-the-box. At least now she didn't have to torture herself. What if she and Greg had gotten married, as she had expected they would after dating for so long? *Then where would I be? Wearing a gag to keep the peace, most likely.*

It helped to remember that, though it was cold comfort compared to the future she'd imagined—including the engagement ring she had felt sure would be on her finger by Christmas morning.

Lauren pushed the thoughts aside. No sense spoiling such a beautiful afternoon outdoors. That was the beauty of a golf course. The setting was a distant, perfect world, and the game required complete focus, if you played it right.

She was eager to tee off, but Joe was fidgeting endlessly as he addressed the ball. Which didn't improve his shot any, she'd noticed. He gazed out at the pin, then down at the ball, shifting and wiggling, drawing the club back in practice swings but never quite committing.

Just when it seemed he would finally take his swing, the oddest sound cut through the silence.

Joe straightened up and lowered his club. "What was that?"

He looked around, and so did Lauren. He was about to speak, but she pressed a finger to her lips.

They heard it again. At first, she thought it was a person hidden in the woods, groaning in pain. Then she realized it wasn't a human sound. She and her sisters had spent many a summer at 4-H camp. She knew a *moo* when she heard one.

"Is there a farm around here? That's definitely a cow."

CHAPTER TWO

*J*OE GAVE HER A LOOK. "HOW COULD THAT BE A COW ON THE golf course? There isn't a farm for miles."

She smiled and pointed. On the far side of the fairway, a large brown-and-white cow daintily stepped out of the woods. It sniffed the air, then headed to the fairway, where, head bent, it began to munch the bright green sod.

"I bet that tastes good. Like prime sirloin. If you're a cow, I mean," Lauren said.

"It costs about as much, too." Joe was clearly upset.

"She prefers the best. Totally bypassed the rough," Lauren observed. "And she's brought a few friends."

They watched in stunned silence as a shaggy gray horse emerged next. Lauren could easily see, even at a distance, that it was on in years. It walked with a limp and had a swayback. The horse was followed by a brown-and-white donkey. *A pirate donkey,* Lauren thought, noticing an eye patch and a battered ear.

After the donkey, two large lop-eared rabbits and several ducks of various sizes leaped and waddled past the larger animals. The ducks dove straight into the water hazard, where they happily quacked and flapped their wings.

Just when Lauren thought the animal parade was over, a large sow trotted out from the brush, as if in a hurry to catch up to the fun. Her big body moved with surprising grace and speed on her small black hooves. She stood at the edge of the rough and sniffed the air, then scuttled up a little hill and onto the putting green, where she grunted and sighed. She rooted the velvety sod with her snout, then chewed a great chunk of it with satisfaction.

"Get off. Get off of there! Scoot! Scram!" Joe ran toward the animals, waving his club. Lauren knew he would never in a million years strike any of them. He was just trying to scare them away.

The ducks took no notice. They swam in small circles and quacked in reply. The horse and donkey did pause grazing for a moment to watch him approach. Then, deciding he was no threat, they returned to their late-afternoon snack.

Joe walked up to the donkey, taking a gentler approach. "You go home now, fella. Go along. Go back to wherever you came from." Joe grabbed the donkey's halter and tried to turn him.

The donkey stared back, then flipped his head and brayed long and loud. "Hee-haw! Heeee-haw!"

The sheer force of his reply, and the sight of his big yellow teeth and pink tongue, made Joe jump back so quickly, he lost his balance. His feet flew out from under him, and he fell flat on his bottom. The donkey stepped forward and gave one last bray for good measure.

Lauren had to put a hand over her mouth to hold back her laughter. She dropped her golf club and ran to help her friend. He was still struggling when she grabbed his arm and helped him to his feet.

"He makes his point, doesn't he?" Joe quickly brushed off his khaki golf pants and jacket, though his back was smeared with mud and a big grass stain.

Other players had also seen the motley animal visitors, and someone must have alerted the groundskeepers. Lauren suddenly saw electric carts flying to the rescue from all directions. The groundskeepers jumped out and surrounded the larger animals, herding them slowly back into the woods.

Two of the groundskeepers hunted down the rabbits, who were obviously tame enough to be tempted closer by bits of lettuce and carrots. The workers then headed for the water hazard and coaxed the ducks to shore with pieces of bread. The entire lot was soon corralled in a small trailer attached to a golf cart, one likely used to haul away leaves and branches.

A few minutes later, the course was quiet again, and animal free. Joe sighed and finally took his shot. Lauren winced, watching with one eye closed as it flew straight up and fell straight back down just a few yards in front of them. He shook his head, looking as if he was finally losing his patience.

"That interruption was enough to break anyone's concentration," she said. He glanced at her but didn't reply.

She cleared her head, took a breath, eyed the pin, and swung. The drive flew straight up the fairway at an impressive height and landed squarely on the putting green, then rolled toward the pin at the perfect speed, stopping less than two feet from the hole. She was almost afraid to look at Joe.

"Lauren? For goodness' sake . . . you almost had a hole in one." Joe stared at her, his mouth agape. "If you won't work at the firm, will you at least give me a few golf lessons?"

Lauren had to smile. A lot of men she knew would have been so intimidated, they would have sunk into a snit. Joe was truly a good sport. And a really nice guy. *Still* a nice guy, she corrected herself.

A cart roared up the path, the sound cutting into their conversation. The little vehicle pulled over and stopped at their tee, and the driver waved to Joe.

"Paul—what a nice surprise." Joe smiled, but Lauren could see the man's appearance had made him a bit anxious. Joe quickly leaned close and whispered, "Paul Hooper. The head of the board here. The club is one of my clients."

Lauren nodded and fixed a pleasant, client-greeting expression on her face.

"Sorry to break into your game, Joe. I know I'm not the first to do that today." Paul began talking as he walked toward them. "You must have seen that pack of animals on the eighth hole?"

"Hard to miss that gang," Joe said.

"They were pretty good sports. They didn't mind us playing through." Lauren had no sooner offered the little joke—very little, she realized too late—than she remembered that Joe should be the only one doing the talking right now.

Paul forced a smile. "Good for you. Most of our members are not nearly as tolerant."

"Of course not," Joe said quickly. "By the way, this is Lauren Willoughby. Lauren, Paul Hooper."

"Nice to meet you." Lauren smiled, trying to say as few words as possible.

"Likewise." Paul nodded, then turned back to Joe. "This isn't the first time we've had these stray beasts wandering in from who knows where." He pointed to the woods, where the animals had come from. "It's a farm or something, on the other side of that wooded patch. I've told the fellow who owns the land to keep his livestock on his side of the property line. He doesn't listen. If he can't control his animals, we'll sue," Paul said decisively. "You'll sue them for us, I mean. I want you to find him, whoever he is, and tell him that."

Sue? That was extreme. Before Lauren realized it, she was jumping in with advice. "Maybe a letter would take care of it? He is your neighbor, Mr. Hooper. There might be some reason, down the road, you'd value his cooperation. And I'm sure you don't want the community at large getting the impression that this club doesn't have compassion for animals?"

Joe glanced at her, and she realized she'd spoken out of turn. Again. She stared at the ground, hoping to look contrite.

Paul looked confused. He looked at Joe as if to say, *Who's the attorney here?*

"Lauren has a good point," Joe said quickly. "It's not only a matter of neighbor relationships, but it could turn into a public relations matter, too. We should approach the property owner in a firm but reasonable way. Enlist cooperation. Only a hint of possible consequences. He'll get the message."

Paul Hooper sighed, the flush in his complexion fading a bit. "I've tried that route, but maybe some legal stationery will work. Copy the board on any correspondence and we'll see what happens."

"Of course," Joe replied.

"Nice to meet you, Ms. Willoughby . . . I assume you're in the legal field as well?"

"I am." Lauren wasn't sure what else to say.

"Lauren just left a big firm in New York. She might come work for me now." Joe smiled, as if he'd finally gained the upper hand.

"Really? Maybe you can solve this problem for us. You seem to have a clear idea of how to handle it."

Lauren felt awkward but knew she deserved it, after jumping in to advise Joe's client before he could. That unfiltered mouth again. *See where it's gotten you now?*

Joe seemed to enjoy seeing her put on the spot. "Excellent idea, Paul," Joe said. "I'll have Lauren work on it right away."

"Great. Keep me posted." Paul turned toward his cart, then stopped and looked back at them. "By the way, I saw that last drive off the tee, Lauren. Not bad." *For a woman,* he meant. "You've set yourself up nicely for an eagle. Think you can make it?"

Lauren almost laughed at the way Paul had praised her shot then undercut the compliment in his next breath.

"Can she make it?" Joe asked. "I'd bet my new clubs on it."

Paul didn't look convinced, but he smiled. "I just got a new set, too. I'll pass on the wager this time. Enjoy the rest of your game."

They watched him hop into the cart and drive away. Lauren's polite smile faded as she turned to face her golf partner. "I'll get her working on it right away?"

Joe shrugged. "Seemed to me that you were champing at the bit to deal with that animal problem. If you'll excuse the pun."

Lauren's eyes grew wide. "I will not," she insisted. "That pun was awful. I'm not champing to do anything."

"I understand. I just threw it out there to get rid of Paul. You're the one who offered the strategy."

"A little problem I have. I talk faster than I think sometimes."

"I would have offered him the same advice. Given the chance," he added, teasing her. He glanced at his watch. "Let's stop at nine. It's getting cold, and I'm not sure I can stand a full eighteen holes of humiliation after you eagle this one." He met her gaze and grinned. "The food here isn't bad. Why don't we figure this out over dinner?"

Lauren hadn't expected a dinner invitation, but once she thought about it, she didn't mind at all. The sun had slipped down in the sky, making her remember it was almost winter. Joe was so easy to be with. And she did owe him an answer about whether she'd help out at his firm while she was in town.

"I'd like that very much. Play on," she said cheerfully.

LAUREN HAD NEVER KNOWN JACK SAWYER TO KEEP FARM ANIMALS, but Paul Hooper claimed the unwanted visitors were coming from Sawyer's Tree Farm. She did recall a big barn on the property, where Jack kept a huge red-and-gold sleigh trimmed with jingling bells and a big, shaggy horse to pull it. He sometimes even kept a pony, to amuse the children who visited the Christmas tree farm's Winter Wonderland.

She had been away a long time. Maybe Jack had started some sort of petting zoo? Or had given up growing trees for tending barnyard animals? Of course, it didn't really matter why the motley crew was living there, so long as they stayed on their side of the property line, chewing their oats and not the golf course sod.

Lauren drove over to Sawyer's on Thursday afternoon, at the end of her first day at Joe's office. She'd dressed to make a good impression on her new colleagues in a sharply cut, ink-blue suit with a pencil skirt, a stark white silk blouse, and black heels. With her long hair swept back in a tight ponytail, pearl earrings were her only adornment.

The outfit was the norm in Manhattan's high-rise offices and meeting rooms, though she had felt a bit overdressed at Joe's firm, where most of the female employees wore tailored pants and sweaters.

Out here, in the open countryside, Lauren knew she looked positively . . . bizarre. As she drew closer to her destination, she wished she'd had time to stop and tone down her look before making the call, or even thought to toss some rain boots or heavy shoes in the back seat this morning. Who knew what she was likely to step in before this was over?

Still, it was best to look businesslike. It would help get her point across, especially since she knew Jack. This wasn't a social call. Paul Hooper expected an immediate resolution, and an apology, as well.

Jack was a friendly, reasonable man. She doubted he would argue with her. She was sure he'd face up to his responsibility and make quick repairs on the fence and keep his four-footed friends on his side of it.

She had faced down some of the toughest corporate attorneys in New York City. So why was she nervous about talking with Jack? Maybe because opposing counsel was usually assumed to be the enemy, and Jack was the cheerful man who sold her family a Christmas tree every year. She'd known him since childhood.

She drove past the sign that read *Sawyer's Tree Farm* and followed a dirt road that led to the barn, some distance from the big yellow farmhouse in front.

The donkey with the eye patch and the old gray horse were trotting about in a small corral. The sight confirmed that she had come to the right place. She spotted a man tending to them. She could see it wasn't Jack, even at a distance.

He hooked a pail of water to the fence, then picked up a pitchfork and began to break apart a bale of hay, the effort outlining his broad shoulders and biceps under a dark blue thermal shirt.

He glanced at the car when she parked and watched her wiggle out of the front seat. Her narrow skirt clung to her hips and legs, and she pushed down the fabric, silently cursing the invention of pantyhose. She grabbed her bag and tried to strike a confident stride—shoulders back, chin up—which was nearly impossible, as her thin heels stuck into the soft earth at every step. She would be lucky if she didn't break off one entirely in the mess.

About halfway to the corral she stopped and waved. "Excuse me. I'm looking for Jack Sawyer. Is he around?"

The man turned and squinted at her. He had dark eyes and looked in need of a shave. Maybe two? His dark hair was cut short on the sides but thick and wavy on top.

"No idea. Check the big house. He lives there with his family."

She tried again. "Yes, I know the Sawyers live there. I've known them a long time."

He seemed puzzled, then annoyed. "Then why are you bothering me?" He attacked the hay bale again, forcing Lauren to take a step back to avoid the flying bits of hay and muck.

She took a breath, holding on to her patience. "I'm here on a business matter. About the farm animals he keeps here now. Like that donkey and horse . . ." She was about to explain more, then shook her head. "It's fine. Sorry to *interrupt* your work."

Lauren did believe that sarcasm was the lowest form of wit, but couldn't help herself this time. *For goodness' sake, you're spreading hay. It's not brain surgery*, she nearly said. If he noticed her tart tone, he didn't react.

As she turned on her heel as smoothly as possible—which was actually not smooth at all—he finally put down the pitchfork and looked at her. Really looked at her.

"If your 'business matter' is about the animals, I'm the one you need to talk to." He was not above a dose of sarcasm either, was he?

She struggled to hide her reaction—so important for a successful negotiation, she'd learned. But what luck, having to deal with this guy instead of good old Jack.

"So you own the animals?"

"I didn't say that. But Jack certainly doesn't."

Was he naturally annoying, or had she pressed some hidden button that set him off? Maybe he had an aversion to women in business suits. She wouldn't be the least bit surprised.

"The animals are housed on Jack's property," she replied.

"It's not Jack's property anymore. I own this parcel now. The corral, the barn, those fields back there . . ." His gloved hand swept across the horizon. Then he turned. "The cottage," he added.

She followed his gaze to a small white cottage a short distance from the barn and corral. A battered pickup was parked in front.

At least now they were getting somewhere. Maybe he didn't work for Jack. She tried to start over. "I'm Lauren Willoughby. I'm sorry, I didn't catch your name?" She tried to muster a polite, amiable tone, but she could see that he knew she was faking it.

"Cole McGuire. You didn't catch it because I didn't give it." He offered a brief gotcha sort of grin.

Okay, we'll skip the niceties. They aren't going to work. Just as well.

"Mr. McGuire, I'm here on behalf of Wagner and Associates, a law firm in town. We represent the Cape Light Golf Club, your neighbors to the west." She paused and pointed to the open field behind the barn and the stand of trees that stood between Cole McGuire's property and the golf club. "I've come because these animals have wandered off your property on at least three occasions and ended up on the golf course. They've disrupted the players and could have caused serious injury with the distraction, and they have also done considerable damage to the greens."

"Disrupted the players? My, my. That is serious." He leaned on the pitchfork and stared at her, his wide mouth pressed into a tight line. A very nice mouth, she couldn't help but notice. She thought he was angry, then noticed the amusement in his eyes. Was he trying very hard not to laugh at her? Seemed so. Which annoyed her even more.

Lauren, get a grip. You're a New York corporate attorney. Are you really going to let this country bumpkin rattle you?

"The courts take property damage seriously, Mr. McGuire."

His eyes widened. "So . . . you're going to sue the animals? Is that why you're here?"

Lauren took a breath to keep herself from losing her temper. How had this gotten so out of control?

"Of course not. I'm here to ask you—or whoever is in charge of their care—to keep them on your property. To figure out how they're getting onto the golf course and make any necessary changes or repairs to fencing that will contain them, by December first. That should be plenty of time. The golf course doesn't want to be a bad neighbor," she added, recalling the soft-soap approach she'd practiced in the car, which had totally flown out of her head once she encountered this guy.

"Good to know. It gives me comfort." He nodded, still secretly laughing at her, she suspected. "The offenders in question belong to the Grateful Paw. It's an organization that rescues animals that have been abandoned or are headed for a slaughterhouse. That sort of thing."

"I'm familiar with that group." Lauren kept her expression blank and businesslike, though it was a surprise to hear the real source of the animals and the problem.

"A woman named Jessica Morgan is in charge. She used to be a bank manager but gave up that career to save animals. An interesting woman," he added in an admiring tone.

An innocent comment, though Lauren couldn't help but feel that he was also saying, *As opposed to a fussbudget like you, totally bent out of shape about a few sweet, old creatures who nibbled some expensive grass.*

Jessica Morgan *was* an interesting woman. She was also Lauren's aunt. And Aunt Jessica had not run the whole bank, just the loan department. But Lauren didn't bother to correct him.

"Jack always helped her out, housing the overflow," Cole McGuire continued. "Especially farm animals. I've continued to do the same."

"That's commendable. But it doesn't change the situation. The animals live on your property, and you need to contain them."

She reached into her bag and pulled out a letter that included everything she'd just explained, in more official language.

He stood back and crossed his arms over his chest. "I was wondering when you'd get to that. Was there ever a lawyer who didn't write a letter?"

No argument there. The profession was prone to setting things down in black and white. But she wouldn't give him the satisfaction of acknowledging his point.

"Here's the one I wrote for you. If you have any questions after reviewing it, feel free to call . . . the firm."

She'd nearly said *call me*. But she caught herself. Right now, she wasn't sure she would take more assignments from Joe.

She held out the letter, hoping that he'd simply agree to mend the fence and that would be the end of it. Though a tiny, mischievous voice did wonder if he would get in touch. Maybe just as an excuse to talk to her again? Or . . . she could find an excuse to call him?

Where in the world had that come from?

He pulled off his work gloves and gazed at the envelope but didn't take it. "Can you drop it in the mailbox? I have to pick up my daughter."

Before she could reply, he'd jabbed the pitchfork into a pile of hay, then hopped over the fence and out of the corral in a smooth, strong motion that stole her breath away.

He yanked on the gate to make sure it was locked, then he pulled a set of keys from the pocket of his down vest. When he looked back at her, they were eye to eye. Lauren found it jarring and realized she had felt safer when he'd been corralled.

"Anything else?" His tone was impatient.

At five-foot-ten and wearing heels, Lauren knew she was hardly a wilting flower. But she still tipped her head back to meet his gaze. The conversation was clearly over.

"That's all. Thank you for your time."

"Then we're square. Watch your step. It's slippery out here. More than you'd expect."

He was talking about the patches of mud on the drive, but she also heard a second meaning. He thought he'd won their little verbal sparring match. The idea irked her.

Not that it mattered—as long he complied with her request and did what he needed to do.

Still, she didn't like anyone thinking they had gotten the upper hand. Especially an intentionally difficult, contrary man, like this one. One who was obviously intimidated by an accomplished woman. She had only been out of the law loop for a few weeks. Had she lost her edge so quickly? *Maybe you really do belong out here in the boondocks,* she scolded herself.

She watched Cole climb into the faded red truck. He started it up and drove off without sparing her a glance.

Feeling a mixture of relief and dismay, she pushed her carefully worded letter into the mailbox in front of the cottage and snapped it closed.

"That's that." She said it out loud and hoped it was true. She didn't like the way Cole McGuire got under her skin.

*　*　*

It was good to be back in the house where she'd grown up, but it felt a little strange to Lauren as well. There was a quote about coming home that she'd heard somewhere. She was fairly certain Nelson Mandela had said it. "There is nothing like returning to a place that remains unchanged to find the ways in which you yourself have altered."

It came to her as she sat at the kitchen table in her old, familiar chair, eating dinner with her mom; her half sister, Betty; and her stepdad, Matt. Lauren and her younger sister, Jillian, both called him Dad, and they thought of him that way, too. Their biological father, Phil Willoughby, had tried his best to be a good parent but had drifted in and out of their lives all the while they were growing up. But since the day her mother had married Dr. Matthew Harding, he had been a solid and loving presence twenty-four-seven. Lauren and her sister never thought of him as a "step" anything. He was their dad and held a place in their hearts just as important as Phil Willoughby's.

Lauren thought of her stepsister, Amanda, and half sister, Betty, in the same way. It had been her friendship with Amanda, a new girl in town when she was just twelve, that had helped bring their parents together.

Once her sisters Jillian and Amanda came home for Thanksgiving, it would feel more normal, she thought. Even though Amanda was married, her sisters would still tease her, argue with her, and put her in her place.

Right now, her parents were giving her so much attention and velvet-glove treatment, Lauren felt as if she had come home to recuperate from an illness. Little Betty—not so little anymore at age eleven—was completely in awe of her just because she'd been living in New York. Betty treated her like a movie star, or a superhero, which was sweet and a great balm to Lauren's confidence. Lauren knew she was still licking her wounds from the law firm and her breakup with Greg. The tender, loving care of her family wasn't the worst thing.

Lost in her thoughts, Lauren had hardly been following the conversation at the table. Her mother's excited tone caught her attention. "I beat out three other bids, Matt. Including the Clam Box," Molly announced. "I thought you'd be proud of me."

"Of course I'm proud, honey," her dad said. "And not surprised at all. Your food is the best anywhere. I'm just not sure how you're going to get it all done. Feeding a movie crew three meals a day, in addition to all the holiday parties you book? Not to mention the regular business at the bakeries, which are both madhouses this time of year."

Matt was right to be concerned. Lauren was used to her mother working around the clock during the holidays. She now owned two bakery-cafés, one in Cape Light and one in Newburyport. She also did a big business catering holiday gatherings. But it sounded as if this year's schedule would be even more intense.

"No worries, Matt. It works out perfectly." As usual, Molly Willoughby was unfazed by what sounded to Lauren like a disaster in the making. Her mom did thrive on chaos—one trait Lauren had happily not inherited. "The movie crew leaves town right before Christmas, so that job barely overlaps with our catering schedule."

Her father looked doubtful. "Are you sure?"

"Absolutely," Molly promised. "We say, 'It's a wrap!' in the business. No pun intended," she added with a cheeky grin.

Lauren saw her father try not to smile and quickly give up on trying to advise his dynamo wife. He gazed at her mom with a tender warmth and a familiar sparkle in his dark eyes. After all their years together, all their ups and downs—and raising four daughters—they were still very much in love.

That's what I want, Lauren thought. *It's probably all for the best that I broke it off with Greg. I never felt that way about him . . . or he about me.* Instead of making her sad, the realization did her heart good, just to remember that love was possible. Rare, she knew. But possible.

Matt sighed and shook his head. "You'll do what you want anyway, Molly. You always do. And you always bite off more than you can chew. Pun totally intended."

Her mom smiled and began to clear the table. She knew she'd won. This round, anyway. "Betty and I have it all under control." Betty Bowman, Lauren knew she meant, who was her mom's business partner—and such a dear friend that Lauren's younger sister was her namesake. "Everybody wants to work on a movie set. We'll find extra help easily."

Lauren rose to help clean up. "I think so, too. The town is struck by movie fever already, and the production company hasn't even arrived yet. When do they come, again?"

"November thirtieth, the Monday after Thanksgiving. Betty thinks we should put Thanksgiving leftovers on the menu for them that first week, like turkey with gravy, stuffing, and sweet potatoes. But I think it would be tacky. The closest I'll get is a turkey wrap with goat cheese and cranberries, maybe. We always have some leftovers from the catering gigs, no matter how carefully we measure," Molly mused.

"Never mind the movie crew, what are *we* doing for Thanksgiving? Are we hosting here again?" her father asked.

"Jessica and Sam offered to have us all over when they heard I got the movie job. But since we'd be bringing most of the food, I figured it will be just as easy to have it here. You and the girls can get the house ready while I'm working." Her mother dumped a pile of pots in the sink, and Lauren slipped on an apron as she headed over to scrub.

"Don't we always?" Lauren filled the sink with water and soap suds. Her mother would leave a long and precise list of orders for them; she had already fussed over the table setting and flowers, as if Martha Stewart would be dropping by to critique her hosting skills. "By the time you come home, everything will be perfect," Lauren promised.

Betty brought a pile of dishes to the counter, and her mother began loading the dishwasher. "Can I go with you, Mom? You said last Thanksgiving that this year I'd be old enough to help."

Molly gently smiled. Lauren knew she was wary of having Betty in the commercial kitchen during such a crazy, stressed time but also didn't want to disappoint her. "We'll see, honey," she said, offering the standard reply of parents who've been asked questions they don't want to answer. "Goodness knows you're the only one of my girls who shows any interest. I have to leave the business to somebody."

She glanced at Lauren, who shrugged and laughed. "Don't look at me. I can hardly work a coffeemaker. I'm a lawyer, remember? I haven't given up on it yet."

"I know, sweetheart." Molly patted her shoulder. "Just teasing. How did it go at Joe's office? I was so distracted by my news, I forgot to ask."

"It was fine." Except for her encounter with Cole McGuire, but she had no intention of going there. "I guess I will do a little work for Joe while I'm here. It's good to keep my hand in."

"Very true. You might end up liking it." Her mother gave her a look, for once not blabbing out everything that she was thinking.

Lauren already knew what she was thinking. Her mom hoped Lauren might enjoy the job at Joe's firm more then she expected—and end up feeling a lot different about Joe, too. Lauren doubted either outcome was likely, but she didn't want to get into that conversation right now. She turned her attention and energy to scrubbing a big iron skillet.

The mention of Joe's firm brought to mind the animal problem. Even though the creatures were living on Cole McGuire's land and he was responsible for their trespassing, Lauren thought her aunt should be aware of the situation, too. Her aunt Jess was one of the sweetest, most reasonable people in the world and would take the golf course's concerns seriously. Unlike McGuire. When the time was right, Lauren would talk to her. Jessica probably knew more about him, too. Lauren had to admit—even if just to herself—that she was curious.

Excuse me? You're looking for warmth, understanding, mutual respect, and compatibility—everything your mom and dad have, remember? I don't see the curt and churlish Mr. McGuire checking off any of those boxes.

She was just bored here, she realized. Already. It was even quieter than she remembered. But things would get livelier when Jillian and Amanda came home. Besides, Lauren knew that a break from city life was the perfect remedy for all she'd been through recently.

But she never wanted to feel so bored she'd have any interest in a guy like Cole McGuire.

CHAPTER THREE

CHARLIE KEPT THE CLAM BOX OPEN ON THANKSGIVING, AT least until five. He knew it was an inconvenience to his wife and children, and even an obligation for them. Some thought his strategy was to catch any stray customers looking for a meal that day, since every other eatery, including his chief rival, Willoughby's Bakery & Café, was closed. But that wasn't the reason at all. He simply believed that everyone should enjoy a good Thanksgiving dinner—from families who couldn't afford a fancy restaurant to the lonely souls who had not received any invitations from relatives or friends.

He wanted the Clam Box diner to be a warm, cozy place where anyone could enjoy roast turkey, stuffing, and all the trimmings. Even if they didn't have a dime in their pocket. That was the best part, Lucy thought as she moved through her own kitchen, taking mugs and dishes out of the cabinets. She was very proud of him for that. They all watched carefully for customers who looked down on their luck and in need of a free meal. When such a guest was spotted, all they found on their check was a smiley face and the words, *We hope you enjoyed your dinner. Happy Thanksgiving!—Charlie Bates and Family.*

Over the years the word of this generosity had gotten out. As Lucy rose at six a.m. on Thanksgiving morning, she expected that today Charlie would be picking up the check for at least half of the customers who came in, maybe even more. He did this quietly, too—for Charlie. Even though touting his charity would have certainly been good publicity.

Charlie was a complicated man, without question. Perhaps the contradictions in his character were the reason he never really got his due for his good deeds and his soft heart. Or maybe because he managed to hide them so well?

As much as Lucy loved having her whole family home for the holiday and only wanted to pamper them, her three children knew they were obliged to help at the diner before enjoying the family dinner that Lucy prepared in advance.

C.J., Jamie, and Zoey took the place of the waitstaff, who couldn't be asked to come in on such a big holiday. Charlie stepped up as cook and captain of the kitchen. Lucy helped a bit in the kitchen and out in the dining room, too, directing her brood. They had all worked at the diner at one time or another, as had some of their boyfriends and girlfriends. Like Zoey's fiancé, James Potter, who was always happy to pitch in on the holiday.

They were all good sports, Lucy thought as she set up the coffeepot and set out a "grab and go" breakfast for them—yogurt containers and a plate of date, nut, and banana muffins that she and Zoey had baked together the night before.

Charlie had left the house at least an hour ago; he was already deep into his cooking in the diner's kitchen. Her children, all in their twenties now, were still fast asleep. They'd all arrived last night and had stayed up late, talking and teasing each other in the usual way.

Her younger son, Jamie, who was twenty-three, had driven up

from Hartford, Connecticut, where he had an entry-level job in the actuarial department of a big insurance company. He'd always been a whiz at math and loved to get lost in numbers. Her older son, C.J., had inherited his father's outgoing personality and talent for glad-handing. He was doing well in his career in advertising and public relations and had been living in Boston for the past five years, since graduating college. Their daughter, Zoey, lived the closest, in Salem. Lucy was secretly thankful, though she'd never pressured her children about anything like that. But she did love having Zoey just about a half hour away, seeing her often for shopping, a movie, or other mother-daughter outings. Zoey had come into their lives only ten years ago, when she was fifteen. Lucy had missed out on raising her but knew that her adopted daughter was as dear to her as either of the boys whom she'd given birth to.

Zoey had started out studying art in college but had found a way to combine that love and her natural insight and empathy for others as an art therapist. Although she had just finished her advanced degree and certification, she already had a good position at a family therapy center in Salem. Her fiancé, James, was a writer. He published articles in magazines and had also had a novel published, based on the story of his great-grandparents, who had come to Cape Light in the early 1900s and started the Potter Orchard.

Even though she lived nearby, Zoey still liked to sleep over in her old room during the holidays. A good thing on Thanksgiving, Lucy thought, since it guaranteed that everyone got to the diner in time.

Lucy glanced up the stairs toward the bedrooms, knowing her kids would be grouchy when she woke them and prodded them to get ready. But Lucy also knew that by the time customers arrived at the diner, her children would be very much in the spirit of the day—grateful for their own blessings and glad to share the bounty.

The family would return home around six o'clock that night, tired but happy, feeling that certain kind of contentment that comes after you've spent time doing good for others. They would sit at their own table, connected by that feeling and truly realizing the ways in which their family had been so richly blessed. Which was what this holiday was all about, wasn't it?

Braced for their protests, Lucy stood at the bottom of the stairs and called out in her best Mom voice—though it was a bit rusty these days, she had to admit.

"C.J.? Jamie? Zoey? Rise and shine. Coffee is ready. Come on down now, everyone."

She drifted back to the kitchen, smiling at the groans and complaints that descended in reply. She loved having her kids home. It was going to be a great day.

ONE OF THE BEST THINGS ABOUT THE HOLIDAYS WAS ALL THE DELI-cious food. It was one of the worst things, too. At least Lauren thought so as she loosened the belt on her dress under the cover of a linen napkin.

Their Thanksgiving dinner was just about over, except for dessert. They were more or less in the seventh-inning stretch, and from the look on every face around the table, Lauren knew she was not alone in feeling stuffed.

Even in a food daze, Lauren still felt happy to be with her "tribe"—especially her sisters Jillian and Amanda, who had arrived yesterday and helped with the preparations, along with Amanda's husband, Gabriel.

Her aunt Jessica and uncle Sam were also there, along with Lauren's three cousins. Darrell was twenty-four, working on his degree in architecture. He was amazingly talented and had already designed an apartment complex that was going to be built by the town. His younger brother, Tyler, fourteen, was just starting high school, and their sister, Lily, was ten, only a year younger than Betty. Those two went to the same school and were as close as sisters.

Her mom had been up at five that morning, supervising deliveries of turkey dinners all over town, but she still looked bright and lovely, seated at the head of the table, in all her glory as the hostess of the family gathering. Lauren wasn't sure where her mother got all her energy and spunk. She tried her best to follow her mom's lead, but it wasn't always easy.

Sam leaned back and patted his stomach. "Just when I think a Thanksgiving feast cannot get any better, you hit new heights, sis. That meal was epic. I even had seconds of the brussels sprouts. And you know how I feel about that vegetable."

Sam, who was hamming it up as usual, looked very fit for a middle-aged guy. He was still working hard in his construction business, though Darrell was involved in the business now, too.

"I also know how you feel about bacon, and I definitely knew which ingredient would win out," her mother replied.

Jessica laughed. "Your sister knows you too well. It took me years to figure out that bacon trick."

"No denying it. I won't even try." Sam grinned, his dimpled smile identical to her mother's, and to her own. "I hear that now they say bacon is good for you."

Her father's face crinkled into an expression that was half-amused and half-perplexed. Lauren could tell his medical sensibilities were doing a backflip. "Bacon? Where in the world did you hear that one?"

Sam shrugged. "Not sure. But if doctors didn't discover that yet, I'm sure someone will soon. Eggs, chocolate, red wine . . . all this other stuff the doctor always said was bad for me turns it out to be good. Why not bacon?"

Her father sighed and seemed about to argue, then sat back and shrugged. "There is a lot of contradictory information out there about nutrition. I'll grant you that."

"But no argument about this dinner, Aunt Molly," Darrell said. "I had seconds of everything."

"Thanks, honey. Hope you left room for dessert. We have plenty of pies," Molly replied. "Apple, coconut custard, pecan, and pumpkin."

Sam raised his hand, as if in school. "A taste of each, please. Except the pumpkin. Unless it has bacon in it."

Her mom laughed. "Sorry, Sam. Maybe I'll experiment and surprise you next year."

Jessica rolled her eyes as she lifted the mostly empty turkey platter off the table. "Don't encourage him, Molly. Please?"

Lauren noticed that Darrell and Tyler both started clearing, too, without being asked, along with her mother, her aunt, herself, and her sisters Amanda and Jillian. Betty and Lily slipped off to Betty's room, already giggling before they'd even made it to the stairway.

Amanda's husband, Gabriel, also helped, stationing himself at the sink in front of a huge pile of pots and pans, while her dad and uncle drifted into the family room to watch football during the intermission between dinner and dessert.

It was a small thing, but it revealed a distinct difference in the generations and what was considered "women's work." Lauren was happy to move around after the long, rich meal. She hoped she could slip out for a walk later and maybe even a few jogs around the neighborhood this weekend.

Back in the city, intense sessions at a high-tech, exclusive fitness club had been a regular part of her routine. Life was different in Cape Light in that respect as well.

With her height and build, keeping her weight down was always a struggle. Lauren had long ago faced the fact that she'd never be a flat-chested, model-thin silhouette. She'd shot up to her full height early—and towered over the boys—which had caused her to be a bit shy in high school. She'd since learned to take pride in her stature and her curves. Still, she did want her expensive wardrobe to fit when this visit was over. Especially the sleek business outfits she would need for interviews come January. She would be apoplectic if they didn't.

As her mother began to unwrap an array of delicious-looking pies, Lauren knew that goal was going to be a challenge.

"Those pies look too beautiful to eat." Jessica stood next to Lauren, also fascinated by the unveiling.

"They do. Though I doubt it will stop any of us. I should just apply a slice or two to my hips."

Aunt Jess laughed and put her arm around Lauren's shoulder. "You're gorgeous, honey. Young women worry way too much about dieting."

Lauren knew that was probably true. "I haven't been working out since I got home. Except for a few rounds of golf. We walked the course, but it's still not great exercise."

Her aunt's expression was suddenly serious. "I've been meaning to speak to you about the golf course. I'm so sorry my animals wandered. Cole McGuire told me that you spoke to him about it."

Lauren had meant to get in touch with her aunt after visiting McGuire, but the week had passed and she'd never gotten around to it. It was one thing to confront a total stranger but another entirely to bother her aunt, who was only trying to make the world a kinder place. And Jessica wasn't responsible for the four-footed trespassing. McGuire was.

"I did visit, on behalf of Joe Wagner's firm. They represent the golf course."

"So I heard. Cole claims the golf course threatened to sue him."

Lauren was shocked by McGuire's misinterpretation. "That's not true at all. He needs to keep the animals on his side of the fence. I did make that clear. But I never said anything about a lawsuit." Lauren paused. "The letter was strong. But he's been warned before. The golf course just wants him to know they mean business this time. I will add that he didn't seem to be taking it all that seriously."

Aunt Jess smiled and rolled her eyes. "Cole is not what I'd call an easygoing guy. He doesn't like anyone telling him what to do."

"I noticed. But it's good to hear you confirm it. Now I won't take it personally. Not that I care one way or the other," she quickly added.

"Maybe I won't send the overflow there this winter," Jessica mused. "I don't want to cause problems for everyone. Though having that extra shelter space did save a lot of lives last year."

"It's not your fault. Send the animals there, please. That's fine," Lauren said quickly. "McGuire is responsible for keeping them under control once they're on his property."

Her aunt still looked concerned. "Are you sure? I'd hate for this to go any further. He's doing us a favor, and he does put in work to take care of the animals while they're sheltered in his barn."

Lauren hadn't thought of that part, how McGuire was contributing his time and maybe even some money toward the cause. That was good of him.

"Don't worry. It will never come to that. I'll make sure," she said, though she wasn't entirely sure she could keep that promise if the situation did escalate and get nastier. "How is the rescue group going? You must take in a lot of animals if you need to bring them to different locations."

Her aunt positively glowed, happy to talk about her favorite topic—aside from Lauren's cousins. "We just won a grant that will carry us through the end of the year. And we've applied for another. But winter is so busy, and we're very low on volunteers. It's hard to find help during the holidays."

"I bet. I can help you sometime. I've only been working a few hours here and there and driving Betty around to music lessons and sports practice to help Mom."

Lauren did have a lot of extra time, but she secretly cringed the moment the offer left her lips. Had she really volunteered to help the Grateful Paw? What was she thinking? She liked animals well enough. Cats, dogs, even her little sister's gerbil. But she was not eager to babysit the sort of barnyard critters her aunt's group specialized in rescuing.

But when she saw Jessica's pleased expression, she knew she'd said the right thing—and had smoothed over their uncomfortable moment.

"That would be super, honey. Thank you so much. I'm going to take you up on that," her aunt warned.

Lauren grinned. "Operators are standing by for your call, Aunt Jess."

A sharp knock sounded on the back door. Lauren's mother didn't look surprised as she sailed across the kitchen, carrying a carafe of coffee into the dining room. "Will you get that, Lauren? We're all set for dessert."

Lauren headed through the mudroom and glanced through the window. It was Joe, holding a big bouquet of autumn flowers. He looked a bit self-conscious but greeted her with a wide smile as she pulled open the door.

"Happy Thanksgiving, Lauren." He leaned forward and gave her a friendly hug.

Lauren had no choice but to hug him back, but she was still unable to hide her surprise. "Hello, Joe . . . What's up?"

"Just stopped by for dessert. Your mom invited me?"

Lauren didn't like it, but she did get it. And she felt bad for making him feel awkward. "Oh . . . right. I know she mentioned it. I totally forgot. Thanks for coming," she said in a politer tone. "The Thanksgiving pie parade is just about to kick off in the dining room. You haven't missed a thing."

She could tell by his expression that he knew her mother hadn't told Lauren to expect him. But as usual, Joe didn't take offense. He looked every inch the prosperous country gentleman in an expensive-looking Donegal tweed sports coat with a dark brown muffler slung around his neck. He removed the muffler and hung it on the coat tree, then handed her the flowers.

"Let's try this again. Happy Thanksgiving, Lauren."

She smiled and accepted the bouquet, trying not to show the reluctance she really felt at the lavish gift. "Thank you, Joe. Happy Thanksgiving. These are lovely."

"I hope you enjoy them." He also had a gold box of chocolates tucked under his arm. For her family, she suspected.

"Let's go inside." She led him into the dining room, where her mother and Aunt Jess presided over the pies and had just begun taking orders.

"Joe, good to see you," her mother greeted him warmly. "I'm so glad you could make it."

"Would anyone in their right mind miss an invitation for dessert at your house, Mrs. Harding?"

"Good point," her mother replied without the slightest trace of modesty. "Just call me Molly, Joe. You two aren't in high school anymore."

"I will, thanks. And thank heaven that phase is over," he added, making everyone laugh.

Her father and sisters—except for Betty, who was just born the year Lauren was a senior—remembered Joe well, and also seemed glad to see him. Jess and Sam knew Joe from church and greeted him warmly. He took a seat next to Lauren and fell into conversation easily, looking quite relaxed with her family.

As the group discussed the movie crew that was due to arrive in town on Monday, her mother met Lauren's gaze across the table. She grinned from ear to ear, the famous Morgan dimples flashing.

Molly looked extremely satisfied. Like a cat who had eaten a canary pie, Lauren thought. Her mother's little matchmaking plan had worked out today. Though Lauren wanted to tell her it wouldn't amount to much.

She liked Joe. She really did. She even enjoyed working at his firm. But Joe was just . . . Joe. Had she worked so hard to move on from her hometown only to circle back and end up here? With a guy who clearly never wanted to leave?

Maybe her parents—especially her mom—thought a relationship with Joe Wagner was a good choice right now, but Lauren didn't agree. Despite how well he fit into her family and how thoughtful and patient he could be. And despite being in the "danger zone"—twenty-nine and totally single—she still could not move Joe's marker from the friend square to the boyfriend square on her game board.

She was also sure that if she tried to explain, her mother's reply would be one of her patent "Sure, honey, we'll see" phrases and smiles. Lauren decided she wouldn't even bother. She sat back and enjoyed her pumpkin pie.

* * *

"THEY'LL TRAMPLE THIS VILLAGE TO SHREDS, LIKE A HERD OF BUF-
falo. They'll leave us in wreck and ruin. Dimwits like Charlie Bates
will be sorry," Lillian predicted. "But it will be too late. Mark my
words."

Lillian could see she'd soured the family's Thanksgiving gathering
with her prediction, but someone needed to voice the truth of the
matter. She'd taken on that mantle before and was not afraid to take
it on again.

She had expected the dinner conversation to turn in this direction
sooner or later, to some chitchat about the imminent arrival of the
movie people. She had strong feelings on the subject. She couldn't help
that.

Her daughter Emily and son-in-law Dan exchanged glances and
shifted uneasily. The younger ones, her granddaughter Sara and Sara's
husband, Luke, looked amused. Jane, her younger granddaughter, just
looked confused.

Lillian's husband, Ezra, sat back in his chair at the opposite end
of their long dining table, which had been carefully laid with her finest Wedgwood china, Waterford crystal, and silver flatware, as the
holiday gathering required. He pushed his glasses to the top of his
nose—a sure sign he was vexed.

"Now, now, Lillian. No need to get up on your high horse. You're
liable to slip off and break a hip." His quip made the others grin,
though none of them dared laugh aloud. "You have to admit, having
a real Hollywood movie filmed in our village is exciting. It doesn't
happen every day."

"I'll admit no such thing. And I'd be happy if it never happened
any day."

High horse, indeed. At least I still have one, she nearly added. *Not like some old people, who have thrown in their saddle and don't care about anything more than keeping up with their TV shows and keeping their pill boxes in order.*

She noticed Luke lean over to his young sister-in-law. "I think it's time to bring in dessert. Want to help me?"

Jane nodded and smiled, and the two slipped off to kitchen. Lillian wasn't surprised. Luke McCallister was a bit of a coward, she had always thought. Not nearly good enough for her granddaughter Sara. She'd never approved of that marriage, though the rest of the family liked him well enough.

"Thank you, Luke and Jane," Emily called after them. "I'll help you in a minute."

"That's fine. Turn tail and run." Lillian pinned Emily with a look. Emily had been mayor of the village for fifteen years before Charlie Bates took over. She should have some answers, if anyone at the table did. "No one wants to talk honestly about this situation. I still can't comprehend how those permits were approved. I wouldn't be surprised if that Bates creature bribed a few board members to push this through."

Emily rolled her eyes and shook her head. Lillian had seen that expression of disbelief before. Her daughter was so naive, even at her age. Always was, always would be.

"Mother, don't be silly. And please don't start spreading rumors about Charlie. I'm the first to admit he has his little schemes and agendas. But in most respects, he's an honest man and aboveboard."

"In most respects? That's threading the needle, dear. I wouldn't put anything past that man. He's a short-order cook with delusions of grandeur. I suppose he thinks this scheme will advance his business interests in some way. Bring a bit of attention to his pathetic diner?" Lillian grunted and sat back. "I can believe anything of Bates. But I can't believe my own family is so giddy and starstruck. So blind to the reality of this . . . impending disaster. I'm glad there are no strangers here to witness this . . . this embarrassment."

Ezra laughed. "That's the first time I've ever heard you admit to that reaction, my dear. Lillian Warwick, embarrassed? Isn't your motto 'Never apologize; never explain'? I don't see how chagrin figures into that philosophy."

Lillian gave him a look, gray eyes narrowed. "I didn't say *I* was embarrassed. I know where I stand. I meant that I'm embarrassed for all of you. When all the fawning and autograph-seeking is over, there will be a reckoning, believe me. I pray there's a brick of Lilac Hall left standing. How in the world did they get permission to put a toe in that house? I have a notion to block their entrance with my own body. I'll lay across the threshold in protest," she declared.

The idea had just come to her. It was a good one, too.

Emily's husband, Dan, leaned over and patted her hand—a gesture Lillian generally found condescending, though she knew he meant no disrespect.

"I was concerned about Lilac Hall, too. But the production company will be closely watched. They've made an ironclad promise that the crew will take extreme care during any filming there. There's been a good deal of research into the experiences of other towns and historic sites that have allowed this group on location. There were very few and very minor complaints reported."

Dan shared Lillian's interest in the town's history. The former owner and publisher of the *Cape Light Messenger*, he'd handed the newspaper over to his daughter Lindsay years ago and embarked on a second career as a writer, with a special interest in local history. He'd published several books so far, all of them well received.

But Dan could hardly share her connection and commitment to

Lilac Hall, which had been the estate of her first husband's family, the Warwicks. Lilac Hall had also been her first home in Cape Light, where she'd made a life as a young bride after eloping with Oliver Warwick and giving up all ties to her own family in order to marry him.

She and Oliver had expected to raise their daughters there, to see them married in the rose arbor and watch their grandchildren play on the long, sloping green lawns. But fate had written a different story for their family, casting them out of that grand home in shame and disgrace after Oliver's tragic misstep. Talk about embarrassment. Dear Ezra didn't know the meaning of the word.

It was all ancient history now. Even Lilac Hall was relegated to those dusty pages. Her husband had been found guilty of stealing from the pension fund of his employees to cover his gambling debts. That was what the newspapers had reported, though the real story had been more complicated and her husband, though a weak man in some ways, had acted with good intentions. Or so he'd believed.

In the end, they'd been forced to sell most of their possessions and give up the family's lavish home and property as well. It had been her idea to sell the mansion and estate to the county as a historical site and, in doing so, save the beautiful buildings and grounds from the wrecking ball and salvage a small part of the family fortune.

Was it any wonder she felt such strong ties to the place? She still sat on the board and fought for its safekeeping, though this movie business was one battle she had not won.

"You all know how I feel about the Hall. I suppose this unfortunate episode wouldn't irk me half as much if that place were not involved. They can tear apart the rest of the town, for all I care."

"Grandma, get a grip." Her granddaughter Sara, who looked so much like herself at that age, with her pale complexion, dark hair, and startling blue eyes, had also inherited her penchant for debate.

Sara was a high-level reporter at the *Boston Globe*. Lillian was very proud of Sara's achievements and kept a scrapbook filled with her articles. However, she kept that hobby—and those warm feelings—mostly under her hat. The young woman thought very well of herself as it was. She didn't need any more of a swelled head, Lillian thought.

"We're not expecting an invasion of barbarians," Sara explained. "These people are professionals, and the publicity will be good for the village. I'm sure that's why Charlie Bates was pushing for the approvals."

"But can anyone tell me *why* it will be good? This village has managed perfectly well since the sixteen hundreds without publicity. I'd be happy if *fewer* people found their way here. Not more."

"Dessert, anyone?" Luke stood between the pocket doors of the dining room, carrying a tray that held an apple pie and a carton of ice cream. "Janie is bringing in the pumpkin."

"I'll start on the apple," Ezra called to him with a grin. "Bring it here, young man." His tone was serious, but everyone knew he was teasing.

"Sorry, Ezra. We have to share," Emily said. "Jane baked them for everyone," Emily added proudly. "You all know the only way I helped was to steer clear of the kitchen."

The rest of the family laughed because it was true. Emily was not much of a cook, a trait she had clearly inherited from her mother. But unlike Lillian, Emily seemed to see the situation as a negative—almost as a character flaw.

Lillian, on the other hand, had never perceived her challenges in the kitchen as a lack of any sort. When she was growing up in a grand house on Boston's Beacon Hill, there were always servants to take care of the domestic chores like cooking, cleaning, washing, and all of that.

Later, after marrying Oliver, she lived in an even grander house and had even more servants to attend to her every need. But even after their financial reversal, she still didn't see her disinterest and lack of inclination for cooking—or any such domestic chores—as a shortcoming.

Did any man think that way, ever? Rich or poor? Did one ever hear a man bemoaning his inability to cook? Of course not. She'd always seen this supposed shortcoming as a freedom. Liberation from a life sentence of producing tasty meals, every day, practically nonstop. Once the line in the sand was drawn, she was off the hook. No one expected her to put together more than the most basic dishes. She was not pressured to turn out meal after meal for her family, like most women of her generation, as if they were performing seals. If anyone wanted to eat restaurant-quality food in her company, they need only get in a car or pick up the telephone. Or they could inform the housekeeper, Estrella, with enough advance notice of their preferences.

And now Emily was encouraging her own daughter into this domestic tyranny. While Lillian silently pondered these questions, her guests happily dug into their dessert and lavishly praised dear little Jane, unmindful of the larger questions. Uncaring that they were encouraging her in such a dangerous direction.

Her slice of pie sat before her, untouched. Lillian stared down at it but did not pick up her fork.

"Don't you like pumpkin pie, Grandma?" Jane asked. "Try some apple. You might like it better."

Lillian turned to her granddaughter and forced a small smile. "I do like pumpkin. I like it very much." She took her fork and tasted a small bite as Jane waited for her reaction.

Lillian nodded her approval. "Just the right amount of spices and sweetening." High praise from her, she knew. But she did feel it was important to be honest. Always. It was an exceedingly good pie. "It's very good," she said.

"Just very good? I'd say it's excellent. And the apple is, too," Ezra said from his end of the table. Lillian could see that her husband had not stressed himself by making a choice between the two but had a slice of each on his dish. "Well done, Jane. Five stars. The highlight of our dinner."

That was Ezra, so lavish in his praise. Her granddaughter did seem to glow at his words. Lillian wondered if he had given her too much positive reinforcement.

"I can see that you are a good cook, Jane," she said. "It's fine for a hobby. Just don't make a profession of it."

"But, Grandma, I want to go to culinary school instead of college. I'm practically decided."

Lillian sat back in her chair, feeling the blood drain from her head. "No one's told me that. When did this all come about?"

Emily pressed her lips together, a sign that she didn't want to react too quickly and say something she would later regret. "Jane loves to cook. And bake," she said finally.

Lillian recalled when that interest had been encouraged—by Jane's birth mother, who had come to town last winter and taken a job at a local inn. Somehow her daughter and granddaughter had navigated those choppy waters. Lillian didn't want to speak of it now.

"We're just exploring options," Emily added. "Visiting schools. Nothing's set in stone."

Lillian sighed. She couldn't fight yet another battle at the table. She could see that Ezra didn't want her to either.

She raised her hands in surrender. "Explore away. Let me know what you find, miss," she said to Jane. "All I know is that in my day, young women aspired to venture out into the world. To take on professions far beyond the reach of apron strings."

Lillian had studied art history in college and found a good job as an assistant museum curator for the Egyptian collection at Boston's Museum of Fine Arts. *Very* assistant, she recalled. Still, it had been difficult to win an interview in the male-dominated profession, even armed with a stellar academic record from Radcliffe College, the all-female annex of Harvard at that time. Her wealthy family's connection had greased the wheels at the museum, though she was certainly more than worthy of the job. She had done very well in her brief tenure, foretelling a bright future in the field. How she often wished she'd stuck with her career and had never been swept off her feet by Oliver Warwick.

No, that wasn't it exactly. She didn't wish for one or the other. She certainly didn't wish away her young love—the brightest moments of her life, perhaps—or the blessing of her two daughters. But she did wish that both paths had been open to her. At least these days, women could have a home life *and* a work life, if they were strong enough to juggle it.

Sara shook her head. "Grandma, you make it sound as if Jane will be walking into a trap if she studies cooking. But don't you see? Your generation and Mom's fought those battles so that women like me and Jane can make any choice we want. Even if that means Jane *wants* to study a 'domestic art' like cooking. By the way, the world of commercial kitchens and celebrity chefs is still a male stronghold. Jane will be in the thick of it if she goes to culinary school."

"Perhaps you have a point," Lillian conceded in atypical fashion. She turned to Jane. "Now I can thoroughly enjoy this pie, since I know you won't be selling yourself short. I may even have a bit of the apple, too. A very small sliver. If your grandfather hasn't eaten it all?" she said as Jane quickly picked up the sterling silver cake server.

Lillian's acquiescence seemed to bring peace to the table. She sensed the tension disperse like a puff of smoke as talk turned to other matters, like a cold snap expected in the coming week and the prospects for Boston's football team, who had gotten off to a poor start.

It had taken them a while, but they'd finally found a topic upon which she had no opinion.

It was after eight o'clock by the time Lucy's family had finished dinner and was ready for dessert. She felt a little surge of warmth as she remembered her children would stay through the weekend and there was no rush. No rush at all.

"Let's cut into some of those pies we brought home, Lucy," Charlie said.

"I was just going to bring them out," Lucy said, rising from her seat.

"I'll help you," Zoey offered.

"Me, too," James added.

"There's apple and pumpkin from the diner. And I made pecan." Lucy glanced over her shoulder at C.J. Predictably, his eyes lit up.

"Thanks, Mom. You're a peach."

She'd stayed up till one the night before last, waiting for C.J.'s favorite pie to come out of the oven, but his delighted expression more than made up for the effort. "You're very welcome, honey. I know how much you like it."

As she slipped into the kitchen, following Zoey and James, she heard Jamie tease his older brother, "You'd better marry someone who can make pecan pie, bro. Or it's not going to work out too well."

Charlie laughed. "Listen to this guy, giving relationship advice. Your mom could hardly boil water when I met her. Everything she knows about cooking, she learned from yours truly."

Zoey was pouring milk into a pitcher and widened her eyes. "Mom, are you really going to let him get away with that?"

Lucy winked at her. "That's not true, Charlie," she called back. "I knew how to cook very well when we met."

She emerged from the kitchen, carrying the pecan pie. Zoey had the coffee and cream, and James followed with the apple and pumpkin pies.

"Sure you did." Charlie rolled his eyes and Lucy laughed.

"I said I knew how. I just didn't like doing it," she added, making her children laugh. "I certainly didn't see myself cooking for a big family back then. Or married to a restaurant owner."

The diner was not quite a restaurant, Lucy knew. But she didn't mind upgrading the establishment for Charlie's benefit.

"Did you want to be an actor, Mom?" Zoey met her gaze and smiled.

"What makes you ask that?"

"Dad told me," Zoey answered. "He showed me that article in the *Messenger.* He said you could have been one of those big-shot actors coming to town."

"Your dad was exaggerating," Lucy said with a fond smile for Charlie. "I never really got too far with acting." She felt a bit embarrassed about that early, naive, and fleeting dream, but she also didn't want to deny it. "But for a while, I thought being onstage was the road for me."

"That's very interesting," James said. "Was this in high school or after?"

"I belonged to the drama club in high school, but I was so shy, I was terrified to perform in front of all the kids I knew. I stuck with the group who worked behind the scenes. With props and prompting lines. After I graduated, I joined the troupe at the community theater. Just for a year or so."

"She was onstage all the time," Charlie said. "Sang and danced, too. Prettiest girl up there. You should have heard her curtain calls. People jumped up in their seats to clap for her."

One person did. Charlie would applaud and cheer so loudly that she felt embarrassed. But in a good way.

She didn't really know Charlie well at the time. He'd been a few years ahead of her in high school. It wasn't until Fran and Tucker began to date that they got to know each other, thrown together by the courtship of their closest friends.

When the Tulleys got married, she was the maid of honor and Charlie was the best man. They were paired off at the wedding, as close as the little plastic figures on top of the cake. That was when their own romance began. Charlie was a very handsome and attentive escort and a surprisingly graceful dancer. It was amazing to her what a tuxedo could do for a man. Cliché or not, the Tulleys' wedding day sparked a romance between them, and every year since, they noted Fran and Tucker's anniversary for their own reasons.

She had almost been done with acting by then, starting to see that her interest was superficial and easily discouraged. But for a brief moment, she'd felt a career onstage was her destiny, however silly the notion seemed later.

After high school graduation, she had decided to hold off on starting college and instead work for a year or so to earn money for tuition and other expenses. Her parents weren't well off, and even the community college she planned to attend was a stretch for the family.

Lucy wasn't sure why she'd tried out that first time. To make up for those high school plays when she'd worked backstage? She won a part in *Oklahoma!* and even had a few lines. That was all it took. She was bitten by the bug.

She juggled her schedule at a few different jobs to fit in rehearsals and performances. She could never wait to get to the theater. That's where she met Craig, and the chemistry seemed instant. At least for her it was, the moment she saw his dark gaze and heard his voice. Lucy felt as if they were meant to be together. Her plans to study nursing faded into the background. She was gripped by a passion for acting— and a passion for the young, handsome actor who had won her heart.

They talked about the future—a future together. How they would go to California and be discovered. It could happen. It only took one lucky break. Or two. Or so they told themselves. Lucy's savings for college started to look like the perfect cushion for their adventure. Craig was saving up for their trip, too, from his part-time jobs. How could she resist such a heady, exciting plan? Or resist the young man who offered it—along with his heart and his soul? She could not. Neither did she doubt him or their love. Not for one single second.

They chose a night in late September to run away together. She waited at their special spot, under a birch tree near a pond, not far from where the Morgans now lived. It was a lovely and deserted spot where they'd picnicked on long summer afternoons or sat gazing at star-filled skies and telling each other everything, all their most intimate feelings and secrets.

She waited hours for him. But Craig never showed up. Finally, she gave up and went home. She hid her suitcase in the garage so that no one could guess her failed plans. It was far harder to hide her broken heart.

The bright lights and applause seemed to mock her after that. But Lucy persisted, unwilling to admit that Craig's betrayal had tainted acting for her. She remained dogged in her ambition to carry out their plans all on her own. She refused to admit, even to herself, that however much she enjoyed performing, maybe it wasn't what she truly wanted to do with her life, and that maybe part of her passion for it had been tied up in her feelings for Craig.

"I did enjoy it. And I had some talent. But it was more of a hobby," she said finally. "I never had the drive, or the talent, it takes to be really successful at it. To be in the movies, say. Or star on Broadway."

"Don't listen to her. You know how modest your mom is," Charlie interrupted. "The problem was, once we met, your mom knew she could never leave me behind. Even for a life of fame and fortune."

"Right, Dad. I'm sure that's exactly what happened," C.J. teased.

Charlie shrugged. "Isn't that so, Lucy? You tell that wise apple of ours."

"Something like that," she replied with a smile.

Charlie had asked her out a dozen times before she agreed. She liked him well enough. It wasn't that. She felt a bit numb inside and didn't want to date anyone. But Charlie was persistent and charming, in his way. He made her laugh and made her feel so special, as if she had stepped down from a cloud. After Craig, her life seemed so bleak, as if she had been living in a vividly colored movie that suddenly turned to grainy black and white.

Somehow, Charlie brought the color back, and the sunshine. She began to accept that sometimes a bad turn in life could lead to something even better. Something she hadn't ever expected or imagined. Like falling in love with Charlie Bates.

"Seriously, kids," she added, "who wouldn't choose the Clam Box over Hollywood?" They all found the question very amusing. Charlie laughed loudest.

"That's exactly my point," he insisted.

Her younger son, Jamie, caught her gaze. "I heard that the movie crew is looking for extras, Mom. Maybe you should try out."

Lucy cringed at the thought. "I don't think so, dear. That ship has sailed, as they say."

"Are you sure, Mom?" Zoey asked. "It might be fun. And I bet you were a good actor."

Lucy smiled at the compliment. "I don't think I could do it now. Even if I wanted to. Guess I'm in a different place. And I have to say that every step in your life, even the disappointments and mistakes, gets you closer to where you're meant to be." Lucy looked around at the faces of her children, whom she loved so much and still wanted to help and guide, even though they were mostly beyond that now. "It was hard to put aside that notion. But I see now that the choice should have been very clear. I was lucky. I took the right path, and I'd never trade the way my life turned out. Not even for fame and fortune."

Zoey reached over and squeezed her hand. "I guess we're all glad you decided not to be a movie star, too."

C.J. stared at his sister across the table. "Speak for yourself. Now I'll never get a Maserati."

C.J. was not nearly as materialistic as he sometimes sounded. Lucy hoped not, anyway—though his profession tended to stress appearances over content. She did worry about that.

"I can give you a bowl of spaghetti, buddy," her husband offered. "Would that help?"

Everyone laughed at the offer, and Lucy had to smile at C.J.'s expression. Some things never changed. That was something else to be thankful for today.

LILLIAN HAD ENJOYED HER FAMILY'S THANKSGIVING VISIT BUT WAS quite tired by the end of it, and a bit short-tempered, too. She could hardly wait for them to finish with their helpfulness. Finally, she shooed them out of the kitchen.

"Thank you all very much. Estrella will take care of the rest. You can all go home now. Please?"

There were hasty but heartfelt farewells. Emily and Jessica dropped by frequently during the week. There was no lack of seeing them. Lillian saw Jane often, too, though she had the busiest schedule of anyone right now. Sara and Luke would stay with Emily a night or two, then return to Boston. Their visits were rare. Sara had always been a big hugger—an expression of affection Ezra enjoyed but Lillian merely tolerated.

"You're coming home for Christmas, aren't you?" Lillian asked mid-embrace. "I'll see you then, dear. Let's not stand in the draft. Drive safely."

She finally shut the front door and turned the lock, leaning heavily on her cane. The sudden silence in the large foyer was nearly deafening. "Good grief, I thought they'd never go."

Ezra stood beside her and laughed. "You always say that, no matter if they stay five hours or five minutes. I had a fine time. I wish we had more family dinners. In the old days, it was every Sunday, without fail. The whole family got together for an early dinner after church. Usually a nice roast and potatoes. Remember?"

"I do. The tradition is not likely to return. I fear it's gone the way of the horse-drawn carriage."

Ezra headed to the kitchen at the back of the house, and Lillian followed with her hobbling step. "Every week was a bit much. I don't mind the holidays, but I do sometimes wish they weren't all squashed together. Christmas is hot on the heels of Thanksgiving, and then *boom* . . . it's over in the blink of an eye, like a big, festive explosion. And after that there's a long, dreary winter to face."

"Very true, dear. Too bad you were not around when Thanksgiving was invented. You could have spread the merrymaking out more evenly. It's a much more sensible approach."

Ezra's wit was so dry, sometimes even she was not sure when he was teasing her.

"Go ahead, mock me. I'm low-hanging fruit. L-O-L, as the kids say." She shot him a look, and he had the grace to color a bit with embarrassment.

"You know I love you, Lily. Love Only Lily—that's my L-O-L," he quipped.

Lillian had no answer for that. Though he did remind her daily how lucky she was that Dr. Ezra Elliot had fallen for her decades ago, at the same time she had met and fallen for Oliver. But Ezra had never given up on her and had finally seized his chance to win her heart. And here they were. Happily married in the third act, for nearly eleven years now. Who would have ever predicted that? L-O-L, indeed.

They'd arrived in the kitchen. Ezra was already perusing the refrigerator, peeking under various wrappings.

"You're not having more food, are you?" Her comment was half-command and half-question.

He didn't seem to hear her, then he turned around, holding a plastic container. "Maybe a bite or two. They say turkey helps you sleep."

"Indigestion certainly doesn't," she replied.

"Can I make you a cup of tea, dear? Ginger will settle your stomach."

"I don't have indigestion, Ezra. I meant that you'll have it if you get into those leftovers." He replied with his usual good-natured grin. She knew that meant he would do as he pleased, thank you very much for the advice. Lillian sighed. "I will pass on the ginger tea. I'm heading upstairs."

Ezra popped open the container of turkey. "Leave the light on for me. I won't be long."

Lillian was making her way out of the kitchen when a cacophony right outside the back door startled her to stillness.

She leaned on her cane and turned her head. "What in the world was that? Did that dimwit Luke pile the garbage so high it's tipped over? What an unholy mess that will be."

Ezra had hurried over to the door and flipped on the outside light. He peered through the small windowpanes. "Maybe an animal got into the trash."

He grabbed his parka and flat tweed cap from the hook by the door, then found a flashlight on the shelf near the laundry room. "Let me see what's going on. I suppose the raccoons are entitled to a Thanksgiving dinner if they can find one."

Only Ezra would say that. Lillian shook her head. "If you do find raccoons, please don't invite any in for dessert."

Ezra laughed quietly as he sauntered out the door. Lillian stayed inside but watched through the glass. It frosted with her breath, and she impatiently cleared the spot with the edge of her sweater sleeve.

It was cold outside, the night sky clear and dark. A thin silver sliver of moon hovered over bare trees like a single Christmas tree ornament hung from a bit of string. No snow yet, but it was almost December. There soon would be. It was winter in New England; snow was a certainty.

She watched Ezra plod out to the trash pails, the beam from the flashlight bobbing with each step. He came to a sudden stop and pointed the light at something down low.

Lately it seemed they needed so many pails. Different types of garbage couldn't touch anymore. It was like separating laundry—there were pails for paper, tinfoil, food trash, bottles, and who knows what else. Lillian had a dickens of a time remembering what went where each time she needed to throw something out. Luckily, Estrella kept it all in order for them.

Ezra was peeking behind a big blue pail, making cooing sounds. She opened the door a crack to hear him clearly. Yes . . . he was calling to something, in a soft, enticing tone.

Was the man stark raving mad? Joking about raccoons was one thing. Coaxing them close was positively crazy.

"Ezra? What are you doing out there? Who—I mean, *what*—are you talking to? Leave those scavengers alone. You'll get rabies, and then where will we be?"

He turned quickly and scowled at her. "Pipe down, Lily. It's just a little dog. He must be lost, poor fellow. We don't want to scare him away."

Why not? she nearly asked. That's what she'd do.

"Let him go, Ezra," she said. "He doesn't need our assistance. You know how people are. Too lazy to walk their pets. They let them wander all over the neighborhood. He's probably on his way home right now."

Ezra had his back turned toward her. If he'd heard a word she'd said, he didn't show it. She took a tentative step out, cane first, her free hand grasping the doorknob. Thank goodness there was no frost on the steps. She hadn't thought of that. She pulled the edges of her cardigan up around her throat. She'd catch her death, and then he would be sorry he'd acted so foolishly.

"Ezra? Come back inside this minute. Leave that animal alone. Send him on his way. I need to get to bed, and you should, too."

Outside without a coat, she felt chilled to the bone. Whatever was she thinking? That man would drive her crazy before it was through, that was a certainty.

When he finally turned, her heart sank. His face was lit up, as if he'd just won a prize of some kind, and his arms were full. Full of white fur, four dangling paws, and a droopy dog head with floppy ears and a nose as black as a piece of coal.

"Stand aside, stand aside," Ezra instructed her. "He jumped right into my arms. He needs our help, Lily. I can't just leave him out there."

Lillian was ready to argue with that assertion, but Ezra was moving like a steam engine. She had no choice but to pull open the door and stand aside as he carried the questionable package in. She followed and shut the door, shivering. "Now look what you've done. I've probably caught something."

Ezra had set the dog down on the floor of the mudroom but remained crouched by its side. He squinted up. "Who told you to go out without your coat? That wasn't very wise."

"I had to see what you were up to. Not that it helped." She took a breath and smoothed down her sweater. "I hope you don't intend to keep that filthy animal in this house. I don't think *that's* very wise," she countered.

Ezra's gaze was fixed on the dog. He gently stroked its head. It wasn't a tiny dog; it was medium sized, with mostly shaggy white fur. The wiry kind, not soft and silky like the fur of an Irish setter or a golden retriever. It had brown coloring on its face, like a mask, that extended over its ears. There were additional brown patches on its back and the tip of its tail, which was wagging wildly. It turned away from

Ezra and stared up at her with dark brown eyes, panting. Then it leaned forward and licked her leg.

Lillian jumped back, as much as she was able, letting out a little shriek. She was instantly embarrassed and annoyed. "For goodness' sake. Hold it back. It attacked me!"

Ezra laughed. "He likes you, Lily. He just gave you a lick. That's what dogs do when they like a person."

She didn't believe that. "More like tasting me for future reference."

Ezra stood up and pressed his hands to the small of his back. She knew he would soon be complaining after squatting down that long.

"Now that you mention it, I'm sure he's hungry. I'll give him a little turkey and some water."

"You'll do no such thing. I don't even know why you took him inside. Out he goes. This instant. He looks well cared for and well fed." That was not entirely true. Still, she held her ground. "He has an owner somewhere. Someone who's probably looking for him right now."

"That might be," Ezra conceded. "But I checked his collar. There are no tags. Maybe there was some ID but it fell off? I think you're right, though, Lily. His owners could be looking for him right now. They might be worried sick that the little fellow is lost. I think we should keep him safe, just for tonight. We can call Jessica tomorrow. She'll know how to figure out where he belongs."

Lillian knew she had painted herself into this corner. She felt stumped and exhausted, too tired to argue any more about the dirty little beast.

"Suit yourself. But that beast doesn't place a paw any farther than that mudroom. We'll die of some dreadful disease. As it is, I need to clean this drool off my leg with alcohol."

Ezra snickered and stared at the floor. The dog sat at his feet, gazing around alertly, first at Ezra, and then at her. The thing seemed to be smiling at her, just the tip of its pink tongue showing, along with a few bright white teeth. It was . . . uncanny.

"Promise me, Ezra," she demanded.

He nodded and offered a serious expression. "On my life, Lily. Not a paw. I'll make him a little bed with some old towels and bring his food and water out here. And shut the door."

"Excellent plan. Why don't you leave a phone so he can call room service if he desires any other comforts during the night?" Without waiting for his answer, she shook her head in frustration and headed for their bedroom.

"Tomorrow morning, bright and early, that dog is gone. No two ways about it," she called back over her shoulder.

"Absolutely. Bright and early," he echoed.

Lillian hoped to heaven he wasn't just humoring her, as he sometimes did. She had seen that look on her husband's face before. A born nurturer, a sucker for any creature in need—sick, wounded, financially troubled, or otherwise. Two-legged or four. Of course, that's why he had been such a wonderful doctor and was still beloved and revered by his former patients. Ezra's nurturing talents aside, she believed what she'd told him. The dog had owners and must be returned to wherever it was he belonged. End of story.

She settled herself on the stair seat, set her cane across her lap, and pressed the remote. The mechanical chair glided up the long staircase, carrying her to the second floor with a gentle whirring sound.

With some effort, she heaved herself up again and headed to their room.

Jessica will know what to do. She'll agree with me. I'll ring her first thing and make her take that dog away. Before Ezra gets any more crazy ideas in that soft head of his.

CHAPTER FOUR

~✦~

"WHERE HAVE YOU BEEN?" LILLIAN LOOKED UP FROM THE newspaper as Ezra entered the house through the side door. She wasn't even dressed yet, but he had already been outside. Bundled up for the cold, he led the little dog in on a leash fashioned from a leather belt.

"What does it look like? I took the dog for a walk. A tired dog is a good dog." He hung up his jacket and hat and pulled off his muffler.

"A tired husband as well," Lillian muttered. "I've spoken to Jessica. She'll be here soon to take that thing away. She totally agrees he must be returned to his rightful owner. The sooner the better. As we agreed, as well," she reminded him.

That wasn't exactly what Jessica had told her. She'd actually said she was very busy this morning with her silly animal rescue tasks and would be by later in the day—if she was able to come at all. Lillian had insisted that she make time, but Jessica, in her sweet, even-tempered way, could be absolutely intractable when she wanted to be. Lillian didn't think it wise to tell Ezra the dog's departure might be delayed. It would only encourage him to get more attached.

Ezra had poured himself a cup of coffee and sat across from her at the table. "All well and true. What if Jessica can't locate the dog's owner? Then what?"

Lillian had finished the news section of the paper and pushed it across the table to him, as was their habit. Ezra, who was always eager to check the headlines, didn't seem to notice.

"What will happen to Teddy then?" Ezra asked.

"Teddy? You've named it? Already?" Lillian peered at him over the edge of her glasses.

Ezra shrugged and sipped his coffee. "I couldn't keep calling him 'Boy.' Certainly not 'it,' like you do." He gave her a sharp look. "I think Teddy suits him. Or maybe just T.R.? He reminds me of Theodore Roosevelt. Small but strong, spunky, and spirited. But a real gentleman in his manner."

Lillian let loose a dramatic sigh and gazed at the ceiling. "Saints preserve me. I'm living with a madman." She pinned her husband with a steely-eyed gaze. "You realize that you're totally anthropomorphizing this animal, don't you? It's a mangy stray dog. A mutt, most likely— not even a pedigree. T.R., indeed."

Ezra had respected her wishes and confined the dog to the mud-room, but instead of keeping the door closed, as she would have preferred, he'd placed a barrier across the threshold with a piece of cardboard that merely blocked the bottom half of the doorway. It was just high enough to reveal the dog's head and shoulders. Lillian pretended to ignore him as he sat there staring at her with those beady brown eyes.

When the dog finally whined, Ezra chuckled. "Poor little chap. He smells your eggs and toast. I bet he'd like a taste."

Ezra eyed the leftovers on her dish. She pulled it back abruptly. "This is human food. It will upset his stomach."

"Nonsense. Dogs can eat scrambled eggs." But Ezra didn't make a move to take her plate and prove his point. Thankfully.

She knew that she would have fought him for it.

Estrella swept into the kitchen, carrying a basket of laundry. She'd been upstairs, making beds and straightening up, as was her routine. She had been with them so many years, Lillian didn't know what they would do without her. Though, much to her embarrassment now, she had objected to Estrella when she'd been hired to help right after Ezra's heart attack. Lillian could now see it was a good thing her husband had prevailed in that argument. He'd been proven right that time, though it was a rare instance.

"Good morning, Mr. Ezra. I see we have a houseguest?" Estrella greeted Ezra with a sunny smile. He was definitely her favorite, though she was always respectful and considerate to both of them. But she did like Ezra better.

"Yes, and one who isn't staying long," Lillian replied. She sighed and focused on the crossword puzzle.

"Isn't he cute?" Ezra said to the housekeeper. "Do you like dogs, Estrella? You're not afraid of them, are you?"

"Not at all. I like dogs very much. Where did he come from?"

"Ezra found him last night, eating from the trash bins. We need to find his owners. Doubtlessly worried sick that he's disappeared. When, in fact, he's being held captive by a self-indulgent old man."

"He's being kept out of the cold and safe from being hit by a car and from bigger animals that might hurt him. And fed proper food," Ezra corrected her.

Estrella looked at Lillian and then at Ezra, as usual showing no reaction to their bickering, which was another reason she had stayed so long in their employment. That was a rare talent indeed, Lillian had always thought.

"Would you like some breakfast, Mr. Ezra?" Estrella asked.

"I would. Just some toast . . . and maybe a scrambled egg?" he added.

"Of course. I will prepare it for you." Estrella disappeared into the kitchen. Lillian looked up to find Ezra smiling.

"I know what you're up to. What do I care? Make the dog sick if you must." Before she could say more, her cell phone buzzed. She squinted down at a text message from Jessica.

On the run more than I thought today. Not sure I can make it over this afternoon for the dog. Will be in touch.

"A note from Jessica," she reported. "She'll be a little later than she thought. But will take the dog today," she insisted, contrary to the message.

"A little later, you say? Good. I have time to give Teddy a bath. He's been living rough, poor fellow. Might as well clean him up if I can. For his homecoming."

Lillian imagined Ezra bathing the dog in the very tub she used and felt her blood pressure rise.

"In the laundry room or basement, I'm sure you mean. I'm going upstairs to dress. I don't want to hear another word about that dog today. Until Jessica comes to remove him."

Without glancing at her husband, she rose from the table and walked out of the room as swiftly as she was able.

She felt the hard edge of her cell phone in her bathrobe pocket. She would call Jessica again once she got upstairs and out of Ezra's earshot.

She obviously didn't understand the crisis here. Jessica had to come today. Immediately. What could be so important that she couldn't come and take the dog?

If she denies me this small request, I must take matters into my own hands. There is always a solution to a problem, if one has nerve and will enough. That dog can be let loose, back into the outdoors, as easily as it was brought into this house.

LAUREN'S AUNT'S CELL PHONE RANG INSISTENTLY, RESTING IN THE cup holder of the van. "Can you check who's calling me, honey? Don't pick up, just tell me who it is."

Lauren picked up the phone and checked the screen. "It's your mother again. Maybe I should answer?"

Jessica shook her head. "No, don't. I know what she's calling about. I just sent her a text. If it's a real emergency, she'll call Emily. I'll get back to her later, once these guys are unloaded and settled down."

Lauren set her aunt's phone down and leaned toward the window, cracked open just a bit for air, despite the chilly weather.

The cargo area, right up to the back of their seats, was filled with animals that she and her aunt had just picked up at a local farm. Most were in plastic and wire crates of various sizes. Sam had fitted the back of the van with a few cushioned partitions where tethered goats stood side by side, braying insistently, like malcontent airline passengers, while ducks quacked and chickens clucked in a barnyard chorus.

Only a small baby pig that Jessica had handled with extra care lay silently in his crate. The crate was tucked between their seats so that Lauren could watch him during the ride.

She wasn't sure how her aunt managed to stay on the road with the racket going on. Or the aroma, eau de barnyard, that filled the small space and wafted up from their clothes, which were splotched with mud and manure.

Lauren considered tossing all her clothes out once she got home—her oldest jeans, a worn-out red sweatshirt with a big lobster across the chest, and an ugly green camouflage vest that her father had stashed in the back of his closet. Her big rubber boots could be hosed off. She'd salvage those at least.

"How's our little friend doing?" Jessica asked, slanting her head toward the piglet.

Lauren peered into the crate. He appeared to be sleeping, breathing deeply, his eyelids—almost translucent—closed tight. His pink skin was so pale, and he was so small. So much like a newborn baby. Her heart melted at the sight.

"He's either carsick or sleeping. Though I can't see how with all the chatter going on back there."

"Babies are like that, right?"

Lauren shrugged. "I wouldn't know. Not firsthand, I mean."

"Not yet," her aunt corrected her. She cast Lauren a knowing glance, then turned back to the road. "It was nice to see Joe Wagner. He's such a nice guy."

She had used the word "nice" two times within one breath to describe Joe, Lauren noticed. And she was hardly the first person Lauren had known to do that. "Yes, he's very *nice*," Lauren echoed, her sarcasm lost on her aunt.

"You two seem to get along so well. How's that going? I mean, you're working at his office and playing golf and all?"

Lauren laughed. "Did Mom ask you to squeeze me for some info?"

Her aunt smiled and shook her head, her dark curls springing from her loose ponytail. "Of course not. I'm just curious. Sorry to be such a nosy old lady."

"You're not," Lauren said. "Old, I mean," she teased her. "I always have fun with Joe. He's easy to be with. Even to work with," she added. "We get along well. We always did. But I don't see any big romance blossoming, if that's what you mean."

Jessica turned to her for a moment, then looked back at the road. "I understand. But you just don't know about these things, honey. I wouldn't be so quick to rule him out."

Lauren had already ruled out Joe as a romantic possibility, for a few reasons. Yet her sisters, mother, and now aunt were all encouraging her to take a second look. Were they seeing something she didn't see? Or just noticing that she was almost thirty, her choices narrowing and her biological clock ticking louder and louder?

The thing about Joe was he looked good on paper—attractive, smart, successful. Easygoing and kind. There were so many good points to recommend him to an unattached woman her age. Still, each time she considered the question, she knew there was simply something missing. Would she feel differently if she gave him more time?

She glanced at her aunt. She didn't want to get into it right now. Jessica seemed to sense that as well.

"It was good of you to help me today, Lauren. I ran through my entire volunteer list before I called you."

"I'm glad you did. This is fun. I bet my sisters aren't even up yet."

"Probably not. I'll get you home shortly. You'll have plenty of time to visit with them."

Lauren didn't doubt it. She had no real plans for the day and was happy to make good on her promise to help the rescue group. Her aunt had received a desperate call late last night. A local farm had to close down and clear the property by December first, only four days from now. The farmer's arrangements for passing on his livestock had fallen through, and all of their noisy passengers would have been sent to slaughterhouses if Grateful Paw hadn't stepped in.

It felt good to help save them. Lauren hadn't expected that part of her morning's work. And they were almost done now. She would help her aunt unload the animals and do whatever was needed to get them settled. Maybe her uncle or cousins would come out to speed that part of the job along? Then she would head home and have a long, hot shower. Next time her aunt tapped her for this gig, she would wear nose plugs—and maybe even earplugs—she decided.

She glanced out the window, checking the road for familiar landmarks. They were driving on the Beach Road, but in the opposite direction from her aunt's house.

"Do you have more animals to pick up, Aunt Jess?"

"I don't think any more would fit, even if I did."

"Why are we driving in this direction? Your house is the other way." Lauren pointed out her window.

"Oh . . . didn't I tell you? There's no room in our barn right now. We're bringing these guys to Sawyer's. To Cole McGuire's barn, I mean. He still has plenty of space there." She turned to Lauren, looking suddenly concerned. "I hope that's not a problem? He promised me that he found the hole in the fence and fixed it."

Lauren shook her head, her stomach knotting. "If he said he did, then he did. Besides, I'm not representing the golf course today. I just want to help you."

"And I'm very grateful," Jessica answered with a smile. "And lucky."

That makes one of us, Lauren answered silently. Of all the days to confront Cole McGuire again . . . She looked and smelled like she'd just rolled around in a hogpen. She glanced down at her clothes and wanted to scream.

What doesn't kill you makes you stronger, she reminded herself. She knew this morning would certainly put that motto to the test.

McGuire was waiting for them, standing just outside the corral near the barn. He waved as the van pulled up.

Lauren took a quick, deep breath and hoped her aunt didn't notice her distress. *It's showtime,* she silently coached herself.

Her aunt had turned the van so that the driver's side faced Cole. He smiled as he greeted her, then noticed Lauren hop out the passenger side. His mouth hung open for a moment, and she felt she'd scored a point or two by catching him off guard.

Jessica was already talking to him about the animals. Lauren masked her emotions with a neutral expression, as she had been trained to do in her work. Then she walked over to join them.

"Good morning, Mr. McGuire," she said politely, the barest note of irony in her tone.

"Ms. Willoughby. Here to check the fence repairs before more animals check in? I believe the deadline is Monday. By the way, that letter from your firm scared the chickens. They haven't laid all week."

"Really? You should speak to the rooster about that," Lauren countered.

Her aunt looked puzzled by the edge in their voices. Lauren hated to stick her in the middle of this, but there was no help for it. She had been perfectly polite and he was still totally disagreeable. As she had expected.

"I know you've met my niece, Cole," Jessica intervened. "She was nice enough to give me a hand this morning. I couldn't find a single volunteer to help today."

He turned back to Lauren. "You told me you knew of Jessica Morgan. You never said she's your aunt."

"No, I didn't. What difference does that make?"

"No difference at all," Jessica cut in. "Cole, can you give us a hand unloading this gang? We'll be out of your way in no time."

He glared at Lauren, then followed Jessica to the back of the van. Her aunt pulled open the doors, climbed into the van, and pushed out a ramp that led from the tailgate to the ground.

"Goats first. Whoever said the squeaky wheel gets the oil was right."

Lauren stood aside as Jessica and Cole dealt with the first goat. The creature stepped into the daylight, its reaction a mixture of confusion and stubbornness, much like a person forced into a big, unexpected change. Lauren could totally relate.

"Come along. Don't be scared. You're going to be fine." Cole coaxed the little goat down the ramp, his manner surprisingly kind and gentle.

He's a lot nicer to animals than to humans, she noticed.

Once he was headed for the barn, Lauren took her turn and carried out two crates of chickens, one in each hand.

"There's a coop next to the barn," her aunt said. "Just pop them inside. We'll check on them later before we go."

Lauren took care of the chickens and, after that, two big lop-eared rabbits. Cole was escorting the second goat, and her aunt was taking care of a pair of ducks.

The van was empty and she had succeeded in avoiding further conversation with him, or even more poisonous looks.

Eager to go, Lauren decided to wait for her aunt inside the van. She expected Jessica and McGuire had to discuss the care of the animals and how long they might stay.

She wondered who paid for their feed and hay and other costs while the animals were housed here. The rescue group probably worked something out with him. Glancing around at the little cottage and beat-up truck, she doubted he could afford to cover all the costs himself.

She slid open the van door and noticed that the crate with the baby pig remained. He was softly grunting and seemed fretful. Lauren lifted the carrier with care. "Hey, there. Don't worry. We won't leave you behind," Lauren cooed to him.

She headed for the barn with slow, steady steps, taking care not to jostle the baby too much. He seemed scared enough as it was.

She had just reached the corral fence when a little girl burst through the cottage door and ran to meet her. Lauren stopped in her tracks at the sight. The little girl looked as if she had stepped off a picture in a storybook, with a red jacket matching the apple-red spots on her cheeks. Her blue eyes were shining, and her long brown hair flew behind her like silk ribbons.

"Hey! . . . Hey, lady! Did you bring us more animals?" the girl called out.

"Yes, we did." Before Lauren could say more, the little girl was right beside her, peering into the crate.

"What's in there? A baby pig? He's so cute." The girl hopped up and down with excitement. Lauren couldn't help but smile.

She crouched down so the girl could see inside the crate clearly. "It is a baby pig. But he's very small and scared. We have to be gentle with him, and talk softly. Loud noises scare him."

The girl suddenly looked very serious. "I'll whisper, is that good?" Lauren could hardly hear her hushed words.

Lauren touched her shoulder. "That's perfect."

"He's so small. Can I pet him?"

Lauren thought that would be all right. The piglet had to be taken from the crate very soon anyway.

"Sure. I'll take him out and you can see him better. Just be gentle. Touch him like your fingers were feathers."

The girl grinned at that idea. Lauren crouched down, set the crate on the ground, unlatched the lid, then lifted out the piglet. He weighed no more than a pound or two. She suddenly realized how fragile and vulnerable he was.

She held him out and the little girl ran her fingertip over the piglet's head. "He's just a little baby," she said, her voice full of awe.

"He is," Lauren agreed. He squirmed in Lauren's grasp, then turned his head and tried to suck the girl's finger. The girl laughed and pulled her hand away. "He's just hungry," Lauren explained.

"Where's his mother?"

"I don't know. My aunt is trying to find him a new mother. There's a pig in your barn named Tilly? My aunt thinks she'll take care of him."

The girl looked concerned. "I hope so. I wish he could find his real mother." Her reply was so serious, Lauren was surprised.

The girl looked up at her. "Are you a farmer? Women can be farmers. I learned that in school."

"That's true." Lauren managed not to laugh. "I'm not a farmer, but I love animals."

"I might be a farmer when I grow up. I love animals, too. Especially pigs." She gently stroked the piglet again. "What's his name?"

Lauren shrugged. "I don't think he has one. Why don't you name him?"

The girl thought about the question for a moment. "My mom had a cat named Mr. Whiskers, but that doesn't seem good for a baby pig."

So there was a mom somewhere? Lauren had already guessed that the girl was Cole McGuire's daughter, the one he had rushed off to pick up at school the other day. Lauren knew it was too quick to assume, but somehow she sensed the little girl's mother was not living here with Cole and the girl.

"What would you name him?" the girl asked.

Lauren didn't have to think about that much. "I'd call him Wilbur. Like the pig in *Charlotte's Web*? Do you know that story?"

The girl shook her head.

"That was my favorite book when I was a kid. Even now," Lauren added. "Wilbur was a lonely little pig without a mother, too," she recalled. "But things turned out all right for him."

"My dad reads to me to a lot, at night before bed. I'll ask him to find that book for us."

"Good idea. I'm sure he can find it at the library."

Lauren couldn't quite picture surly Cole McGuire reading bedtime stories. *But wonders never cease in this world*, she reminded herself.

She noticed her aunt and Cole emerge from the barn. As his gaze settled on her and his daughter, he frowned, then walked quickly toward them.

She couldn't quite fathom his reaction, though he certainly had one. She stood up, the piglet cradled in her arms. Was he concerned— or even angry—to find his daughter talking so freely with a stranger? Parents were very cautious these days, she knew, and with good reason.

"I was just showing your daughter the piglet. She was very excited to see him," Lauren explained.

He nodded, his mouth a tight line. "Phoebe, let Lauren bring the piglet into the barn now. You can see him later."

"Can I just go with her and watch? Please?"

Absolutely, Lauren was about to blurt out. But she caught herself, for once, and instead waited to hear his response.

"Yes, of course. We'll go together. Jessica made a spot for the piglet with Tilly. Let's see if she likes him."

Phoebe ran and practically skipped ahead, too excited to keep pace with the slow, plodding adults.

Lauren couldn't help but smile as she watched her. "How old is she?"

"She's five years old."

"She's adorable. We had a very nice conversation."

He answered with a curious look. "I noticed."

Lauren didn't know what to say after that. Jessica was standing in the open doorway of the barn, waiting for them, with Phoebe hopping at her side.

"Here he comes, our little charmer. Tilly will fall in love with him," Jessica predicted.

Lauren hoped that was so. She didn't know much about these things and wondered what would happen to the little pig if the sow didn't nurture him. He felt so fragile, nestling into the warmth of her arms.

"You'll be just fine, Wilbur," she whispered, hoping that no one noticed.

In the shadowy barn, Lauren handed Wilbur over to Jessica, who stood in the pigpen with a large sow who was covered with black spots.

"Tilly's just had a litter," her aunt explained. "I hope she takes to him."

She set the piglet down next to the sow, who was lying on her side, feeding her offspring. Jessica set him among the brood and watched while he found a spot to eat. Tilly sniffed him curiously, then lowered her head again.

"So far, so good. I hope her maternal instincts take over." Jessica looked up at Cole and Phoebe. "You'll have to watch that he's fitting in with the litter and getting enough to eat. And that the other pigs aren't pushing him around too much. He's much smaller than they are," she warned. "If she doesn't take to him and protect him, someone will have to bottle-feed him for a while. He's still young and at risk if he's not nursed properly."

"I'll watch him, Mrs. Morgan. I love him already." Phoebe's tone was definite and touched Lauren's heart.

Jessica rested her hand on Phoebe's shoulder and smiled. "Thank you, honey. I won't worry one bit with you watching over him."

Her aunt glanced around the barn at the other animals. "Everyone looks very cozy. Thanks for putting down fresh straw, Cole. I have a few bales at home to bring you but needed the space in the van for the animals. I'll bring them next time."

"No worries—whenever you get to it."

They headed out of the barn. Lauren was eager to go home. She climbed into the van while her aunt gave McGuire a few more instructions.

"Don't worry. I know what to do, and I'll call you with any questions," he replied.

He leaned over and looked into the van as Lauren was clicking her seat belt shut. "No more runaways. Even the one-eyed donkey. Though he'd love to work on his putting."

Lauren tried not to laugh. "Why don't you take him to mini-golf? There's a cute one on the turnpike. It has a *Star Wars* theme."

He rubbed his hand over his mouth and stepped back as Jessica climbed into the van and shut her door. Lauren could tell he, too, was trying not laugh.

Phoebe had been the last to leave the barn and now clung to Cole's leg. She peeked around her father and shyly waved. Lauren wondered what had happened to her loquacious side, but little kids could be like that—bold one minute, timid the next. She really was adorable, either way.

As they pulled out to the main road, her aunt said, "I know he comes across a little brusque at times, but Cole is a good guy. He's been through a lot."

Was it so obvious she'd been thinking of him? Lauren decided Jessica had not guessed that but just wanted to defuse the tension between them. Lauren was curious about Cole but didn't want her aunt to get the wrong idea. A bad divorce is what she guessed Aunt Jess meant by "he's been through a lot." It was fine to leave it at that.

"As long as he's repaired the fence and keeps the animals contained, I don't care what sort of guy he is," Lauren said honestly. "His daughter is sweet."

"You were a big hit with her. Phoebe is usually very shy. More than shy," Jess noted. "She'll barely speak to most people. Even if they're familiar."

So that's why he'd given her odd looks after she spoke with Phoebe. "Baby animals are a good conversation starter," Lauren said. "Not so much at a cocktail party, but works like a charm with a five-year-old."

"I've gone over plenty of times with animals. She's curious but sticks like Velcro to her father and hardly says a word."

Lauren didn't get that. Children usually loved her aunt. She knew how to talk to them, having brought up three of her own. Lauren did believe that children and dogs know who their friends are, and she did love the little ones; she had even considered becoming a teacher instead of an attorney. Maybe Phoebe had picked up on that. Children were sensitive, and Cole McGuire's daughter seemed even more sensitive than usual.

When Lauren imagined having children of her own, there was

always a little girl in the picture, though she was sure she would adore either a daughter *or* a son if and when she was ever blessed with a baby. The "if and when" part had come to the forefront lately. She tried not to think about it or see herself facing some baby-making deadline. But it was hard to put the issue aside when so many of her friends, and her sisters, not only talked about the question but were starting families left and right.

One life crisis at a time, Lauren reminded herself as she stared out at the passing scenery on the Beach Road. Bare trees and stretches of golden marsh grass rushed by, distracting her from worrisome thoughts. It really was so pretty here, she realized.

If I have to figure out my entire life over again, at least I picked a good spot for it.

"You're not wearing *that*, are you?"

Only her sister Jillian could get away with that line. Or their mother. Jillian had a touch of Molly in her personality, too. Though Lauren had inherited the complete software. Amanda, on the other hand, was too considerate to put an outfit critique quite that succinctly.

But Lauren could tell from the expressions on both of their faces as they lounged across her bed that the clothes she'd chosen for her dinner date with Joe did not merit the sister seal of approval. She sat at the dressing table and started on her makeup, determined to weather the protest.

"Black leggings, boots, and a black sweater. It's more than a Saturday-night outfit. In New York, it's a uniform," Lauren countered. "In fact, there might be a law there that everyone under forty has to dress like this at least once a week."

Jillian rolled her eyes. "Spare me the city snobbery. I know we're only country mice, but you look like a Ninja warrior. Or maybe a bank robber? You're not planning on wearing a black ski mask with that, are you?"

Amanda grinned. "What about that wrap dress you had on the other day? That color looks super on you, Lauren."

"The wrap dress! Good idea. You look fantastic in that," Jillian agreed.

Lauren liked the dress and knew that she looked especially attractive in it. It emphasized the positive aspects of her figure and disguised the *less* than positive. But she also had her reasons for not fussing, even though it was Saturday night.

"I purposely went low-key. I don't want to give Joe any ideas," she admitted. "I'm not even sure why I agreed to go out with him again. I'd rather stay home with you guys and play Scrabble."

Jillian sat up, bouncing Amanda. "Wow, don't get too excited. I know he's a lawyer, but he doesn't seem that boring."

"I never thought Joe Wagner was boring." Amanda had been in the same year at school as Lauren and had known Joe well back then, too. "He was always fun to be around, and he seems the same. Just older. And successful," she added, "lawyer or not."

Lauren paused, mascara wand in hand. "You forgot to say, *He's such a nice guy.*"

Amanda met her gaze in the mirror. She knew Lauren well. "I didn't want to remind you. I have a feeling his niceness still counts against him. Though I can't really understand why. Especially considering what you just went through with that stupid Greg. Who was anything but nice to you."

Lauren knew that was true. She wasn't sure either.

"You should definitely know better by now and give good old Joe another look," Jillian added.

Lauren had picked up a lipstick, but Jillian's words gave her pause.

"Eyes or lips," Amanda warned, reminding her of the classic makeup rule. "That jungle red will definitely give him ideas. Though I think he has a few already."

Lauren stared at the lipstick for a moment and set it down. She turned to them. "How do I manage to dress myself every day without step-by-step directions from you two? It's positively amazing."

"Not very well, truth be told," Jillian muttered. She tried to stifle a smile but couldn't stop it. "I'm sorry. You set me up for that one."

Lauren was miffed by the comment for a moment, then couldn't help laughing. But just to show she wasn't taking any sibling guff, she picked up a stuffed dog from the dresser and threw it at her younger sister. Jillian deftly blocked the attack with her arm, and the toy bounced off Amanda, who sat back in surprise.

"You guys! We're not in middle school anymore, remember?"

Jillian ignored her and retaliated with a bed pillow. It landed squarely on the dressing table, and a cloud of face powder flew up and settled on the front of Lauren's black sweater and all over her face.

Lauren blinked and stood up, then stared down at herself. That was the end of her Ninja look. She'd be wearing the wrap dress after all.

"Nice move, Jill. I hope you realize that you're paying the dry-cleaning bill."

"Sorry!" Jillian held her hands up in a sign of surrender as she and Amanda huddled together on the bed, reduced to a fit of giggling. "You should see yourself. It was so worth it."

Lauren glanced at her reflection and started laughing, too.

"I have half a mind to go downstairs just like this. But I know you guys won't let me."

"I dare you," Jillian said.

"It won't make any difference to Joe," Amanda said.

"He'll still think you look great."

Lauren knew that was true. And it gave her pause. If she still thought of Joe as just a pal after tonight, she'd better let him know. Before their high school reunion got out of control.

CHAPTER FIVE

I SAW HIM, LUCY. HE STOOD AS CLOSE TO ME AS YOU ARE
right now. He spoke to me, too," Fran reported in a breathless voice. "Real nice. Just like a regular guy."

Lucy had been careful to avoid the movie insanity that had struck
the town that morning, and she had almost succeeded. She wouldn't
have stopped in the village at all, but just as she was leaving the house,
Rosemary Holmes called and asked if Lucy would kindly pick up a
book of stamps at the post office on the way over. Rosemary had a pile
of thank-you cards to mail and no one else to buy her stamps. The idea
of refusing or pointing out that such an errand was not part of her job
never crossed Lucy's mind.

As long as she avoided the diner—where she knew Charlie was in
overdrive—she figured she'd be fine.

Several huge trailer trucks from the production company, filled
with equipment and who knows what, had pulled into the village lot
by the harbor late last night and covered nearly every spot. She saw a
few people from the crew near the trucks, though she'd heard that the
filming had started at Lilac Hall. There was more equipment there,

she imagined, as well as the fancy trailers belonging to the movie stars. She didn't let her thoughts wander too far in that direction.

Fran's eyes were bright and her cheeks tinged with pink, maybe from running to catch up with Lucy. Or maybe from her morning's adventure.

"I can't believe you went to Lilac Hall this morning, Fran. What time did you get up?"

"Half past five. There was already a crowd when I got there. The stars took forever to come out of their trailers, and then there was another wait to get an autograph. But it was worth it. Craig was so nice. Not snobby at all, just like a regular guy."

Lucy rolled her eyes. "He puts his pants on one leg at a time. Just like Tucker. He didn't descend off a cloud."

Fran laughed. "You know how I love Tucker. But I'm the first to say there a big difference between my husband and Craig Hamilton. Look, he gave me his autograph."

Fran had been clutching a book to her chest and Lucy finally saw the cover: *Scene by Scene*, Craig Hamilton's memoir, which had been published a few months ago. Lucy had known that Fran was reading it. Fran had offered to lend it to her, but Lucy had claimed she had no interest—though she had leafed through it surreptitiously in a book-store one night, feeling a mixture of relief and anger when she discovered that she had not been mentioned, even in passing.

Had their relationship meant so little to him? She had faced that hard truth long ago, but it was still difficult to see the proof in black and white.

Fran read the inscription aloud. "'Thank you for sharing your beautiful village with us. Best wishes, Craig Hamilton.'"

"Very nice. But I wouldn't get too excited. He probably wrote the same thing a hundred times today."

Fran gazed at the page, then finally closed the book. "I know. Even so, I think it was a very gracious thing to say. He's got class. You have to grant him that."

Lucy wasn't willing to grant him anything. "Did he remember you?"

"If he did, he hid it well . . . But I know he'd remember you, Lucy. How could he ever forget?"

"Right. Like I'm going to get up before dawn and stand in line to find out. That's the last thing I'd ever do."

Fran touched her arm. She looked so sympathetic, Lucy felt terrible snarling at her. "I know, honey. Don't be silly. That's not what I mean at all. I'm just saying you should see him. Send him a note or something. I'm sure if you got in touch, he'd reply. After all this time, wouldn't it help to talk to him? To finally have some answers? I bet he'd be willing if you asked. I bet he wants to talk to you, too."

"Oh, Fran. What answer do I need to hear? Why a guy who made a lot of promises and plans left a nineteen-year-old girl waiting all night under a birch tree? Do you think there's some mysterious thing that happened that I don't know? He was struck on the head and got amnesia? Or was run down by a bus and couldn't get a message to me?"

Fran gripped Lucy's arm. "Isn't there a famous movie where that happens? With Cary Grant and Deborah Kerr? They were supposed to meet at the Statue of Liberty."

"The Empire State Building," Lucy corrected her. "She gets hit by a car crossing the street and ends up in a wheelchair."

"But Cary Grant still loves her," Fran pointed out.

"Why are we even talking about this? I have to get to work."

Fran looked suddenly contrite. "I'm sorry, Lu. I know I'm being a pest. It's just that if I were in your shoes, I would figure out a way to see him and have my say. There must be things you want to say that have been brewing inside you for years. Even if you don't care why he did what he did. There must be things you want to get off your chest."

Lucy knew that was true. Then decided, as she always did, there would be no point in telling him off. It wouldn't change anything. It wouldn't soothe or reassure that naive, loyal little girl who'd stood under that tree all night. That girl was gone. The woman who remained didn't need or want a thing from that man.

"All I would say is, 'Thanks. You did me the best favor of my life.'" Even if she had felt like a bug squashed on a windshield at the time. "My life turned out fine. Better than fine. It's all ancient history, Fran. If he wants *my* autograph, he knows where to find me."

Fran looked like she was about to say more, but then she nodded and stepped back. "You're right, Lucy. It works both ways. I bet, with Google and all, he knows you still live here. After what he did, he should make the move to get in touch. Maybe if he does, you'll feel differently. I won't say any more about it," she quickly added. "I promise."

"Thank you, Fran . . . I'm going to hold you to it this time," Lucy insisted.

The friends hugged and headed separate ways to get on with their Mondays. Lucy's head was spinning. Leave it to Fran. Lucy had never even considered that Craig might get in touch with her. Now that the possibility was on the table, she felt even more unnerved about his presence in the town.

Even if he knows I'm still here, he won't have the nerve. He'll be too embarrassed about how he ditched me. He might act all nice and "regular guy-ish" with his fans, but he is a movie star. He's got to have some ego and pride. He's not going to lower himself to apologize to a little, ordinary person like me.

Though the idea of it had struck her cold with dread, Lucy knew the notion was laughable. Craig Hamilton was not going to seek her out. It would be an easy thing to avoid him for the next two or three weeks. Then she would shut the door again on her memories of that chapter of her life. Shut the door and forget it had ever happened. Just as she had all these long years.

"Didn't expect to see you back so early. Did they postpone the closing?" Joe was standing in the law office's reception area, and he looked up from a pile of message slips in his hand.

"Not at all. It's signed, sealed, and delivered," Lauren reported as she sailed into the office.

She'd gone straight to a house closing at a local bank that morning. Contracts 101 for her, though Joe had expected the assignment to be challenging after the inspection reported an ailing furnace.

"Of course, they brought up the furnace first thing," she added. "But I negotiated a sum for repair or replacement to be held in escrow. No other surprises. Everyone left happy."

Joe looked happy, too, and rewarded her with a sunny smile. "Good job. And fast. Maybe I need to find more work for you than I expected."

The dispute had been a no-brainer, not a deal breaker, Lauren thought, but it was still nice to be praised.

She had actually been glad for the appointment out of the office this morning. She had felt a bit nervous last night, wondering how it would be between her and Joe in the workplace after their date on Saturday night. Despite her qualms, she'd genuinely enjoyed herself and found that they still had a lot to talk about over dinner, just like old times. When he drove her back to her parents' house, there had been an awkward moment as they said good night. But ever the gentleman, Joe simply leaned over and kissed her on the cheek, in a re-strained and mostly friendly way. Then he smiled and said, "I know you have your plans and don't intend to stay, Lauren. But things can change. I want you to know I'm willing to wait and see how it goes."

"Umm. Okay, Joe." Lauren had not known how to answer him beyond that—for once in her life, she was at a loss for words. She squeezed his hand and headed for the front door.

She was glad to see her sisters were not up waiting for her report. Though on the other hand, she wouldn't have minded some help interpreting Joe's promise.

She did see a recurring theme in his words—he was still willing to wait for her feelings about him to change. Was he foolish to keep hoping? Or did he see something between them that she was unable, or not quite ready, to see?

This morning, she found him as friendly as ever but all business, which was a relief.

"Speaking of more assignments, Paul Hooper at the club just got in touch. The board isn't satisfied with McGuire patching the fence. They want to be reimbursed for the damage caused by the 'all you can eat' sod buffet."

"Really?" Lauren felt uneasy at that news. The client had asked for and received a solution. She didn't like to hear that they were back-tracking and asking for more. "They should have stated that up front, don't you think?"

Joe didn't answer. "Let's step into my office," he said smoothly. "I'll show you the message."

Lauren followed Joe into his spacious office, decorated in a traditional style with a big wooden desk and leather chairs. A dark green area rug with a Persian pattern and high wooden bookcases filled with law books completed the decor. His many diplomas, certifications, and professional awards covered a wall behind the desk. The opposite wall, above a tufted leather couch, displayed photographs of the village taken in the 1800s, along with more recent photos—scenic shots from his travels to distant places.

At least he left Cape Light once in a while, Lauren reflected, then felt a bit mean at the silent but snide observation.

Joe took the chair behind his desk, the high, tufted chair like a leather throne. He riffled through papers on the blotter. "It's a small town, Lauren. We need to be careful when we discuss our clients, even in the office."

Lauren knew he was right. "Sorry. I should have waited to vent in private. But it really isn't fair."

He glanced at her curiously, then handed over a printout of Paul Hooper's email. "That's an odd thing to say. This is what they want. At least, what they want us to ask for. You need to go back to McGuire and make him understand that it's the principle of the thing. And that the animals did real damage to the course."

Lauren glanced down at the email, which included an estimate to repair the greens where the animals had dug and dined. Her eyes grew wide at the bottom line.

"This number is a little high, don't you think? I mean, it's not like McGuire's property is a business with insurance or deep pockets. He's a private individual. Living in a tiny cottage next to a barn," she added. "You ought to see what he drives around in."

Her defense of Cole McGuire surprised her. But despite her pit bull training, Lauren had always been informed by a strong sense of justice and fair play. From sports fields to courtrooms, she believed everyone should play by the rules. Demanding such a hefty sum after saying the repair was adequate was simply not fair. And it was an outlandish demand as well, she thought.

"Does Hooper understand that the animals don't even belong to McGuire?" Not that she wanted to see the country club turn on her aunt and Grateful Paw.

"Yes, he understands that. But, as you pointed out, the animals were in his care, and the fence and the hole belonged to him. He's responsible for the damage the animals did."

Lauren felt stung, hearing her own argument tossed back at her—a fairly solid one, too. "Listen, we both know that at this time of year, and later, in the spring, golf courses need a ton of maintenance. Slabs of sod are replaced routinely from the wear and tear of players and golf carts, not just damage from animals. I bet the club would have needed to work on those greens anyway, whether or not the animals had visited."

Joe gazed at her and sat back. He seemed curious and just on the very edge of losing his patience. "So you're saying the course needs the work anyway, and the board is trying to get McGuire to pay for it?"

Lauren shrugged. "Not exactly . . . but I do think they're pressing him for an unfair share of the costs. I bet they have a mammoth amount in their budget for maintaining the grounds. They don't need his money," she said bluntly. "I think this request is just . . . mean-spirited."

Joe took a breath. Then he shook his head as he pulled the email back to his side of the desk. "Fine. If that's the way you feel, I'll handle it. No problem."

Lauren sat up sharply. She didn't like that idea, for a few reasons. She wasn't some shrinking violet who needed a man to sweep in and do the heavy lifting. She was a smart attorney and a tough one and was determined to maintain that reputation. Even way out here in the middle of nowhere.

And if anyone was going back to Cole McGuire with an additional and outlandish demand, it was her. Not Joe. McGuire would think she was too chicken to face him, or embarrassed. She didn't know why his opinion should matter, but it did. She was embarrassed, but she would figure out some way to smooth it over.

Maybe it was because of Phoebe. The man couldn't be so awful if he had a little girl as sweet as that. Could he?

She wasn't sure why; she just didn't like the idea of jerking McGuire around—which is what this demand from the club was when you boiled it down.

"I started it. I'll finish it," she told Joe. "I'll write McGuire a letter asking for the damages. A strong letter. I'll run it by you."

"Good plan." Joe looked satisfied by her answer. Had he purposely goaded her into sticking with this issue? Lauren had never thought of him as a manipulative person, but she supposed every attorney had a few tricks up their sleeve. Even one as *nice* as Joe. "We'll send it overnight, signature required," he said.

"Of course," she answered.

She rose from her seat and grabbed her briefcase, then plucked the sheet of paper with the email from Joe's desk.

Writing this letter was the last thing she felt like doing right now, but Lauren had always found it was best to start with the most distasteful task on a to-do list and get it over with.

"For pity's sake, Jessica. What took you so long?" Lillian squinted down at the slim gold watch on her wrist. "I've been waiting hours. Days, actually. I shudder to imagine what would happen if we had a *real* emergency. Do you realize that I've been calling you since Friday morning?"

"I do, Mother. You used up the entire message space on my phone. Twice."

"Don't be so glib. It's totally unnecessary, and unbecoming as well. Do you want some lunch? We've put it off."

Jessica was used to her mother's tirades and her many strategies to induce guilt. She greeted the onslaught with a smile and walked into the foyer. "No, thank you. I have more stops to make. How are you today? I'm a bit tired from relocating an entire farm full of animals. Sorry I didn't have time to deal with your little dog."

"It's hardly 'my' dog. It's a stray mongrel—though Ezra fawns over the beast as if it had just won best in show at Westminster."

Jessica had already gathered from the many messages that her mother wanted the dog out and Ezra wanted to keep him. She really had been busy relocating the farm animals but had hoped that over the weekend, her mother would ease up and Ezra might win this argument. No such luck, it seemed.

"Did you even try to find the dog's owner?"

"I did try," Jessica replied. "I searched all the notices about lost dogs online, left posts at different sites, called shelters and even the police station to see if anyone has been looking for him. So far, there are no reports of a dog like this. I'll take him to a vet today and have him scanned for a chip."

"A chip? What's that? Is it contagious?"

Jessica laughed. "It's a tiny device slipped under the dog's skin that identifies the owner and gives contact information. Most owners these days chip their pets just in case they run away."

Lillian looked happy to hear the explanation. "Tell that to Ezra. He's gotten too attached. I've warned him the dog must be returned to his real home."

"If we can find his home," Jessica said. "Where is this mangy little beast?" She imitated her mother's disparaging tone and was rewarded with a sharp look.

"Confined to the mudroom. Where else? If Ezra had his way, that thing would sit between us on the silk brocade couch every night, watching TV and eating bonbons. As it is, Ezra coops himself up out there most of the day and the evening, ever since his little friend arrived."

Jessica nearly laughed. "If I didn't know better, I'd say you sound jealous, Mother."

Her mother bristled. "Don't be ridiculous."

She stabbed her cane into the thick Oriental rug and turned, then headed for the back of the house. Jessica followed, feeling twinges of sympathy for Ezra. He would be the most perfect dog owner in the world. He had so much love to give.

She decided not to tease her mother anymore if she could help it. Perhaps she could plead Ezra's case and her mother would reconsider keeping the dog.

When they reached the mudroom, they found the passage to the kitchen blocked by a piece of cardboard. Jessica moved it aside, but they didn't enter right away. She saw the dog sitting at Ezra's feet as the old man carefully brushed out his coat in gentle, smooth strokes. "My, my . . . you're looking very smart today, Teddy. But what's this? A bit of mud on your tail? How did that happen? Before we know it, you'll need another bath."

"Jessica is here," her mother announced. "She says the dog might have a little microscopic tag in its fur with the owner's phone number on it. That would solve everything, wouldn't it?"

That wasn't *exactly* what she'd said, but Jessica didn't bother to sort out her mother's mangled explanation. Lillian had caught the gist, and Ezra's expression fell at the news.

"I don't doubt someone out there misses him. How could they not?" Ezra put the brush aside. He stood up to face them. "What sort of dog do you think he is, Jess? I see a lot of terrier, but likely something else. Australian cattle dog, maybe?"

Jessica looked the dog over and agreed. "Terrier definitely. The rest is hard to say. He does seem to have a bit of hound in him."

"He's a mutt. Plain and simple. Do we need to go into the fine points?" her mother cut in impatiently.

"Whatever the lineage, he comes from good-natured stock, and smart. He's been no trouble at all. And wonderful company. Pets are good for your health, they say. Especially at our age," Ezra said to his wife. "They help in all sorts of ways. Even lower your blood pressure."

Her mother rolled her eyes. "That depends on the patient. This one has been raising mine. Given the choice, I'd rather take pills."

The dog sensed he was being discussed, as most dogs will, Jessica knew. He walked over to Lillian and sat down at her feet, then gazed up at her with pure adoration. Jessica almost laughed out loud. "It looks to me like Ezra has been caring for him, but he has as real thing for you, Mother."

Lillian jumped back and made a huffy sound. "You're all imagining that. He knows I don't like him. He just wants to annoy me."

"Nonsense. He's smitten. He wants to win you over, Lily. Reminds me of myself, during our courtship." Ezra glanced at Jessica and winked. Then he sighed and leaned down to clip a leash to the dog's collar. He petted the dog's head with a slow, affectionate hand. Despite his jovial tone, it was no secret that Ezra was very sad to see the dog go.

"Goodbye, Teddy. I hope you've been happy here. You're a very good dog. Don't let anyone tell you otherwise. It has been a pleasure to get to know you."

Jessica felt a catch in her throat. She looked over at her mother, wondering if there might be some eleventh-hour reprieve. But her mother's expression was blank, her chin high, her gray-blue eyes steely with resolve.

Ezra saw it, too. Jessica realized that they'd been having this discussion about keeping the dog for several days now, and her mother had won.

"What will happen now? Where will you take him?" Ezra asked. "If the owner isn't found, I mean."

"I've identified a very good home, an older couple, here in town. They have several pets. They'll treat him like a king."

"That's some consolation." Ezra's eyes were clouding with tears. Jessica could barely look at him. "Sounds like they will *both* give him all the love and care he deserves." He cast a meaningful look in her mother's direction, but her mother ignored him.

"Good luck, my friend," he said, patting the dog's head one last time.

The dog leaned back and licked Ezra's hand. Ezra nodded but didn't say more. He took out a hanky and dabbed his eyes, then handed the leash to Jessica.

"You take him now. I need to go upstairs." She saw a tear slide down his cheek, but she didn't know what to say.

She listened for the sound of Ezra's steps on the staircase, then turned to her mother. "Mother, really . . . why can't you just keep this little dog? Ezra is heartbroken," she said quietly.

"For pity's sake." Lillian waved her hand. "He'll get over it soon enough. I don't want a pet of any kind, and if I did, it certainly wouldn't be this one. Besides, you said it yourself, you can find the owner with that chippy thing. Once Ezra hears the dog has been returned to his real home, how he can complain about not keeping it?"

Her mother had a point. Ezra would still be sad, but that outcome would be easier to accept. "All right. I'll let you know what happens."

"I really don't care," Lillian replied quickly. "Just don't bring the dog back here. If you can't find the owner, bring him to those new people. Directly," she emphasized. "I don't want to see that animal again. That's final."

Jessica couldn't argue with those instructions. Her mother was many things, but being wishy-washy about her needs or directives was never one of them.

The shaggy terrier mix stared up at her curiously. "That's the plan," Jessica told him. "Say goodbye, Teddy."

She knew it would annoy her mother, but she couldn't help using the name Ezra had come up with. It did suit the dog well.

Teddy smiled and wagged his tail, happily answering to his new name.

LAUREN KNEW THAT SHE SHOULDN'T HAVE BEEN HELPING COLE MC-Guire. It was highly unethical to act against her client's interests. But wouldn't it be better to get something for the golf club by letting him know there was room to negotiate than to get nothing by simply dumping this outrageous demand in his lap? The guy was wound tight enough already. She had no doubt the country club's latest demand would set him off like a box of Fourth of July fireworks.

She was actually doing the club a favor by hand-delivering the letter and taking the time to talk to him about it, she decided as the tree farm came into view. Though she wouldn't bill the firm for the extra visit. For some reason, she didn't want Joe to know she hadn't followed his instructions exactly and mailed the letter special delivery.

A small, niggling voice insisted that was what she should do: *It's not too late to turn around and play this by the book.*

But she'd already turned up the bumpy gravel drive and spotted Cole and Phoebe in the corral. Cole was near the barn saddling a horse. Phoebe was petting the donkey, his head sunk into a bucket of oats. She noticed the approaching car and ran over to the fence rail to see who was coming.

Lauren's heart felt a little ping of affection. Her worries about her decision to visit flew out of her head. She parked the car near the corral and grabbed her briefcase. The truth was, she had been looking for an excuse to come back. She had found a worn copy of *Charlotte's Web* in her old bedroom and hoped there would be some opportunity to give it to Phoebe. Just a little thing. No big deal.

But first she had the letter to deliver. The assignment was a high hurdle. No question.

She took a breath, tossed her shoulders back, and stepped out, dressed a bit better for the visit today in gray pants, short black boots, and a white turtleneck under her wool peacoat.

Phoebe stared at her a moment, then offered a brilliant smile. "Pig Lady! You look so different." She climbed up on the fence rail so she could see Lauren better. "You look really pretty."

"Thanks, honey. I took a bath. I smell better, too. At least, I hope so." Lauren loved her nickname and the compliment. "How's Wilbur doing?"

Phoebe's expression turned serious. "Not so good. Tilly doesn't like him. His feelings are hurt," she added in a whisper. Lauren bet that was true. She felt bad about the news.

Cole McGuire glanced over his shoulder but didn't deign to greet her. He yanked on the saddle cinch, then walked to the other side of the horse.

You could at least acknowledge my existence, for goodness' sake, she silently scolded him.

"Jessica showed us how to feed him with a bottle," Phoebe continued. "We keep him in the house, and I get to take care of him like a baby, so that part is fun."

"I bet he loves that."

"He does," Phoebe agreed in serious tone. "We made him a nice bed. He's having a nap. Maybe you can see him later."

Lauren doubted her visiting would last that long once Phoebe's father learned why she'd come. But she didn't want to hurt Phoebe's feelings. "I'd love to see him again. But don't wake him up. Babies need their sleep."

Cole appeared behind his daughter. Hands on hips, he looked her up and down. Did he think she looked pretty, too? Did he at least think she smelled better?

"Lauren Willoughby," he announced in a formal tone. "Have you come for the cow? Jessica said she found a home and was sending someone to pick her up."

He knew very well that was not possibly the reason she was there, not in this outfit. She offered a polite smile. "I'd love to give the cow a lift. But I'm borrowing my mom's car today, and she doesn't even allow breath mints in it. Much less a passenger chewing cud."

His mouth—a very nice mouth, she noticed, and not for the first time—pulled to the side. She could see he was trying not to laugh. Score one for the visiting team.

He yanked off his work gloves. "So, what brings you back to the animal annex?"

During the drive from town, she'd practiced exactly what she wanted to say. But her brain screen went blank as he simply stared at her, waiting.

He had definitely taken a bath. And shaved. Overall, he looked about ten times better than he had on her last two visits, dressed in a dark green barn coat with brown leather trim, newish-looking jeans that fit his lean build perfectly, and a neatly pressed denim shirt.

She lifted her chin and looked him in the eye. "I have another message from the country club. But I want to talk about it first."

"A thank-you note? That's touching. But unnecessary, honestly."

She didn't answer or even react. She wasn't going to encourage his sarcastic digs, though she knew she was not blameless on that score.

"I fixed the blasted fence last week," he nearly shouted at her. "If they found more animals on their silly, sacred sod, don't look at me. Don't those people have better things to worry about than their stupid grass?"

"I assured them the fence was repaired and you were totally co-operating." She hoped a calm, even tone would remind him to rein in his reaction.

He did stop to take a breath, muttering as he glanced away from her. His gaze caught Phoebe, who was hanging out with the donkey again. "It's almost time, honey. Why don't you go inside and get your gear?"

"Okay, Daddy." Phoebe ran to the gate, and Cole opened it for her, then stepped out behind her and latched it again.

As he watched his daughter run to the house, he said, "So, what is this all about? In ten words or less."

She gave him a look. Was he suggesting attorneys were overly verbose? He was probably right, but she wouldn't give him the satisfaction of agreeing.

As succinctly as she could, she explained that the club had tallied the cost of repairing the turf that was grazed and trampled and wanted him to pay for it. She paused and named the figure, then quickly added, "But here's the thing—"

"What? You've got to be kidding." He stared at her for a moment, in shock. Before she could voice her conciliatory suggestion, his tone grew even louder and sharper. "Is this your idea? Trying to score a few points for your client?"

"Absolutely not." She hadn't intended to raise her voice but could hear it getting louder. Why was this man such a dolt? Couldn't he see she was trying to help him? "I tried to persuade the lead attorney at the firm not to go forward with this. But he didn't agree and I have to convey the client's wishes. I'm sure the request is a financial burden. I get that. If you'd calm down for a moment, we can figure out a counteroffer. You can pay in installments," she added. "I also think Grateful Paw bears some responsibility. I know my aunt. She won't want you to be stuck with this bill, no matter how slim their resources are."

Lauren stepped back, trying to gauge how her little speech had been received. Cole stared at her, his dark eyes wide with surprise. Was he shocked that she was willing to help him? To offer a plan to work out the problem?

He suddenly smiled and shook his head, looking incredulous. "I can pay for the stupid sod, don't worry. I could buy that whole club out from under that smug, self-satisfied lot."

Lauren sincerely doubted that but didn't argue. Clearly the man's pride was hurt by her mentioning an economic burden and installments. Did he even have a job, aside from helping Jack around the tree farm? It didn't seem so.

"The money is not the point," he added.

Lauren struggled to hide her reaction. People always said that, especially when the money was exactly the point.

"This is the most petty, selfish thing I ever heard of. These are poor, dumb animals who were either abandoned or barely escaped the slaughterhouse. They nibbled a few stalks of grass. Play golf all you want, but get the bigger picture, for pity's sake. Those people don't realize how good they have it, racing around in golf carts, chasing a little white ball all day. Most people are working hard to keep a roof over their head and put food on the table for their family. Or wish that they even had a job," he railed.

The question had clearly hit a hot button for him. Was he working hard to provide those basic needs? Or wishing he had a job? Even so, Lauren did agree, though she wouldn't have put it quite that way. The whole situation had been blown out of proportion.

"I understand your point," she said, trying to keep things on track and, perhaps, steer him back to the notion of some compromise.

"Well, thank you very much, at least, for that, Ms. Willoughby."

So, they were back to surnames. She blinked but kept a straight face.

"My answer is no. I could use . . . more colorful language? But let's leave it at that."

"That's your answer—you won't pay any damages?"

"Not a penny."

"Okay, but there will be another letter, stating that the club will file suit and take this to court."

She doubted the case would get very far. But she couldn't admit that. Even floating the compromise suggestion was cutting it close to the ethics line.

"You probably need to hire an attorney," she told him. "Though I'm sure this can all be worked out with a phone call. Or two," she added, calculating in his dark scowl.

"I get it. Thanks for your concern."

She wasn't sure he did. He was certainly stubborn. But he did have solid principles and good values. She admired that.

"Are we done here?" he asked.

Lauren nodded. "I just need to give you the letter and you need to sign for it, please," she noted. "It's basically what we just discussed. Don't let the chickens read it. You'll be eating cereal for a week."

He spared a smile at her quip as she reached into her bag and pulled out a folder. It held the letter and a form for his signature of receipt.

But something else flew out as well and landed at his feet. He bent down first and picked it up. She felt embarrassed as he inspected the cover of the little chapter book. "*Charlotte's Web*? I'd take you for a fan of self-help . . . or romance novels?"

Lauren didn't like his guess, even though it was mostly on target. That irked her even more.

"It's for your daughter. She told me she didn't know the story. About the baby pig?" He answered with a puzzled stare, and she wondered if he didn't know the book either. He was probably the product of a deprived childhood. Maybe that explained his difficult personality? "I thought she might like it."

He nodded, holding the book at arm's length. "Sure. I know it. Thanks . . . But I don't think she's ready for this one yet."

He reached out, intending to give it back, when Phoebe walked out of the cottage. Dressed for horseback riding, she cradled Wilbur in her arms. "He just woke up, Lauren. You said you wanted to see him."

"I'd love to see him. Be careful. No rush." She glanced at Cole McGuire. He stuck the book in the big patch pocket of his jacket. The delay of her departure seemed to be annoying him. She was happy about that, at least.

Phoebe came toward them with a stately step, her gaze fixed on Wilbur. When she reached Lauren, she held out the pig, who squirmed in his thin blanket. "Oh, wow. He looks like he grew an inch since Friday. You must be taking very good care of him."

Phoebe smiled. "We are. Me and Dad," she noted. "Want to hold him? He's cuddly but wiggles a lot."

"I'd love to hold him. For a minute," she added, glancing up at Cole, who stood watching over them. His expression had softened, and it looked as if he wasn't so angry anymore. Or in such a hurry to get rid of her. Was he suddenly able to separate Lauren from the job she had to do?

Maybe that's what bothered her the most. She didn't want Cole judging and disliking her just for being the messenger of this news, though that sort of thing had never bothered her before, she realized.

She crouched down to Phoebe's level and held the little pig in her arms. He turned on his belly and started crawling up her shoulder, then found an earring and began nibbling on it.

"Whoa there, fella. Those are good earrings. Not pig kibble."

Her reaction made Phoebe laugh. Cole laughed, too. He rested a hand on Lauren's shoulder. "Here, let me take him. He's stronger than you think."

Lauren stood up and handed Wilbur over. Their eyes met for a moment and he smiled. Really smiled. She felt her knees turn to water and hoped her reaction didn't show.

She heard a vehicle coming down the drive and turned toward it, wondering if it was Jack Sawyer. She would have liked to say hello to him. But she saw a woman in the driver's seat of a long white truck. A very pretty woman, she noticed, who waved and smiled happily as she parked next to Lauren's Volvo.

"Hi, everybody. Ready for your lesson, Phoebe?" the woman called as she hopped down from the cab.

Her long honey-blond hair was pulled back in a ponytail, which emphasized her fine features and large blue eyes. She wore a thin, quilted vest over a black turtleneck, with tan riding breeches and high boots. She had the ideal figure for spandex, Lauren noticed. Her own body put the elastic content of such garments to the test.

"Hi, Phoebe." The woman leaned over and gave the little girl a special smile.

Phoebe seemed shy again and moved closer to her father. "Say hello to Jen, honey," he coaxed.

"Hi, Jen. Want to see our pig? Lauren gave him to us."

"We're watching him for Grateful Paw," Cole filled in. He glanced at Lauren, seeming amused by her being identified as the source of Wilbur. "I'll put him in the house. Be right back."

"That's fine, Cole. Phoebe and I will get started." Jen turned back to Phoebe with another gentle smile. "Where's your helmet, honey? You know we need that."

"Oh, right. It's in the barn. I'll find it. Daddy put the saddle on Buster." Phoebe ran to the gate and Jen lifted the latch for her.

Lauren was about to say goodbye to Phoebe. She felt out of place here, with a riding lesson about to start. But Phoebe turned once she was inside in the corral and called back to her.

"Want to watch me ride Buster, Lauren? I can ride him with no one holding on."

Lauren sighed and smiled. The invitation was impossible to resist. "Really? That's amazing. I want to see that, for sure."

Phoebe headed off to find her helmet, and Lauren found herself alone with Jen. She expected the other woman to follow Phoebe, but Jen turned to face her, offering a friendly smile. She had beautiful white teeth. *Is she younger than me? Maybe a year or so.*

"I don't think we've met. I'm Jen Bennet."

"Nice to meet you. Lauren Willoughby." She left it at that, having no reason in the world to explain her connection to the McGuires. A silence fell between them. "Has Phoebe been riding for very long?"

"A few months. Since she and Cole moved here. I'm actually a therapist, not just a riding instructor."

"Oh . . . interesting," Lauren replied. She had heard of special therapy that involved animals, and horses in particular. Patients who'd experienced trauma of some kind were able to recover through contact with and caring for horses.

She wondered why dear little Phoebe needed the sessions, but of course, she couldn't ask. "Is it helping her?" she did ask, then wondered if that was too private a question as well.

"Her progress has been encouraging." Jen nodded, her expression thoughtful.

Lauren wanted to dislike her. And dismiss her. She was so attractive and kind, and spoke in such a gentle, thoughtful way. Nothing like Lauren's own harsh braying. And now it turned out she wasn't some airheaded Barbie doll riding instructor. She was an actual therapist. Lauren couldn't dislike her, for some odd reason. She seemed so . . . sincere.

"That's good to hear. Phoebe is such a sweetheart."

Jen answered with a wide smile. "That she is. She's my favorite," she whispered in a playful way. "Don't tell my other clients."

"I found it." Phoebe ran out of the barn waving a black riding helmet, then stuck it on her head and struggled to fasten the strap below her chin.

"That's my cue," Jen said.

"Sure. See you."

Cole came out of the house and headed straight to the corral. He leaned on the rail and waved at Phoebe as Jen helped her into the saddle.

Lauren checked her watch, feeling uneasy standing there. But she needed to keep her promise to the little girl. She wasn't going to run away just because it suddenly seemed obvious that Jen's visit was the reason Cole McGuire had cleaned up his act today and looked so well-groomed and well-dressed.

She felt like a fool, thinking for one minute that he could have any interest in her.

Phoebe sat atop the horse, with Jen holding a lead. Buster began a slow circle around the corral. "Good job, Phoebe. Don't look down. Look ahead and sit up straight," Jen reminded her.

Phoebe nodded and corrected her posture. Then she met Lauren's gaze and waved. "See me, Lauren?"

Lauren waved back. "I see you, honey. You're doing great."

Cole turned, as if he'd just remembered she was still there.

"I have to go," Lauren said. "Please tell Phoebe I said goodbye."

"I will." He waved briefly, then turned to watch his daughter and Jen again. Lauren headed to her car.

She drove off the property quickly, eager to put space between herself and Cole McGuire. It was too late to return to Joe's office. That was some relief. Her head spun with a million different feelings, and she could hardly see straight.

Stop the madness, Lauren. I can't believe you're getting yourself tied in a knot about this nutcase. How ridiculous is it to be attracted to him . . . and jealous of some horsey babe? Well, not a "babe," exactly—a woman with an impressive degree. Who looks like a model in her jodhpurs and boots.

You should be grateful for this dash of cold water. Cole McGuire definitely has some baggage. A therapist would be a perfect match.

You are not now, and will not ever be, attracted to him.

Case closed.

Chapter Six

HERE YOU ARE. WHAT TOOK YOU SO LONG?" Charlie was carrying a tray loaded with breakfast orders but stopped in his tracks as Lucy walked through the door.

He was in his battlefield commander mode today, and she excused him for his rude greeting. She knew by now that he didn't really mean it. Dealing with a rush like this shorthanded was bound to make anyone anxious.

"Visiting a patient. I told you I had to make a call this morning. And I'm here now, so calm down a little, please? Take a breath or two. Remember?"

She had taught him some stress-reduction techniques to help him feel calmer. But he never remembered to use them when the time came.

"Right, right . . . sorry, I forgot. Deep breaths." He nodded and pantomimed deep breathing. "Meanwhile, please get your apron on? The plates are backed up at the window like rush hour on I-95."

Lucy headed to the kitchen. "I can only stay an hour or two," she reminded him, though he didn't seem to hear her.

"More coffee at table three," he called back as he swooped around the room, delivering dishes of eggs and hash browns and platters of the pancake special.

Lucy slipped behind the crowded counter, where Tucker sat sipping his coffee. "Charlie was right," he said. "The movie crew has put us on the map. The town is crawling with celebrity hounds."

"*You* were right, Tucker. Who needs all these people? It's a madhouse in here. You should see Willoughby's. There's a line out the door. Don't tell Charlie, but it looks like we only got the overflow."

Tucker chuckled. "Why burst his balloon? He hasn't been this happy since he beat Emily Warwick in the last election."

Lucy had to agree with that observation. Charlie had made a few runs at it and had finally won the mayor's seat. You had to give Charlie a gold medal for persistence. No one could deny that.

"Lucy? Cut the chitchat, please. I need some backup, honey."

Lucy rolled her eyes as Tucker offered a knowing smile. She pushed through the kitchen doors and shed her coat and scarf, then wrapped a blue Clam Box apron over the white top and pants she wore for nursing visits. It was not the first time she was struck by the irony that she'd traded one uniform for another. *Traded up*, she reminded herself.

But here she was this morning. The diner's devoted full-time waitress Trudy had called Charlie last night with the news that she was knocked off her feet with a bad cold. He'd been perfectly sympathetic on the phone—for Charlie—but had unraveled shortly after that as he checked with all the employees on his backup list.

Lucy had been working on her patient files and barely peeked up from the laptop screen. But she had overheard the calls and knew he would get to her in the end.

It was hard to refuse him. The diner was the mainstay of the family's income. She had always felt it was both right and fair to contribute if she could. Even their boys worked there in the summer and on school vacations, though it didn't seem likely that either would take over when—or if—Charlie retired. Not the way Charlie had happily taken the helm of the Clam Box from his father, Otto, long ago.

It happened that she did have a few hours free in her schedule today. One of her patients had taken a bad turn and been readmitted to the hospital, and another had received an all-clear from her doctor and no longer required Lucy's visits. The main office would fill the space soon, but she hadn't been assigned any new patients yet.

The thought had occurred to her that Charlie would not be any the wiser if she claimed she had no time free. But she couldn't do that to him. She agreed to rearrange her appointments and come in during the morning rush, which had made him so happy and relieved, he hugged her. "You're the best, Lu. I can always count on you, honey. When things settle down, we'll go out for a nice dinner. You pick the spot. Anywhere you want," he promised.

"You didn't forget our anniversary or my birthday," Lucy mused with a laugh. "If that's what you're worried about?"

He looked hurt by her suggestion. "Of course I didn't. I know that. But, now that you mention it, maybe this time can count as sort of a spare tire, in case I do."

He winked, and she had to laugh again as she turned back to her work. That was typical Charlie logic if ever she'd heard it. She'd heard that "night out" offer before, too, and wondered if they would follow through this time.

Either way, it was nice of him to say. Charlie had his faults, but didn't everyone? He had a good heart, and underneath his bluster and impatience, he was a genuinely kind man with a soft side that he hid well.

Life with Charlie was never boring. No matter how unreasonable he could be, she always knew he loved fiercely—his family, his business, his hometown, and her. Once Charlie had made up his mind that she was the one for him, he'd gone the distance to win her heart. He didn't care who knew it. She still had to admire that quality, when so many people she had known in her life had not been nearly as consistent or dependable. For better or worse, you always knew where you stood with Charlie. That was saying something.

But this morning, as Lucy fastened the apron strings around her slim waist, she didn't feel quite as generous toward her husband. She was, in fact, wondering why she'd agreed to come in. He had known for months that the diner would be overflowing with customers when the film crew came. He should have hired extra help, the way he did in the summer. Not expect her to drop everything and wait tables.

"Hey, Lucy." Tim the cook took a second from his work at the stove to greet her. "I'd say 'order up,' but I can barely fit another dish up there. I'm leaving these pancakes for table five here in the kitchen."

"No worries, I'm on it." Out at the pass-through window, she checked the order slips against the dishes and arranged as many as she could safely carry on a big round tray.

She knew the diner so well, she swiftly swept through the room, setting down plates in front of grateful customers with flawless accuracy.

"Here you go, cheese omelet with wheat toast. Oatmeal with bananas and raisins. Here's the OJ. More coffee on the way," she promised, moving gracefully to the next table.

A few minutes later, the window was cleared, and all the tables were caught up with coffee and ice water. Lucy slipped behind the counter and began tallying up checks.

"Seems to be slowing down," Charlie said to Tucker. The police officer had just finished his breakfast and looked ready to go. "Though

I expect a second wave. Someone said they just took a break filming at Lilac Hall. That's when the fans run into town for a bite."

Lucy hadn't seen many familiar faces in the diner this morning, except for Reverend Ben, having breakfast with two ladies from church, Vera Plante and Sophie Potter.

"You'd think people would have better things to do than chase around after movie stars," Charlie marveled. "Don't these folks have to be at work?" Lucy had wondered about that, too. There were a lot of seniors, but still, some people must have taken vacation days for the adventure.

Tucker shook his head. "The diner is getting a lot of business from the situation. That's good."

"Wait till the stars stop by. You'll see lines out the door with people waiting to brush shoulders or even breathe the same air."

Tucker placed his hat squarely on his head and made sure it was settled just right. "Don't the actors eat on the movie set? Isn't that why they hire someone to bring in the food?"

Whoops, that was a sore point. Charlie had wanted to cater, but Molly Willoughby had won the job. Tucker must have forgotten. Lucy filled an urn with fresh coffee, preparing to make a refill run through the room.

"They'll be sick of Willoughby's food in a week," Charlie predicted. "How many arugula and goat cheese wraps can a person eat? Even Hollywood people can only stand so much of that frou-frou food before they're craving a burger and fries or a bowl of chowder. Or good old bacon and eggs? Sooner or later, even an actor wants good, honest food, Clam Box food. I know they will."

Tucker offered his ever-tolerant smile. Then Lucy saw his eyes bug out and his mouth drop open in a fishlike expression.

She followed his gaze to the door, where the bell above was still jingling. A customer had just walked in. He paused and looked around. He wore a black baseball hat, sunglasses, and a battered, aviator-style dark brown leather jacket that Lucy knew cost extra for the vintage distressed look.

She bit down on her lip and heard the blood pound in her ears. The clatter of customers melted away. She had no sense of her surroundings, or even of time passing, as she watched the man pull off his cap and run a hand through a head of thick brown hair threaded with gray.

That is not a toupee, she nearly shouted at Tucker. *Or a weave either.*

Their eyes met, and he smiled, very slightly. Or maybe she was imagining that? Lucy wasn't sure. She did know she felt the room spin. She looked down at the floor and gripped the edge of the counter.

No one seemed to notice. Customers were jumping up from their seats. "Look who just came in—Craig Hamilton!"

"Right there. Look, it's him, Hamilton," someone else shouted out.

Charlie stood frozen in shock at the sight, then nearly knocked her over as he ran to greet their honored guest. Lucy fled in the other direction, pushing through the kitchen doors.

She found Tim and the rest of the kitchen staff lined up at the pass-through window, gawking at the movie star. She ran into the restroom and splashed her face with cold water, then nearly screamed at her reflection in the tiny mirror.

"Of all the days. Why here? Why now? Mother of pearl, look at me. I knew this would happen. I just knew it. Why in heaven's name did I ever come here today?"

She ran a comb through her hair and clipped it up again, at the back of her head, then dashed on a bit of lipstick. She tossed the tube back into her purse. There was nothing in her handbag likely to make her look thirty years younger, that was for sure.

She pulled on her coat, then picked up her purse and briefcase. Charlie was going to scream when he caught sight of her leaving, but she was just going to have to weather his reaction. At least she would be going out looking a bit better and more professional than she had when Craig Hamilton walked in.

Lucy peeked out through the tiny window in the swinging door. Most of the diners were crowded around a front table. She could see Charlie there as well but couldn't pick out the actor.

He was being mobbed by admirers. Well, almost mobbed. *That will teach him to come in here.* Assuming he didn't like that sort of thing. Maybe he did. Maybe that's why he'd come in the first place, seeking the attention of his adoring fans?

She certainly wasn't going to stop to ask and was thankful for the cover. She took a breath, steeled herself, and stepped out, heading for the door with long, fast strides.

She almost made it, too. Until Charlie caught sight of her. "Lucy! For pity's sake, where are you going?"

Lucy pulled open the door and called back over her shoulder, "I'm not a waitress, Charlie. I'm a registered nurse. I've got patients to take care of. You know that."

She only caught a glimpse of Charlie's expression. He looked miffed but was struggling to control his temper in front of his honored guest. She just hoped that the honored guest had heard her parting words. It was impossible to say.

She could barely see the top of his head. His fans clustered around three deep, holding out menus and place mats, and even copies of his autobiography, for him to sign.

"Now, now, don't crowd the man. Step back, please. Give him some air." Charlie waved his hands as if directing traffic. "Tucker? A little help here?"

As Tucker ran over, Lucy made her escape, daring one last backward glance. The autograph seekers blocked Craig from her sight—and her from his sight as well, she realized. *A small mercy*, she thought, as she ran out the door and down the street to her car.

She reached into her tote for her keys and realized that her hands were shaking. When she finally pulled the key ring out, it clattered to the sidewalk.

She bent to retrieve it, but another hand was there first, a man's hand. It held the keys out to her. She saw dark shoes and suit pants—and felt terrified to lift her gaze.

"Lucy? Are you all right?" Reverend Ben asked quietly.

Lucy sighed with relief at the sound of the familiar voice. "I'm fine. Just in a rush." She forced a smile. "I promised Charlie I'd help out this morning. He's so shorthanded. But I just remembered I need to see a patient all the way out in Rockport."

It wasn't *entirely* a lie. She did have an appointment in Rockport, but not until much later that afternoon. She braced herself, wondering if she'd be struck by lightning right in the middle of Main Street for fibbing to a minister.

Reverend Ben smiled but watched her curiously. She could tell he wasn't fooled by her flimsy excuse. "Drive carefully. It would be a hardship all over town to have our best nurse on the sidelines right now," he said kindly.

"Thanks, Reverend. I will," she promised. He did have a point. She was so distracted and addlepated. She needed to calm herself for a minute before she got behind the wheel.

"And if there's anything else on your mind—or anything you'd like to chat about—you know my door is always open," he added.

She knew that was true. Lucy had sought his wise counsel many times when she felt stuck, was facing a hard decision, or was trying to solve a seemingly insolvable problem. Reverend Ben had helped her, and helped Charlie, too—if he'd ever admit it—to sort out their stalemates about Lucy pursuing her college degree. Or adopting their daughter, Zoey, a runaway teen they had taken in one cold, snowy night.

Reverend Ben never told her what to do. He did help you ask the right questions in your mind and heart and find your true feelings so you came to your own solution. One that always made you feel as if you had known the answer all along but had just been unable to see it. And he did advise you to pray about your problems, to talk things out with God and ask for His help. Which Lucy often did, not just about problems but about situations in her life that made her feel happy and grateful.

The wise, caring minister could not help with this one, she knew. It was hers and hers alone to navigate.

"I'll remember, Reverend. If something comes up, I mean. Enjoy your day," she added.

"You as well, Lucy." He nodded and headed toward the village green and the old stone church. Lucy slipped behind the wheel, feeling uneasy and nearly found out.

She had always imagined that if she saw Craig again, she would be much cooler and calmer. Not running like a scared rabbit. But here she was, shivering. Or just about.

Fran had been right, as much as Lucy hated to admit it. If Craig Hamilton meant so little to her, if she was really totally over it, how could she have reacted the way she just did?

She still had feelings for him—whatever they were: anger, disillusionment, regret? *But that still doesn't mean I need, or want, to talk to him.*

The words echoed in her head, as if she were silently arguing with someone. *Like Fran*, she thought.

Maybe she was ashamed? Embarrassed that after all this time, Craig Hamilton could find her right where he'd left her? After all their big plans. Plans that he had carried through on, and so successfully. *He probably thinks he ruined my life*, she reflected. *Even though it isn't true. Not one bit.*

Lucy knew that she alone had made her choices and she alone was responsible for them, for better or worse. By and large, she was happy and grateful for the life she'd made with Charlie. She didn't have anything to prove to anyone. Even Craig Hamilton. Though part of her still felt as if she did. A small part that niggled at her.

She wished he had never come here and stirred up all these feelings, all these memories. It didn't seem fair. But life wasn't always fair. Reverend Ben's appearance did remind her that life's speed bumps and detours happen for a reason, though that reason is rarely clear at the time.

Lucy started up the car and headed toward the slow route to Rockport. She would take her time and pick up some supplies on the way. If she arrived early for the appointment, she would have a cup of tea and walk on the dock with all the art stalls. The long drive would calm her, too, and would provide the perfect time to have a talk with God about the situation.

I wish I knew why you've thrown Craig Hamilton in my path after all this time, she silently prayed. *I don't have a clue what to do about it. Or what you're trying to tell me. If there's something you want me to do about this, God, could you please make it a little more obvious?*

*   *   *

JOE KNOCKED ON LAUREN'S OFFICE DOOR, THEN WALKED IN. HE WAS carrying a file in one hand and looked excited about something. But not in a good way. Lauren put down the document she'd been reviewing. "What's up?"

"Didn't McGuire tell you he's a client of Perry, Cook and Doyle?"

Lauren recognized the name of one of Boston's oldest and most prestigious law firms. But she couldn't quite put those names together with Cole McGuire.

"He certainly did not. I think I would have remembered that."

"It must have slipped his mind. Or he was playing games with you, big-time. Lawrence Perry just called me. Lawrence Perry, *personally*," he repeated.

Lauren knew what that meant to Joe. He couldn't have been more impressed if he'd been contacted by the head of the CIA.

"He sure slapped us down." For once, Joe's good spirits failed him.

Was he blaming her for this gaffe? Did he think she'd somehow missed this important information?

"Joe, take my word for it, McGuire couldn't afford five minutes with Perry's outer-office receptionist. Someone must be doing the guy a favor. A friend of a friend of a brother-in-law's cousin's college roommate's father type of connection?"

Joe blinked, trying to follow her convoluted explanation. "I get the point. Nonetheless, somewhere along those six degrees of separation, McGuire is connected. Perry made me feel like a fool for putting forward this complaint."

She had told Joe the demands were unreasonable. But she didn't remind him of that. "How did you leave it?"

"I've already called Paul Hooper. I strongly advised him to drop the issue, and he agreed. The board members don't need bad word of mouth in that circle. Even way out here. I hope you didn't mind me jumping in?"

In most any other situation like this, Lauren would have felt disrespected and annoyed, and she would have told Joe so in no uncertain terms. But she actually felt relieved.

"Not at all. I understand the urgency. I'll call McGuire and let him know the golf club has backed off."

"That's all right. Perry will tell him. From what you've said about the guy, I'm sure he'll be very smug about this little victory. No point getting our noses rubbed in it. All's well that ends well?"

"No point at all." Lauren could already picture Cole McGuire's smug grin, though she wasn't sure she agreed with the rest. It seemed that now there would be no further contact between them on this issue. Which probably meant no contact at all. It was an ending, but not a good one, from her point of view.

Joe sat on the edge of her desk and handed her the file he was holding. "Besides, I have a new assignment for you."

"You do?" Lauren still had qualms about taking more work at the firm. If she had to be perfectly honest, maybe the only reason she had continued this week was the unsettled situation with Cole McGuire. This, despite the pep talk she'd given herself after leaving his property on Monday afternoon.

But it didn't seem the right time to have that conversation with Joe. And the light in his eyes made her curious about this new assignment.

"Before you say anything, I want you to read this file. It's mainly an interview with the client, Madeleine Belkin. She created software at a firm in Burlington called Dendur Software. Her job was eliminated when the company had to tighten its belt. She later found out that two men at her level, who had been kept on, had been at the firm a shorter time and had come to their jobs with fewer credentials and less experience. And they're making substantially higher salaries."

Lauren could feel her blood pressure rise as she listened to the story. "And her claims have been substantiated with records from the company?"

"To some degree. Of course, if we decide to take her on and go forward, there's a lot more work to do."

Lauren didn't doubt that was true. Discrimination and disparities in the workplace happened all the time. Despite laws about equal opportunity, equal work, and equal pay, on average, most women earned anywhere between 20 to 50 percent less than a man for the same work at the same job.

The courts seemed to accept this double standard, and such matters were often hard to prove. Employees shied away from complaints, fearing to be labeled as troublemakers in their industry, and companies had very broad rights to hire and fire as they saw fit.

Just hearing the vague outline of her situation already made Lauren angry on Madeleine Belkin's behalf. But the attorney, trained to smell a winning case, sniffed and sniffed.

"Would she be willing to settle for damages, or does she want her day in court?" Lauren felt a bit cold asking, but she did want to know before she read the file.

"She's not sure. She is sure that she wants the world to know how Dendur Software treats their female employees."

Lauren pulled the file closer but didn't open it. "Sure, I'll take a look."

Joe gazed at her curiously. "Okay, thanks. But I'd thought you'd jump up in your chair over a case like this."

"Why? Employment law isn't really my thing."

"No, but being a woman who more than holds her own in the workplace—and on the golf course—certainly is."

Lauren wasn't sure if she should take his words as a compliment or an admonishment. "I like to think that I do. But that doesn't mean I want to fly into a courtroom wearing a cape and boots."

"That's too bad. I think I'd like to see that."

Lauren felt herself blush and hated the reaction. "What I mean is, I'm sure that there are plenty of lawyers who specialize in women's rights in and around Boston and they're proud to wear that outfit. And wield a shield and thunderbolt, too."

"I don't doubt it. But for some reason, this fell our way, and I offered to help. Or at least consider her situation and advise her?" He paused and smiled. "You know, that old friend of a friend of a brother-in-law's cousin's father thing?"

Lauren laughed. "Don't forget the ex–college roommate. I'll tell you what I think tomorrow, first thing."

Joe looked satisfied. "I look forward to it."

Was he mocking her? Not exactly, Lauren decided as she watched him go. He still seemed to think he was dangling a ball of catnip under her nose, despite her disclaimers. She would have to see if he was right and her feminist ire won out over her reservations.

LILLIAN GAZED AT HER HUSBAND ACROSS THE TABLE. STILL UNSHAVEN and in his bathrobe, he'd barely picked at his breakfast. With his head bent so low that she only saw the top of his mostly bald scalp, he was totally engrossed in a thick book. Or he was pretending to be, just to annoy her and avoid conversation.

By this time of the day, Ezra was always showered, clean shaven, and dressed for the day in one of his many tweed sport coats, oxford-cloth shirts, and signature bow ties, whether or not there were appointments on the docket. He took pride in his appearance and appreciated fine clothing—a trait of his she'd always admired.

He only came downstairs in this state of dishevelment when he was ill, and she knew that today he was in perfect health. Physically, anyway.

Are you going to pout again all day? When is this mood going to lift? It's positively . . . self-indulgent. I've lost my patience entirely.

She had a mind to scold him soundly in just that way but decided to hold her tongue. For once. She had already conveyed that message during the last few days, though not quite so harshly. It had only made matters worse.

Instead she said, "Would you like more coffee? I'll ask Estrella to make another pot."

Ezra shook his head without looking up. Not even sparing a "No thank you."

"Do you really need to read a book at the table?"

"You're reading the newspaper."

"That's different."

He turned a page but still didn't lift his head. "I don't see how."

She wouldn't waste her breath explaining. He was just being obstinate. And cranky. She knew why, too. Like a thick black cloud, the mood had descended the moment Jessica had taken that infernal dog away. Five days past and counting. How much longer would this go on?

Ezra knew very well that they both read the morning paper at the table, *together*. That's why it was different. Affably sharing bits of news, editorials, and tidbits they came across in the pages. Discussing reviews of the latest books and plays, or reports of a new art exhibit. Even though it was harder and harder to avail themselves of these cultural events, they did enjoy keeping up and discussing them.

She and Ezra shared an intellectual rapport she had never known with her first husband, Oliver. Nor had she missed it at the time, she had to admit.

Oliver had cut a bold figure, handsome and charming, totally disarming her with his confidence and devil-may-care attitude. A war hero and heir to a fortune, he'd swept her off her feet. He persuaded her to elope, and so they did one snowy Christmas Eve. He'd brought her straight back to Cape Light, to live with his family in Lilac Hall, a home and estate so grand even her staid Boston Brahmin clan could not have helped but be impressed. But she'd never had the chance to impress them with her new home or new position as the wife of the wealthiest, most prominent businessman for miles around. Her parents had strongly disapproved of Oliver and had forbidden her to see him. The Warwick fortune was amassed during Prohibition, with questionable business dealings, and Oliver, they believed, was entirely unsuitable—his reputation tainted with scandal and even a divorce. When they heard of the marriage, they cut off all ties, a punishment that had pained her and still did, even now.

Lillian had always believed that someday her mother and father would come around. Her mother at the very least? But only her younger sister, Beth, who had been so dear to her, had kept in touch, secretly, until her early and unfortunate death.

Ezra and Oliver had grown up together, friendly rivals all through childhood. They'd both served their country admirably in World War II. Oliver had won medals on the battlefield for his bravery and came home with the scars to show for it. Ezra had worked as a medic at makeshift hospitals, tending to the wounded under the most crude and stressful conditions. Saving some, he'd told her once, but losing many more. He had been awarded no medals for that grueling service but never begrudged his fellow soldiers for their honors or regretted his contribution.

She had met them both at the same time, as a very young woman, visiting the seaside village one summer. There had been a cousin who lived in Newburyport, a sweet but flighty blond. Lillian couldn't recall her name now. She hated when that happened. It would come to her later. When she wasn't thinking about it.

Ezra had also courted her, in his way. But his kind, bookish personality was no match for Oliver's dashing charm and utter confidence.

She recalled how Ezra had once taken her to the opera in Boston. He was a doctor at Children's Hospital, and she was working at the Museum of Fine Arts as an assistant curator for the Egyptian collection. They had seen *Turandot*, a wonderful performance. The lead soprano had been excellent, Lillian recalled. Still, the entire evening, all she could think of was Oliver and their parallels to the plight of the coldhearted princess and the condemned man who had melted her heart.

She'd often wondered what her life would have been like if she had taken the path not followed, if she'd become Mrs. Ezra Elliot over sixty years ago. She would have lived the life of a country doctor's wife. All things considered, she doubted her family would have found Ezra, with his blue-collar background and college tuition paid by the GI Bill, any more acceptable than the dapper and wealthy Oliver Warwick, despite Ezra's degree from Tufts University and graduation with honors from Harvard Medical School.

There would have been children. Ezra loved them and had always wanted a family but claimed he'd never met the "right" girl. That girl had married his friend Oliver. Everyone in town knew that.

She would not have held her prestigious position in the town's "first family" if she had married Ezra. Neither would she have suffered the humiliation of Oliver's later disgrace and the loss of his family's fortune. To his everlasting credit, Ezra had been among the few who had stood by them, and stood up for them, when it seemed all but a handful in the town were ready to tar and feather her first husband for his misdeeds. Reverend Ben Lewis was new to the church and village, but he had spoken for Oliver, shielding the family as well. He had reminded the villagers of their better natures, and of the question of casting the first stone.

After that sad time, and in all the years that followed, Ezra had been a stalwart friend to her and her family.

There had come a point when they'd realized there was no good reason not to be married. She had come to love him dearly, and he had always loved her. Ezra prized her good points and tolerated her imperfections. Perhaps he saw, as few did, that what made Lillian unlikeable to many were the very strengths that had helped her survive. She had not been born this way, but time and experience had shaped her, like the rocks at the edge of the sea. She made no apologies for who she was, and she never would.

He was a man with enough confidence and sense of self-worth to marry a strong woman who was not prone to apologies. Oliver had been, as well. But she loved Ezra in a different way. Was either way better? She could never say.

How the years since had passed so quickly, she would never understand. But here she was, over half a century later, Mrs. Ezra Elliot. And content with that choice. Quite blessed, she knew, truly, by her husband's persistence and lifelong loyalty to her. For reasons she didn't quite understand.

What would Oliver have been like, had they ever made it this far?

He had died soon after his fall from grace. The stress and strain of his failures had worn out his heart. No mystery there.

It was always hard to imagine Oliver at this stage of life. Gray and shrunken, infirm, moving through the day like an inchworm. He was that rare type, a brilliant, fast-burning light; a colorful flare shot across the dark sky on a summer night. An awe-inspiring show, never designed to burn long and steady. Ezra was just the opposite, she reflected, gazing at him.

He cleared his throat and turned the page, then scratched his bearded chin in an absentminded way. *I hope those whiskers are bothering you*, she said silently. *Enough to go back upstairs and promptly remove them.*

"The weekend crossword looks challenging," she reported. "The theme is 'Foreign Affairs.' I wonder what that means?"

Of course, she had some idea. It was a play on words. Doubtlessly there would be questions about political events, and the royals, and maybe even one about Ingrid Bergman running off with that famous Italian film director. What his name again? Ezra would remember.

She waited for him to answer her first question, tossed out like a bit of bait.

He was too much of a gentleman to ignore her completely, though the book provided an acceptable excuse to disengage and wasn't totally humiliating to her either. That's the way Ezra was, thoughtful even when he was angry.

"I suppose, if you work on it, the meaning will become apparent," he answered finally.

Did that mean he *wasn't* going to work on it with her? They always worked on the puzzle together. He knew that. Especially the weekend edition. The situation was grave indeed. Even worse than she'd thought.

She steadied herself. Perhaps if she solicited his aid with a clue or two, he might become engaged despite himself and rise out of this dreadful funk.

She didn't know what else to do. He had to break sooner or later. No one could keep this up forever.

"The schedule is out for the symphony. Should we get a subscription this season? The problem is getting into the city and back, of course." She paused and watched him. "I wondered if we should get a ticket for Estrella as well. She could drive us in and out."

Ezra peered up. Finally, she'd said something so outrageous and out of character, he deigned to give her his full attention.

"Estrella prefers the opera. I'd invite her to that." He delivered the message and looked down at the book again.

"Interesting. Does she really? I had no idea."

"I'm not surprised to hear that. Do you ever talk to her about anything except how you prefer your eggs cooked? Or how you like the linen closet arranged?"

He turned the page and propped up the book on his juice glass.

She sighed, feeling totally exasperated. She looked back at the newspaper but couldn't focus. Not with Ezra acting this way.

"What are you reading? I can't see the cover."

He held the cover up so she could read the book's title. Another tome about Theodore Roosevelt? She thought he'd read every one written by now. Obviously not. T.R., in a classic pose, graced the cover, wearing his Rough Rider uniform and smiling widely under his iconic mustache.

She decided not to comment, lest the very name sparked a discussion of the four-footed namesake. The creature who had caused all this trouble and unrest.

The phone rang. The handset was closer to Ezra, but he ignored it. Lillian leaned over and picked it up. She saw Jessica's name and number on the screen. Finally, some decent conversation.

"Good morning, Mother. Did I wake you?"

"Of course not. We're dressed and ready for the day. At least, one of us is," she added.

"I'm just calling about church tomorrow. It's my turn to pick you up. I just wanted to know if you planned on going."

"Certainly, we do . . . Just a minute." She looked across at Ezra. "Church tomorrow, Ezra. Jessica's picking us up."

"You can go. I'll play it by ear."

"What does that mean, *play it by ear*?"

He shrugged. "What does it sound like?"

She did hope his ear told him go. Whenever he got like this, which was not often, Sunday service always snapped him out of it. Ezra was so well-liked, and greeted so fondly by everyone at church, that it was hard for him to maintain a grouchy countenance. He automatically reverted to his normal, affable self, and by the time they got home, he usually forgot whatever he'd been mad about—or at least, took a perspective of greater equanimity. She was, in fact, counting on that antidote, since so far, all else had failed.

"Ezra seems unsure, but he'll probably come, too," she said. Had Jessica even heard her? There was the oddest sound on the line. Like . . . whining machinery. "Whatever is that sound? Where in the world are you?"

"In my van. On the way to Carlisle. We're delivering a pair of goats to a new home."

Lillian took a breath. All that education, a master's degree in finance, a solid career in banking. Jessica would have been bank manager in a year or two, no question. Pearls before swine, literally.

"I see. That explains it. I can barely hear a word you're saying."

"I can't talk long. I'll pick you up at the usual time," Jessica replied. "By the way, please tell Ezra that Teddy is doing well with his new owners. Everyone is getting along perfectly," she added, referring to the couple's other pets. "They kept the name Ezra chose. They said it suits him."

"That is good news. Ezra will be happy to hear it."

The chippy thing had not been found under the dog's fur, so his real owners could not be located. Jessica had placed him with an older couple who lived near her, out in the woods—the sort of neighborhood where animals belonged, if you were going to keep one.

Jessica had mentioned a small chance that the dog's placement might not stick. The couple also owned another dog and two cats. Who could live in such a menagerie? You might as well move into the zoo. There was some question of whether Teddy would get along with his siblings, but it seemed it was all working out.

Lillian was happy to hear that the last possibility of Ezra lobbying to bring the dog back had gone up in a puff of cat hair. She said goodbye to her daughter and set down the phone.

"I'll be happy to hear what?" Ezra put the book aside and looked at her.

"Jessica said the dog is adjusting well to his new home. All the animals are getting along, and his new owners kept the name you came up with."

He scowled and looked away. He took a sip of coffee and put the cup down again, then rose abruptly from his chair. "I'm going for a walk."

"Good idea. Some fresh air will do you good. I hear the town is crowded with all the movie fans."

"Well then, I'll walk around them. What do I care?"

"Don't be cross. Do wear your hat and gloves. Estrella said it's cold out. And some real clothes, of course," she muttered in a lower tone.

He tucked the book under his arm and went upstairs. He made a sound as he passed her, but she couldn't tell if it was an actual remark or just wholesale grunting. Perhaps it was best that she hadn't heard it clearly.

No doubt that fresh air and exercise would do him good. Clear the cobwebs. Perhaps he'd come to terms with the news that the last hope of the dog's return was now off the table.

She did feel sorry for him. But it couldn't be helped. The sooner he accepted the situation and moved on, the better.

A few minutes later, she heard Ezra come down the stairs. He soon headed for the mudroom, where he put on his hat and coat. Lillian pretended to be reading the newspaper, wondering if he would talk to her this time.

But he left the house by the side door, without even asking if she wanted anything from the pharmacy or post office or needed a library book returned. He really was not himself at all. She was starting to worry.

She picked up the paper and maneuvered into the living room, where she sat in her favorite chair. She was tempted to start the cross-word but decided to hold off on a solo flight until Ezra got back. He might feel better when he got back, and then they could work on it together. As they always did.

She had just started a new collection of short stories, about a woman who lived in Maine named Olive Kitteridge. Fairly dark, but well-observed and exquisite writing, she thought.

She had only advanced a page or two when she heard a key turn in the front door's lock and then heard the door open.

"Emily? Is that you?" Her daughters both had house keys, and she knew it couldn't be Jessica, off on her goat delivery. They were usually polite enough to ring the doorbell before letting themselves in. Whatever could be the rush?

"It's me," Ezra called out.

"Did you forget something?" Lillian rose with the aid of her cane and walked to the foyer to meet him. She was encouraged by his tone. The air had done him good already, it seemed.

"No, but I found something," he reported. "Found someone, just about sitting on our doorstep."

Lillian entered the foyer and saw Ezra standing in front of the door, his arms full of . . . dog.

Not just any dog. *The* dog. That Teddy.

"What in heaven's name? . . . Ezra, how did you get that dog back? You didn't call those people who took him in, did you?"

Her mind spun with possibilities and secret schemes.

He laughed. "Of course not. Are you daft? I don't even know their name. Looks like Teddy ran away from his new home. He obviously likes it better here."

"Because he gets more attention, that's the reason. You positively spoil him. He's an only dog here, and over there, one of many. No mystery, I'd say."

"Lillian, you're too hard on him. He likes us. I think he likes you even more than me. Look at the way he gazes at you."

Lillian had noticed that the dog was staring at her and wagging his tail furiously, wearing that uncanny smile, too.

He looked as if he wanted to jump into *her* arms. Heaven forbid.

"I bet if I let him loose, he'd run right to you."

Lillian jumped back. "Don't you dare. Straight to the mudroom. Get that cardboard up again. I'll call Jessica. She'll let his new owners know. At least we know where he belongs this time. They must be very worried about him," she added.

She was assuming that, even though she knew for sure that those people were extremely irresponsible. The dog had only been with them five days. How could they have lost it already?

With that houseful of creatures crawling around, maybe they hadn't even noticed he was missing. But she didn't say that aloud, knowing that it would only encourage Ezra to keep him.

"They can pick him up right away," she said.

"I could have predicted you'd say that."

He sighed as he walked past her, cradling the little hound like a baby. The dog rested his head in the crook of Ezra's arm and gazed back at her until they disappeared into the kitchen.

You never know what will happen when you get up in the morning. Lillian had heard it said, and it was still true. She did hope that by the end of the day, Teddy the dog would once again be banished from her home.

This time, once and for all.

CHAPTER SEVEN

⌒

*Y*OU HAD TO LOVE A GUY WHO ORDERED THE "SUSHI BOAT."
And then didn't seem the least bit embarrassed when all of
their fellow diners turned to watch the waitress carry the elaborate
entrée to their table. Was he always like this on a date? Or was this
bon vivant persona for her benefit?

Lauren had not intended to go out with Joe two weekends in a
row. But when he'd asked last week if she was free, she thought some
private time out of the office might provide a good moment to explain
why she didn't want to take any more assignments from his firm.

For one thing, the hours spent working were seriously cutting into
her job search. At this rate, she would still be home at Easter. For
another, their growing closeness as colleagues was giving him ideas.
He had already had those ideas before she'd set foot in his firm, and
spending so much time together at the office only encouraged him in
that direction.

Lauren had decided it was best to step back and disentangle,
though she truly enjoyed and appreciated his friendship and company.

How boring the last few weeks here would have been if they hadn't renewed their connection.

It was a fine line, and Lauren wasn't sure she could make it from one end to the other without falling off and hurting his feelings, which was the last thing she wanted to do. No matter how many times he assured her that he valued her honesty and up-front personality, no one likes to be romantically rejected. She knew that firsthand.

Then he had dumped that file about Madeleine Belkin and Dendur Software on her desk. She'd read it, met with Madeleine, and mulled over the pros and cons of representing her. And finally ended up taking on the case, much to Joe's delight. He had, after all, predicted that she would.

The "It's not you, it's me and my job search" talk that she had planned was canned. Stored, more accurately, for some future meeting. And here they were, at a Japanese restaurant in Newburyport, where the sleek decor combined shades of cool gray, creamy white, and black lacquered wood to create a sophisticated, upscale setting.

They'd shared a few appetizers and sushi and sashimi for two, artfully arranged on a large bamboo boat, tasting as good as, and possibly better than, most she'd eaten in New York.

Joe insisted on ending the meal with a shared dessert as well: a dish of green tea ice cream, fried. She had never understood the point of frying ice cream. Or flavoring it with tea. Lauren preferred her ice cream far less gourmet—plain old vanilla, slightly melted and swimming in hot fudge sauce.

If Joe was trying to show her that life in "the sticks" did not lack gourmet dining and civilized comforts, he was doing a good job. A transparent job, Lauren silently qualified, but a good one nonetheless.

Their conversation ranged from recent films to golf to the news—

carefully skirting political potholes—and then on to an update on their high school classmates. A "Where are they now?" rundown.

Many had moved away for a time after college but had returned to the area to settle down and raise their families. Most had not ventured beyond Boston. Lauren wasn't surprised. In many ways, Boston and Cape Light and the surrounding villages were easier—and more attractive—places to settle. New York was exciting and stimulating, but it wasn't easy.

What she had found surprising was that a guy like Joe, with so much to offer some lucky woman, had not married yet. She was sure from all he'd said, and not said, that he was not avoiding marriage, like some men, but would race to the altar if he found the right woman. And wanted to have children, as well.

Emboldened by the tiny but potent glasses of sake, she decided to ask outright. "Well, that catches us up on most of our classmates. But what about you, Joe? Any serious relationships in college or since? I can't imagine that the single ladies in this town aren't tracking you with GPS."

He blushed, which she thought was cute. "There has been a serious relationship. Or two. A few near misses with matrimony, I guess you'd say."

"Near misses? You make your love life sound like a runway at Logan Airport."

He looked a bit embarrassed but laughed. "I guess I've realized that any of those relationships wouldn't have been right for the long run. Breaking up was painful at the time, but it was the the best thing—for my former girlfriends and for me."

"I understand."

"Is that how you feel about the guy you mentioned? Who broke up with you back in New York?"

Lauren sighed. "I haven't quite turned that corner yet. But I can see it, not too far up the road."

He took another spoonful of the ice cream. "It takes time to get past these things, but you're doing well if you already feel that much better."

She appreciated his encouraging reply. Then she realized he had turned the conversation back to her again, a little trick she had noticed him playing from time to time. Was she so interesting? She hardly thought so.

"Back to you," she said boldly. "I just find it surprising that you're not married yet. It sounds like you'd like to be."

He nodded. "I would like to get married. I'm more than ready."

"Just haven't met the right person?"

"I wouldn't say that's the problem, exactly." He gazed at her, his words hanging in the air.

For pity's sake, Lauren-Big-Mouth. This is just what you didn't want to happen—a full-blown, all-the-cards-on-the-table talk about Joe's feelings for you.

She wracked her brains for a quick, diverting answer. "Sure, well . . . I bet there's a busload of wonderful, accomplished women around here with a lot to offer. It shouldn't be a problem meeting someone," she rambled. "I really was impressed by Madeleine Belkin," she added, trying to cut across to an entirely new tract of conversation. "I was on the fence about taking the case, as you know. But talking with her face-to-face made all the difference."

Joe squinted, then smiled. He knew what she was doing but was letting her get away with it. "I thought you two would get along. She's the very definition of 'still waters run deep.'"

A perfect assessment of Lauren's new client, and Lauren wondered what that made her. Noisy waters run shallow?

"She's a very thoughtful person and a very principled one," Lauren said. "I believe she's following through on this action, at a high personal cost, for the sake of other women at that company and in the industry. My hat is off to her."

He sat back and quietly clapped. "Well done. Your closing argument is practically written already. I have a good feeling about this."

Lauren nearly said, "Me, too." But in truth, she wasn't entirely sure if she could win justice for Madeleine from the corporate villains. Funny how she was usually fighting on the opposite side. It did feel different, and good, to be championing the little guy. The little gal, in fact.

"So, has Madeleine's case changed your mind any about working for a Chihuahua-sized law firm?"

He lobbed the forgotten insult back so casually, Lauren had to laugh. "I believe the record will show that I never actually said that. *You* called the firm a Chihuahua."

"So I did—though it had been clearly implied," he added in a very lawyerly way. "But you haven't answered the question."

"I wouldn't say one way is any better than the other, Joe. It's just . . . different. I can see that practicing out here, a person can have a real life—marriage, kids, dogs, the works," she said honestly. "In the city, it's doable but a lot more challenging."

New York firms expected you to clock longer billable hours, and there was more juggling, expense, and intense competition. New York was a pressure cooker.

"I'd like to say I'd miss the culture scene, but Boston has more of that than I'm likely to ever indulge in," she admitted. "I'm happy most of the time to crash on the couch and binge on Netflix or Amazon, and you can do that anywhere."

Joe laughed. "That's about all I can handle after a day at the office. I love British mysteries. Everything sounds so much more intelligent and interesting when it's said with a British accent, don't you think?"

"Absolutely. Though I do turn on the subtitles," she confessed. She was glad to be off the topics of marriage, children, and finding the right person to share the rest of her life with. She thought she had found the right person, and he had turned out to be a callow, shallow commitment-phobe. She felt so confused and didn't trust her judgment at all right now.

She certainly didn't want to jump on the first reliable-looking log—or sushi boat—that floated past, giving in to a panic about approaching thirty and being left alone on the riverbank.

Was Joe a convenient log . . . or a really great guy offering her a wonderful and satisfying life? Had she said too much? Been too honest again? She never meant she could see herself working at his law firm forever and going home with him to veg out and watch Netflix. And take care of their kids.

The possible advantages of making a life here with Joe, or anyone for that matter, were obvious. But Lauren knew that she hadn't given up on New York yet and would not let herself be defeated. It wasn't a defeat, just a setback, she reminded herself. *You're only resting here before going back into the ring. You can get knocked down in the fight, that's all right. As long as you get up.*

Joe didn't seem to understand that yet. Or want to accept it. *He believes he can change your mind. So be it. That's on him. Someday soon, you may need to make it clear.* But this was not the moment.

When she got home, she found her mother in the kitchen, working at the kitchen table on her laptop. Most of the lights in the house were off and it seemed that everyone else was asleep.

Her mom's reading glasses, which were a new addition since Lauren's last visit, were sliding down her nose, and she barely seemed to notice Lauren come in and put the kettle on.

"Hi, honey. Did you have a good time with Joe?" she asked, tapping away furiously.

"It was fine. We had some really good Japanese food. Want some tea?"

"Um . . . no thanks. You go ahead. There's some chocolate cake in the fridge. Betty asked me to bring one home. But I bet you had dessert already."

Lauren so wanted the cake but decided to skip it. She'd been indulging way too much lately, and there was still Christmas to get through. *Eat through*, more like, at this house.

"So, your night out was just 'fine'? That's it?"

Her mom didn't let a tiny nuance slip past, did she?

"It was fun, I meant." The kettle called, and Lauren poured hot water into a big mug. *Best to change the subject*, she thought. "What are you up to? Catching up on work?"

"Nothing important, just making a list."

One of her Master Lists, Lauren had no doubt—her mother's foolproof method for prioritizing every task she had to complete or supervise over the coming weeks.

The system was first developed when Lauren and Jill were kids and lived with their mom in a small apartment above the hardware store on Main Street. Those days, right after her parents split up, were difficult and confusing for everyone. She and Jill missed their carefree, fun-loving father, who was as playful as a big Labrador. Looking back, she could see that her dad had never been a mature, responsible partner. He had failed and hurt her mother, and the dissolution of their marriage had caused a shell to harden around her mother's heart and tainted her spirit with bitterness. But only for a time.

Molly would not be kept down or shortchange herself and her future by taking on the role of a victim. She now insisted that the breakup was one of the best things that had ever happened to her. Forced to fend for herself and her girls, she had worked a million different jobs, often two or three at the same time—from cleaning houses to driving school buses to stocking supermarket shelves and baking muffins all night. Then she'd be out at dawn to make deliveries all over town.

No one would have predicted that a young woman who had barely graduated high school and then married at eighteen would turn out to be the town's foremost and most successful entrepreneur, male or female.

Lauren deeply admired her mother and all the hard work and sacrifices she had made for her family. Molly's success was more than well-earned and well-deserved. Lauren knew that she and her mother shared so many traits, good and not so good. But she would never change a thing about her mom. Or herself. She had learned that from her mother as well.

She was so proud of her mom and wanted her mom to be proud of her, too. Maybe that was also a reason she couldn't turn tail on New York. She would always feel the city had beat her. Her mother would approve of her decision either way. But Lauren felt slinking away from that challenge was something her mother would never do. Molly Willoughby Harding set a high bar. But that was a good thing. "A woman's reach should exceed her grasp." Lauren knew that was not the poetic quote exactly, but it was the version she preferred.

Lauren sat down at the table with her tea. "One of your big, *big* lists. Right?"

"That's right. It's just a habit. It feels so good when I check things off. Sometimes I add items that I've already taken care of, just to get that little *ping* of reinforcement. Those good brain chemicals?"

"Mom, you didn't have to tell me that." Lauren laughed and shook her head.

"Try it, honey. It works." Her mother stopped typing and looked at her over the edge of her glasses. "What's up, Buttercup? You seem in a quiet mood. Did you and Joe really have a good time? Or maybe . . . some sort of serious talk?"

Leave it to her mom to hit the bull's-eye with one dart. Not exactly the bull's-eye, but close enough.

"We didn't. But we probably should have. I didn't have the heart, or the nerve, tonight. But I will need to do that, and soon. Especially if I keep working at his firm."

"And going out to dinner with him. Oh, and playing golf," her mother added. "Did it ever occur to you that he's getting the 'wrong' idea because you're giving it to him?"

Lauren was about to deny the accusation, but then she nodded. "Umm . . . now that you mention it . . . it's complicated. I don't mean to. I just enjoy hanging out with him. As a friend," she insisted. "I'm sure I've told him that and made my feelings clear."

Had she really? Thinking back, she *had* hinted, but some guys—especially guys like Joe, who wore their hearts on their sleeves and sallied forth like knights trying to win fair maidens—didn't get the hint, or even want to.

"Fine. Then you've been honest. But are you sure that's all you're feeling? Wait, you don't have to answer that. It looks to me like you don't even know. What I will say is that many a wonderful romance has started off as friendship. And being friends with your main squeeze is important, Lauren. I'm sure you know that? Granted, you and Joe go back so long, one would think if that apple was going to fall, it would have by now. He's certainly given the tree a good shake. But this could be the lucky shot he's been waiting for," her mother mused. "And you'll both look back and laugh and see that it was meant to be all along, and say, 'Hey, it was just a matter of timing.'"

"You really think so?"

Her mother shrugged, totally frustrating her. "What do I know, honey? If it's meant to be, it will be. You will feel that in your bones. Down to your toes. That light bulb will go off and you'll just . . . know."

"But I thought I knew with Greg. I thought I felt all those things," Lauren insisted. "He turned out to be Mr. Totally Wrong."

"He *was* Mr. Totally Wrong. I could have told you that, if you'd ever asked."

Lauren felt a little jolt at her mother's bluntness, like she had stuck her finger in the toaster for just a second. She was about to protest, then realized that this was probably how other people felt talking to her. She wasn't sure she liked being on the receiving end.

"I wished you'd told me that two years ago. It could have saved a lot of time and energy." And heartache and disappointment.

"I wish I could have, honey," her mom said sincerely. "But—and you'll see when you're a mom—parents can't live their kids' lives for them. Sometimes it's like riding a roller coaster and not being allowed to scream. And you know how I feel about roller coasters."

Molly hated roller coasters, and the analogy made Lauren smile. "Have we taken you and Dad on that sort of ride a lot?"

"Rarely, thank heavens." Her mother looked toward the ceiling with gratitude. "But I think you know what I mean. If I had raised objections to Greg, would you have listened?"

Lauren knew the answer to that. So did her mom.

"At a certain time, I had to accept that you and your sisters must learn by the consequences of your own choices. Just like I did. My point is, you can't overthink these things, sweetheart. Believe me. I know it's hard for you. We're so much the same, it's scary." Molly shook her head and made a face. "But sometimes you just need to let go and go with the flow. Isn't that what kids say?"

"Kids who grew up in the nineteen sixties, you mean?" Lauren corrected her with a laugh. "I get your point." She paused and stirred her tea. "Is that how it was when you met Matt? Jill and I were too young to know what was really going on."

"Good thing, too. I think we both knew, from the first minute we met, that we wanted to be together. But your stepdad and I hit some rough sledding on the way to the altar. We even split up for a while. We finally realized that what we had together was too wonderful to lose. We knew our love was more important than any complications or roadblocks that our minds had conjured up. I think all that silly stuff was just about being scared to take a chance and try again. We'd both been hurt, in different ways. But what would life be if we never took a leap and trusted that wings would sprout on the way down?"

"Right," Lauren quietly agreed.

Lauren knew how her mother had been hurt by her first marriage. And Matt's first wife had died of cancer when Amanda was barely eleven years old. He'd come to Cape Light to start over and had taken over Ezra Elliot's practice when the town's favorite doctor had retired.

Her mother reached over and grasped her hand. "Don't worry, honey. You'll know what to do when the time comes."

"About Joe, you mean?"

"About Joe, about a new job, about everything. I've no doubt the pieces will fall into place perfectly." Lauren knew her mother's assurances were totally illogical and even unlikely. But hearing them did make her feel better. "Right now, I think you should just relax. Enjoy your visit and the holidays. Whenever I have a big problem with the business, or even a recipe, the answer always comes to me when I'm not thinking about it. When I'm in the shower or washing dishes. It's weird, but it's just how it works." Her mother smiled at her softly in the low, warm light.

"Thanks, Mom. I'll try to remember." Lauren grinned. "Is that a hint you want me to help more around the house?"

"Hey, there's an idea. By the way, you can leave a quarter in that jar on the counter," her mother teased, returning to her list making.

"A quarter? Lucy in the *Peanuts* comic only charges five cents."

"I charge more for my quality products, Lauren. You know that."

Lauren laughed as she headed to her room. "Right. The secret to your success."

"If you bake it, they will buy it." Her mom looked up at her for a moment. "By the way, are you coming to church with us tomorrow? It would be nice. We all missed the service last Sunday with your sisters getting ready to go."

Lauren never went to church in the city. But she knew it would make her parents happy if she joined them and Betty tomorrow. She wanted to get up early and jog a few miles anyway, before the day got away from her. This was a good reason to set her alarm.

"Sure, I'll tag along," she agreed. "I haven't been to church in a long time."

"I bet." Her mother's gaze was fixed on the computer screen. "Maybe some insights into your questions will strike, heaven-sent, during the service."

Was her mother joking? Molly had a sharp sense of humor, but she was never really irreverent when it came to church.

"You never know." Lauren meant it sincerely. She said good night and headed for her room.

FOR LAUREN, WALKING INTO THE OLD STONE CHURCH ON THE VIL-lage green the next morning felt strange and yet amazingly familiar. The smell of the damp stone outside, and then, within, the floor polish mingled with the fragrant pine and greenery that decorated the church for Christmas, brought back a flood of memories.

So many friendly faces greeted her with warm smiles—Sophie Potter, Vera Plante, Grace and Digger Hegman. Lucy Bates and her husband, Charlie, who ran the Clam Box diner and was mayor of the town now. Lauren saw Lucy wave to her friend Fran Tulley, who had saved her a seat. Fran's husband, Tucker, was the quintessential friendly policeman and still had not retired from the force, Lauren had no-ticed. He was also the church's head deacon. He roamed the aisles with Lauren's uncle Sam.

Lucy had remained remarkably pretty, Lauren thought. She looked wonderful in a sea-blue sheath dress, black patent heels, and the perfect touch of makeup. Lauren almost didn't recognize her, re-calling Charlie Bates's wife in her waitress uniform. Though she did remember that Lucy was a nurse now and had been for many years.

Grace Hegman waved at Lauren shyly as she helped her father, Digger, into a seat in a back row. Digger had been a fisherman and clammer in his day, renowned for his ability to find the shellfish. The Clam Whisperer, some would say. Lauren suddenly recalled how his daughter, Grace, a quiet, modest woman, had once made a very grand gesture, gifting Lauren with a piano.

The instrument had been stored deep in the barn behind The Bramble, the antique shop Grace ran with her father's help. They lived in an apartment above the store. Lauren had found the piano while visiting her uncle Sam, who'd had a workshop on the other side of the storage space. Not only had she loved playing at the time, but the old upright was especially intriguing. The wood surface had been painted pale yellow and covered with a garden of colorful flowers. By Grace herself, Lauren later learned.

Grace had caught her testing the keys without permission and scared the living daylights of her. The piano had belonged to Grace's daughter, who had died years before in an accident. She had been about Lauren's age, or even younger, at the time. Lauren hadn't had any way of knowing that, of course. There had been words between Grace and her uncle, she recalled, and she remembered apologizing.

After some time and thought, and a talk with Reverend Ben's wife, Carolyn—who was Lauren's piano teacher—Grace had a change of heart. She insisted that the cherished instrument be passed on to Lauren and Jillian, little girls who would learn and make lovely music on it, as she thought her daughter would have wanted. Lauren had been thrilled. She knew that her mother couldn't even afford to rent a piano.

Of course, she and her mother had thanked Grace for the gift, but it wasn't until years later that Lauren realized how hard it must have been for Grace to part with the treasure, one of her last souvenirs of her beloved child.

It was an uncommon and even heroic act of kindness. But it didn't seem uncommon at all when Lauren looked around the congregation, most of whom she'd known since childhood. So many had grown old and frail, but she knew that deep inside, their spirits were still strong. The church had provided good role models for her while she was growing up, seemingly ordinary people she could still admire and be inspired by, she realized.

Her family walked to their favorite seats, on the left side of the altar about halfway to the front. Lauren sat at the end of the row, with her mother sitting between her and her younger sister Betty. Her dad was all the way on the other end of the family. Still, there was one seat left next to her.

She gazed around the church, admiring the stained glass windows, which were rarely found in a church this old, but had been installed during the 1800s. Seven years ago, a violent storm had nearly destroyed them, and a stained glass artist had been hired to perform the painstaking repairs. It just so happened that at the time, her sister Amanda was working part-time as the choir director and practicing her cello day and night in the sanctuary. Like a melody written by some unseen hand, a romance had developed between Amanda and her captive audience, Gabriel Bailey, the stained glass artist. By the time Amanda had won a seat as first cello with the Portland Symphony, she and Gabriel had fallen in love. They'd been happily married now for five years. Lauren knew her parents hoped to hear they were going have grandchildren soon. Jillian had confided that she had a serious relationship now, too.

Lauren was happy for both of her sisters. But, as she studied the sparkling bits of light captured in the mosaic of colored glass, she did wonder when her chance would come.

She heard voices in the center aisle and saw Lillian Warwick-Elliot being escorted to a pew front and center by Lauren's aunt Jessica and uncle Sam. It took one escort alone to remove her fur coat, which had to weigh a ton. Lauren wondered where Lillian's husband, Dr. Elliot, was this morning. Resting at home, perhaps? Living with a woman like Lillian had to be a strain on anybody, and even more so on an old guy like Ezra.

Lillian was probably the person Lauren would least like to emulate in her old age. At any age. The haughty old dame and her mother got along like oil and water and never missed a chance to lock horns. Lauren would have liked to say that Lillian instigated these petty battles, but she knew her mom was just as bad. Something about the sour old lady never failed to push Molly's buttons. Probably because Lillian never missed a chance to insult her mother's cooking or remind Molly that she was once Lillian's cleaning lady. Until her mom had dumped a pail of water over Lillian's head. Or so the tall tale went. Lauren doubted it had ever been that bad. Sam tended to exaggerate the details each time he told the story. Still, Lauren had no doubt it was a humdinger of an argument.

But Lillian was family—Molly was Sam's sister, and Sam had married Jessica, Lillian's daughter. Besides, Lauren had been taught to respect adults. Even if her mom did not always follow the rules she set for her children.

The big wreath outside on the church's large wooden doors and the decorations inside the sanctuary had set Lauren in a Christmas mood and a more charitable state of mind. She hadn't really felt that way so far, even though Main Street was decked out with lights and displays in all the windows.

Her gaze rested on the altar table, decorated with a white cloth and candles surrounded by a ring of pine branches. There were four large blue candles in a separate arrangement as well, one for each week of Advent. The first was lit last Sunday, and today, the second would be.

The organ sounded the opening note of the first hymn, "Watchman, Tell Us of the Night," and the congregation rose. She noticed that her uncle, who was a deacon, quickly led a man and a little girl up the center aisle to empty seats just behind Jessica. It was Cole McGuire and Phoebe, which was a surprise; Lauren would never have taken Cole for the churchgoing type. Maybe that was unfair, since she would never label herself that way either, though she did approve of giving children some spiritual background and religious education.

"Just so you have something to rebel against later," her mother would tell her and Jillian each time they questioned going to service and Sunday School.

Molly had been joking, of course. Lauren had never really rebelled, but after she left for college, she only attended church when she came home on holidays. Someday, when she had her own children, she would feel differently, she expected.

She held open her hymnal but sang along in a halfhearted way. Suddenly, she heard a deep baritone voice singing the lyrics loud and clear, and very close. She turned to find Joe slipping into the empty seat next to her. He stood by her side and reached over with his left hand to share her hymnal.

She turned to catch his eye, unable to hide her surprise. Joe smiled and kept singing. As if there was nothing unusual about them attending a service together. Or even standing this way, practically cheek to cheek.

Joe was giving the church ladies something to talk about at coffee hour, Lauren had no doubt. She loved Sophie, Vera, Grace, and the others, but their eyesight was still sharp and always on the lookout for interesting "news," especially of the romantic variety. She would not be surprised if one of them asked her mother—in a nice way, of course—about her and Joe, or if any "big news" was expected this Christmas.

When the hymn concluded, everyone took their seats. A young couple had come up to the altar to light the Advent candle. Lauren recognized Jack Sawyer's son, David, and his wife, Christine. They had a little boy about five years old, and Christine held a baby in her arms.

They took turns reading the liturgy, even their son, and then David held the boy up to light the candle. Joe was smiling and looked touched by the scene. Lauren could guess what he was thinking. She didn't doubt he would like to be in David's place one day.

They took their seats again and Lauren saw Jack and Julie Sawyer in the same pew, along with Julie's daughter, Kate. She also realized David was sitting next to Cole. The two men seemed very friendly, and she wondered if David was Cole McGuire's connection to Cape Light and that was how Cole came to buy a piece of Jack's property.

She was suddenly glad that Cole was sitting in front of her and hadn't noticed her there. She didn't think he had, anyway. If he'd been sitting behind her, he'd get the wrong impression about her and Joe.

Which made no difference at all, she reminded herself. But she was still relieved it hadn't turned out that way.

Reverend Ben began the service with announcements. "There's a meeting of the Christmas Fair committee after the service. Please see Sophie Potter if you'd like to take part. And rehearsals for the pageant begin today as well. Parents and children, please meet in the sanctuary after coffee hour."

He left the pulpit and walked to the center of the sanctuary to lead the opening prayer. Lauren followed along in her program—until her mother's pointy elbow jabbed her in the ribs.

"The movie people are here," Molly whispered. "They just walked in and sat in the back row. I think Craig Hamilton is there, too."

Now, there's a guy she never expected to see in church this morning, never mind Cole McGuire. Lauren turned her head, as inconspicuously as she could—though as a soft buzz of whispers echoed around the sanctuary, she soon realized that the entire congregation was doing the same.

Yes, it was definitely the movie star, along with a few other actors she recognized, and some people from the crew, she assumed. Luckily, no one was really gawking.

Reverend Ben seemed aware of the distraction but continued with the liturgy in his patient, steady way. Tucker Tulley read the day's verse from the Old Testament and the minister returned to the pulpit to read the New Testament Scripture and deliver his sermon. In keeping with the Advent season, his theme was preparing for Christmas—in the spiritual sense, but with consideration of everyone's practical concerns, too.

Lauren had come to appreciate how Reverend Ben managed to bring home his spiritual insights in a way anyone could understand and relate to. That was truly a gift, she thought.

She found his analogy to an expectant mother preparing for the birth of her child an original way to speak about Christmas, but when you thought about it, the day was really about Mary giving birth to her son.

He spoke about Christmas not as a holiday of indulgence and gift giving but as the celebration of a new start, a fresh slate. The idea struck a chord for her. Wasn't that what she was trying to do in her own life right now?

Was it really a fresh start if she rested up here, only to run straight into the same brick wall? What would be the point of that? she asked herself.

The next time will be different, another voice insisted. *You have to go back. You can't let the city beat you. You can scale the wall this time. Up and over, girl. You just need to be sharper, be tougher, and try harder.*

Unless you want to end up married to good old Joe? Running his Chihuahua-sized law firm? Is that the sort of change you want? She shook her head, trying to clear the rambling thoughts. There were other possibilities, surely?

She realized she had missed the end of the sermon when she heard Reverend Ben say, "And now it's time to share our joys and concerns." He walked front and center again, coming closer to the congregation. "We'll start with our concerns."

A few hands rose, and church members asked for prayers for family and friends battling illness, career problems, financial stress, the loss of loved ones, and even dealing with depression and addiction.

This was a time when Lauren always counted her blessings. It also reminded her of the old motto her mother had taught them: *Be kind to all you meet. You have no idea what troubles they might be facing today.*

She was surprised to see Lillian seek the minister's attention. Covered with large, sparkling rings, the wrinkled hand rose just a bit, shifted above her head, in the exact way the Queen Mum had waved to her subjects.

"Lillian? Do you have a concern?" Reverend Ben recognized her, and she rose, leaning on her cane. Her voice was surprisingly strong when she spoke.

"I'm requesting prayers for my husband, Ezra. He's not been himself the past week or so. I suppose you could say that he's had a . . . disappointment. He's quite sad and not bouncing back in his usual way. I am worried about him," she said finally.

People were sometimes vague in the way they worded these requests, Lauren had noticed. To maintain privacy, of course. God knew what they were talking about; that was the main thing.

"Our prayers are with Ezra, and with you, as he faces this challenge," Reverend Ben assured Lillian. "We pray that he's feeling better and recovers from this setback very soon."

The minister seemed about to move on to the joys when another, much smaller hand rose. Lauren realized it was Phoebe. The little girl looked adorable today in a bright red coat with a black velvet collar, her long hair plaited in two shiny braids. Had Cole done that for her? What a dad.

Or maybe a woman "friend" of his had worked on the hairdo? A friend like . . . Jen Bennet?

Reverend Ben smiled and walked closer. "Yes, dear? Do you have a prayer request?"

Phoebe seemed about to lose her nerve. Lauren saw her father quietly assure her. "We need prayers for Wilbur," Phoebe said. "He has a bad cold. He's very sick."

Lauren felt her heart clutch. Wilbur was sick? She hoped it wasn't as serious as Phoebe made it sound.

"Prayers for your friend Wilbur, who has a bad cold. Is that correct?"

"Yes, he's my friend. But he's a pig, too. A piglet, I mean."

A few soft laughs rose from the pews. Reverend Ben's expression remained perfectly serious. He had a wonderful way with children. He was never condescending.

"I understand. All of God's creatures deserve our prayers and concern," he told Phoebe. "We pray for Wilbur's speedy and thorough recovery. And give gratitude for the love and care you're showing him."

Lauren watched Phoebe sit down, her head bowed as her father leaned over and whispered to her, his arm around her shoulder.

Reverend Ben went on to the blessings, large and small, that had brought the congregation joy during the past week. Triumphs of children and grandchildren—honor roll citations, sports team victories, and winning the lead role in a school play. There were announcements of engagements, weddings, and births, as well as simple joys, like a reunion with relatives who lived at a distance, or even meeting a movie star and getting his autograph.

Fran Tulley announced that coup, looking straight at Craig Hamilton with a big grin. Lucy Bates, who sat beside her, bowed her head, Lauren noticed, looking embarrassed for her friend.

The actor had the grace to rise in his seat a bit. He smiled and called out to Fran, "My pleasure to meet you as well."

The congregation responded with a round of applause, and Joe leaned over and whispered, "We enjoy full and colorful lives out here, Lauren. Wouldn't you agree?"

She knew he was teasing. Mostly. "Can't argue with that," she whispered back.

"Want to have brunch after the service? We can drive by the movie set and see if they're filming today."

Lauren considered the offer. Her first thought was to make an excuse about needing to get home. She'd just spent time with Joe last night. Today as well seemed a bit . . . much?

Then she remembered her mother's advice about going with the flow. "Sounds like fun. Maybe I can get Hamilton's autograph, too."

When the service ended, they slipped out of their row on the left aisle. Lauren was glad of that, knowing that Cole and Phoebe would walk down the center aisle to leave the sanctuary and she could easily avoid running into them.

She would have liked to talk to Phoebe and hear more about Wilbur, but no way could that happen without dealing with Cole.

She and Joe had made it to the narthex, where, a short distance away, Reverend Ben was stationed at the center exit to the sanctuary, a line of church members waiting to greet him. She noticed her aunt Jess in line, her expression serious as she talked with Cole. Lauren looked away quickly, turning her back to them. Hopefully, they hadn't noticed her and she could make a quick escape.

Where had Joe run off to? She walked a few steps more into the crowd but didn't spot him.

She felt a tug on her coat and turned to find Phoebe. "Lauren, I have to tell you something."

Lauren crouched down to talk to her. She looked so upset. "About Wilbur? I just heard. I'm sorry he's sick, honey," she said sincerely. "But your dad can take him to a veterinarian. I'm sure my aunt Jessica knows someone to call."

Phoebe swallowed, fighting back tears. "Yes, Daddy said he will. Jessica can't come but she's telling him what to do."

Lauren didn't like hearing that her aunt couldn't visit Wilbur. She was sure Aunt Jess would know how to whip up some herbal chest rub, or some pig equivalent of the same. Did pigs like chicken soup? Probably not, she realized.

Phoebe did not look the least bit comforted by Lauren's suggestions. She was staring straight ahead, fighting back tears. Lauren leaned over and gave her a hug. "Don't cry, honey. We all get the sniffles now and then. I bet when you have a cold and you stay home from school a day or two, then you feel better again, right?"

She felt Phoebe nod into her shoulder. "I guess so," she mumbled. "But he's so little."

That was true. The piglet was probably vulnerable to infections at this stage of life. Since he did not have the benefit of the built-in immunities of his mother's milk, he'd be even more so.

Lauren wondered what more she could say that might comfort Phoebe. She stood up and found Jessica and Cole McGuire standing next to her. Phoebe drifted over to her father. Cole rested his hands on her shoulders, but his gaze was fixed on Lauren. She was an expert at reading body language and facial expressions, but she didn't have a clue as to what he was thinking.

"How is Wilbur doing?" Lauren asked her aunt. "I hear he has a cold?"

"It seems to have settled in his chest. I called my vet early this morning, and she's going to visit him later. I'm busy with my mom right now and I have to get a cow to a farm near Deerfield this afternoon," Jessica said, mentioning a small town in western Massachusetts at least two hours away. "I was wondering if you'd be able to help Cole and Phoebe take care of the little guy today? They really need some backup."

Lauren glanced at Cole and then at Phoebe, whose doleful expression lit up with hope at Jessica's suggestion.

"I do have some plans," Lauren began, suddenly recalling Joe's offer of brunch and celebrity hounding. It was easy to forget about the poor guy once Cole stepped into view. No disrespect—just a stone-cold fact.

"I understand," Cole said quickly. "We shouldn't have bothered you."

Phoebe looked very worried and stared up at her, practically holding her breath.

"It's no bother. No big plans that can't be changed. But I don't know the first thing about animal husbandry."

"I bet you know something. All those summers at 4-H camp?" her aunt reminded her. "We just need you to give him basic care for the cold and keep your eye on him. I'm sure you can do it."

"I guess I can manage that. But do you really need two adults to nurse him? We'll take shifts or something?" She looked back at Cole and he finally picked up on her quizzical stare.

"The problem is," Cole explained, "I have an important business meeting today, a teleconference that will take most of the afternoon. Phoebe was going to visit with David and Christine Sawyer. But even if Phoebe stays home, I can't watch the pig."

"I'm staying home with Wilbur," Phoebe piped up.

Lauren suddenly got it. But who has a business meeting on a Sunday afternoon? She wasn't entirely buying his excuse, but when she felt Phoebe lean toward her and tug on the edge of her coat, she sighed and knew she was all in.

"Sure, I'd love to help Wilbur," she replied, mostly to Phoebe, who jumped up and down and actually clapped her hands.

Cole looked relieved as well and *almost* smiled. Her aunt Jess sighed with relief and touched her arm. "Thank you, honey. You're a good sport. Just for that, you get a free Grateful Paw T-shirt."

"I saw those shirts in the last issue of *Vogue*. Paw prints are in this season."

Her quip broke the tension and made everyone smile—until Joe suddenly appeared.

"Hi, Joe," Jessica greeted him, then met Lauren's eyes, suddenly realizing what Lauren's ill-fated plans had been about.

"Hi, Mrs. Morgan." He smiled at Cole and offered his hand. "Joe Wagner, a friend of Lauren's."

"Cole McGuire," he replied, and shook Joe's hand.

"Oh . . . interesting." Joe's smile never faded but Lauren could almost hear the wheels in his head spin. "I'm the annoying Wagner, of Wagner and Associates. We represent the country club."

"Right. I sort of put that together." Cole did not add *Good to meet you* or any other false social nicety. "That's all sod under the bridge to me."

Lauren stifled a grin and glanced at Joe's reaction.

"Absolutely," Joe agreed. He said nothing more but looked at Lauren. "Ready to go? I made a reservation at the Inn on Angel Island. I thought the drive out there would be fun."

Lauren looked up at him, then back at her aunt, Cole, and Phoebe. "Excuse us for a minute, will you?"

"We have to get back home anyway. Maybe we'll see you." Cole began to guide Phoebe toward the big, arched doors.

"Text me, honey," her aunt said as she followed them.

When Lauren turned back to Joe, he looked confused. "What's up?"

"I need to do a favor for . . . for my aunt," she said, deciding that was the best way to frame the situation. "Remember when that little girl announced her pet pig was sick?"

Joe smiled. "That was so cute."

"It was, and she's a dear. The piglet belongs to my aunt's rescue group. The little girl and her dad are just taking care of it for a while. I've been volunteering for my aunt, and she asked if I could help this afternoon and watch the pig a bit. The little girl's dad has some business obligation. Seems like they need me there right away. So brunch won't work out, I'm afraid."

She waited for his reaction.

"Sure, I understand. I can come with you. I don't mind."

His offer blindsided her. Now what?

"Gee, thanks, Joe. That's so sweet of you. But I barely know Cole McGuire. I don't feel comfortable inviting anyone to his house. Especially with this teleconference going on. He seems very stressed about it. He probably doesn't even want me there."

She wasn't so sure about the first part of her excuse, but the last part was probably true, she reminded herself. Though the larger truth was that she knew Joe's appearance would send a message that they were a package deal—a message she did not want to send to either Joe or Cole.

Was Joe reading the subtext here? Or at least suspecting her ulterior motives for excluding him?

Joe hesitated a moment, then said, "McGuire does seem tightly wound, now that you mention it. No worries. Good luck with the little guy. Keep me posted."

He smiled, then kissed her cheek. Lauren felt bad for backing out of their plans, but also relieved. It wasn't as if they'd had some long-standing big date planned.

But she had just pushed him aside in order to nurse a sick pig—and to spend time with another guy and the guy's daughter. No man, however even-tempered, could feel good about that.

"Thanks, Joe. See you at the office tomorrow."

An important meeting with Madeleine Belkin was scheduled for early Monday morning and was at the top of Lauren's priority list.

He nodded and headed for the coffee hour. "See you then. Have fun now."

The zinger was so unlike Joe. Still, it was good to know he was not a total saint.

She felt a twinge of guilt as she headed outside, but quickly swept it aside as she eagerly texted her aunt to confirm that she could indeed rush to Wilbur's rescue.

CHAPTER EIGHT

*L*UCY HAD ALMOST SKIPPED CHURCH THAT MORNING. A floor nurse at the hospital had called very early to ask if she could fill in a shift later in the day and Lucy had agreed. Her patient load with the visiting nurse service was still relatively light, and she had offered to help her old colleagues during the holidays. With Christmas shopping coming up, the extra money would come in handy, too.

She did expect to be working most Sundays until Christmas, so she did her best to attend the morning's service. The possibility that the movie people would come, too, had never once crossed her mind. Especially Craig. Though he had attended church when they were young.

The congregation had been surprised and pleased to welcome the glamorous visitors. Lucy had been surprised and horrified. Her thoughts jumped like drops of water on a hot griddle at the sight, though she knew it would be easy to avoid him with all the church members crowding around the celebrities at the end of the service.

To be on the safe side, she hid out in the kitchen, helping Claire

North and her husband, Nolan Porter, with the coffee hour service and cleanup. Claire and Nolan were rarely seen at the church, compared to their dedicated membership in years past. The couple had mostly retired from overseeing the Inn on Angel Island. They'd been catching up on their travel bucket list this last year, though they had returned just before Thanksgiving to share the holidays with the Merritts, who still owned the inn. Liza, Daniel, and their children were like family to Claire and Nolan, and Lucy wasn't surprised to see the older couple back, at least for a few weeks.

The kitchen afforded a view of the parking lot; standing at the sink, it was easy to spot the movie people as they left the church and climbed into their big SUVs. Lucy hadn't spotted Craig, but she assumed she'd missed him. Still, she dried the last platter with unnecessary care, searched for the last paper plate and cup, and chitchatted with Claire as they tidied the fellowship-hour supply closet. Until, finally, she felt the coast was clear.

"Thanks so much for your help, Lucy." Claire pulled off her apron, her cheeks tinged with pink after all their kitchen work. "You'd think running coffee hour would be a snap for me, after all those years at the inn. But it's always more than I remember."

"You served a three-course gourmet breakfast out there. Most of us get by with a percolator and a box of donuts," Lucy teased.

She was exaggerating, but the inn's famed cook did go the distance for the weekly social hour.

Claire blushed at the compliment. "Cooking never seems like work to me. Though I'm glad that Nolan and I have retired. This past year has been a wonderful adventure."

"So I've heard. Good for you. It's exactly what I'd like to be doing at your stage of life."

After living in the Southwest for many years, Liza Merritt and her husband had returned last Christmas to take over the inn once more, and the older couple had taken off for distant places that Lucy had always longed to visit, in Europe and even Africa. In the warmer months, Claire and Nolan had stayed closer to home, helping at the inn during the busy weeks while fitting in trips all along the East Coast on their sailboat. It seemed like a perfect life to Lucy.

"Are you coming to the meeting for the Christmas Fair?" Claire checked her watch. "It's probably started by now."

Lucy folded a dish towel and hung it on a rack near the sink. "Wish I could, but I have to be at work in a little while. I need to run home and change."

"No apologies necessary, dear. Your nursing is very important work." Claire grabbed her handbag and smoothed down her cardigan. "See you soon. Have a good day."

Claire was the type of person who, in her quiet way, always made others feel good about themselves. She took the time to see people clearly. Lucy thought it was a true gift.

We all have our gifts and talents, she reflected. *Satisfaction in life comes from figuring out how to grow and express them. How to balance what we need to do with what we want to do.*

She smiled at her philosophical mood as she slipped on her coat. It so wasn't like her. But church did push her thoughts in the big-picture direction. She was glad now that she'd made the time this morning to come here.

She pushed open the glass door and flipped her collar up as she headed to her car. A brisk wind swept off the harbor, which was just behind the church. The waves were choppy today, capped with white foam. Bands of clouds scudded over a deep blue sky.

It was a pretty day, and she wouldn't mind the drive up to South-port. The time alone, to center herself and recharge, was always welcome. If she hoofed it home and changed quickly, she would have a leisurely trip and little traffic on the thruway.

"Lucy? Lucy, wait a minute, please . . ." a man's voice called to her from the church. Her breath caught in her throat and she slowly turned.

Craig Hamilton. She could have screamed. What was he still doing here? She didn't want this. Not one bit.

She turned her back to him and felt the urge to run the short distance to her car, jump in, and race out of the lot. But as she heard his quick steps on the gravel and his harsh breath as he ran to reach her, the idea of sneaking away again seemed silly and immature.

She was cornered and had no choice but face him. She finally turned, mesmerized by the sight of his approach. She felt as if she couldn't breathe, then scolded herself for getting so unhinged.

Stay strong. If ever you needed to find a poker face and not be swayed, this is the moment.

"I've been watching for you. I almost gave up," he admitted in a breathless voice.

She so wished that he had.

"Here I am," she said flatly.

"So I see. Thank you for not running off." He took a deep breath, gazing at her as he got his bearings.

He looked so different, but the same, too. It was funny, like an optical illusion that kept switching before her eyes from a vision of his younger self to this version: the same smile, the same features, but much older.

But not so old that he'd lost his good looks. She hated to admit it, but he hadn't lost them in the least.

She crossed her arms over her chest. "I'm sorry, but I have to get to work. At Southport Hospital," she added, hoping he knew she didn't mean the diner.

"Right. You're a nurse now."

"That's right." Lucy nodded, feeling embarrassed now that she'd shouted out the information at the diner Thursday morning—for his benefit, of course.

"That's wonderful. I bet you're great at your job."

"I try," she said in a clipped tone.

He gazed down for a moment, as if he'd forgotten what he was planning to say. Or was he losing his nerve?

He looked up again. "I don't want to make you late. But I'd like it very much if you could see your way to having a talk with me sometime while I'm here. I'd like to meet you for coffee, or something? Anywhere you want."

"And talk about what, Craig? I'm a nurse. I'm married to Charlie Bates, who owns the diner and is the town's mayor. I have three kids, two sons and a daughter. Not much more to report." She shrugged. "Your life is an open book, literally. Not that I've read it, or plan to," she added, sounding far colder than she intended.

Her sharp reply caught him off balance. Did he think he could just smile and toss her a few compliments, and she'd turn to mush— like she used to?

"I deserve that. You have every right to be angry. Every right not to speak to me ever again. But I wish you would. Just once. There are things that need saying. I can see by your reaction that the past isn't over for you yet either."

"Whoa, there . . . That's a big assumption. And totally wrong. If I don't seem eager to talk, it's because the past *is* over for me. Completely. The book is closed, and there's no use opening it again. I don't see any benefit. Not for me."

He didn't answer right away but looked past her for a moment, out at the harbor and horizon. "All right," he said finally. "If that's how you feel. I feel just the opposite. I've thought about you a lot, Lucy. About the past. Especially lately. All my missteps and mistakes. I keep thinking I'm going to write you a letter. I've written it a thousand times in my head."

His confession was flattering. She couldn't deny it. She felt herself softening to his request but forced herself to pull back. She didn't owe him a thing after what he'd done to her. She didn't have to help him for one second to make it right. It wasn't her problem if he felt bad now for his "missteps and mistakes." It wasn't her job to fix that.

"I think you mean well. But the time for talking is past. It's passed for me, I know that. Maybe you should have written that letter right after you left, when I was tying myself up in knots, trying to understand why you did. Frankly, the reasons don't matter to me now. Offering to dredge it all up . . . well, that's too little, too late."

He looked stunned by her reply. She could see in his expression that he was shocked by her words and her manner, as if he didn't recognize her anymore. Well, she'd changed. That was true. Though it wasn't at all like her to say something so cold, and even cruel, to anyone. It felt as if another woman had taken over her body and her tongue. A woman who was angry and hurt—and had not a drop of forgiveness in her heart.

Craig took a step back, his warm, beseeching expression going blank. "I'm sorry, Lucy. I shouldn't have bothered you. I should have realized . . ." His words trailed off, his apology unfinished.

For a man who expressed himself so smoothly on a film screen, in real life, he stumbled over his lines. "I won't bother you again, I promise. But if you ever want to talk to me while I'm here, or anytime, I'd be very grateful." He reached into his pocket and then held out a slip of paper. "Here's my cell number. Call or text anytime."

She glanced at his outstretched hand and met his gaze, some small voice urging her to relent, to show the man a little mercy. He did seem sincere. But a louder voice ordered her to grasp her righteous flag and march on.

She dug her own hands into her pockets and stepped back.

"Goodbye, Craig." She almost added *It was nice to see you again* automatically. But it had not been nice. It had been painful—more than she'd ever expected it could be. Not after all the time that had passed.

She turned away from him quickly and hugged her arms to herself as she ran against the wind to her car, feeling a genuine and deep ache in her heart.

Once she had slipped behind the wheel, she couldn't start the car. She just stared out the windshield at the harbor. How odd. With all the times she had pictured seeing him again—and she had pictured it, though she hated to admit it—she had never once expected it would feel this way.

"I finally reached Alice," Lauren's aunt Jessica said, mentioning the veterinarian, Dr. Ackroyd, who had been donating her services to Grateful Paw for years. "She should be there within the hour. In the meantime, set up a vaporizer. Just plain water; none of that mentholated stuff. Put it near Wilbur's bed so he's breathing in the warm, moist air. But not too close."

Lauren had her phone on speaker as she wandered around Cole's kitchen looking for a pad and pen to take down Jessica's instructions. Phoebe was sitting on a kitchen chair, a towel on her lap, and Wilbur was curled into a cozy ball on the towel. The girl gazed down at him, stroking his forehead with one fingertip and murmuring encouraging words.

He looked listless, his eyes half-shut, his breath labored. Phoebe had offered him his bottle when she got home, but he didn't want to eat. *Bad sign for a pig,* Lauren thought.

"I don't even know if Cole has a vaporizer."

"Of course he does. It's standard kid equipment. They give you one when you leave the maternity ward," her aunt insisted. "I know Wilbur isn't interested in food, but see if you can get him to take some water. Bottled water, room temperature. If he gets dehydrated, he'll have to go into an animal hospital."

Phoebe's eyes grew wide and glassy. "No! No hospital. He's not going there. Ever!" she shouted.

Lauren was alarmed at her response. She did not seem like the sort of child to shout and act out that way. Not at all. The situation had upset her deeply, Lauren realized. She'd been dumb to have this conversation on speaker, with Phoebe hearing every word.

She picked up the phone and turned off the speaker. "Deal breaker for Phoebe. I'd better get him to drink. Can I flavor the water with something?"

"Such as?"

"I don't know. What do pigs like to eat?"

"Practically anything. But maybe just a touch of organic honey? Manuka is best, if they've got it. It's antiviral and might give him a little energy."

When had her financial-whiz aunt turned into such an earth mother? *Could that possibly happen to me . . . if I stick around here too long?*

"I'll ask. And on the slim chance there's no vaporizer, we'll run up to a store and get one."

"Great. I've got to go. My passenger is getting restless back there. I need to pull over and see what's going on."

Lauren heard a low, unhappy *Moo-oo-oo* in the background.

"Sounds like she needs to stretch her legs." She could only imagine Aunt Jess pulling into a highway rest stop and leading a cow from the van into the dog-walking area. She might make the evening news. Wouldn't Lillian Warwick be proud of that?

"Let me know what Alice says." Jessica said goodbye and hung up.

Phoebe sat with her head lowered, and Lauren leaned way down to catch her gaze. "An animal doctor is coming very soon to see Wilbur. In the meantime, there are a few things to try that might make him feel better."

Phoebe's expression brightened a bit. "Can I help?"

"Absolutely. I can't pull this off without you, pal. Jessica said to see if he'll drink some water with a tiny touch of honey. Do you think there's any in the house?"

Phoebe nodded and pointed to a cabinet near the refrigerator. The kitchen was old and cozy. The knotty pine cabinets and dark green countertops reminded Lauren of her grandma Morgan's house. She pulled open a door and saw a neat array of spices and baking supplies. A jar of honey sat right beside it. Organic, too, though not the "manuka" her aunt had prescribed. Whatever that was.

"Great. Where's his bottle? I'll whip this up and you can feed it to him."

Phoebe smiled at the plan, then leaned down to talk to Wilbur. "You're going to have a treat, Wilbur. You must be thirsty. Please drink it," she added in a solemn voice.

Phoebe hadn't mentioned the hospital again, but Lauren could tell she was thinking about it.

Cole had disappeared into another part of the cottage shortly after she'd arrived. He returned to the kitchen just as Lauren was about to fill Wilbur's bottle from a dispenser of spring water she'd found near the back door.

"Wilbur needs water. Or he'll be sent to the hospital. But we won't let him go there. Right, Daddy?" Phoebe asked before Cole was even all the way in the room.

He rested his hand on her head for a moment. "We'll do our best to keep him home with us, honey. You know that."

"The vet is coming soon," Lauren reported. "Do you have a vaporizer? My aunt said to set one up for him."

"It's in a closet somewhere. I'll find it. Then I'd better get to the meeting. Sorry," he added, with atypical concern.

"Sure. No problem."

His brash, contrary side must be in the laundry today, she decided. It had been nowhere to be seen since she'd arrived. So far, anyway.

Cole started to set off on the vaporizer hunt, then stopped in the doorway. "Thanks again for helping us. I'm sure you had better things to do."

She considered acting as if the visit was a great inconvenience and sacrifice for her but knew she couldn't pull off the charade, since she was actually happy to be there. "I'm the Pig Lady, remember? This is what we do."

Hearing the nickname she'd devised made Phoebe smile. Cole smiled, too. Really smiled. Lauren felt as if she'd been hit by a mega-blast of sunshine.

Wilbur's bottle dangled in her hand and she suddenly realized it was dripping. "Where did I put the lid for this thing?" she mumbled, wandering back to the counter.

"You forgot the honey," Phoebe said.

"Oh . . . right. It needs honey. Just a touch." She felt Cole watching as she looked around for the jar and then mixed the honey into the water. She kept her focus on her task, waiting to hear his footsteps disappear down the hall.

Thank goodness he'll be shut up in his office for a few hours. I don't think I'd make it otherwise.

A short time later, the vaporizer was spurting a cloud of steam toward the kitchen ceiling and Wilbur was sipping his honey water.

When the bottle was more than half empty, Lauren said, "I think that's good for now. We don't want him to get a tummy ache. Let's see what the vet says."

Phoebe agreed and put the bottle aside. It was hard to tell if Wilbur was relieved by the misty air, though Lauren knew her smooth blown-out hairstyle was getting wavier by the minute. The piglet squirmed a bit in Phoebe's lap, and she put him down on his bed. He walked in a small circle, then lay down again with a raspy sigh. Lauren was worried, but she was determined to keep a brave face for Phoebe's sake.

"What should we do now?" Phoebe stared at the piglet, her chin propped in one hand.

There didn't seem to be anything more they could do. That was the frustrating thing when someone you loved was sick. There was so little you could do for them except keep them comfortable and cheerful.

"Do you have some crayons and paper? We can draw pictures and happy signs for him, to cheer him up," Lauren said. "And make him some get-well cards from the other animals? I'm sure they all want him to feel better."

Phoebe sat up, suddenly brighter. "Great idea. I'll go get my crayons right now."

Cole appeared in the doorway, and Phoebe rushed past him. "I need to get my crayons. We're making Wilbur get-well cards."

He cast Lauren a questioning look. "To cheer him up," she explained.

He pressed his lips together to keep from smiling. "Whose idea was that?"

"Mine?" she said quietly. "It might cheer up Phoebe, too. She's taking this so much to heart. She got very upset when Jessica suggested that Wilbur might need care in an animal hospital," she added in a quieter voice.

"I'm sure she did." His expression was solemn. He glanced over his shoulder. "She has her reasons. I hope it doesn't come to that either. When does the vet get here?"

"Any minute. She just sent a text. She's been held up on another call. I thought your meeting was about to start?"

"They have some company business to take care of first. I'll go back in a few minutes."

"I'm just curious, what sort of company has a big teleconference meeting on a Sunday afternoon?"

"It's Monday in Auckland."

"Oh, right. So it is." She glanced at her watch. "I set my watch for Europe and Australia but somehow forgot to set it for New Zealand." She shrugged, as if she, too, always thought in such global dimensions.

So he wasn't a down-and-out farmhand, as she'd first assumed. Or even a struggling home-based entrepreneur, which had been her second guess this morning. She was about to ask what he did for a living, but a knock sounded on the back door. Lauren turned and saw a woman peering through the glass. "That must be the vet. I'll get it."

"Thanks. I'd better head back." He gave a thumbs-up sign. "Wishing Wilbur luck."

"Aren't we all," Lauren replied as she ran to the door.

"Lauren? Your aunt Jess sent me. Sorry I'm late." Dr. Ackroyd was not tall but looked strong. She had a round face and dark hair threaded with gray pulled into a long ponytail. Her skin looked as if she spent too much time outdoors in the sun and wind but didn't care; little crinkles showed at the corners of her bright blue eyes.

The vet slipped off a heavy tan field coat and draped it on a chair, then rolled up the sleeves of her denim shirt. She gazed down at Wilbur, who was lying on his side, struggling for breath. "There's my little patient."

"Yes. His name is Wilbur."

"So I've heard. Where can I wash up? . . . I ought to take these boots off first, I suppose." Her dark green, knee-high rubber boots were caked with mud, but Lauren didn't want her to go to the trouble.

"It's all right. I'll clean up later."

The vet smiled briefly and washed her hands in the sink. Then she set her bag on the table and opened it. She was pulling out a stethoscope when Phoebe ran into the room, a pile of paper and a pink plastic box pressed to her chest.

"Are you the doctor?"

"Yes, I am. Are you Wilbur's owner?"

"Sort of. He really belongs to Jessica. But I take care of him. And I love him."

"I get it." Dr. Ackroyd nodded. "You're doing a good job, too. Let's see how he feels." She picked Wilbur up by the back of his neck with one hand, set him on the table, and began an examination. Lauren watched as she did everything a doctor would do to a human patient—listened to his heart and his breathing, looked into his mouth, checked his ears. She took his temperature, too. Wilbur squirmed, but Dr. Ackroyd controlled him with an easy touch.

She gazed at the thermometer and frowned. "He has a fever. We have to get that down."

Lauren nodded and felt Phoebe take her hand. Her heart did a little flip-flop, and she looked down at the little girl. "Don't worry. The doctor will tell us what to do."

Dr. Ackroyd glanced at Lauren. She could tell the vet was concerned about Wilbur's state but had the good sense and sensitivity not to scare Phoebe.

"Will he need to go the animal hospital? He can't go," Phoebe said flatly.

Dr. Ackroyd glanced at her. "That depends on what happens today and tonight. Wilbur has an infection in his lungs. He's very young and not very strong," she added in a frank tone. "The next twelve hours are crucial. I'm going to give him a shot. It won't hurt him much, just a pinch," she promised. "And I'm going to remove some of the mucus from his lungs so he can get a good breath. Right now, he feels like he's underwater. He's not going to like that part. He'll put up a fuss," Dr. Ackroyd predicted. "But he won't survive otherwise."

Phoebe nodded. Lauren could see she understood.

The doctor quickly gave Wilbur his shot. Then she took a rubber instrument from her bag. It looked like a medicine dropper with a big ball on one end. She held Wilbur very close and tipped his head back. He squirmed and squealed, but she somehow eased the tube down his throat and sucked up the liquid blocking his lungs.

When the procedure was over, he coughed a bit, and Dr. Ackroyd petted and soothed him. "There, there, my friend. You must feel better after that?"

The piglet stalked around the table. He shook his head, making his ears flap, then trotted straight to Phoebe and nuzzled her.

"He must feel a little better. He hardly noticed me today before now," Phoebe said.

"I have some medicine here for him. I'll write down the dosage." The doctor searched her bag and found a small bottle of liquid. Lauren saw that it was given with a dropper.

"What can we do for him? Besides the medicine, I mean."

"A quick bath might help. Tepid water—not too cold, not too hot. It should bring his temperature down."

Phoebe looked happy at that news.

"Dry him well. Wrap him in a towel or blanket for a few minutes after, if he'll tolerate that. Don't let him get chilled. Keep offering water. He needs fluids, and some food if he'll take it. But water is more important right now. And you need to keep track of his temperature. Take it every hour. I'll leave the thermometer."

Luckily, it was the electronic kind that could be inserted into Wilbur's ear. The directions for his care sounded simple, but the doctor's warning about this being such a critical time for him made Lauren nervous.

Dr. Ackroyd must have read her thoughts. "Don't worry, I'll write it all down. And I'll check in to see how he's doing. Call anytime with any questions. Or if he takes a turn," she added, careful again not to sound too dire.

A few minutes later, the veterinarian was packed up and ready to go. Lauren stood at the door, holding the instructions and the medicine bottle—and wishing the wise, calm woman could stay and see Wilbur through this. Maybe it would be best if the vet took Wilbur with her and cared for him at her animal clinic, even if just overnight? Though Lauren would never say that aloud to Phoebe.

Once the vet was gone, Lauren turned to Phoebe, who held Wilbur in her arms again. "Well, we have our orders from Dr. Ackroyd. Let's start with the bath."

The notion of a slippery pig was a cliché but she expected Wilbur would be hard to handle, even feeling ill.

"There's a sink near the washer on the screened-in porch," Phoebe said. "I'll show you."

Phoebe carried Wilbur to a small space at the side of the house that had once been an open porch but was now enclosed to provide a small laundry and utility room, and Lauren followed. She ran the water, making sure it was just right. Phoebe left to find towels and returned with enough for a family of four to spend a week at the beach. She set them on the washer, next to Lauren. "He can't get a chill, remember?"

"I do. Good job."

Phoebe pulled over a chair and climbed up so she could help. Wilbur seemed surprised at first to be submerged up to his shoulders in the water but appeared to like it.

"Pigs can swim, you know. I read it in a book," Phoebe said.

"I didn't know that," Lauren replied honestly. "You can give him swimming lessons sometime when he feels better."

They weren't supposed to use soap, but streamed capfuls of water over his back and head, careful not to get it in his ears.

Lauren did it first, then let Phoebe take charge. "Very good. I think he likes it."

"I think so, too. The next time, I'll give him a bubble bath. He'll love that."

Lauren hoped there was a next time. She so hoped he made it.

The pig was soon back in the cozy kitchen, swaddled in towels, snug as bug. The bath had tired him a bit, along with his encounter with the formidable Dr. Ackroyd. He lay in Phoebe's lap again and took a little more water with honey. His eyes closed as he sipped from the bottle.

"I think he feels better," Phoebe said quietly.

"I think so, too." Lauren wasn't really sure but didn't want to worry Phoebe. She pressed her hand to his back and then his belly. "His skin feels a little cooler. Maybe the fever went down. That's good."

She checked the time. It was almost six o'clock. Where had the afternoon gone? Cole's meeting had started at three. She wondered how much longer it would last. And how long she would wind up nursing Wilbur. She hadn't even considered that.

Lauren pulled up a chair next to Phoebe and put her arm around the little girl's shoulder. The bottle was finished, and Phoebe had put it aside. "Do you want me to hold him now? Are you tired?"

The little girl leaned against Lauren and sighed.

"It's okay. I'm not tired," she insisted, right before she yawned.

They sat close together that way for a while. Phoebe's eyes closed, and Lauren's did, too.

A sound in the doorway roused her, and she turned. Cole was watching them. She wasn't sure how long he'd been standing there. "How's the patient? Any better?"

"We think so," Lauren replied in a tentative tone.

Phoebe woke up and blinked. "We gave him a bath. To bring his fever down. The doctor said," she reported.

"That makes sense. It always helped you when you were a baby." Cole met Lauren's gaze, and she could tell he wanted the doctor's bottom line on Wilbur's chances but wouldn't ask in front of Phoebe.

The alarm on Lauren's phone sounded. "Time to take Wilbur's temperature. We'll see if the medicine and bath helped."

Phoebe laid Wilbur on his bed, and Lauren found the thermometer, then placed it in his ear, as the doctor had taught her. Phoebe and Cole were both on the floor with her, helping in the operation.

"Can someone hold his head steady until this thing beeps?"

Cole reached over and held Wilbur, his face so close to hers, she could feel his breath in her hair. She willed herself to stare straight ahead, though it seemed like an hour until the thermometer sounded.

She leaned back and sighed, struggling to read the temperature.

"Still above normal, but it went down almost two degrees. Good news, right?"

"Very good news." Cole looked as relieved as she felt.

Phoebe jumped up and clapped, startling the pig a bit. "He's almost better," she declared.

Lauren sure hoped so. "Definitely on the right track."

CHAPTER NINE

~~~~~~~

COLE STOOD UP AND RUBBED HIS HANDS TOGETHER. "Who's hungry? I'm thinking of pancakes."

Phoebe's face lit up. She looked delighted but turned to Lauren. "Do you like pancakes? Because we have to eat something that you like. You're the guest."

Lauren laughed. "I am? I didn't know that," she said honestly. She really hadn't expected to stay this long, and certainly not for dinner, too.

"I hope you can stay," Cole added quickly. "Please do. I don't have to make pancakes. You are the guest. I should have asked you first."

"I love breakfast for dinner. Though my pancakes stink. They come out all lumpy and burnt."

"My dad makes the best," Phoebe promised.

The questions seemed decided, and the treat seemed to distract Phoebe from Wilbur's troubles, at least for a while. Cole asked Phoebe to help him cook, and even let her crack the eggs.

Good ploy, Lauren wanted to tell him. While they cooked, Lauren set the table. The kitchen smelled delicious, and Lauren realized that she had skipped lunch and was very hungry.

Cole was an efficient and able cook. They were soon enjoying a feast of pancakes, with all the trimmings.

"I like sliced bananas and cinnamon on top," Phoebe explained as she sprinkled the spice over her dish.

Lauren stared at her wide-eyed. "You're kidding, right? I love bananas and cinnamon on my pancakes, *too*. My sisters always made fun of me for that."

Phoebe giggled and handed her the cinnamon shaker. "How many sisters are there? A lot?"

Cole cast her a curious and playful look. "Yes, Lauren, how many sisters do you have?"

"Three. Amanda, who's six months younger. Jillian is two years younger. And Betty is eleven."

"So you're the biggest sister," Phoebe said.

She was, in fact, literally and figuratively. "That's right," she said. "I'm the totally big sister."

Cole had made coffee, the perfect fit with the pancakes. He took a sip. "That explains a lot."

She gave him a look, guessing he meant it explained why she was so assertive—"bossy," some might say.

Phoebe sighed and stuck her fork in an apple chunk. "I wish I had a sister. Or a brother. I'd like a sister better, though."

She slid a glance at her father, who, for once, was at a loss for a clever reply.

"That's funny, because when I was your age, I used to wish I was an only child," Lauren replied. "I love them all to pieces, but there are good things and bad things about having so many siblings."

Cole looked grateful to her for picking up the slack. "And you have some very nice friends at school, Phoebe," he reminded her. "And cousins."

Lauren knew that friends and cousins were not quite the same as siblings, but it was a touchy subject. Cole could get married again, to a woman with children, or a new baby could arrive in that new family. *He could remarry* very *easily*, she thought, peering at him as she poured a dash of milk in her coffee.

"How's Wilbur?" Lauren asked, to change the subject. "Maybe he wants more water?"

Phoebe was done with her meal and slipped off her chair to check the pig. She sat by his bed and petted his head. "He feels warm again," she reported.

Lauren wasn't happy to hear that. "I think it's time for his medicine. I'll give him the dose and you can give him some water. Then we'll take his temperature."

"Good plan." Cole rose and began to clear the dishes. "After that, I think it's bedtime. School tomorrow, remember?"

Phoebe sighed but nodded. Had any kid in the world ever forgotten on a Sunday night that there was school the next morning? Lauren did not think so.

Wilbur took his medicine easily. Lauren suspected it tasted good to him. She fixed a bottle of water with honey and let Phoebe feed it to him while she helped clean up the kitchen.

When Phoebe was done with Wilbur's feeding, Cole said, "Now run up and brush your teeth and get pj's on. I'll come and tuck you in."

"But I have to say good night to Lauren. You're not going home yet, are you?"

Lauren was drying the last pan and hooked it on a rack on the wall. "I'll be right here, sweetie. No worries."

Cole looked relieved to hear that, too. Or was that the interpretation of her hopeful imagination?

"Go ahead now. Scoot. It's getting late," he told his daughter. He listened for her footsteps on the stairs, then said, "What do you think about Wilbur, really?"

Lauren sighed and looked for the thermometer. "I'm worried. I think his fever is up again. I was waiting for the meds to kick in, but I think we can take his temperature now and see what's going on."

"Sure. I'll hold him," he offered.

They crouched on the floor again with the piglet, and Lauren worked the thermometer while Cole held the patient still.

Even before it beeped, Lauren could see the numbers rising. "Not good news. It's jumped again. It's as high as when the doctor was here." She sat back on her heels. "Don't tell Phoebe."

He sat back, too, and petted the piglet, who looked listless. "Of course not. What should we do?"

"Another bath might help. It did before. I'll check with the vet while you get Phoebe to sleep. I don't think she should know we need to bathe him again. It might worry her."

"Right." He seemed relieved to let her take the lead. She was surprised at that, all things considered.

As they both came to their feet, they heard Phoebe's light step on the stairs. She looked unbelievably adorable in a big white robe over pink pajamas that had a purple unicorn print. Her fluffy slippers had animal faces and scuffed across the kitchen floor.

"Love those pj's. Where can I get some?" Lauren asked, making her giggle again.

"At the store," Phoebe said, as if anyone would know that. She bent down and very gently kissed the top of Wilbur's head. "Feel better, Wilbur. Everyone in church said prayers for you."

Lauren suddenly remembered that and couldn't help sending up a quick, silent prayer herself. *Please, God, don't let Phoebe wake up tomorrow and find that this little guy has gone to Pig Heaven. Please?*

That was all she could manage before she was nearly knocked off her feet by Phoebe's massive hug around her legs. "Good night, Lauren. Thank you for taking care of Wilbur with me. We never got to draw pictures for him."

Lauren leaned over and hugged her back, running her hand over the little girl's soft hair. "You're right. We'll do that another day, okay?"

Phoebe looked up and nodded. "Okay."

Cole walked over and extended his hand. "Come on now, sweetie. Let's go up."

Lauren stepped back and waved. "Good night, Phoebe. Sweet dreams."

As Cole led Phoebe upstairs, Lauren dialed the vet. Dr. Ackroyd was concerned but didn't change her instructions except to add that she wanted a report every hour and that if Wilbur's temperature went over a certain number, Lauren was to call right away.

Lauren ran the bath and set up towels again. When Cole returned, they gave Wilbur another bath, and Lauren kept him warm and cozy while Cole refilled the vaporizer.

"His skin is a little cooler, I hope," she said. "We need to wait to take his temperature."

She sat near the table with the piglet on her lap. Cole took a chair nearby. "You don't have to stay. I can take it from here. It's getting late. We've imposed on you enough."

She looked up and met his eyes, trying to gauge if he wanted to get rid of her or was just being polite. The latter, she decided. "I can stay. It's not that late . . . unless you need to be well rested for kindergarten."

He laughed and sat back. "That's true. But anytime you want to go, feel free. Tomorrow is Monday for grown-ups, too."

Lauren did have an important and early meeting at Joe's firm on her schedule and still hadn't prepared for it. But Wilbur's outcome seemed more important.

"The vet said the next twelve hours are critical. I feel like I can't leave, not knowing if he's going to make it or not," she admitted. "Not that I don't trust you to take care of him."

"I understand. It's good of you to care so much. Did you have a lot of pets growing up? You seem comfortable with animals."

"We had this zany chocolate Lab mix named Barkley. He was mostly Jillian's. How about you?"

"My sister had allergies. So we had gerbils."

"Gerbils can be fun." Lauren grinned.

"My wife loved animals. We had a cat and were about to get a dog for Phoebe when Amy got sick. After that, our lives were turned upside down."

Got sick? Lauren's brain flipped a switch. She had assumed Cole was divorced. The news that he was a widower was a game changer. No wonder he'd looked disturbed by the idea of reading Phoebe *Charlotte's Web*. Everyone knew that Charlotte, the spider, died at the end. Lauren felt awful now for pushing it on him; but how could she have guessed?

"You lost your wife to an illness? I'm so sorry."

He took a breath and nodded. "Cancer. Very fast moving, too. A blessing, in a strange way, and that made it even harder."

She knew that she couldn't even begin to imagine and didn't know what to say.

"Phoebe was only four when it started. Amy was gone about six months after the diagnosis. Poor Phoebe didn't understand what was happening. You can understand why she's so horrified at the idea of anyone she loves going to a hospital."

Lauren suddenly understood that reaction and so many other things about Phoebe—and Cole—she had misread. "Wilbur getting sick makes her remember all that," she said. "It must be awful for her."

"I'm sure it does. Though she hasn't mentioned her mother. Not so far. I blame myself. When I told your aunt that I would continue keeping the animals for her, I never realized it might create this sort of problem."

"Of course you didn't. Not too many people would. There's always the risk of being hurt once you form an attachment to anything, a pet or a person." *Once you fall in love*, she could have added. "But how can you protect Phoebe from that forever? Would you even want to?"

She stopped herself, realizing that, once again, her mouth had run ahead of her filter and she had probably said too much. Way too much to a man who must still be grieving and hardly needed her advice on how to raise his daughter.

But he didn't look annoyed with her. "I've thought of it that way, too. And she's so full of love. Just like Amy. Who could stop her? But now that it's actually happening, I feel differently. Maybe I shouldn't have taken this little piglet into the house and treated him like a pet. What if he doesn't make it? What am I going to tell her tomorrow?"

"I have no idea," she answered truthfully. "We just have to make sure that doesn't happen." She looked down at the baby pig. "We have to save you, Wilbur. For Phoebe. I'm not going anywhere until I'm sure you're out of the woods."

Cole offered a small smile. "Since you feel that way about it, guess I'll make more coffee."

As he put on a fresh pot, Lauren asked, "Where were you living before you came to Cape Light?"

"In Boston. I'm a financial analyst." He named one of the top

Boston finance firms. Lauren was impressed. "My wife was an illustrator. She was able to work from home when Phoebe came, which she loved. And it was easy for me, too. Too easy," he added.

"Why do you say that? Or is that question too personal? I have a bad habit of that. Ask first, think later."

He turned and smiled at her over his shoulder. "Yeah, I noticed. Now that you mention it."

Lauren felt herself blush. "Sorry."

"That's okay. I know you're a lawyer, and a sharp one," he added. "I expect a lot of questions."

"That's a relief."

He shook his head. "Are you always so . . . blunt?"

She took a moment to answer, wondering if the truth would hurt her chances with him. But really, she had no choice but to be honest. "Uh . . . yeah. I am. Is that a problem?"

"Not at all. I find it amazingly refreshing." He brought over two mugs of coffee and set one at her place. "To answer your question, counselor, it was too easy for me with Amy at home all the time because I was a workaholic. After she got sick, I saw how much I had missed out on and how little I'd been around for her, or for Phoebe. I can never get that time back. It's something I'll always regret."

She could see his sadness and her heart went out to him.

"We miss her a lot," he admitted. "Sometimes, Phoebe is so much like her mother, it's eerie."

"She's a wonderful little girl. Your wife must have been an amazing woman."

"She was. But not so you'd notice right off. She was quiet and kind. A very thoughtful and sensitive person. She was a wonderful artist. She painted the walls of Phoebe's room with all sorts of animals and flowers. That was one thing we both hated about leaving the house in Belmont. Phoebe had to leave those murals behind. But I took a lot of photos for her. I even considered hiring someone to reproduce the paintings. But that wouldn't be the same, right?"

"No, it wouldn't," she agreed.

Amy McGuire did sound amazing. *And the complete opposite of me in temperament and personality,* Lauren reflected.

"You made a big change, coming out here," she observed in a mild tone, careful not to ask any more invasive questions.

You don't need to grill the poor man like he's on the witness stand, for goodness' sake.

"I had to do something. I thought it might help Phoebe to come to a new place, where everything didn't carry a reminder of her mother. I know David Sawyer through some mutual friends. I heard that his father was selling this property. I didn't really know much about the town or the area, except that it's so quiet and pretty around here. But it seemed a good place to start over, and I thought it was worth a try."

Lauren thought of her own life and how she was trying to start over, too. It was encouraging to hear that Cole had taken a chance and it had turned out to be the right choice.

"Seems like you were right," she said.

"Seems so. And I'm grateful. Phoebe was very withdrawn after we lost Amy. She hardly spoke or related to anyone. Not even me. She's gotten a lot better since we came here. We may not stay forever. But I can see it was the right choice for now."

His expression brightened as he spoke of his daughter's progress. Lauren now understood Jen Bennet's role in their lives, too, though she hoped it wasn't as more than a therapist for Phoebe.

"So you work remotely?" she asked.

"Yes, I started my own firm, McGuire Financial Consulting. I make my own schedule, centered around Phoebe. I advise charities and not-for-profit organizations on how to handle their assets and investments. I decided to use my superpowers for good," he added with a grin. "How about you, Lauren? You stick out like a shotgun in a flyswatter shop at Wagner and Associates. If you don't mind me saying."

Lauren felt a jolt at his blunt analogy, then had to laugh. "I don't mind. Especially after all my nosy questions. I'm just helping out there for a few weeks. Joe's an old friend from high school. I came home for a visit between gigs, you might say."

"I see." He met her gaze, and she knew he could see a lot more than she'd just reported.

"I really live in New York. I mean, I *was* living there and intend to return in January. I guess you could say I had a setback in my career plans," she added. "I worked my tail off at my former law firm but was told at my last review that I was no longer on track to make partner. I had to leave. So that means I have to try somewhere else. Those are the rules of the game."

"Rough rules, tough game," he offered with a note of sympathy. "I will say, if you came up short, I'd hate to meet the attorneys who do make it. I'd be shivering in my boots."

She met his gaze and smiled. "That's a nice compliment, thanks." She sighed. In for a penny, in for a pound. He'd told her all about his life. She decided to tell him the whole story of her New York adventure.

"There was another reason I needed a break. My relationship crashed and burned. I'd been with a guy for almost two years, and we decided it just wasn't, you know . . . right." She paused. This part was harder to talk about. "*He* decided," she added.

"More fool him."

It was nice of Cole to say that. But she had been nursing his daughter's sick piglet all day. He was bound to be nice to her because of that, she reminded herself.

"I didn't see it that way at the time. But maybe it was a lucky escape? My sisters—and my mom—just admitted that they never liked him."

"Really? What did you say?"

"I told them they'd better speak up promptly about the next guy. I'm getting too old to waste any more time."

Cole laughed again. "Lauren, as I said before, you're very refreshing. And you're not old. Not at all."

"Thanks. My mother says to just go with the flow. I mean, what a retro slogan, right? What does that even mean?"

Before he could answer, her phone alarm pinged, and they both looked at Wilbur. "Time for his temperature. Fingers crossed."

He gave her a weary smile and showed her his crossed fingers. It was odd how she felt so in sync with him tonight when just days ago they were sniping at each other, bitter adversaries. She liked this a lot better. And she hoped he did, too.

The hours passed as they tended to Wilbur, giving him medicine and more baths, checking his temperature. They had to call the vet two more times during the night, fearing the worst when his fever kept shooting up. At one point, the poor little thing even shivered uncontrollably. Lauren feared the end was coming and fought back tears.

Cole brought in pillows and quilts, and they took turns watching over him and dozing off on the kitchen floor.

LAUREN FELT A CRAMP IN HER NECK AND OPENED HER EYES SLOWLY. A beam of sunlight squeezing through a gap in the curtains made her squint. She realized she had fallen into a deep sleep. Much deeper than she had intended. She checked her phone and saw she had slept right through the five o'clock alarm.

Cole had missed it, too. He was slumped over the kitchen table, his head resting on his folded arms, lightly snoring.

She turned and quickly checked Wilbur's bed, and her breath caught in her chest. It was empty.

How could that be? Struck with horror, she jumped up, her sock-covered feet slipping on the floor.

"Cole, get up. Wilbur is gone. I don't see him anywhere."

Cole slowly roused; he looked dazed. He squinted at her as she ran around the kitchen, searching for the pig.

She looked under the kitchen chairs and an old-fashioned hutch that had ample space beneath it for a piglet to hide.

She once had a friend with an ailing cat that had crawled off to die when the time came, settling in the back of a closet. Is that what had happened? Dear heaven, she hoped not.

Cole swiftly joined the search. "Are you sure? Maybe he's snuggled in the towels down there?"

He looked alarmed and totally disarming with his bedhead and bearded face. Lauren knew that she must look like the Crypt Keeper but couldn't stop to worry about it.

There had been a baby gate across the kitchen doorway during Wilbur's stay, but when he got sick, no one paid attention to keeping it in place. It hung open, accusing them. The pig could be anywhere in the house by now.

"I'll search the porch," she suggested. "You check the rest of the house. He's got to be somewhere. I mean, the car keys are still here."

A small spot of humor. Very small. *Didn't help either*, she reflected as she ran out to the small screened-in porch near the kitchen, which had many more piglet-sized nooks and crannies. She used the light from her phone to peer into the small, dark spaces.

"Wilbur? Wilbur, honey? Where are you?" Lauren called softly. "Please come out."

After a thorough search of her assigned territory, she had to admit he was nowhere to be seen.

She met Cole in the kitchen. She could see from his expression he had found no sign of the runaway patient either.

"What in heaven's name do we do now?" she wondered.

"I don't know. I suppose he could have gotten outside, though I don't see how."

Outside, in his state? On a frigid night in December? That scenario would likely spell the end for him, Lauren thought sadly.

"I sure hope not," she replied in a quiet voice.

Cole stared at her and took a deep breath.

They heard Phoebe's steps on the stairs. Lauren's heart skipped a beat.

"Phoebe's up," he whispered. "Blast it all. She never gets up this early."

Lauren swallowed hard. "We just have to tell her the truth. I mean, it's your call. Entirely. But she'll see that he's gone right away."

He let out a long, frustrated sigh and ran a hand through his hair. "I know, I know. Let me think a second before you say anything."

Lauren nodded. "Of course."

Phoebe was steps from the kitchen, and they both held their breath, waiting for her.

"Look who I found in my bedroom! He woke me up. He nearly jumped in my bed, Daddy. I think he's hungry."

Phoebe walked in, holding Wilbur in her arms. He was licking her chin and looked as lively and healthy and in "the piggy pink" as Lauren had ever seen him.

Cole practically collapsed with relief and clung to a kitchen chair. Lauren didn't feel much better and leaned heavily on the refrigerator. "For goodness' sake. We were looking all over for him. We didn't know where he'd gone," she admitted.

"He must feel a lot better if he made it all the way up the stairs." Cole walked over to Phoebe and took a closer look. "Hey, Wilbur. Happy Monday."

Wilbur gave a snorty-sounding *oink*, and everyone laughed. "I'll take his temperature in a minute," Lauren said. "But I think the medicine must have finally taken hold. Seems he's on the mend."

"Excellent diagnosis, Dr. Willoughby," Cole teased her with a warm smile.

"Pig Lady, please. That's my official title, and proud of it. Especially after last night."

"You earned it," he said. "Hey, we'll get you a special T-shirt for Christmas."

"And I'll cherish it always." Lauren meant it, too.

Feeling elated over Wilbur's dramatic recovery, they rushed to feed him and keep up with his medication. Lauren reported in to Dr. Ackroyd while Phoebe hurriedly ate a bowl of cereal and got ready for school.

Lauren freshened up in the bathroom, but it wasn't much help. When she emerged, she realized there was no time to stop home and change. She had to go straight to Joe's office.

They left the cottage together. Cole and Phoebe headed to school in his truck and Lauren headed to the village. Phoebe had bid her goodbye with another huge hug and even a kiss on the cheek this time.

Lauren thought she could live off the sweetness for months, like Wilbur's bottles of honey water.

She waved to them as she drove off the property. She liked the feeling of being on good terms with Cole. Better than good terms. Last night she'd felt genuinely close to him. Open and honest. As if something was happening between them. Something important. Or something that could be, given time?

Had he felt that way, too? She didn't dare hope. But, of course, she couldn't help wishing. And calculating how long it might be before she saw Cole McGuire again.

CHAPTER TEN

ORRY I'M LATE, EVERYONE. I HAD AN EMERGENCY." LAU-
ren swept into the meeting wearing the same clothes she'd
had on at church the day before: a thick, cream-colored cowl-neck
sweater, jeans, and her peacoat. She was sure Joe noticed. He stared at
her and cleared his throat. Of course, he wouldn't ask in front of a
client how that had happened. If he had the nerve to ask at all.

Madeleine Belkin offered a calm smile. She didn't seem to think
there was anything unusual about her new attorney's casual appearance, though she herself was dressed in a turtleneck sweater, tweed
skirt, and black blazer, looking polished and professional yet relaxed.
Lauren liked that.

Lauren had already spoken to her once on the phone at length and
had gotten the impression that Madeleine was the type of person who
was focused not on appearances or the trappings of things but on what
was inside. She wrote code for software, so she naturally had a logical,
mathematical mind. Lauren liked that about her, too. But she still
wasn't sure that Madeleine understood what she was taking on—or
the possible consequences.

"We were just discussing the materials we need to gather to back up Madeleine's claim against Dendur, as well as any possible witnesses that might support her assertions about their compensation practices," Joe said.

"Right. I've made a list for discovery." Lauren slipped copies from a folder and gave one to each of them. "But before we go over it, I think we should talk about the big picture, Madeleine."

"And by that you mean—" Joe cut in.

"I want to be sure that Madeleine has a clear idea of what she's getting into."

"All right. And call me Maddie. Please."

Her soft, clear voice threw Lauren off for a moment, but she quickly gathered her thoughts. "Dendur is a big player in your field, Maddie. If they decide not to settle quietly and fight you, this action will get a lot of attention. Not on the evening news, but certainly in your industry. In fact, even if they try to keep a lid on it, people talk. You'll get a reputation as a whistleblower and a troublemaker, or as someone who isn't a team player. However they want to say it. They'll find other ways to impugn your character, too. Even if you're a saint. You'd be surprised how damaging and hurtful mere hearsay or distortions— or straight-up slander—can feel. Other companies may not want to hire you."

Joe had been staring at her, his expression growing darker. "Lauren, do you really have to go there right now? We haven't even gotten started."

"Which is why this is the best time to go there, Joe. Before we've all invested a lot of energy and effort."

He was as annoyed with her as she'd ever seen him. Was it really because of her stern warning to Maddie Belkin, which might scare her off as a client? Or because he knew where she went yesterday afternoon after she broke their date? And here she was, Monday morning, in the same outfit.

Lauren brushed the questions aside. She sincerely wanted this principled, well-intentioned woman to understand there was a rough road ahead and there would be unforeseen consequences of following through on this complaint. She wanted her to understand that a sense of justice and fairness was admirable, but it wouldn't protect her like a magic shield. Instead, it would make her a more visible target.

Joe turned to Maddie and offered a conciliatory smile. "We don't mean to confuse you. But we took on your case quickly and haven't had time to get our ducks in a row. You're brave to bring this inequity to light. All Lauren is trying to say is that she hopes you've considered the possible downside. Not everyone will look on your action favorably—even though they should."

That wasn't what she had wanted to say. It was a watered-down version. But it was Joe's firm, and he had the right. Or at least he definitely thought he did.

"I understand," Maddie assured them. "I really do."

"I'm sure you think you do," Lauren pressed on. "But since you've never gone through this, you may be unpleasantly surprised. Pursuing this claim will probably upend your life. It's not too late to think about it more before you go forward."

Joe shot her another quelling look. Obviously, her blunt, straightforward manner did not seem that attractive to him this morning.

"But we'll be with you every step of the way," he said. "We're the front line, fighting that dragon. You're very brave to take this on, for yourself and the other women in your field. You should be proud. And you really don't need to worry," he added, undercutting Lauren's advice.

She suddenly noticed how he was gazing at Maddie, waiting for her answer with a soft expression she'd only seen when . . . when he looked at her?

Did Joe have a crush on their new client? She was very attractive; Lauren had already noticed that. And she was clearly intelligent, with degrees from prestigious universities, and surprisingly well-spoken for a math person. During a routine gathering of background information, she had told them she wasn't married and had no steady relationship.

Even though Lauren doubted that she wanted to be with Joe— especially this morning—she felt stung to realize he could fall for someone else. She could see all the signs.

She had to laugh at herself. *It's not enough that the poor man grovels at your feet and you don't want to date him. You don't want him dating anyone else either.*

Of course, if Maddie became their client, Joe wouldn't date her until the case was concluded. Doing so would be really bad form, if not a violation of some ethical rule. It was possible he didn't even realize his own feelings yet.

"I have given the question serious thought," Maddie finally replied. "And while I haven't gone through this situation personally, I can see from the news, and even experiences of women I know, that it's not going to be easy. I'm prepared for that. Luckily, I just landed a new job at a start-up in cybersecurity. I was totally open with them about what I think of Dendur and what I plan to do about it. They're fine with it."

Joe replied with his trademark mile-wide smile. "Just what we want to hear, Maddie."

He cast Lauren a smug look. "Lauren, do you want to move forward with your list now?"

Lauren kept a straight face, though she wanted to smack him.

"Absolutely. Seems like we're all on the same page. That's all I wanted to know."

The meeting went longer than she expected but was productive. Maddie was a huge help in the fact-finding phase and even supplied names and contact information for other women who had left Dendur because of similar treatment.

If they could show a pattern, the company wouldn't be able to talk its way out of Maddie's accusations so easily. Lauren's attention was captured by the case more than she'd expected, and she was enjoying it more than any case in a long time.

Joe strolled into her office in the late afternoon. He had an extra coffee drink in hand and set the cup on her desk. "Cappuccino. With cinnamon on top, as you like it, ma'am."

She smiled and flipped the lid. "Thanks, I can use this."

He sat in the armchair across from her desk. "Sorry if I snapped at you this morning. I just thought you came on a little strong. I didn't want you to dissuade her from going forward."

She looked up at him. "I was trying to. Well, not entirely. I did want to test her resolve. We'll be with her 'every step of the way,'" she said, purposely echoing his promise, "in a deposition room or a courtroom. But Dendur's attorneys will go at her hammer and tongs, and she's the only one who can answer. And she's the only one who will have to deal with whatever gossip and bad-mouthing Dendur spreads about her professional skills and even her personal life. You know how these things go, Joe."

He didn't look happy with her answer. "Of course I do. But I think she's tough. In a quiet, self-reliant way. I think she'll make an excellent witness, if it comes to that."

Whoa, now she knew he was smitten, though Lauren doubted he realized it.

"She convinced me, too. I just wanted to make sure she knew the downside going in. It's only fair. I'm representing her, right? I mean, you asked me to do this? If you want to take the case, it's fine. I'm happy to play second fiddle and just back you up."

He laughed, back to his usual good humor. "When were you ever happy to play second *anything*, Lauren?"

"I'm serious, Joe." She was, too. "I can see that you've taken a special interest. Which is great. But I can't do my best work with someone watching over my shoulder."

He looked taken aback by her words. But he didn't rush to reply. "I understand. I won't hover. But I hope there will be a . . . synergy? You told me yourself this isn't your usual territory. I think we need to strategize. Two heads are better than one."

She couldn't argue with that. "Of course I'll be happy to have your advice and input. No question."

He smiled, looking pleased that the situation was resolved. "So, how did your emergency turn out? The little pig isn't heading for the sausage factory, I hope?"

She knew he meant no harm by the joke. But she thought of Wilbur as more than a pig, and the gallows humor appalled her.

"It was touch-and-go for a while, but he miraculously survived. We stayed up all night checking his temperature and giving him medicine. Phoebe lost her mother about two years ago," she added. "It would have been very hard for her to lose the piglet."

"Wow, that's too bad. Poor kid," Joe said with sincere sympathy. "You did a good deed, then. Good for you."

"Thanks. It was exhausting but worth it."

She didn't owe Joe an explanation about her relationship with Cole McGuire, but she wanted him to know that it had been a totally innocent evening.

"You must be beat. Why don't you leave? It's almost five."

She sighed. "It does feel like an unusually long day. I think I will."

Joe said good night and left her office. Lauren saved her work and snapped her laptop shut, then checked her phone for the umpteenth time.

Still no message from Cole. She wondered if she should send one, asking how Wilbur was doing. But she decided she didn't want to be pushy. For once.

Had she just imagined they'd grown closer? Maybe that feeling was all on her side. Then again, the day hadn't even passed. She would give him time to get in touch. It wouldn't help to seem too eager. Men were like timid woodland creatures. They did get startled easily.

Truth was, she felt a bit blindsided by her sudden change of heart. Had these feelings been simmering under the surface all the while—like a tsunami forming in the depths of the ocean? Maybe Cole felt the same way and was trying to process it. Lauren knew that she was an "adult portion" and not to everyone's taste. Then again, he had told her that she was "refreshing." Twice. That had to count for something good, right?

LAUREN WAS WORKING AT HER DESK ON WEDNESDAY AFTERNOON when her phone lit up with an incoming call. The screen said *Cole McGuire*, and she nearly jumped in her chair.

She took a deep breath and let it ring a few times. She couldn't sound nervous or even annoyed that he hadn't called before now. It had only been three days, she reminded herself. *It's your problem if you obsessed about hearing from him every second.*

Finally, she decided to grab it before he gave up. "Hey, Cole. What's up?" she said, trying to strike a cool, friendly tone.

"Lauren? It's Aunt Jess. I'm at Cole's house and my phone went dead. But I thought you'd like to know that Wilbur is doing absolutely great. He's making a super recovery. Dr. Ackroyd was here and she's amazed."

Lauren could hear Cole and Phoebe talking in the background. She pictured them in their cozy kitchen and wished she were there, too.

"Wow. That's great. I was wondering. I meant to call," she added, purposely vague about whether she meant to call her aunt or Cole.

"I can't thank you enough, honey. Wait, hold on, someone wants to speak to you."

Lauren sat back, her heart pounding. She prepared her cool, friendly voice for Cole but wasn't sure she could pull it off.

"Hi, Pig Lady. It's Phoebe."

Phoebe's sweet greeting almost made up for her crashing disappointment. "Hi, honey. Good to hear your voice. I hear Wilbur is back to his old tricks."

"He doesn't really have any old tricks, but I'm trying to teach him some. He's very frisky. You'd never guess he was so sick."

"That's great news. I'm so happy to hear it."

"When can you come and see us? We can still draw the pictures. Dad said Wilbur doesn't need a get-well card anymore, but it can say 'Congratulations!'"

Lauren had almost forgotten about Wilbur's cards. "That's a great idea. I'd like to come see him very soon." *But your father needs to invite me* was the unspoken truth of the matter. "We'll figure it out," she promised, knowing she sounded like her own mother now.

Phoebe simply answered, "Okay," though she did sound a bit disappointed. "Goodbye."

"Bye, Phoebe," Lauren replied, feeling her hurt melt a little.

She waited, wondering if Phoebe was going to end the call. Then she heard the phone switching hands again. Was it Cole now? Please?

"I just wanted to say goodbye, honey," her aunt said. "Thanks again."

"No problem, Aunt Jess. Nursing Wilbur was a truly memorable experience." She offered the line in a joking way, though she meant so much more.

Her aunt laughed and ended the call. Lauren put the phone aside, and a wave of disappointment swept over her.

Cole was there. She had heard his voice. So near, yet so far. Maybe he'd been embarrassed to ask for the phone in front of her aunt?

You wish. Don't make excuses for him. Face it. You felt something and he didn't. He's just not that into you, as they say. Though it sure felt like he was getting there.

She didn't know what to think. Had she just imagined the attraction and intimacy sparking between them? Maybe he had felt a connection but she'd made too much of it in her mind.

Either way, the pretext she might use to call him—checking up on Wilbur—was off the table now. He'd had a chance to talk to her, but he hadn't taken it. There didn't seem to be any moves left for her on the board. Game over, she realized.

TWO WEEKS UNTIL CHRISTMAS, TO THE DAY. LUCY WAS USUALLY done with her shopping by now, but not this year. Her friends, Fran especially, swore by shopping online and the overnight delivery. But Lucy liked to see and touch the gifts she chose. She didn't like the mall much either, though for some gifts it was a necessary evil. She tried to give the shops in the village and in Newburyport her business when she could, though the prices could be a little higher. It was convenient and even pleasant to walk down Main Street with her list, going from shop to shop. All the store windows looked so pretty this time of year, and they made her feel more Christmassy. Even if the stores might be a little more crowded with the movie fans around and because it was Friday, she had to take advantage of a small window of free time today. She had agreed to cover a few shifts at the hospital next week and was juggling those hours with the appointments for her private patients. She had high hopes of getting most of her list checked off today.

But the carefully planned excursion did not go well from the start. The movie crew was filming at the harbor—how in the world had she missed news of that? She found Main Street blocked to traffic, with signs rerouting drivers. She followed a trail of cars that moved at a snail's pace through the side roads, all the while wondering if she should just turn around and go home.

Almost half an hour later, she found a parking space several blocks from the village. She grabbed her purse and headed for the shops. *My step tracker will look good tonight*, she told herself. She had planned to visit Grace Hegman's antique store first, but she found she was emerging at Bayview, which ran along the shore and intersected Main Street at the harbor and green.

She walked at a fast pace, right past Willoughby's Bakery & Café, which still had a line of customers waiting. The closer she got to Main Street and the harbor, the thicker the crowd. She could see the movie equipment set up near a dock. There was yellow tape keeping the onlookers back at a safe distance.

Tucker stood by with other uniformed officers, making sure no one snuck over the barrier. She heard someone call her name, and Fran ran toward her from across the street.

"Lucy, did you come to see them filming? They picked some extras for this scene. You won't believe it. Digger and Reverend Ben. And Sophie Potter." Fran stood before her, practically breathless. "They're in full costume and makeup. It's a riot."

Lucy could only imagine. The film was a historical one, set in the 1800s. A family story, she'd heard, though she had purposely avoided learning anything more.

"Did you try out? Tell the truth." Lucy was just joking, but Fran was so starstruck, she may have.

"I did," she admitted. "They didn't want me. I don't have the historical look, I guess." She shrugged. "Maybe that's a compliment at our age?"

Lucy laughed. "I think it is. Definitely."

"Well, enjoy. I have to get to work," Fran said.

"Really? What's the occasion?" Fran's movie fan needs seemed to be her priority lately. Luckily, she'd been at Bowman Realty for ages and more or less made her own hours.

"Very funny. I'm running an open house today." Fran checked the time and tossed her phone back in her big purse. "But you should watch the filming for a minute or two. You don't want to miss this. I guarantee it."

"Maybe I will. See you later. And good luck with the open house. I hope you reel in a big fish."

"Me, too." They hugged, and Fran ran up the street and disappeared around the corner, headed for Bowman Realty. Lucy continued toward the harbor and the crowd. Though the wind off the water was cold and sharp, the onlookers, bundled in parkas and scarves, did not seem discouraged by the weather.

Lucy wouldn't wait in the cold to watch, but since she was walking past anyway, she would stop for a little while. She did want to see her friends and neighbors transformed for the film. There would be little to no chance of running into Craig, she decided. He might not even be there. Even she knew that not all the actors were needed for every scene of a movie. It looked as if the celebrities were being kept at a safe distance from the "little people."

But as she walked up to the gathering, she heard a woman say, "Look, it's Craig Hamilton. He's coming out of his trailer!"

Lucy turned and saw him walk down the narrow steps of a long luxury trailer—not your ordinary RV. It was parked in the lot next to the harbor, alongside three others. People around her clapped and called out. Just before he turned to them, she ducked behind a tall older man, though there was little chance he'd notice her at this distance, and in such a crowd.

Craig Hamilton answered his fans with a wave and a smile. Dressed in his costume, with hair and makeup done, he looked dashing, as if he'd stepped out of the pages of a romantic novel. The elegant attire for a gentleman of that day suited him—a black morning coat with tails and a high collar, a burgundy vest, and a white jabot tie. Tan trousers were tucked into high black boots, and a black silk top hat was the crowning touch.

Lucy loved the clothes of that era, for both men and women, though she imagined it was a tyranny to wear such a complicated outfit, and uncomfortable, too. The women's dresses had stays and impossible undergarments. Thank goodness clothes were much simpler now.

Craig was guided to the dock by a very frazzled-looking little man with a clipboard and headset. The whole crew was running around adjusting lights and other equipment. There were squares of reflective material set up all around, too, and wires and cables everywhere. It was amazing how much was out of sight when you saw a movie. Lucy wasn't sure she would ever look at a film the same way again.

She saw a camera that was so huge a man was riding on it. It seemed to move on motorized wheels. There was a woman sitting in a tall chair in the back with a large video monitor in front of it. She was having a very serious-looking conversation with a young man who wore his long hair in braids and was paying close attention as the woman spoke. Lucy got the feeling she was the director.

The village residents were in costume now, too. The man with the clipboard gathered them around and gave them instructions. They listened and nodded, but even at a distance, they looked a little nervous, Lucy thought. Sophie wore a bonnet tied with a wide ribbon under her chin and carried a basket over one arm. Digger's appearance was not changed much at all, except for a long canvas coat and knee-high boots. He seemed to be in charge of a pushcart loaded with fish. *Real fish?* she wondered. Looked like it.

Reverend Ben wore a long black cassock and the wide-brimmed clergyman's hat of the era. He had a Bible tucked under his arm and looked the most calm and comfortable.

They were each led to a different spot on the dock, like pieces on a chessboard. A very, very detailed chessboard, Lucy thought. Craig Hamilton and another actor stood on the dock while a woman busily powdered their noses, then looked them over carefully. Another actor was in a small boat.

The man talking to the director shouted, "Quiet on the set!" in a loud, booming voice. And it was suddenly very quiet and still. Even in the milling crowd, everyone seemed to hush and hold their breath. A seagull swooped right over the set and let out a loud caw, and Lucy heard a snicker behind her.

The man shouted again, "Roll sound!"

"Sound is speeding!" called a voice from the right.

"Camera?" the man said.

"Camera rolling!"

Lucy didn't want to be fascinated, but she was. There was something thrilling about watching a movie being made. She could see now why Fran had morphed into a total fan.

A girl holding a clapboard ran up in front of the camera aimed at Craig. "Scene 21A, Take One. Marker." *SLAP*—she clacked down on the board and quickly moved off the set.

"Action!" the director shouted.

The actor in the boat called to Craig and tossed the boat line to the dock. Craig grabbed it and tied it up. Lucy heard his voice as he recited his dialogue—until the words were lost in a sudden spasm of coughing.

"Hold for sound!" the woman holding the boom pole called, but the coughing continued.

"Cut. Cut!" the director shouted. Two assistants ran up to Craig and stood by. The coughing had stopped, but his eyes bugged out and he grabbed at his throat, clawing at the elaborately knotted tie. Even from a distance his panicked, shocked expression was clear.

The director jumped down from her chair, shouting, "Call an ambulance!" Then the entire crew rushed to help.

Craig stumbled forward, and someone grabbed his arm just in time to save him from falling into the water. He dropped to his knees, a soft landing, as he crumpled on the dock and was suddenly out of sight.

The onlookers reacted with gasps. "Did you see that?"

"What happened to him?"

"Is he sick?"

"Looks like a heart attack or something."

Lucy pushed forward as far as she could go, straining to see what was going on. With a shaky hand, she pulled out her phone and dialed 911.

A few police officers had run up to the set, and others stayed to keep the onlookers back. But most people had the good sense to stay out of the way.

The operator came on, and Lucy gave her name and location. "A man on the dock just collapsed. Send an ambulance immediately."

The operator asked her to hold, then told her a call was already in and help was on the way.

Lucy felt relieved. The fire station was just down Main Street, and she'd barely ended the call before she heard a siren roaring their way.

She craned her neck to see what was going on. Craig was stretched out on the dock, and it appeared that one of the members of the movie crew was giving him mouth-to-mouth resuscitation. She had heard that movie crews always had medical professionals on-site and felt encouraged by the immediate attention. It could make a world of difference, depending on what had happened to him.

The ambulance roared up, and everyone made way for it to pass. She watched as Craig was lifted onto a gurney, his face covered with an oxygen mask, then loaded into the vehicle.

"Geez, looks bad," someone said. "What do you think happened to him?"

Lucy wished she knew. It appeared that he was conscious. She had to count that on the plus side, though she still felt stunned as the ambulance sped past them again and disappeared down Bayview Street, headed for the highway.

The crowd quickly dispersed. Lucy felt oddly disoriented. What had just happened? Was he going to survive?

She drifted across the street and stared out at the choppy blue waves in the harbor. She suddenly felt as if she might cry.

That's just plain silly, Lucy. Get a grip. It could have been . . . a peanut allergy, for all you know. Though even that situation was life-threatening if not addressed promptly and properly. But Lucy had been trained not to overreact. A minor, easily treatable problem could often present as a health crisis.

Still, she didn't know what to do. What to feel. She'd willed herself to shut down so totally to Craig Hamilton, even after his plea for sympathy Sunday. But she had to admit the sight of him being lifted into the ambulance really got to her.

Maybe he had some ongoing medical condition. That might explain his reflection on the past, and his regrets. *Everyone our age starts to feel that way a bit. We become aware of the big picture, and our mortality.* She certainly felt aware of his right now.

If she'd known this was going to happen, would she have been kinder to him? Would she have shown him at least a hint of compassion? *Without a doubt,* she answered honestly.

She had already been feeling guilty for the way she'd spoken to him, even before this emergency. Not for what she'd said—she'd been honest and had no regrets about that—but for the way she had said it. She could have been kinder.

She'd had time to think since Sunday and had to give him credit for approaching her. It couldn't have been easy after all these years. She still didn't want to dig around in all that ancient muck. She couldn't see any point to it.

She tucked her bag under her arm and headed back to her car. She was in no mood for Christmas shopping now. That was the last thing she wanted to do. She wished she knew what had happened to him. But no one did. Not yet.

Tucker would have some sense of it, having been front and center on the scene. He would tell Fran, or even Charlie. She'd hear some news that way, probably by the end of the day.

There would be an item in the newspaper about it tomorrow, too, though she doubted medical details would be disclosed. But she had a shift coming up at the hospital soon. That was probably the best route to real information.

Southport Hospital rarely admitted celebrities of Craig's caliber, which meant that despite patient privacy laws, the staff would be buzzing about his situation. She would hear the entire chart, top to bottom. She felt a bit better knowing that and thought she might even call a friend she knew was working at the hospital today. She still had no intention of getting in touch with Craig to "talk things out," but she did want to know what had sent him to the hospital and what medical issues he was dealing with. From a safe distance.

"Is the dog at your house? Have you seen him around the neighborhood?" Jessica sounded panicked, which was not her style at all.

Lillian felt annoyed. "Have they really lost track of that silly animal again? I thought you said that you found responsible owners. They appear to be the very opposite."

She had returned the irritating creature on Saturday afternoon, and it was only Friday. Couldn't those people keep track of their dog for an entire week? The feckless owners had come around, all smiles and apologies, and had almost seemed to find it amusing that their new pet had run off.

"They're doing their best, Mother. The property is completely fenced. But he seems to have dug a hole when they weren't looking."

Resourceful little creature, she'd give him that. Still, she was losing her patience with this comedy of errors. And she was starting to feel warm in her coat and hat, with her purse strap over her shoulder and her gloves in hand.

"We haven't seen him. And we're on our way out to do some

Christmas shopping. We should be gone all day." *No help forthcoming from this quarter* is what she hoped to convey.

"All right. Then I guess I'll miss seeing you today. I'm going to come by and look around your neighborhood. It seems to be Teddy's favorite destination."

"What can I say? He prefers the better neighborhoods. To his credit."

Providence Street was among the best, if not the very best address in the village. The classic and beautifully maintained grand old houses that lined the street, Lillian's mansard-roofed Victorian among them, were the jewels in the crown of Cape Light. Lillian had always thought so.

Though her family had had to leave Lilac Hall, at least she'd managed to land them here; it was some small recompense. Of course the dog liked this part of town better than out on the Beach Road—the armpit of nowhere, if you asked her. But she didn't tell Jessica that. Her daughter thought that wild territory was paradise on Earth. And after the way she'd been raised. It was that husband of hers. He'd brainwashed her, clearly. It was like shouting down a well, trying to advise those two. Better to save her breath.

"Is that all?" she asked Jessica.

"Yes. That's it. Keep a lookout, will you, please?"

"Indeed I will. I'll chase him away with a broom if I see him."

"Tell Ezra. He'll help me."

"Goodbye, Jessica. Good luck with your . . . task." Lillian ended the call and suddenly realized that if she played her cards right, Ezra would be none the wiser.

Unfortunately, he'd been standing near enough to hear the conversation as he searched around for the reusable tote bags he insisted on using when they went to the stores these days. She knew that he'd heard more than enough by the look on his face. "Was that Jessica about Teddy? Has he run away again?"

Lillian was about to reply, but the look on her husband's face gave her pause. It was as if some inner light that had been switched off since Saturday was suddenly turned on. Glowing brilliantly, too.

The real Ezra had returned, which was a great relief to her—though the reason was impossibly annoying.

"Yes, the dog is lost. Again. His owners are totally irresponsible. Jessica says she's going to find new ones. Someplace distant, this time."

Ezra set the pile of neatly folded bags on the table. "That's not what she said. I heard her. Or at least enough of the conversation to know that part isn't so."

He walked into the mudroom, sat on the bench, and began to exchange his good shoes for heavy walkers.

"What are you doing? You don't need to wear those ghastly shoes to the shops. They're full of mud."

"They'll have more on them by the time I'm through. I'm not going to the shops. Change of plans, dear."

"You're not going out to look for that dog. Are you?"

"That's exactly what I'm doing." He glanced up at her briefly, then chose a heavier muffler for his neck and that awful plaid hat with the earflaps. He looked like a cross between Sherlock Holmes and Mr. Magoo. She wouldn't be seen with him in that thing.

"You'll never find him. He could be anywhere. All you'll do is tramp around in the cold and catch a chill. They say it's going to snow."

"Not until tonight. All the more reason to get him inside as soon as I can."

"And what about you? Anything could happen to you out there. It's not worth the risk. All for a silly dog."

He ignored her and walked back into the kitchen. Was she making any headway at all?

He opened the refrigerator, found a dish of leftovers, and filled a sandwich bag with meat scraps. He stuck that in his pocket, along with a few dog biscuits from the cupboard.

He already had a dog leash—the one he'd bought during the few days the dog had been stranded with them—slung around his neck.

"Of course he keeps coming back here. You spoil him. I bet his real owners don't stuff him with table scraps."

"It's not the treats, Lillian. Face it, he likes us. He belongs here. He likes you most of all."

Lillian jumped back and stuck out her chin. "Don't insult me with such foolishness. He doesn't belong here. We've been all through that."

"He does. You'll see." He filled another pocket with tissues and took a pill with a sip of water.

She decided to try another tack. "So you're leaving me flat. Is that it? When will we do our Christmas shopping?"

"Plenty of time for that. This is an emergency. I'll be in touch," he promised. "Maybe Emily will take you out. Why don't you call her?"

"Sure. And maybe I'll saunter down Main Street with a rose between my teeth," she answered tartly.

Her older daughter, Emily, had to be the busiest person in the universe, even though she was no longer mayor. Busier than God, Lillian sometimes said.

"See you later, dear," Ezra said cheerfully.

"I hope so. And in one piece. And without that dog," she called after him. "Don't bring him back here. Call Jessica to meet you and take him back."

Ezra did not answer. The side door closed, and the house was very quiet and still. *Too quiet*, she thought as she ambled toward the living room. She pressed a few buttons on their music thing, and the loud, full notes of an opera filled the silence.

What had she found? She wasn't even sure, though she used to be able to identify every aria after only a note or two. What did it matter? It was always about love—love or death. Or both. This one was about the former. A love that made you lose your senses and drove you to mad, absurd, and desperate acts.

Ezra was in love. That was it. She'd hit it on the head. She felt like calling someone to share the insight, but no one would understand. She'd sound like a raving old bat. Now that she saw it clearly, it explained everything.

Ezra had fallen in love with that ridiculous Teddy—her flop-eared rival—and had lost his judgment completely. In the opera, these affairs of the heart never ended well. Lillian knew this one wouldn't either.

CHAPTER ELEVEN

⌒✕

*L*AUREN WASN'T SURE IF SHE'D AGREED TO HELP HER AUNT with the rescue animals again out of boredom or from a need for some strenuous exercise in the fresh air. Or was it because the day and night spent caring for Wilbur had hooked her, and now she had to live up to her title as the Pig Lady?

I'm worried about you. Honestly, she told herself as she headed for the old barn on the spacious property that Sam and Jessica owned.

Sam had bought the house and lot on the outskirts of the village long before he and Jessica had even begun dating. The house had been deserted, a boarded-up, decrepit Queen Anne that most new owners would have knocked down in a heartbeat. It took a rare and imaginative soul like her uncle to see the beauty hidden under a moldy roof, peeling paint, rotten shingles, and all the rest. It had taken a skilled craftsman, which he was as well, to restore the house to its full glory. Which he'd done, practically all on his own.

Sam and Jess had lived there happily for years, raising a growing family. But when a fire ravaged the home and consumed almost everything the family owned, they had somehow managed to rebuild an exact replica. "With better wiring and plumbing," her uncle always added. The insurance policy had failed to supply the means for the project, but to everyone's surprise, a generous gift from Jessica's mother, Lillian, had answered their prayers.

Lillian was a complicated woman. Just when you thought you had her all figured out, she'd make some grand gesture and confuse everyone. She still made it no secret that she didn't like the house, in its past or present version, or the woodsy setting.

Lauren thought it was lovely—if a person wanted to live around here. There was even a pond on the edge of the property, its shoreline shared by a few neighbors. She had happy memories of swimming and boating there in the summer and ice-skating in the winter with her sisters and cousins. Jessica's youngest, Lily, who was close to her little sister Betty in age, still had skating and swimming parties with Betty and their friends.

Lauren found her aunt in one of the horse stalls, brushing down the sleek coat of a chestnut mare with one hand and talking on the phone with the other.

"I'm sorry, Mother. If Ezra wants to search for the dog, I can't stop him . . . I do know how cold it is. I'm outside right now." She paused. Lauren could hear Lillian voicing a reply, even though the phone wasn't on speaker.

"All right, I'll call him, if you really want me to. I doubt it will do any good," Jessica said. "I'll let you know."

She ended the call and greeted Lauren with a frustrated expression. "My mother is in a tizzy. That little dog Ezra found was placed in a new home, but he keeps running away. Straight to Providence Street the first time. He's taken off again but hasn't shown up there. Ezra was out looking all day yesterday, and into the night. He went out early again today. My mother's beside herself."

"It is very cold for an old person to be outside all day," Lauren conceded. "He made flyers. I saw one this morning when I stopped in my mom's bakery. I guess he's posting them all over."

"Bless that man. I meant to do that but never got around to it." Her aunt had finished with the horse. She cleaned out the brush and stepped out of the stall. "I wish I could drive around to look," Jessica said, "but there's so much to do here. We just got a huge donation of hay and feed. I have to deliver it to the people who are holding animals for us." *Like Cole McGuire*, Lauren thought. "And we need to muck out these stalls and lay down fresh straw."

"That's why I'm here?" Lauren asked with a grin.

"If you're up for it. There are easier tasks."

Less distasteful, she really meant. Lauren was tempted to volunteer for the deliveries but decided that move would be too obvious. To both Cole and her aunt.

Never one to back down from a challenge, Lauren pulled out a pair of leather work gloves she'd swiped from her father's workbench. "You forget, digging through manure is a big part of my job, Aunt Jess. I'm no stranger to the stuff."

Her aunt laughed and rested a hand on her shoulder. "Lauren, you're one of a kind. Scratch that, you're actually just like your mother, but she's definitely a unicorn."

"So that makes me a unicorn two-point-oh?"

"At least two-point-oh." Her aunt found her a pitchfork and shovel and showed her where to leave the dirty straw.

Lauren slipped off her jacket. The barn was heated a bit for the animals, but fresh air flowed through the open doors, and her aunt had opened the shuttered windows, too. She liked working in the cool air; even the tangy barn smell had an earthy honesty about it. She'd been through a hectic, demanding workweek. Immersing herself in a purely physical and mindless activity was the perfect antidote. If she still lived in the city, she would be hitting the gym right now for a long, challenging workout—an intense spin class, followed by sprints on the treadmill and lifting some free weights. Mucking out barn stalls was somewhat equivalent, if you put your back into it, she decided.

She'd finished with the first stall and had just started on the second when a red pickup truck pulled up and parked between the house and barn.

Lauren's stomach turned in a knot. She knew who drove that truck. He quickly hopped out of the driver's side and went around to help Phoebe out of her car seat.

Jessica was outside the barn, and they talked for a moment. Lauren felt as if she were hiding—cowering, actually—in the shadowy barn. Then she rallied. *Why are you hiding? You have nothing to be ashamed of. He's the one who should have gotten in touch. Even if only to thank you again for helping Wilbur.*

And you look like a farmhand and smell like one, too, she added in a silent singsong voice as she tried to straighten herself up a bit.

No hope for that. She pulled on her jacket and stepped outside. Cole was already walking toward the barn. To seek her out, or to load his pickup with his share of the donations? She wasn't sure. His serious expression wasn't giving much away.

But someone was thrilled to see her.

"Lauren—it's me. Phoebe. Remember?"

Coming from an adult, the question would have been sarcastic, but Lauren knew the little girl meant it sincerely. She crouched down and opened her arms for a hug. "What a question! How could I ever forget you, you silly thing?"

Phoebe hugged her tight, which was a very sweet feeling, then stepped back. "Why didn't you come back? You said you would."

Lauren felt sorry for disappointing her. She shouldn't have done that, no matter what had—or had not—gone on with Cole.

"I'm sorry, honey. I meant to. But I had a lot of work this week. My aunt Jess kept me up with Wilbur's progress, though. Sounds like he's totally well again."

"He got bigger, too. Daddy said he might have to live in the barn soon." She seemed sad about that. "But not right away. He misses you."

Bigger in a week? It was possible for a piglet, she supposed. She was touched to hear Wilbur missed her. At least two members of that household did. It was probably too much to ask that she'd won over three out of three.

"I have to visit him. Before he forgets all about *me*." She stood up but held Phoebe's hand. "I'll come by in a few days. I promise."

As she came to her feet, her youngest cousin, Lily, ran to greet Phoebe. "Want to help me feed the rabbits? My mom said we can let them hop around the barnyard a little."

Phoebe's face lit up at the invitation from the older girl. But she glanced back at Lauren, looking torn.

Lauren smiled and touched her shoulder. "Go ahead. Those bunnies are hungry. I'll be here."

As Phoebe ran off, she noticed Cole standing near, his hands in the pockets of his barn coat. "Guess Phoebe gave you the update on Wilbur?"

"She did. My aunt kept me up on the patient's news this week, too. Sorry I didn't touch base. I was so busy at work. Great to hear the little guy pulled through."

"With bacon flying, you might say." His reply made her smile despite herself. "We just swung by to pick up some hay. Your aunt got a big donation this morning."

"Yup, heard about that, too." She didn't mean to sound sarcastic, but she was standing practically hip deep in it.

"Hey, let me help. I can muck out with you. Looks like Phoebe wants to stay awhile." He turned, looking for another pitchfork, and found one hanging on the barn wall.

"I'm fine. Really."

He ignored her, his guilt about not calling her prodding him, she suspected. He found a pair of gloves and began to work beside her in the same stall, which suddenly felt very small.

After a few minutes, he paused, slipped off his barn coat, and hung it on a hook. "Lauren?"

She stopped working and turned to him. "Yes?" Had he remembered some appointment he needed to keep or errand he needed to run?

"I want to apologize. For not getting in touch this week, I mean. I was swamped with that Auckland project, working all sorts of crazy hours—"

She raised her hand. "No worries. I get it." She paused and glanced down at the pile of manure that had amassed between them. "I've been shoveling this stuff all morning. You don't need to add to it, Cole."

He had the grace to blush, then laughed. "You called me on that one."

"You don't owe me an explanation." She shrugged. "We're both grown-ups."

"One of us is." He stared at her and sighed. "You scare me. To be totally honest. But I've decided that's okay. I might even like it."

His words surprised her, right to her toes. "I do? I mean, you do?" She paused. "I don't understand. What are you trying to say?"

"I didn't call because I rarely confide that much about myself to anyone. Especially a woman I've just met. Now you know all about me, and I'm not sure I like that. But I like you," he added quickly. "I wanted you to know all that stuff about me. But it felt strange after. I didn't like that part. But I've been thinking about you. A lot."

She liked hearing him say that. A lot. It made up for everything. "I understand. I really do," she assured him. "I usually don't download my life history either." Especially about her spectacular failures in work and relationships. *And on a first date*, she nearly added, though she caught herself in time. Their time together watching over Wilbur had hardly been that. "It felt jarring afterward to me, too. I mean, we barely know each other."

His shoulders relaxed and his expression softened. "I wouldn't say that. We met almost a month ago."

"Has it been that long?" Lauren acted like she hadn't been aware, though she had, in fact, counted the days.

Cole met her gaze and held it, his expression warm. Lauren felt better about everything. The pungent scent in the horse stall seemed like a garden breeze on a spring day.

The sound of gravel crunching in the driveway broke the spell, and she dropped straight down to earth when she recognized her mother's huge white SUV pulling up and parking right behind Cole's truck.

What was her mom doing here today? Why wasn't she overworking herself at the bakery, as usual?

The passenger-side doors flew open and Lauren's little sister Betty jumped out, along with two of her friends. They ran to meet up with Lily and Phoebe, who were in the front of the barn wrangling huge lop-eared rabbits under Jessica's watchful eye.

Her mother climbed out, waved to her sister-in-law, then headed straight to Lauren.

"Hey, honey. I wondered where you disappeared to this morning." She paused, fanned her hand near her nose, and took in Lauren, mucking out the stalls. "I know you want to make a career move, sweetie, but don't you think this is a little . . . drastic?"

Lauren hated herself for her adolescent eye roll but couldn't control it. "Funny, Mom. Who let you out of the bakery?"

"Just dropping off your sister and her friends, since you weren't available. They're going ice-skating with Lily."

Before Lauren could stop her, her mom turned to Cole. "Hi, I'm Lauren's mom, Molly Harding." She held out her hand and Cole shook it. He seemed amused by her mother already. *A good sign*, Lauren thought. Guys who met her mom were either charmed or terrified.

"Cole McGuire. Good to meet you."

"McGuire . . . the Pig Guy? I've heard a lot about you."

"About Wilbur, she means," Lauren quickly interjected. She gave her mom a look, but her mother ignored her. She hadn't confided anything about Cole to her mother, except to explain why she wasn't coming home Sunday night. But it never took Molly long to connect the dots. Lauren knew she couldn't get around that.

"Yes, about the little pig. He sounds so cute," her mother said in an overly sweet tone. "And about your little girl, too. She sounds adorable."

Cole smiled. "She is."

"I'd love to meet her sometime." Her mother looked at Lauren. Lauren stared back, hoping to convey the message that if her mother *dared* to invite them to dinner without her approval, she would never, *ever* forgive her.

"Phoebe is playing with Lily and the girls. Feeding the rabbits," Lauren cut in.

Her mother paused. She seemed to understand the look, but

would she charge ahead anyway? "That's all right. Don't disturb them. I have to run. Some other time," she said decisively. She smiled at Cole. "Nice to meet you, Cole."

"Good to meet you, too, Mrs. Harding."

Her mother glowed with her triumph. "Call me Molly. Everyone does." She looked back at Lauren. "I don't know when I'll be home; I hope you can start dinner. And leave those boots outside the door before you go inside, please."

With a little wave, Molly trotted out of the barn and headed toward Jessica.

Lauren stood simmering and speechless. She turned to Cole. "That was my mom. In all her glory." Almost all her glory, Lauren silently amended. All in all, she felt relieved that her mother had not been quite as nosy and embarrassing as she could have been, meeting Cole for the first time. She was sure that her mother sensed Lauren's attraction to him in her uncanny, intuitive Mom way.

"I've heard a lot about her. It was nice to finally meet her."

"She has a reputation, that's for sure. I love her to pieces, but she can get out of control."

"You seem to keep her in hand."

"Barely." She sighed and picked up her pitchfork. "My family is crazy."

"I'm getting the idea. I'll proceed with caution," he promised.

His reply surprised her. She hadn't tossed out the comment about her family thinking he'd ever meet them. But it seemed he thought he would, sooner or later.

She didn't know what to say to that.

They made short work of clearing out the rest of the stalls and putting down fresh hay. Then they joined her aunt and the pack of little girls who were gliding—with a range of skill—across the frozen pond. Jessica had found Phoebe a set of skates that fit well, but she sat close to Jessica, inside a gazebo perched at the water's edge, seeming too shy to join in the fun.

"How's it going, honey? Don't you want to skate?"

"Lily offered to take her out. I did, too. But she wanted to wait for you, Cole," Jessica said.

"Me? I'm like Frankenstein on ice. I don't have any skates."

"What's your shoe size? We're well stocked," Jessica said.

"Ten," Cole answered.

"How about you, Lauren?"

Lauren hadn't expected to skate, but Phoebe tugged her hand—and, simultaneously, her heartstrings.

"Oh, about a nine. And a half—or a ten, maybe? Ladies' ten, I mean." She avoided Cole's gaze, embarrassed by her shoe size. When they were growing up, her sisters had called her Big Foot. "But you'd look silly on smaller feet," her mom would say, trying to comfort her. "You'd tip over."

"No worries. We have skates for everyone." Jessica headed for a little shed a short distance up the path from the pond. She soon returned, and everyone got busy lacing up and wobbling around on the ground.

Lauren hadn't been on skates in years. She expected to fall flat on her bottom. A few times. She just hoped nothing horribly embarrassing happened, like hearing her jeans split open, or causing a huge crack in the ice.

But there seemed no choice but to get out there as Phoebe gazed up at her, ready to go. She wanted to hold Cole's hand on one side and Lauren's on the other.

They stepped out onto the ice gingerly, and Lauren found that her body remembered what to do faster than her mind did. She offered silent thanks for her innate athletic ability. Maybe this wouldn't be so bad after all?

Cole had not exaggerated when he'd called himself Frankenstein on ice. His knees remained stiff and he practically clomped from place to place.

It didn't take long before he ended up in a heap on the ice, with his arms waving like a wind turbine and a shout of "Whoooaaa!" that made Phoebe laugh out loud.

Lauren quickly glided over. "Are you hurt?"

"Only my pride," he admitted, scrambling to rise. She extended her hand and yanked him to his feet.

He sighed and brushed off his pants. "Maybe I'll just watch awhile."

"Okay. You get your sea legs back. Phoebe and I will take a spin around the pond. Ready, Phoebe?"

Phoebe looked excited and scared, too. "I'll try."

Lauren extended her hand, and they took off slowly while Lauren gave her a few simple instructions: First, to look up at where she was going, not stare at her feet. Next, to shift her weight from one foot to the other and so push herself forward in a gliding motion.

"The straighter the blade is turned, the faster you'll go. If you want to slow down, make a V with your feet, like this, and dig the side of the blade into the ice a little."

Phoebe tried—not perfectly at first, of course. But with Lauren holding her steady, she was definitely getting the idea and had greatly improved by the time they returned to their starting point.

"I can skate, Daddy. Did you see?"

"I did. You look like a pro. Now you can teach me, kiddo."

"Lauren can," Phoebe said brightly. The older girls were calling her again and she wobbled off to join them.

Cole smiled at Lauren. "I'm game if you are. I warn you, it won't be as easy as it was with Phoebe."

She extended her hand. "Okay, Frank. I'm no Olympic champion, but I can show you the basics. Follow my instructions and don't get overconfident?"

"Wouldn't dream of it."

They started off slowly, with Cole gripping her hand. It was a far different feeling than holding Phoebe's, she reflected. She delivered the same basics and a few more advanced tips. He moved in a slower, stiffer way than the little girl, but that was to be expected. What she didn't expect was that almost every time she glanced his way, she found him looking at her. "It helps to keep your chin up and look straight ahead?"

"Wasn't I doing that?"

"Not exactly. And don't lean too far forward, or you'll—" But before she could explain what would happen, it did and he started falling face-first, his arms swinging wildly again.

Lauren quickly tugged him back, and he slung his arms around her for balance. They ended up spinning in a circle, a totally unintended advanced move.

"Wow, look at us," he said, gazing around. "Is anyone getting this on video?"

"We'd go viral on YouTube. Unidentified skaters turn into human gyroscope," she announced in a wry tone.

He starting laughing as they continued to spin. "You're an armful," he said decisively. "I like that, too."

Lauren blushed at his admission. He wasn't as tall as Joe, but tall enough, with broad shoulders and a heavier build. He was just right for her.

They finally slowed down and came to a stop, both breathless. He could have let her go, but he didn't. He gazed into her eyes and smiled. "I think I like skating more than I remembered."

"Me, too," she agreed.

Moments later, they continued around the pond, not talking, just gliding side by side. Their metal blades scraped the ice in a perfect rhythm, and frosty puffs of their breath mingled in the cold air.

Lauren gazed at the blue sky and sunshine that filtered through the winter woods. The mellow light seemed to flow right through her, and she felt happy. Happier than she'd been for a long time. This day had turned out to be much different than she'd expected. And far better than she could ever have imagined.

Was this what her mom called "going with the flow"? If so, she would have to try it more often.

REVEREND BEN ALWAYS MADE TIME TO VISIT MEMBERS OF THE CONGRE-gation who were ill, especially if they were in the hospital. On Saturday afternoon, he went to visit George Krueger, who owned Krueger's Hard-ware on Main Street. George had been suffering from a kidney stone and had gone in for a treatment to have it pulverized with a laser beam.

He found the patient in good spirits; the procedure had been simple and successful. George's doctor had just stopped by to say that George was perfectly on track with his recovery.

"A zap or two, the doctor got rid of the whole thing. Like my grandson playing a video game," George reported. "I'll be home in a day or two. Fine with me. That movie star down the hall is getting the lion's share of attention. We poor mortals need to press the bell for a nurse till our fingers fall off."

Ben doubted that was true. He knew the hospital staff gave excellent and equal attention to all their patients. But he didn't debate the point. "Is Craig Hamilton on this floor?" he said instead.

"End of the hall. A huge room, all to himself. I've heard he gets special food, too. There's a bodyguard, sits in a chair by the door all day, looking at his phone and reading a book. Well, there must be more than one, right?"

"Right," Ben agreed. "I suppose there are shifts for security guards. Mr. Hamilton must be watched day and night."

"I'm surprised they didn't put him in a helicopter and fly him down to Boston. But I heard it's just pacemaker problem. Poor guy needed a little tune-up."

Ben wasn't sure if the patient gossip was reliable, but the explanation did seem logical. "I haven't heard any specifics, except that he's improved."

"You ought to see him. I don't think he's had many visitors. Maybe a few of the movie people? But the trip isn't exactly convenient for them."

"No, it isn't," Ben agreed. The trip to Southport Hospital from Cape Light could easily be an hour, or more in traffic.

George nodded. "He's a long way from home, I'll say that."

Ben realized he should have noticed that, too, and he should have remembered that famous people feel the same as ordinary people do. Rushed to a hospital with a health emergency, and so far from his loved ones, Craig Hamilton was probably lonely and anxious, the same as anyone else would feel in the situation.

"That's a good idea, George. I will try to see him."

They talked a little more about news of the village and the congregation. Then Ben led them in a prayer, and he gave George a blessing for the sick.

"Thank you, Reverend. I'll be over this in no time, but prayers help, too."

"Always," Ben agreed.

As he left George's room, Ben glanced down the corridor, crowded with linen carts and medical machinery. At the very end of the hall, he saw a man in a dark suit sitting in a chair by the very last doorway. Ben hesitated a moment, wondering if the actor might take him for another autograph hound, one wearing a clerical collar.

But it was his duty to offer his support and solace to the sick, whether that person was a queen or a homeless person sleeping on the street. Or a famous actor. *We are all equal in God's sight, and we all need His love and comfort.*

When he reached the security guard, he said, "I'm Reverend Ben Lewis. I've met Mr. Hamilton, in Cape Light. I just stopped by to see if he'd like a visit. Some pastoral care?"

The man frowned. "I have instructions that he doesn't want to be disturbed. But I'll ask. Can you show me some ID, sir?"

Ben fumbled with his wallet and produced his license and proof that he was clergy.

The guard rose and entered Hamilton's room, leaving the door open partway. Ben stood at the gap and peered in. It was indeed a large room. Craig Hamilton's bed faced the hallway, and the movie star peered at him over the guard's shoulder. Ben thought he was going to refuse the visit, then Craig's face lit with recognition.

He sat up and waved Ben forward. "Come in, Reverend. What a surprise."

Ben stepped forward and smiled. "I was visiting a member of the congregation down the hall. I just came by to see how you're doing, and offer my support. I'm sure your fellow actors and coworkers are concerned about you. But you are far from your home."

"That's kind of you." The actor sat back against the pillows. Wearing a hospital gown, with his thick hair mussed and a few days' growth of beard, he looked like any other patient. A bit sad and confused, another middle-aged man swept off his feet by an unexpected turn in his health and well-being. Ben's heart went out to him.

"I was just on the phone with my wife. I made light of this for her sake. Our daughter, Kate, is expecting our first grandchild any minute. I hate to miss the big moment and would never drag my wife away to be at my bedside instead."

"Some people wouldn't be so considerate."

"Oh, this is nothing. It's happened before. I'll be fine in a day or so."

"What is your condition, if I may ask?" Ben didn't mean to pry and would certainly keep the information confidential. "We clergymen are professional secret keepers," he added.

The actor smiled. "No big mystery. My pacemaker gets out of whack every once in a while. A specialist reset the gadget this morning, but I need to stay here until Monday, to make sure it's set right and working with the medications I take."

"I understand. I have a heart condition myself. Had it so long now, I completely forget. Don't tell my doctor that," he admitted.

"Your secret's safe with me," Craig Hamilton promised with a small smile. "I don't know about you, but this getting-older business has thrown me for a loop. First the heart thing." He touched his chest. "Now a grandchild coming. I'm thrilled, honestly," he added quickly. "But no getting away from it, time is passing, Reverend. When a publisher offered a book contract for my memoirs, I was flattered. But the exercise was . . . enlightening? It made me think about a lot of things I'd brushed aside and stuffed in the back of my memory closet.

But you can't just shake things off. Not important things." He met Ben's gaze a moment, then looked away.

"I agree. It doesn't work like that. We are the sum total of our actions and our choices. That's what I believe, anyway."

"I've come to see it that way, too. Sorry for getting all philosophical with you," Craig said, with a self-conscious grin. "I've been alone in this room too long, watching the news."

"Not a problem for me, Mr. Hamilton. That's sort of my job. I'm the perfect person to get philosophical with." Or spiritual, as the case might be. "When I had a heart attack, I reflected on my past, too. And I had some regrets. Some moments that I wish now I could go back to and do over. I think that's only natural. We're only human. God didn't make us perfect."

Craig Hamilton had been listening with interest, and now, his eyes crinkled with a questioning look. "That's sure true. But why is that, do you think? Seems to me He could have easily made us perfect. Endowed us with the wisdom to make the right decisions and choices in our life and never look back with regrets."

Ben had wondered about that, too. "I'm not sure. Sometimes, I think it's just so we can practice forgiveness. So we can see our faults and forgive ourselves, and in doing so, learn to forgive others. To accept each other without judgment, as He accepts us, with love and compassion."

The actor didn't answer for a moment. He stared at his feet under the thin white blanket. "That explanation makes me feel a bit better. About the mistakes I've made, I mean."

He looked back up at Ben. "Let me ask you something else. Suppose you knew you'd done someone wrong, hurt them badly. And you were sorry for that. Truly sorry. And you tried to apologize, sincerely.

But they wouldn't even hear you out. No matter what you said. They wouldn't let you apologize. They wouldn't . . . take it in. What are you supposed to do then, Reverend?"

Ben had heard many such hypothetical questions during his years. The details didn't matter. He neither needed nor wanted to know the specifics.

"You've taken responsibility. You've been honest. With yourself and the other person. And you seem genuinely sorry for the pain you've caused."

"I am, Reverend. Truly. I've done all those things."

"I have sympathy for your frustration. And sympathy for the person that you've wronged as well. Asking for forgiveness involves empathy. On the part of the asker, I mean. Imagine how hurt that person must be, if you've done all that and they still won't accept the apology. Or even hear you out."

Craig looked surprised at his reply at first, then thoughtful. "I wondered if the person was just acting that way out of spite. Trying to get back at me."

Ben nodded. "I understand. But still, try to empathize. What sort of pain are they feeling if they need to inflict more on you?" He paused, watching as the actor took in his words. "Atonement requires sincerity, commitment, and patience. Maybe patience most of all," the minister added. "Forgiveness is a process. Think of the way water wears down a stone. It rarely happens that a person forgives us for a serious wrong when we apologize the first time. I don't mean apologies for silly things, like eating the last oatmeal cookie or leaving your socks in the middle of the bedroom floor."

"You do that, too? I thought ministers were above such mortal failings."

"So did my wife. Until we got married." Ben laughed. "But, returning to my point, we must accept that the other person deserves all the time it might take to open their heart and let go of a grievance. A person carrying a grudge who can't forgive is only hurting themself. They're carrying around a heavy load that's weighing them down. But they don't realize that. They feel righteous in their anger. We might need to apologize again and again. And sometimes, on the other side, a person may need to forgive again and again and again, until they finally reach bottom and get there. That's been my experience, anyway."

Ben waited for Hamilton to reply. Again, he seemed lost in thought. "It took me so long to work up the courage to offer my apology. Years," the actor admitted. "I see now I was just thinking of myself, my struggle to face and admit what I did—and apologize to her." It was a woman. Ben had suspected as much. But he didn't interrupt. It still didn't matter who or when. "I was only focusing on my feelings. As usual. What I was going through. I guess I did expect her to at least hear me out. I never expected the reaction I got. It made me scared to try again. No, not scared," he corrected. "It made me feel that it was pointless to try again."

"It's never pointless. Blessed are the peacemakers," Ben reminded the movie star. "God can see your effort. And your sincerity. Ask for His forgiveness for hurting that person. And pray for His help. Ask Him for the perfect words to reach that person and to help them have a change of heart. For both your sakes."

"Thank you, Reverend. I'm not much of a churchgoer these days. But as I get older, I'm more prone to think about these matters and questions. God and heaven. Mortality and all that."

Reverend Ben smiled. "If you're ever of a mind to talk more about 'all that,' my door is always open. I'll pray for your continued recovery and a healthy, easy birth for your grandchild, Mr. Hamilton. God bless you and your family."

The actor answered with a wide, warm smile, his eyes shining. He suddenly looked like his movie star self again. "Thank you, Reverend. Thank you very much. I don't care if the baby is a girl or a boy. I'll be thrilled as long as the baby is healthy. And please," he added, "call me Craig."

"I will, Craig. I hope to see you again before you go."

They said goodbye, and Reverend Ben headed out of the hospital, feeling satisfied with a good day's work, for a minister. He felt he had helped Craig Hamilton with his concerns and the questions that weighed heavy on his mind and heart—and perhaps had even contributed to this health problem?

He sympathized with the actor's quandary. It was frustrating to apologize to someone who wouldn't accept the gesture. But the path to forgiveness was rarely a straight road, or a smooth one. Craig Hamilton had faced the fact that he'd caused someone pain, and now, regretting that, he was in pain, too. Ben hoped that, with God's help, the actor and the person he had wronged would arrive at a peaceful resolution.

CHAPTER TWELVE

B Y THE TIME LUCY ARRIVED AT THE HOSPITAL ON SUNDAY
to cover a late shift, she knew Craig Hamilton's diagno-
sis and also knew he was still in the hospital. She hated to be distracted
while tending to her patients. The slightest slip of her concentration
could cause a serious error in their medication or treatment. She consciously held fast to her focus all day. But as soon as there was the tini-
est bit of downtime, the question of whether or not to visit Craig took
over her thoughts.

She had come on duty at six in the evening and had a half hour
break at midnight for "lunch," which always struck her as silly, even
though she sometimes packed a sandwich. She was working on the
fourth floor, where the rooms were filled with a mix of postoperative
patients. She had heard that the actor was on the third floor, one she
could avoid, though the nearest nurses' lounge was there. She could
take her break in a corner of the lobby, which would be deserted now,
or even out in her car. But going to such extremes to avoid his floor
seemed silly.

The elevator doors slid open on the third floor, and she got out.

The nurses' lounge was to the right, but to the left, at the very end of the hall, she saw a man in a dark suit sitting at a patient's door, a newspaper spread out in front of him.

It had to be Craig's room. Of course he'd need security. The realization was some relief. Even if she wanted to see him, she probably couldn't get past the bodyguard.

She strolled down the hall, impulse overtaking good sense. It was so late. She was sure she would find the room dark and Craig fast asleep. She would just walk by and peek in. Once the guard saw her uniform, she doubted he would even notice her.

But as Lucy neared the room, she could see that a low light was still on, and she heard a television. She walked by as inconspicuously as possible and saw Craig, sitting up in bed, wearing glasses with thick black frames, an open book in his hands.

The guard glanced at her and then back at the newspaper. Lucy turned at the end of the hall. There was no place else to go. As she walked back toward the room, the guard looked up at her. "Do you need to see Mr. Hamilton? I thought he had a different nurse tonight."

"He does. I mean, I am a nurse here," she added quickly, hoping the man didn't think she stole the uniform to get into the movie star's room. "I'm just not *his* nurse."

The guard had looked suspicious, but now relaxed. "I see. He doesn't want to be disturbed."

"I'm sure. I wasn't trying to meet him," she practically whispered. Craig hadn't noticed her talking to the guard, and she wanted to leave before he did.

"Thanks," she added as she walked away, even though she wasn't sure what she was thanking him for. She said things like that all time. "Thanks" for no reason at all. And "Sorry." Her daughter, Zoey, was working with her on that.

Lucy had almost reached the elevator when the guard stood up and called to her. "Nurse?" She stopped and turned to face him. "Mr. Hamilton would like to see you," he said.

Lucy's heart jumped up to her throat. "He wants to see me? Or he just needs a nurse?"

"Is your name Lucy?"

She thought of making the excuse that she had to get back to work, even though she had plenty of time left in her break. She bit her lower lip and nodded. "Yes, it is."

She walked back to the room, and the guard stepped aside as she entered. Craig was sitting up in bed. He had turned off the television and taken off his glasses.

"Lucy, it's good to see you. Thanks for visiting me."

"It's no big deal. I'm working on the next floor." She tried to make light of the gesture. "I heard you're doing well."

"My doctor here is pleased. He's been conferring with my specialists at home. They all agree I can come out tomorrow morning and get back to work."

"Are you sure that's wise?"

"My pacemaker just needed a small adjustment. I've held up production long enough. They've been shooting around me the last few days. Every minute counts in this business."

"I can just imagine." She had always thought of successful actors as having pampered and even luxurious lives. She'd never considered the pressure they were under to work within strict deadlines, with any wasted time a great cost to the film's budget.

"It sounds very stressful."

"Sometimes it is," he agreed. "But I thrive on it."

He seemed to believe that, but Lucy thought the pressure and stress had to have contributed to his heart episode.

How about the way you treated him Sunday? That didn't help.

"Well, I just wanted to see if you were all right." She started backing toward the door, then paused. "I do want to say that I'm sorry for the way I spoke to you on Sunday. That wasn't like me. And it wasn't right."

He looked surprised, and pleased, too. "Does that mean you accept my apology? Or will you at least talk to me about what happened between us, way back when?"

Lucy shook her head. "You hurt me, badly. But I got over it. I'm happy with my life. I don't need to stir all that up again. And your apology . . ." Her voice trailed off. She was sorry to see him sitting in a hospital bed. But she wasn't going to lie just to make him feel good. "That's beside the point for me. Now, I mean," she added.

He sighed, a long, noisy breath. She could tell he felt frustrated with her, but she couldn't help that. Then he nodded, finally looking as if he accepted her decision.

"All right. If that's how you feel, Lucy, I won't argue with you." He offered a small smile. "A very wise man told me yesterday that I needed to have patience with this." His expression turned serious again. "I know you don't forgive me. Maybe you never will. But please know one thing—I am truly sorry, with all my heart. I have to say that disappointing you, Lucy, leaving you waiting me for that night, was probably the worst thing I ever did to anyone in my life. I know it's my deepest regret. And I know I can never go back and change what happened. But I would give anything to do it over. To do it differently."

Did that mean he would have kept his promise and met her that night, and they would have run off into the sunset? She'd had a while to think about it and had decided that would have probably been a mistake, too.

She took a breath and raised her chin. "We rarely get do-overs in this life, but that's a nice thought, Craig. You take care. Good luck with the rest of the movie."

She turned and left the room without meeting his glance. She walked toward the elevator, barely dodging the janitor who mopped the corridor at this time of night. Her head was spinning, and she couldn't return to work yet. She sought refuge in the nurses' lounge. The room was empty, luckily. She made herself a cup of tea and fell into a plastic chair.

He would have done it over, really? What did he mean by that? Lucy knew she would never ask him. She didn't want to know now. What would be the point?

They had been so young and naive. They wouldn't have gotten very far or stayed together long, she always told herself. It was all for the best. Or maybe that was just sour grapes?

The thoughts swirled in her head, so many questions unanswered. The big clock on the wall reported she still had six whole minutes to pull herself together.

It would have to be enough.

"What do you think of shopping today, Ezra? It's Monday; the shops will be empty. Well, compared to the weekend." The crowds had been his excuse for the last few days, but Lillian knew it was something else altogether. "We can get out early. Have lunch somewhere nice," she added.

"Perhaps." He'd been reading a section of the newspaper. He glanced up at her. "I have to pick up another order of flyers at the print shop. I'm going to put them up around Essex, too. I could do that later in the afternoon, I suppose. After the shopping."

His reply infuriated her. "Can't you take a day off from dog hunting? Why can't his real owners hunt for him?"

Ezra shrugged. "I expect they are looking. We've only spoken once or twice, but that's a good point. We should coordinate, so we're not covering the same ground and duplicating efforts."

"That's not what I meant and you know it. They're not looking nearly as hard as you for a good reason. They don't want that dog back. He must be a troublesome creature. Perhaps he chews things up, or he's not housebroken."

Ezra nearly laughed. "We had him here for several days, Lillian. He was perfectly behaved."

"Of course he was, out in the mudroom. What damage could he do out there?" She sighed. "So, you're willing to pencil me in for a few hours this morning for shopping, is that it? No commitment to lunch?"

"Let's start with the shopping and see how the day goes."

She took a deep breath, trying to summon some patience and gratitude for this shred of a compromise.

The phone rang, and Ezra grabbed it. It had rested only inches from his hand ever since the dog hunt began.

"Yes, this is Dr. Elliot," he replied to the caller. "Oh my. That's excellent news. Let me get a pad and pen. I'll take down the information."

He hopped from his chair to the counter, then said, "Which direction was he headed? Did you notice?"

Lillian simmered. Another dog sighting. Another wild-goose chase for her husband. He would hang up the phone and run to don his parka and hat, then race out of the house, not to be seen again until dinnertime—if even then.

Where will this end, dear Lord? Honestly, I'm asking for some help here.

"A man on Bayview said he spotted Teddy this morning," Ezra reported, moments after hanging up. "He was sure of it. Seems the little scamp tipped over his trash pails. I guess the poor boy is hungry. Hate to think of what he's been surviving on the last few days."

Ezra had already dashed off to dress in his warm clothes. She followed him to the mudroom and leaned on her cane. "So you're racing out to track down this hot lead? Like a detective on call all hours of the night and day?"

Ezra was changing his good shoes for his waterproof walkers. "This is important to me, Lillian. I've tried to explain. If you can't understand, well . . . I think it's just willfulness on your part."

He slung the dog's leash around his neck and headed to the kitchen to stock his pockets. The meat scraps were already in a little plastic sandwich bag. He removed the bag from the fridge and added to that his phone and wallet, a handful of tissues, and a few cough drops. "I'll be in touch."

"I hope so. I suppose I won't see you until dinner," she said, more to herself than to him.

"Perhaps not. Keep the home fires burning, dear. And say a prayer."

A prayer that you'll get over this insanity, she replied silently as he slipped out the door.

LUCY HAD A LONG BREAK BETWEEN HER PRIVATE PATIENTS ON MONday. She sat in Willoughby's Bakery & Café with her laptop, working on her records. Charlie wouldn't have liked to see her giving business to his competition, but it was far easier and more convenient to sit here than try to work at the diner or go all the way home. And prettier, too, she thought. Molly and Betty Bowman decorated their cafés in a very tasteful way, like French bistros, Lucy thought, with small marble tables and tile floors and beautiful showcases of foods, cakes, and breads. Their shop in Newburyport was just the same.

And the food was delicious and a lot more appetizing than the diner's, though she felt guilty for that disloyalty, too.

She'd found a cozy spot in the corner, next to the big window that framed a view of the harbor. The neighborhood was quieter that it had been on Friday. But the bakery was busy, with customers coming in for lunch and mothers pushing baby strollers and leading toddlers by the hand.

"Lucy? I see you hiding over there."

Lucy looked up to find Fran walking toward her, carrying a white bag of take-out food.

"You caught me," she confessed as they kissed each other on the cheek. "I had a few minutes to catch up on paperwork. If I dare to stick a toe in the diner lately, Charlie is liable to wrap an apron around me."

Her description made Fran laugh, though she knew it was true. "No worries, my friend. I'll never tell him you hang out here. I thought you were back at the hospital this week."

"Just a few shifts, to fill in. I was there last night." She paused, wondering how much she should say.

But her friend was already doing the math as she sat down opposite Lucy. "You were on duty last night? Craig was still there, I heard. He was just released this morning. Did you see him?"

Lucy was not surprised at her questions. Fran never wasted time getting to the point. "I didn't intend to. But, yeah, I did see him."

Fran looked pleased by the report. She flipped off the cover of her soup. "Glad to hear it. That's progress."

"I was just passing his room, to check if he was all right. I didn't even expect him to be awake. It was after midnight."

"So did you speak to him, finally?"

Lucy suddenly realized that she'd never told Fran how Craig had caught up with her after church that Sunday and what he'd said. "I did, a little. But it wasn't the first time."

Fran lifted her head and stared at her, wide-eyed. "*What?* Why didn't you tell me?"

"Oh, I don't know. I didn't tell anyone." She knew Fran wanted to say *I'm not anyone* and was thankful she did not.

Instead, Fran said, "So, when was this first time? Start at the beginning. Tell me everything."

Lucy wanted to laugh at her serious expression. "Did you learn these interrogation techniques from Tucker? Where's your pad and pencil? Don't you need to take some notes?"

Fran spread a bit of butter on a brioche roll she'd set beside her soup. "You're wasting valuable time, Lucy. I have to get back to the office soon, but you're not getting out of here until I hear the full story."

Lucy felt cornered, but it was also a relief. The situation had been simmering inside her for over a week now and she hadn't shared it with anyone. Fran was the perfect confidante and might even give her some sound advice.

She quickly told her friend how Craig had waited for her after church two Sundays ago and what he'd said—and her reaction.

"I wasn't even sure I wanted to visit him at the hospital. But once I was on his floor, it felt inevitable. He was very nice to me," she added. "I give him credit, after the things I said. But I still can't agree to rehash the past, Fran. Despite all his fine words—and some things he said really surprised me—I can't even say, *I accept your apology.* I don't think I do. And I won't lie. What would be the point?"

Fran had finished most of her soup. "It sounds to me like he's really sorry. That must mean something to you?"

"It does, I won't deny it. It makes me feel . . . better. A little," she added. "But it doesn't make up for what he did."

To that girl, she wanted to say. That sweet, trusting girl who believed that he made the sun come up in the morning. The girl who had just about put her entire life in his hands. She really did see her younger self as another person entirely, a vulnerable, naive young woman whom she needed to protect and comfort. And whom she needed to champion now.

Fran pulled a chocolate chip cookie from the white bag. "Want a bite?" Lucy shook her head. "You know what I think?"

"I do," Lucy said. "But you'll tell me anyway."

"Aren't you even curious to hear what he has to say? His explanation? His side of the story? You just told me he said things that surprised you. So it seems you don't know it all."

Lucy shifted uneasily, then stared out the window. She had imagined every possible version. There was nothing—or very little?—he could add at this point. "Maybe I don't. But whatever he says, it won't change anything."

"I think you're wrong. It might melt that icy heart. When it comes to Craig, I mean. Is that what you're afraid of? Because it seems to me that you're afraid of something. That's what all this stubbornness is about, isn't it?"

"Oh, Fran." Lucy shook her head. "You always had a flair for melodrama. I don't need to wallow in the past. If he does, fine. I don't. He said his piece. And he heard my reaction. That's that."

"He didn't say his piece. That's the point. No, wait. The point is that you're making a mistake."

Lucy didn't agree. That's what counted. "The movie people are leaving in a few days. On the weekend, I heard. They'll pack up and go, and everything will get back to normal. It will be as if he never came here. Nothing happened. Nothing's changed."

"You know that's not true. Your life is different already. You're different. Not that it shows," Fran said, "but inside. He apologized to you. More than apologized. Sounds to me like the man bared his soul. That must have changed your feelings about him a little? Made a tiny tweak in the story you tell yourself about the past? Show some compassion, Lucy. It's not like you to act this way."

When had her friend gotten so smart about people—and how their hearts and minds really worked? Secretly, Lucy agreed with her. But she knew that if she admitted it, Fran would never give up.

"I don't act this way usually. That's true. But this is different."

Fran stared at her, then sighed. "I know I keep saying this, but I wish you'd listen. If you don't talk things out with him, you'll be sorry."

"I won't be, Fran," she quietly insisted. But somewhere between last Sunday and last night at the hospital, something deep inside had shifted. Very slightly. But she did feel that inner emotional scale, which weighed the pros and cons of the question, tilting now in Craig's favor.

Maybe she could find a drop of forgiveness in her heart? She wasn't sure what to do. The clock was ticking down. Was it pressuring her to act—or counting down the hours she still needed to hang tough?

Maybe she should just concentrate on her work and getting ready for Christmas and let time take care of this problem. Wouldn't that be the easiest solution for all?

JOE HAD LEFT TOWN THE WEEK PRIOR, ON THURSDAY, TO VISIT HIS mother, who now lived in Scottsdale, Arizona. She'd retired there with his stepfather. Saturday was his mother's birthday and so he had skipped a visit at Thanksgiving in favor of this trip.

Lauren found his absence a relief. Their work relationship had gotten a little tense after the confusing meeting with Maddie Belkin last Monday. With Joe out of town, she didn't have to dodge unwanted dinner invitations.

He did call once a day to check up on things. But he hadn't called her on the weekend, which was also a relief.

She had hoped that the wonderful ice-skating interlude with Cole would extend into an impromptu Saturday-night date. But Cole had to bring Phoebe to a party at David and Christine Sawyer's, and Lauren was a bit disappointed when he left her with the standard parting promise of "I'll call you." She'd heard that one before.

But he did call on Sunday evening, much to her delight and relief. He asked her out to dinner for the following Saturday night. She had hoped to see him sooner, but there was Phoebe to consider. Lauren knew it was probably hard to leave her with a sitter during the school week.

It's best not to rush these things and *If it's meant to be, it's meant to be* were her favorite mantras as the week started. Still, she couldn't help feeling that her days in Cape Light were slipping by. How much time would she spend with Cole and Phoebe before she had to go?

She arrived at the law firm very early on Wednesday, even before the receptionist. Joe was already there. She left her coat and briefcase in her office, then peeked into his office. He sat behind a pile of papers and mail, a stack of pink message slips in the center of it all.

"I wasn't gone that long. I'll be digging out all week."

"That's what you get for sneaking off to play golf in Scottsdale."

"I didn't sneak off. I was visiting my mother, for her birthday." He looked a little miffed at the accusation, then grinned. "Can I help it if she and my stepdad are obsessed with the game? You should see the course they brought me to. I thought I had died and gone to heaven."

Lauren laughed. "The ever-so-slight tan line across your forehead from the baseball cap—dead giveaway."

"You got me, Miss Marple. Guilty as charged." He leaned back in his leather chair. "By the way, how's your investigation into Dendur Software going? Dig up any dirt to confirm Maddie's story?"

Lauren had made progress but had not shared much on the phone, preferring to tell him in person. "I've spoken to both of the women who Maddie claimed received the same treatment from Dendur— lower salary for the same work, men who were less qualified being promoted over them or kept on when the positions of female coworkers were cut."

"Really? What did these women say?"

"They told stories similar to Maddie's, once I got them talking. They all seemed impressed that she was taking a stand." And had seemed a bit embarrassed, or at least regretful, that they'd given up without a fight, Lauren had thought. "I think hearing she's come forward and is going after Dendur made a big impression. Maybe even gave them hope. So far, only one has agreed to give us an affidavit."

"Give it time. You might win the other woman over. Even one voice corroborating Maddie's claim helps."

"That's just it, Joe. Both of these women know *other* women who experienced the same treatment, and they gave me more names. This thing is mushrooming."

Joe's eyes grew wide. "How big?"

"I'm not sure yet, but certainly more than we expected. Definitely potential for a class action suit. I have to follow through now, don't you think? They may want to join Maddie's suit, not just corroborate her story."

"Have you asked them?"

"I wanted to ask you first. Then we need to run it by Maddie."

"Of course. Let's see what the next group has to say. If their stories are substantial enough, I mean. This case has to be solid, or we'll get slapped off like pesky mosquitos."

"Nobody is slapping me off of anything," Lauren promised as she rose from her chair. "I'll keep you posted. I'll line up the calls."

He leaned forward. "Great work. Really. Why don't we get together for dinner one night, Lauren, and you can bring me up to speed? How does tomorrow look?"

Lauren felt a knot in her chest. She liked working with Joe, but this was the part she was not liking lately. Especially now that her relationship with Cole seemed to be more than a hopeful wish.

"Betty has her holiday band concert at school. I promised her I'd go."

He shrugged. "Sounds cute. How about Friday?" She was relieved he had not offered to join her. Thankfully, a middle-grade band concert really was a bridge too far, even for Joe.

"Decorating the tree that night. Family ritual." She stressed the word "family," hoping he'd get the hint—no non–fam members allowed.

"Oh, I see." He sat back, his eyes narrowing. "Should I go for the third swing? Your curve ball is pretty sharp this morning. I'm afraid to ask about Saturday."

Lauren didn't know what to say. Actually, she did know, but she wasn't sure if this was the time to say it.

"Hey, remember when we were in high school and I'd ask you to do things with me and you'd say you were sorry, but you had to wash your hair that night?" Joe grinned, remembering, but she could sense the excuse still stung.

"I do," she answered in serious tone. "That wasn't an excuse either. Nice hair was a really big deal back then."

"It was," he agreed. "But how about now? I get the feeling you're going to say that again. That you have to wash your hair Saturday night?"

She sighed, then stepped over and closed the office door. Joe watched her. "Or something like that," he added. "And I'm not going to like the reason any better."

She sat down in the chair across from him again. "I'm sorry, Joe. The thing is, I don't think it's a good idea for us to keep dating. I don't want to lead you on and give you false hopes."

He ducked his head. "I see. I was wondering about that."

"You were?" She hadn't seen much evidence of it. "Wondering since when?"

"Since that day you dropped me like a hot potato to take care of a pig. I mean, turn the sound off, Lauren, and look at the picture. It sends a message."

Lauren frowned. Poor Joe. She had sent him a message that day, loud and clear, without really meaning to.

"So, are you seeing him now? Cole McGuire, I mean. You once described him as the most difficult, contrary being on the planet. I guess you forgot that part?"

She had said that about him. Couldn't deny it. "We are sort of seeing each other. It's early days. Very early," she emphasized. "The thing is, it did make me think. If I could even accept a date with someone else, am I really the right person for you? I mean, you deserve someone who's over the moon about you. Who wouldn't give another guy a second glance. I'm honored that you even think of me in a serious way. Any woman in her right mind would scoop you up in a heartbeat."

"Any woman but you." His words sounded harsh, but his expression was still warm and even understanding.

"I'm sorry, Joe. I really am. I wouldn't hurt you for the world." *And my life would be so easy if I could have fallen for you and made a place for myself in this firm. And made a home with you in this village.*

"But it don't mean a thing if it ain't got that swing?" he finished for her. "At least you've been honest. As always."

"I owed you that."

"I had to try. You were the one that got away. Now I won't have to wonder anymore what might have been between us. That's something."

"You'll find someone, Joe. Someone who's perfect for you. And she'll be a very lucky woman. And I'll always be your friend."

"I'll be yours, too. After I get over being kicked to the curb," he joked in a halfhearted way.

It seemed he had no hard feelings. He was really being great about this, and Lauren felt so relieved that she'd cleared the air. But where did that leave their business relationship? Would he ask her to give up the work she'd been doing here? That would hurt. She really wanted to pursue the Belkin case and had already put a lot into it.

"Will you keep your hand in here?" he asked.

"Sure. I was hoping that would be okay with you. I don't want to leave the Belkin case when things are just falling into place."

"That's some cold comfort." He paused. "Guess you still have your mind set on New York?"

"I do." Lauren nodded as if there was no question, though she hadn't done much about applying for a new job yet.

"Well, even if you can't see a future for you and me, maybe your mind will change about joining the firm. You would be a real asset to this team."

She thought that was very big of him, all things considered. "Thank you, Joe. If my mind changes, you'll be the first to know." She felt the familiar impulse to hug him, to show she still cared. But he remained behind his desk, and it seemed best that way. She rose and left the room, feeling shaky. She had not planned to have that talk with him today, though she knew it had to happen sooner or later.

Even if things had not taken a positive turn with Cole, Joe was not the one for her. She didn't have to think about it. She just knew.

Her mother was right *again*.

CHAPTER THIRTEEN

THE DINER WAS AMAZINGLY QUIET FOR A SATURDAY MORN-
ing. Quiet and snug, Lucy thought, gazing at the fresh layer
of snow outside, barely disturbed yet by footprints or shovels. Her
Scandinavian grandmother called it "hygge"—a general feeling of
warmth and coziness. That's what she felt here today.

A wave of flurries that had begun on Friday afternoon and continued through the night had covered the village with a sugary white
blanket a few inches deep. Enough to slow people down as they dug
out, cleaned off their cars, and recalculated their day, but Lucy didn't
think it would stop most from Christmas shopping and taking care
of other holiday errands. It was the last weekend left. Christmas was
this coming Friday.

Whenever there was snow, even a small amount, Charlie ran up
to his office at the village hall to supervise the response and cleanup,
making sure the snowplows were out clearing streets and no one was
stranded without power or heat.

He'd left the house before dawn, and his absence made the diner
quieter, too. If she had to be there at all, the situation was ideal.

She was surprised to see Dr. Elliot enter. He and Lillian never came to eat there together, though he sometimes did on his own. He stomped bits of snow off his boots at the door, then looked around for a table. She almost didn't recognize him, bundled in a big green parka, muffler, and a plaid hat with ear flaps, so that only his wire-rimmed glasses showed.

She had seen the impressive outfit earlier in the week, when he'd stopped to leave flyers. *LOST DOG—REWARD!* the notice read in bold red letters. *Medium size. White. Mixed-breed terrier. Answers to Teddy. Friendly to all. All info welcome.*

A big color photo of the dog was placed in the center. The dog looked very cute and bright. Ezra's phone number was below, along with the word *REWARD* again.

She had felt so bad for him, she'd taken a pile of the flyers and taped them all over the diner, even in the restrooms. The little dog's photo competed for attention with Charlie's overwrought Christmas decorations, but that couldn't be helped.

Ezra headed to a table by the window, and she gave him a minute to take off his heavy clothing and settle in. Of course, under the Artic expedition outerwear, he wore a tweed sports coat, a cashmere sweater, and a button-down shirt with a red bow tie. She imagined he wore the same outfit to the beach. The man didn't seem to know the meaning of casual attire. But it would have seemed very odd, at this point, to see him dressed any other way.

By the time she approached with a menu and a coffeepot, a large map was spread over the table, alongside his cell phone and a few fine-point mechanical pencils.

"Coffee, Ezra?"

"Had my quota for today, thank you. I would like some tea, please. With lemon and honey?"

Her well-trained ear picked up a slight rasp in his voice, but she wouldn't ask about it. He was a doctor; he could tell if he was coming down with a cold.

"I'll bring it right out. We have some special oatmeal this morning, with apples, cranberries, walnuts, and cinnamon sugar. It's very good," she coaxed him.

"That sounds perfect. A small orange juice on the side, please. It's not as cold out as you'd expect. I think this white stuff will melt down in a day or two."

"Hope so," Lucy agreed.

"I'm surprised to see you here, Lucy. Fitting in the diner around your nursing shifts?"

Ezra, bless his heart, was one of the few in town who could remember that waitressing was no longer her real job. "Juggling is more like it. Charlie needs some help with all the movie fans in town. It won't be this busy much longer."

Lucy was relieved about that. Lack of time had settled the question about whether or not to see Craig Hamilton again, for better or worse. Right now, she felt it was all for the best. She was eager to shut the door, once and for all, on that episode in her life.

"I heard the production group is due to leave today. I never did get to see any of the filming. Too busy with more important matters," he said.

"Any sign of your dog, Ezra?"

If he had found Teddy, Lucy was sure he wouldn't have looked so glum. But she wondered if there was any progress in the search.

"There have been sightings. Two, maybe three. It's encouraging. The flyers have helped. But by the time people call and I get there, he's moved on. I'm tracking his movements on this map. Assumed movements, of course, because some sightings have been at a distance and could have been another dog. But I have to work with what I have. Never thought the art of triangulation would come in handy when I was forced to learn it as a Scout. But here you are. Everything you know comes in handy sooner or later, Lucy. If you live long enough."

"That's probably true." Ezra was a clever man. She enjoyed chatting with him.

She gazed down at the map. It showed the village and the surrounding area. Ezra had marked red dots and dates on certain streets in the village and beyond and had connected them with green lines, which created myriad triangles.

He pointed into the center of a triangle. "I'm trying to narrow down the search area. I'm afraid that he's sick or injured. Or he lost his way and he's found shelter somewhere. Around here, maybe?" He pointed with his pencil. "Under a porch or in a shed?" He took out his phone. "My grandson showed me something called 'Google Earth.' It's a roving eye up in the sky. A satellite picture of everywhere. In real time. You just type in an address. Look, here's the diner."

Lucy looked at his phone screen. "Well, I'll be. That's the Clam Box, all right."

"I check this, too, whenever I get a call."

Lucy was impressed. For an old person, Ezra wasn't afraid to explore technology. She couldn't say the same for herself, more than forty years younger than him.

"Teddy's run away before but he certainly knows his way to Providence Street. There must be a reason he hasn't returned by now. Unless he did come back at some point and I missed him."

Ezra sounded worried by the myriad of possibilities. Lucy could think of a few that were even more dire than those he'd mentioned. Hit by a car? Attacked by a bigger animal? Of course, she would never add to his fears.

"Maybe someone took him in and they haven't seen your flyers, and they don't know how and where to return him."

He nodded. "Could be. I've left my name and number at all the shelters. And I posted flyers in Hamilton and Essex, too. Dogs can travel miles. You'd be amazed." He sighed. "He's not even my dog. Not really. But it feels to me as if he is. I can't rest until I know he's safe."

"You care enough to make the effort, Ezra. That's what really counts. I think that little dog is truly blessed to have you working so hard to find him. And you will be, too." She patted his shoulder. "I'll be right back with your oatmeal."

"Thank you, dear. Bedside or tableside, you're an angel. And that's a fact."

His compliment touched her heart. It was good to see him finally smile, too, even if only for a moment.

She'd just served Dr. Elliot his breakfast when Charlie burst through the door. He wore a thick fisherman sweater with a down vest on top, a traffic-stopping shade of orange. Lucy suspected it was a gift from some utility worker, but it looked very official and was just the right touch for a man in charge of a community emergency. His dark blue baseball cap was marked with the Clam Box logo, of course. He was rarely without it.

He'd had all sorts of diner souvenir items made—T-shirts, hats, aprons, and mugs—though they didn't sell much. He'd even considered stamping something about the movie on the items. But the cost was too expensive. He did have a plan to persuade the movie stars to autograph a few shirts and aprons, but so far, that hadn't come together.

He pulled off a pair of heavy gloves and rubbed his hands together as he walked toward her. Lucy guessed he'd done some "boots on the ground" mayoring today with the snow-clearing crews. Charlie wasn't above pitching in if help was needed, and she gave him credit for it. Her husband was a down-to-earth guy, scornful of what he called "airs." People liked that about him. She did, too. Most of the time.

"Wait till you hear this. You'll never guess who just got in touch with me."

Lucy stood stone still, coffeepot in hand. She didn't have a clue but knew it had to be good. Charlie looked like he'd just won the lottery.

"I can't imagine. Who?"

He took out his phone and showed her the text. "Adam Cook, from the movie crew. He's in charge of hotel accommodations and the catering and all that. He said the snow delayed their schedule, and they need to stay a few days longer than expected. Molly Willoughby is all booked up with parties and didn't plan on feeding them past breakfast this morning. So guess who gets the job, after all?"

Lucy's calm and contented mood shattered, as if she'd just dropped a tray of water glasses.

"The diner. You, I mean," she said.

"That's right." He grinned from ear to ear and patted her cheek. "We made it after all, honey. Just the tail end, but it's something." He tossed his gloves on the counter. "Where's a pad and pen? I need to take a quick inventory and figure out what we're going to feed them."

Lucy wasn't surprised to hear he didn't know. That was Charlie. He often worked backward to catch up with some overzealous promise, dragging everyone else along to help him make good on it.

For some reason that she didn't entirely understand, feeding the movie crew was important to him. But she wasn't going to rob him of this small victory and joy. He was absolutely thrilled. She felt just the opposite.

"So how will this work? We'll be delivering the food to the set, right?"

"Sure. We'll set up a buffet for breakfast and lunch. But Adam and I decided the crew could take meals here, too. They can just walk in and sign the check, and I'll tally up the cost. With a discount, of course," he added.

"I see." Lucy nodded. She felt a little numb at the news. Just when she thought she was free and clear, this had to happen. It was bad enough the snow had delayed the crew from leaving town, but now they'd all be in here eating, and she'd agreed to help Charlie over the weekend—all day today and part of Sunday.

She wasn't sure what she would do if Craig came in, but she'd think of something. Hide in the kitchen? Plead a migraine? Even if he took dinners at the inn, he'd still be in town a few more days and was likely to visit the diner sooner or later.

She could already imagine what Fran was going to say about all this. *It's a sign from the universe! Another chance to change your mind, Lucy!*

Or something like that.

Well, I'm not changing my mind, she nearly said aloud as she clipped an order to the wheel at the pass-through.

Charlie looked up from the pad. "Spaghetti and meatballs? All you can eat?"

Lucy wasn't sure what he was talking about. Then she realized he was proposing the menu for tonight's dinner for the movie crew. "Sounds good to me," she replied, though Italian cuisine was hardly the diner's strong point.

Right now, that was the least of her concerns.

*   *   *

On Saturday evening, Cole appeared at Lauren's house right on time. Luckily, her mother was still working and her father and Betty had gone to the middle school for a basketball game.

Lauren was relieved that there would not be any awkward moments of small talk with her family. She already felt as if she was in high school, fretting over her outfit and appearance while she got ready.

Where's the fashion police when you really need them? she'd asked herself, thinking of the way her two sisters had critiqued her look before her date with Joe on Thanksgiving weekend. Now, feeling completely stressed and confused, which wasn't like her at all, she did a quick FaceTime with Amanda, who helped her sort out the perfect outfit—a burgundy turtleneck, jeans, and black boots. Amanda insisted she looked great and as if she hadn't tried that hard. Lauren liked that message.

When she answered the door, Cole looked as if he had tried, wearing a leather jacket and jeans, with a black turtleneck underneath. He also looked so handsome that she didn't even notice the blue Volvo in the driveway, not until he politely opened the passenger-side door for her.

"What's this? I was looking forward to a ride in that comfy-looking red pickup truck. Country music on the radio? A hound dog in the cargo area?" She glanced at the back seat with dismay, and he laughed.

"I can find some country music if you want. This is my socializing car. I keep it in a shed behind the barn. I don't take it out much."

"It's very nice. Very comfortable. Though I would like a ride in that old truck sometime."

"Sure thing. You bring the hound dog." Cole turned to her briefly and smiled. Lauren felt a current of attraction down to her toes. Were they really on a date? Finally? She'd imagined this moment so many times. It was hard to believe it was really happening.

Here you are, Lauren. Try to relax and enjoy it?

Cole had chosen a French restaurant in Newburyport, a casual café with great reviews for its food and atmosphere. "We have some time before the reservation," he said, as they parked on a cobblestone street in the center of the village. "I thought we could stroll around and do some Christmas shopping?"

"Great idea. I still have so much left on my list." Lauren winced. "I'll be shopping online and hitting 'Express Ship' until the last possible minute."

"You have a big family to cover. I just have Phoebe and a few nieces and nephews."

"Thanks for the excuse, but I've always been a last-minute shopper. I generally operate best with a deadline."

She hadn't meant to be amusing; she was just telling the truth. But the admission made him chuckle.

He quickly walked to her side of the car and opened the door. Lauren felt perfectly capable of opening her own doors and such. But she was still impressed by his manners.

She climbed out of the car and flipped up the collar of her black wool coat. The style was sleek and figure-flattering, especially when worn with high boots. As she slung her big striped scarf around her neck, she found Cole smiling at her.

He offered his hand, and it seemed the most natural thing in the world to take it. "Off we go, then. Which way? You choose."

There were shops in both directions, and Lauren hadn't been to

Newburyport in a while. The feeling of Cole's strong, warm hand entwined with hers was also very distracting. She pointed to the left, totally unsure of what they might find. They fell into step together and walked forward.

It had been a good guess. She quickly noticed the perfect gift for her sister Amanda. In a shop window hung a long black velvet dress with a V-neck, trimmed with black satin piping.

"My sister Amanda would love that dress," she said. "She's a musician and plays the cello in an orchestra. She needs a lot of formal outfits for performances."

She quickly went inside, then wondered if Cole would be bored and prefer to move on and meet her later. But he was happy to follow. There was a section with clothing for men, and he browsed while she talked with a saleswoman, who suggested that Lauren try on the dress herself to figure out the right size.

Lauren was standing in front of a long mirror, right outside the dressing room, when she saw Cole's reflection just behind her. "What do you think?" she asked.

"If your sister looks anything like you in it, she'll get a standing ovation."

Lauren felt herself blush and saw the evidence of her reaction reflected in the mirror. She wasn't sure what to say.

"We do look alike. Which is funny, since Amanda is my stepsister. It's Jillian and I who have the same parents."

"Interesting." Cole nodded, a funny little smile on his face as he watched her slip away from the mirror and back into the dressing room.

They proceeded down the street, and Cole bought official Red Sox jerseys for his twin nephews, who were ten and huge baseball fans. His sister and her family lived in Connecticut, and he often spent time with them over the holidays. But this year they were spending both Christmas Eve and Christmas Day in Vermont with her in-laws.

"They plan to stop for a visit on their way home, so we'll have Christmas twice," he said. "Phoebe's excited to see her cousins and get more presents, of course."

"I bet she is." It sounded as though Cole and Phoebe might be alone on the holiday, and she thought about inviting them to her family's Christmas Eve party. But it was way too early in their relationship to even consider such a thing.

Why don't you get through your first date with the guy, Lauren? Maybe by Groundhog Day it will be time for an invite to meet the clan? If the relationship lasted that long. Her self-imposed deadline to return to New York loomed ahead.

They passed a shop that sold riding gear—fancy blazers and footwear for equestrians. Cole paused to look in the window, which was beautifully decorated with fake snow and an exceptionally fit-looking Santa wearing a red hunting jacket, black top hat, and high black boots. He sat astride a saddled reindeer, racing through the night.

"Does Phoebe need anything for her riding lessons?" Lauren wasn't sure what to get the little girl and thought some accessory might be a good idea.

"She did ask Santa for real riding boots. Jen Bennet helped me find a good pair. And some jodhpurs, too."

"That sounds great," Lauren said in a bright voice. "I can just see her in all the official gear."

Secretly, she cringed when he mentioned the pretty therapist's name. Lauren could picture Jen riding to the rescue the minute she left for New York—that is, if Jen and Cole weren't already involved? But posing that question was too blunt a move, even for her.

"I wouldn't know the first thing about picking out riding boots," she added.

Cole seemed to sense her unease and smiled. He took her hand again and tugged her down the street. "I wouldn't either. Jen sent me to a shop like this in Hamilton. Her boyfriend owns it. He's an awesome horseman and polo player. I'm going to take Phoebe to watch him play sometime."

Lauren felt a smile stretch from one side of her face to the other. "It's exciting. Betty and I watched a match last year. They play right on Hamilton's village green in the spring."

He nodded and caught her gaze. "So I've heard."

They worked their way down the street. Lauren bought a few Christmas ornaments in a store that stocked handmade items from around the world. Cole found an antique shop and bought his sister a beautiful teapot. They took a moment to admire a grand old church at the top of a hill that overlooked the harbor. The tall spire was filled with light and had served as a landmark for sailors for centuries, as brilliant a beacon as any lighthouse.

At the next corner, they found their restaurant, arriving right on time. The hostess showed them to a table in the corner, and Lauren was glad for the quiet and privacy. She had a lot of questions for Cole and didn't want to shout over a noisy dining room.

And you don't want to interrogate the poor guy either, she reminded her lawyerly side. *That would really blow it, Lauren.*

It turned out Cole had many questions for her, too. Lauren was flattered by his interest in hearing about what she was like in high school, her favorite books and movies, and the highs and lows of her college days.

"I probably shouldn't be admitting this to anyone, but sometimes,

I feel like a real imposter," she confided. "I mean, am I really a full-fledged, bona fide grown-up? I know I am on paper. But I don't always feel that way. Being a kid doesn't feel that long ago."

Cole laughed. "I know what you mean. It's scary. Sometimes I could swear I was still sixteen. A part of me will probably always feel that way, even when I'm sixty. I guess Phoebe was the game changer. Once you're responsible for another human being, it's different. Or it should be."

Life gets more serious, he meant. Decisions and choices matter more. Or, at least, have a wider impact. You're not just living for yourself anymore.

"I think I understand. But I'm sure that until I'm blessed with children myself, I can't really know what it's like. Not completely."

"No, not completely. Otherwise, a lot of people would *not* become parents, believe me. Raising Phoebe is the scariest, most challenging thing I've ever done. And the most wonderful thing, too. I didn't really get being a parent, at first. Oh, I loved her like crazy. But since Amy died, I really get it. And nothing else in my life will ever come close. Not my job, not anything."

"You're a great dad," Lauren said quietly. "I'm not just saying that."

"Thanks." He met her gaze in the candlelight. "I think you'll be a great mom someday, too."

Their waiter arrived with the main course, and Lauren was glad for a break from the serious conversation, though it was wonderful to sit and talk to Cole with such openness and honesty. And warmth. If only there could be more evenings like this one. The closer she felt to him, the more the question of their future seemed to creep up behind her and cast a cold shadow on their evening.

Cole had ordered steak au poivre with pommes frites and happily dug into the perfectly grilled beef, which was topped with a creamy peppercorn sauce. Thin, crisp french fries were piled beside it. Lauren's dish, sole almondine, was more delicate. It smelled delicious, and the first bite was sublime.

They ate in a silence for a few moments, until Cole said, "Any new developments in your job search?"

"I must admit I haven't been that proactive about hunting down leads. Assignments at Joe Wagner's firm have kept me busy. He even offered me a job there."

Cole smiled. "I'm not surprised. What did you say?"

"I was flattered, of course. It's always flattering to be wanted. But I don't think it's the right place for me. I was honest with Joe, and he seemed to understand."

"I understand, too. You were right not to take it. I bet you could do any job there with one hand tied behind your back and a blindfold on. Which isn't necessarily a good thing."

The image made her laugh. "Far from a good thing, I'd say. Though I guess some people don't mind taking the easy road, for whatever reason. For me, it would be a recipe for utter boredom. I'd love to do what you did, Cole. You seem excited about your work and how you're using your skills to do some good in the world. I'd like to find an area of law that I feel passionately about, too. Actually, I may be getting close. There's a case at Joe's firm I've been working on. The client is a woman who's been treated unfairly by her employer. Several women now, it turns out."

She quickly described Madeleine Belkin's claim, without breaching her privacy or that of any of the other women involved. "It's the first case I've felt excited about in a long time. We meet with the attorneys who represent the former employer next week. I'm a little nervous, but psyched, too."

"Yes, I can see that," he replied. "Your eyes have that tiger glow.

The opposing counsel better watch out." His warning made her laugh. "Sounds like you're on the right track. I can't say it was easy for me," he added, "but I did figure it out. And I understand what you're going through. I admire that you've taken on the struggle and aren't just ignoring or bottling up those feelings—which is what a lot of people do, because they're afraid to make a change. You'll figure it out."

Lauren felt encouraged by his words. "Thanks. Lately, it seems like my life is a big snow globe and someone shook it up like crazy. Everything is still swirling around inside, one blurry mess that may never settle."

He smiled and took her hand. "It's not that bad. Honestly. You know what the French say? 'If you want to make an omelet, you have to break some eggs.'"

Lauren laughed. "Good reminder. Actually, it was Lenin who said that, on the way to start the Russian Revolution. He was hiding in Paris, in a boxcar. Maybe that's why you thought it was someone French?"

"I think it's just the reference to an omelet." Cole grinned. "I've never heard that story about Lenin. Tell me the truth—are you a *Jeopardy!* champion in disguise?"

She shook her head and laughed. "Just a European history major in disguise. You studied finance and can be excused."

"Thanks. I appreciate that." The dessert menu had arrived, and Cole scanned the choices with a serious expression. He looked up and said, "I guess that means you probably won't stick around much longer. I mean, if you turned down a job with Wagner, it's unlikely."

It sounded as if he really cared about her answer, and she was taken by surprise. She wasn't sure how to respond.

"Yes, it's unlikely," she said finally.

He nodded. "I thought so. I just wanted to be sure."

He seemed sad, and she suddenly felt bad she hadn't offered more hope or shaded the truth just a tiny bit. But she had to be honest with him.

His phone buzzed with a text message and he quickly checked it. "Sorry, it's Phoebe's babysitter. I'd better call."

He stepped away from the table for privacy, and Lauren was happy to have a few moments to get her emotions under control.

Her reply to his question had been the equivalent of saying that following her bliss would lead her away from Cape Light—and away from him and Phoebe. And when things were suddenly going so well between them. She hadn't felt so head over heels for anyone in a long, long time. Maybe never. She really couldn't say what it was about Cole. In some inexplicable way, he just seemed to be the one for her.

Could she possibly trust this crazy feeling that she couldn't even explain to herself? Was she willing to toss aside her career goals for the slim possibility that they might have a future together? It seemed like a very big if, especially in light of what she'd just been through with Greg. She and Cole didn't even know each other that well. It would be a gamble to stay because of him, and one that broke all the rules she'd set for herself.

Her mom's words came back to her. "You can't overthink these things." Lauren had to admit she was doing exactly that.

Cole returned from his phone call with a cheery smile, and their awkward moment was forgotten. "You'll never guess what that conversation was about."

"Wilbur wants to stay up late to watch a show on Animal Planet?"

"Not quite. Phoebe told the sitter Wilbur is allowed to have a bowl of ice cream with her as a bedtime snack."

"He isn't?" She really couldn't see the problem. What was the world coming to when a piglet needed to watch his calories? "I thought it was his job to eat a lot of fattening stuff."

"He's not supposed to have people food. I'm afraid we've spoiled him."

"Look at the little guy. It's hard to resist spoiling him." She could still remember how cute Wilbur had been the night they had all taken care of him, so cuddly in his towel after a bath.

"The 'little' guy is getting bigger every day. I have to talk to Phoebe about relocating Wilbur to the barn. That's not going to be easy."

Lauren didn't think it would be either. "Maybe you can get her a puppy when the time comes. My aunt has plenty."

He looked terrified at the suggestion. "I know you think that's a great solution . . . and it does make a kind of sense. But please, don't mention that in front Phoebe. All I need is a puppy *and* a piglet running around that tiny house right now. It's hard enough to get any work done."

She smothered a laugh with her dessert menu. "My lips are sealed. Except for the occasional *oink*. And I'll have the crème brûlée, please," she added, setting the menu down.

"There's something we can agree on. I will as well."

He smiled into her eyes, and she could barely recall that there had ever been a moment of tension between them. She secretly cringed to recall the rocky start of their relationship. But she did know she'd been drawn to him from the beginning.

Can you really walk away from this so easily? Are you a total fool, Lauren?

It wasn't even Christmas. Maybe by some miracle everything would work out and she wouldn't be forced to make these difficult choices.

Right. And I bet you still believe in Santa, a little voice chided her. *This is what being a grown-up means. Do you get it now?*

LILLIAN CAME DOWNSTAIRS SUNDAY MORNING DRESSED FOR CHURCH. There wasn't much time for breakfast, but she had to eat something or risk feeling light-headed and even faint. To hear Ezra tell it, that old hobgoblin low blood sugar lurked in the shadows ready to pounce, especially on seniors.

He had come down before her in his bathrobe but was still at the table sipping a cup of tea. Not his usual coffee, she noticed. Bad sign.

"Are you coming to church today? Emily will be here shortly."

"I intended to, but I'm dragging this morning. I didn't sleep well." His explanation was interrupted by a sudden cough. He covered his mouth with his elbow to keep the germs in check.

"I'm not surprised. You were coughing all night. You've got a cold from chasing after that dog. What did you expect?"

Ezra glanced at her, then stirred his tea. "I expected to find him. Why else would I have been out there?"

She hadn't meant that. He knew it. She also knew he would never admit he'd been on a wild-goose chase and had made himself physically—not to mention emotionally—sick over it.

"You must stay home and rest. I'll bring back chicken soup. Emily will know where to buy some that's as good as homemade." Willoughby's, probably, though Lillian hated to give the place the credit.

"And cough drops, please," he said, his throat thick and sounding sore.

"Absolutely. Bed rest and liquids. Keep your head elevated. I hope you don't have a fever." Lillian stepped over and pressed her hand to his forehead. She couldn't really tell if he was feverish or not, they kept the house so warm. "We'll see Dr. Harding tomorrow if it gets worse. I hope you've learned a lesson. Finally. Will you die of pneumonia over this silly creature?"

She guessed that by now the dog had already met with some unhappy end. Wasn't it just as well that Ezra give up without knowing for sure that sad conclusion to this story?

He wasn't being logical. That was the problem. But he had lost all reason the moment he'd set eyes on the blasted canine.

Ezra rose and tightened the sash on his robe. "I won't catch pneumonia, Lillian. We've had the vaccine, remember? I will see Harding if needed. It's just a cold. Leave me be."

He walked past her, looking so sad and beaten, she felt alarmed. Where had her Ezra gone? This bleak, possessed soul—a wraith of a man—had somehow stolen his place.

"Ezra, before you go up, I have something to say . . ." She followed him as quickly as she was able.

He was already seated in the mechanical chair. She didn't like to see that. He always climbed the stairs on his own, strictly adhering to a "use it or lose it" philosophy, unless he felt particularly tired or weak.

"If this is about Christmas shopping, spare me. I actually have very little say in the choices, when you come right down to it. Just be done with it and put my name on the packages."

"It's not about the gifts for the children. But, perhaps, one for you," she began. "I've been thinking—if you feel this strongly about having an animal in the house, I might see my way to taking in one that we agree on. A very miniature poodle type, perhaps? Or one of those teacup sort of dogs? They barely weigh a pound or two. I thought Jessica could advise us. We could look into it, in the New Year," she clarified, not entirely sure she was ready to commit to the idea, though she did want him to know she was at least willing to try to strike a compromise.

Ezra stared at her in shock, his mouth agape, and she felt a spark of triumph in her bold move. He knew her so well, she hardly ever caught him unawares.

"Does the idea appeal? I'm not made of stone. I can see that this situation has torn you in two."

"Bully for you, Lily. If you can see that much, I'm surprised you don't see that I only want my dog. Teddy. Not some yippy little bit of fluff with a bow in its fur. Can we have Teddy if I can find him? That's the question."

She sighed and closed her eyes, struggling to hold on to her last shred of patience. That was the question, indeed. Couldn't he see that Teddy was gone? Disappeared? Vanished? Finito? The question of Teddy was actually irrelevant. But she could hardly deal him those harsh truths right now.

"I'm trying to compromise, Ezra. What more can you ask?"

Ezra pressed the button on the automatic chair, the sound of the motor nearly drowning out her words.

"I'll be straight home after the service," she shouted over the noise. "I'd better find you here nursing that cold, not traipsing around in the woods somewhere."

The chair had reached the landing and the noise stopped. Lillian heard him blow his nose in answer.

Sunday's frenzy at the diner more than made up for Saturday's lull. Lucy had planned to pull off her apron at a quarter to nine and dash up to church, but she was unable to swim against the tide of the breakfast rush. After a while, she gave up.

They were serving not only many in the crew but everyone who had heard the movie people were eating at the Clam Box now. It was absolute mayhem for a while. Charlie had also sent a breakfast buffet to the set, which would be followed by lunch. He had miscalculated their inventory, and a lot of items on the menu were eighty-sixed, which Lucy thought was embarrassing.

The nonstop race from the dining room to the kitchen and back again distracted her a bit from watching the door. She dreaded the sight of Craig entering and strained to hear a word or two of his whereabouts. She assumed he was on the set. With any luck, the director would keep him so busy, making up for the time he'd been in the hospital, that he wouldn't make it to the diner until tonight—if at all.

Even the slim possibility of having to face him again had her nerves in a knot. When Charlie came up behind her at the ice machine, she nearly jumped out of her skin.

Caught up by some new affront, he didn't even notice. "Lucy, get this. Of all the luck, I just heard the big names—like Hamilton and his costars, and the director, too—are bunked at the Angel Island Inn now and are taking meals there. We're just getting the worker bees."

Lucy could have dropped to her knees with relief. "Really? Who told you that?"

"One of the sound engineers. It will be harder to get those T-shirts and aprons autographed. Maybe I should deliver the breakfast and lunch buffets to the set this week and track down the big names. I just heard they're not leaving until Wednesday."

Would Charlie really do that? Craig would certainly know the shameless autograph hunter was her husband. She cringed with embarrassment at the possibility.

"I don't know if that will work, Charlie. You should see the security Hamilton had at the hospital. I doubt you'd get within twenty feet of him."

He rubbed his chin, considering her warning. "I didn't think of that. Maybe you're right. I suppose he could still come in here. He might get tired of the food at the inn."

Claire North, the inn's head cook, was one of the best in all of New England. She had been profiled in all sorts of travel magazines. Claire was mostly retired now, but Lucy had heard that the new cook, Kerry Redmond, was in the same league. If Craig got tired of their food that quickly, he ought to go back to the hospital for tests.

She glanced at Charlie, scooped ice into a row of pitchers, and carried them away.

So Craig wouldn't come to the diner after all. She felt almost dizzy with relief as the message sank in. But she was disappointed, too. And it was hard to admit that, even to herself. But it was final now. Craig would leave town in a few days, and she would not see him again. She would miss the once-in-a-lifetime chance that had been dropped in her lap, as Fran would say, like a gift she refused to open.

That's what would happen now. It felt . . . anticlimactic. But this was what she wanted, Lucy reminded herself. Wasn't it?

LILLIAN WAS PERFECTLY ABLE TO GET INTO HER HOUSE ON HER OWN, but Emily insisted on helping. She did need someone to carry the packages while she concentrated on maneuvering the cane. If she didn't focus, it sometimes got away from her, especially outdoors when the ground was icy.

She stepped inside and called out before she'd even taken off her coat, "Ezra? I'm back. Are you upstairs sleeping? We brought soup.

And some of those French rolls you like, from the bakery. And a chocolate cupcake," she added.

The sweet was Emily's idea. Ezra did love cupcakes, and it would cheer him up.

The house was silent. "He's not answering," she said to Emily.

"Maybe he's asleep, Mother. That's the best thing for a bad cold."

"I suppose. Why don't you run up and check on him? I'll take the soup into the kitchen and warm it up."

Emily headed for the staircase. Better to send a neutral emissary, Lillian thought. Ezra was so cross with her. If she'd gone up to coax him down, he might just roll over out of spite.

She made her way into the kitchen and set the bakery bag on the counter. She rarely used the stove these days. They even had an electric thing to heat water for tea. It went off automatically, so one couldn't burn the house down or die in one's bed from a leaky gas burner.

She searched around a cupboard and found a small pot that would do. Then she pulled open a drawer for the big cooking spoon. And there it was, in plain view. Right next to her days-of-the-week a.m.-and-p.m. pill container was a note from Ezra, written in big letters on a sheet from a yellow legal pad.

Had a call about Teddy. Too promising to miss. I have gone
to investigate. I have my cell phone and will be home
shortly. Please don't worry about me.

—Ezra

Lillian felt her heart skip a beat and her blood rush to her head. She pressed her hand to her chest and gripped the counter for support.

Emily found her that way as she walked into the kitchen. "Mother, what is it? You're pale as a sheet. Sit down, please."

"It's Ezra. He's lost his mind," she managed as Emily helped her to a chair. "He's going to die of pneumonia, and I'll have a stroke. All because of a mangy little dog."

She handed Emily the note. "He's gone out again, with a fever. And who knows what else is wrong with him. When I specifically told him to stay put. This behavior beggars belief."

"He cares so much, he's not thinking about himself," Emily said.

"He'll put himself in the hospital and they'll have to strap him to the bed like a mental patient."

"I hope not." Emily sounded worried. "I'll go out and look for him. Where do you suppose he's headed?"

Lillian threw up her hands. "I haven't the foggiest. If I knew, I'd go myself and drag him back by the scruff of his neck."

"Let me make a call or two. Maybe one of the officers out on patrol has seen him." Emily pulled out her phone and stepped into the dining room. She had been long gone from the village hall, but she still had connections. She'd been respected and even beloved as mayor. Lillian had been so proud. She never could understand why her daughter had stepped down. That lowdown diner owner Bates finally beat her in an election, after years of trying, but only by a handful of votes.

Lillian had always thought Emily could bounce back and win again by a landslide once the town had a taste of Charlie Bates as mayor. But the thrill was gone for Emily. She had moved on to other things. She did seem happier out of office. Certainly more relaxed and patient, at any rate.

"If you do see him, Tucker," Lillian heard her saying, "please tell him that my mother is worried and encourage him to come home. He has a bad cold and he shouldn't really be out."

She returned to the kitchen. "The police are going to look for him. They'll spot him soon, I'm sure."

Lillian sighed. "I hope it's soon enough."

Before she could say more, she heard someone at the side door, using a key. The door opened, and there was Ezra, muffled to within an inch of his life. All she could see of his face were his blue eyes behind his glasses. But that was enough. They looked bright with fever.

He glanced at her. "You found my note?"

"I did," she said simply. "Come in, come in. You must be chilled to the bone. We have your soup. Emily will heat it."

"How do you feel, Ezra?" Emily asked. "You don't look well."

"About the same as this morning, I suppose." It took a while for Ezra to remove his layers of warm clothing. Then he walked with weary steps into the kitchen, hardly able to lift his feet.

"You look worse to me. Much worse." When Lillian pressed her hand to his forehead, he didn't bat an eye or raise his usual objections.

"Good gravy! You're burning up. Straight to bed. Emily, please get him upstairs and put a cool compress on his head. I'll bring some water and aspirin. And hot tea."

Ezra submitted to their care without a word. That worried Lillian even more, enough to drive all thought of scolding him for this outrageous behavior clear out of her head.

CHAPTER FOURTEEN

HE DOOR TO JOE'S OFFICE WAS PARTLY OPEN, BUT LAUREN knocked anyway. It was after six on Tuesday night, and the rest of the staff had gone home. Lauren would have gone straight home herself after a nerve-racking rush-hour drive back from Boston but had driven past the office and seen Joe's car parked in front. She wanted to deliver her news face-to-face.

He looked up, surprised to see her. Then he stood up from his chair, his eyes questioning. "How did it go? Why didn't you call? I was waiting."

She could see he was braced for bad news. Why else would she have delayed reporting in? Lauren tried to keep a straight face as she delivered a summary of her meeting with the attorneys who represented Dendur Software.

"They want to settle out of court. They tried to lowball us with six figures, but I got them up to seven, eventually. There are still a few details to iron out, but they'll confirm the important points of the offer in writing promptly. The email might already be in my inbox."

Joe pressed his hands to his desk for support. "You're joking. Right?"

She shook her head, her smile so wide it hurt. "I was surprised, too. To put it mildly. Especially after their hard-nosed attitude over the phone." Just setting up a meeting with the law firm that represented Dendur had taken major negotiating skills. "Are you sorry now that you didn't come? I never meant to cut you out."

"I know. I do regret that I missed it," he admitted. "But it was the first meeting. It's a sizing-up-the-competition thing. Usually."

They had discussed going together but had decided Lauren would fly solo for this first meeting, which they had both predicted would be preliminary and nonproductive. They had expected that the opposition would simply gauge how seriously Dendur should take the claim— which was no longer just Maddie's claim, but that of three other former female employees.

"I never expected a deal to be struck this fast, believe me," Lauren said honestly.

"And they never expected to face such a tough negotiator, I'd bet." His praise made her feel good. "The affidavits of the other women obviously pushed them to get out in front on this."

"Seems so." She flopped into a chair, feeling weary but victorious. "They were looking down the barrel of a class action suit and didn't like the view. All the same, they did move quickly. But once a bombshell like this hits, some companies want to clean it up quickly, before the New Year."

"Whatever the reason, you did well today, Lauren. It's an awesome victory for Maddie and the rest of our clients. For all the women in their profession, too."

Lauren did feel that way. She'd used her superpowers for good, as Cole would say.

She reached into her briefcase and handed Joe her notes. "When it was over, I thought I should have pressed for more. But I did my best."

Joe glanced down at her hastily scribbled pages, the major points of the offer circled and underlined, including the settlement figure.

His eyes went wide again. "Whoa . . . I'd say you did great. I doubt I could have squeezed out that number." He looked up at her. "We should call Maddie. And the other clients. We should celebrate."

Lauren nodded and smiled. "Absolutely. But maybe not tonight? I mean, not for me." She felt as if she'd gone eleven rounds in the heavyweight ring. "Why don't you tell Maddie the good news, and I'll call her tomorrow?"

Lauren was Maddie's attorney, but Joe was the head of the firm. All things considered, it seemed right that he should tell her about their victory. When Lauren saw his pleased expression, she added, "Maybe you and Maddie should go out tonight to celebrate? You can go over the settlement with her."

They still needed Maddie and the other clients to approve the deal Lauren had negotiated, and the sooner the better.

"You really don't mind?" Joe said.

"Not at all. If it weren't for Maddie, this injustice would never have been brought to light. I think she deserves some special acknowledgment."

"I think so, too," he agreed.

Lauren left his office with the distinct feeling that Joe meant more than what he'd said. She hoped so. And she hoped his evening with Maddie was the start of something more than their attorney-client relationship.

That would feel like a victory as well—but one she would celebrate privately.

* * *

LUCY HAD BEEN CALLED IN FOR A SHIFT AT THE HOSPITAL ON TUESDAY morning, and she clocked out at five. With the rush-hour traffic, she didn't reach the highway exit for the village until well after seven. Not that getting home late tonight mattered much. Charlie was still at the dinner. The boys and Zoey wouldn't be home until Christmas Eve on Thursday. Of course, she still had plenty on her to-do list before their visit—cleaning the house, shopping, and cooking, not to mention baking the Christmas cookies they loved . . . and expected to find piles of. It never really seemed like work, though, because she loved having them at home so much.

There was one task on the list unconnected to her family, or even to Christmas. "A secret mission," she called it privately. After refusing to see or talk to Craig Hamilton, she had surprised herself one sleepless night and decided to write him a letter, so she could put all her feelings and recollections—and conclusions—on paper. The same kind of letter he'd told her he'd wanted to write but never had.

She had not intended to give it to him. She just thought the exercise would be a good way to exorcise the troubling feelings and memories that filled her head. But once she sat down and set pen to paper, *Why not share it with him?* she asked herself. He'd told her that he wanted to know her side of things. It was certainly easier to be honest—totally honest—when she wasn't facing him.

In the middle of the night, she sat and set it all down, a pot of tea at hand. Charlie was upstairs, deeply asleep, without the slightest idea of what she was going through as she relived the headiest, most emotional days of her life. *Among the most*, she qualified. Certainly among the most painful.

When she was finally done, with the pages folded and slipped into a clean, white envelope, Lucy had felt immeasurably better, as if a weight had lifted off her shoulders—and her heart. She decided there and then that she wouldn't tuck the letter into the back of a drawer or toss it in the trash. She would make sure Craig received it before he left, which she guessed would be Wednesday, or even Thursday, Christmas Eve.

She had heard the cast and crew were at a wrap dinner at the Spoon Harbor Inn tonight. She could leave the letter at the Inn on Angel Island, where he was staying, without risk of running into him. If she ran into Claire North, or Liza Merritt, who owned the inn, she would just say the actor had left something at the diner. That was a plausible excuse.

She turned off the highway and headed for the island. The detour wouldn't take long, but the adventure was nerve-racking. It would be worth it, she decided as she drove across the narrow land bridge and the island loomed large in her view. Lucy congratulated herself for devising this solution and for finding the courage to carry it out. It was the right thing to do.

The beautiful inn shone like a guiding star in the dark, clear night. All the windows on the lower floor were filled with warm, yellow light, and small white candles glowed in the windows above. Swoops of pine garlands and big wreaths decorated the wide porch. She had forgotten how lovely the inn looked during the holidays. At least Craig had landed in a comfortable and even elegant place after his hospital stay.

She had considered leaving the letter in the mailbox on the side of the road, then worried that it might not be given to him before he left. She parked her car in the curving drive and climbed up the steps to the front door. Should she knock and leave it with Claire or Nolan? Or step inside for a moment and drop it on a hall table?

While Lucy stood silently debating, the sound of heavy footsteps coming up the porch steps made her turn. She nearly gasped out loud when she recognized Craig.

"Hello, Lucy." He tilted his head to the side, obviously surprised to see her.

Caught off guard, she could hardly find her voice. "Hello, Craig. I didn't expect to see you here. Isn't there a party tonight for the cast and crew?"

"There is. But I felt a little done in after the shooting today and decided to skip it. Besides, it's not a wrap for me. I need to stay a few more days to film the scenes I missed while I was sick."

Lucy hadn't even thought of that. "But how can you do that with most everyone else gone?"

He smiled. "The magic of the movies—and computers. They somehow manage to patch me in. I'm not sure I understand it myself, but no one seems the wiser when they watch the film."

"Interesting." She felt the sharp edge of the envelope in her pocket and had the impulse to just pull it out, shove it at him, and run away.

But he sought her gaze and held it, and she felt frozen in place. "I've just been for a walk; it's a beautiful night. Did you come to see Claire? Or Liza? I think they're out."

"Uh . . . no," she answered honestly. She took a breath. "I came to drop something off. For you, actually." She pulled out the letter and showed it to him. "I didn't expect to see you. I thought the coast was clear. I know I was obstinate about speaking to you. But I hope this makes up for that. At least a little."

He took the envelope from her hand and gazed down at it. "It's a letter," she explained.

He smiled. "I noticed. Thank you. Thank you very much."

His expression was so surprised and his tone so warm and sincere that she felt the last shred of resistance, and even anger, melt away.

"I'm sorry, Craig. For the way I've acted toward you since you came here, and for the things I've said. I'm sorry that I couldn't find it in my heart to accept your apology. Or even let you have your say. That was selfish. And mean-spirited. I'm not usually like that," she added quietly.

"I'd never use those words to describe you, Lucy. Even now. You don't need to apologize to me, not after what I did."

"I'm not so sure. I think I just wanted to hurt you. I know that sounds so immature. But I can't deny it."

Before he could reply, she added, "Look, I wrote a whole long letter, probably saying more than you even want to know about how I feel now and what I felt then. The long and the short of it is, I accept your apology. I want you to know that I tried to understand why you did what you did. We were very young, Craig. Too young for the plans and commitment we made with each other."

"You were my first love, Lucy. I loved you with all my heart. But we *were* young," he agreed. "When I really considered the consequences of taking you away from here—from your family and friends and everything you held dear—I couldn't do it. I was afraid I wasn't enough for that bargain. I was afraid that I couldn't make you happy. I'd persuaded you to leave and acted as if I had all the answers—as if it would be so easy to find our way in California and make it as actors. I made some big promises, didn't I?"

"But you are a success, Craig. That wasn't an empty promise."

"You're too kind. Always were. I beat the odds, somehow, but it wasn't easy. It was hard work, with a lot of rejections, and I often doubted I could make it. But ultimately, I was lucky." He paused, gathering his thoughts. "What I'm trying to say is, you trusted me. I was older and should have known better. When it came right down to the wire, I got cold feet. All I could think of was how much you'd regret leaving with me and how I'd ruin your life. I was afraid that in time, you'd end up hating me." He swallowed hard and shook his head. "Instead, I took the coward's way out and did something that made you hate me immediately, not one far-off day when our plans didn't turn out as we'd imagined. When you realized that I don't have all the answers."

"I never hated you," she insisted. Then had to smile. "Well, maybe for a minute or two."

They both laughed, but she also felt tears fill her eyes and hoped he didn't notice in the dim light. Hearing his side of their story had moved her, more than she ever expected.

"It took me a long time to see it, Craig. But you did the right thing. You did it the wrong way," she added, in a tone a bit sharper than she'd intended. "But maybe it was the only way you could have managed at the time. I can see that now."

He looked surprised by her insight. "I think so, too . . . I wish I'd been braver. What made it even harder was knowing, even on that night, that part of me will always love you. Despite everything that happened between us, and everything that's happened to me since, you'll always have a special place in my heart, Lucy. Nothing can ever change that."

She was speechless at his admission. "Thank you for saying that. You didn't have to."

"I did. It's true," he insisted. "I wish I'd told you long before now. And apologized before now, too."

"Well, maybe what always kept me so mad at you is that, deep down, I've always known that you have a place in my heart, too. I really hated that," she added with a laugh, "but it's true."

He laughed with her, and she could see that his eyes were shining with unshed tears, too. He still had the letter in his hand, and he slipped it into the breast pocket of his jacket. "I'm going to read this carefully. A few times. I can't tell you what it means to me. And what it means to have this talk tonight. Thank you, Lucy."

"You don't have to thank me. I'm happy I came. Finally." She stepped back, struggling to calm her emotions. "What will you do for Christmas? Will you work straight through?"

"We'll take Christmas Day off. A handful of us will be here, and Claire's cooking us a special dinner. My wife wanted to come East, but our daughter is expecting our first grandchild any minute. At least one of us needs to be there, right?"

"Right," she agreed. Lucy felt bad for him. "It must be hard on you, missing Christmas with your family and the baby's arrival, too."

"It's not what I want. But it comes with the territory. We're used to it by now."

His family, he meant. Lucy knew she wouldn't have liked that part of being married to a famous actor, having a husband who was always traveling for his career and missing such important moments.

Who knows what would have happened if they had stayed together? The strain of that life may have taken its toll. Or they might have married too young and started a family, and Craig might have never pursued acting with the focus and commitment needed to become a big star.

It was impossible to know now how the story might have gone. And she didn't dwell on the path not taken.

At least he would be among friends on Christmas, and the inn was a lovely place to celebrate the day, albeit quietly.

He gazed at her. "I'd invite you in, but I think you'd decline."

"I would," she agreed, "though it's good of you to offer."

"I may not see you before I go, Lucy. You stay well. I know you'll always be beautiful in my eyes, inside and out." He leaned forward and gave her brief but tight hug.

She hugged him back, and a bittersweet feeling swept through her heart. "Thank you, Craig. Take care of yourself."

"I will," he promised, as he stepped back. "You, too."

She couldn't summon up the word "goodbye," so she just said, "Good night."

Then she ran down the steps to her car and pulled away. She glanced back once and saw him, silhouetted by the porch light. He was still standing there, watching as she drove off into the night.

THE MINUTE SHE GOT HOME, LAUREN TOOK A LONG, HOT SHOWER and pulled on cozy sweats and fluffy slippers. She felt exhausted but content, like a warrior who had returned from a good day on the battlefield. Her dad was watching TV, and Betty was doing homework in her room, a final quiz before the Christmas break.

In the midst of a dinner salad she tossed together, Lauren called the other clients involved in the Dendur Software case. They would receive documentation as soon as the details were worked out, but all the women reacted with surprise and gratitude at the news of the offer.

Not one had expected to win justice against the corporation, even though they knew their claims were valid. It felt good to tell them right could prevail, and the little guy—or gal—could win some of the time.

Cole was the last call she made, from the privacy of her room. He had sent a text earlier in the day, to find out how the meeting had gone. It was thoughtful of him to remember she was facing such a big day. It made her feel that they were growing closer, which she wanted— when she forced herself not to think of the complications and challenges that waited down that road, and not so far off either. Sometimes she felt they were practically in view.

He let her tell the whole story, without interruption, which must have been an act of will. She was so tired, she heard herself rambling.

"I'm proud of you. But not surprised. You were very intimidating representing the golf club, in your high heels and power suit."

"I *was* going for intimidating, now that you mention it. I'm lucky I didn't slip in the mud and fall flat on my . . . suit. Right in front of you."

"I was wishing that you would," he admitted with a laugh. "But you were really on fire with this case. I saw that when you talked about it Saturday night. Maybe this is what you've been looking for, Lauren, an area of law you feel passionate about. Maybe this is where you should look for a new job."

Lauren had already come to that conclusion. She'd even applied for a position at a firm in New York that specialized in employee rights, especially the rights of women in the workforce. But for some reason, she wasn't ready to tell Cole about that possibility. She was afraid of where the conversation would lead.

"Listen, what are you and Phoebe doing for Christmas Eve? My parents always have a huge party. Family, friends, everyone. No pressure, but would you like to come? My mom suggested it," she added, hoping he wouldn't think she was moving too fast with their relationship. Coming to a family gathering on a holiday was big. And even though Lauren had thought of it, she hadn't had the courage to follow through until her mother voiced the suggestion and then more or less nagged Lauren to get an answer.

She was still of two minds about asking and now waited, holding her breath.

"That sounds fun. I bet there'll be some great food."

"You can count on that. And way more than needed."

"We'd love to come. Thanks for thinking of us. But I think Phoebe and I should keep the traditions we set with Amy. We would always put up our tree on Christmas Eve and get ready for Santa Claus. This year, moving to a new place, it's important for Phoebe that we keep things the same. She's already talking about the night's agenda. If we do something different, she might think I've forgotten about her mom. Does that make any sense?"

"It makes a lot of sense. I totally understand. It might be confusing and send the wrong message."

"I'm sorry to turn you down, but I think it might."

Lauren felt disappointed that Cole and Phoebe would not be at the party, but also relieved. Their presence would have created a lot of pressure for her. Everyone in her family—especially her sisters and mom—would make assumptions and ask too many questions. Cole would have felt pressured, too. Considering that she still planned to leave in January, or sometime soon after, it was best not to get in that deep.

"I have a little gift for Phoebe. And one for Wilbur," she told him. She had one for Cole, too, though she wasn't ready to admit that. "Can I drop them off on Christmas Day?"

After the Christmas Eve bash, her family gathered again at Jessica and Sam's house in the early evening on Christmas for a casual dinner. There would be plenty of time to see Cole and Phoebe before that.

"Please do. We have a few little things for you, too. If the glue dries in time," he teased.

She laughed and wondered how she was going to leave here when the holidays were over and her break in Cape Light finally came to an end.

CHAPTER FIFTEEN

⤙✦⤚

*L*UCY WAS ALWAYS TAKEN OVER BY A CERTAIN FEELING AT church on Christmas Eve. She waited for the service to begin and gazed around at familiar faces, everyone dressed in their best. She returned greetings and good wishes. So many of the regular churchgoers were there, accompanied by children and grandchildren, and even friends and relatives who had come from afar to celebrate the holiday.

The sanctuary was decked out in finery befitting the celebration, with swooping pine garlands and dozens of red and white poinsettias arranged around the altar. It was one of the few evening services of the year, and she loved how candles glowed in every corner and the images on the stained glass windows reflected deep, rich, jewel-like colors.

She sat with her three children, all of them looking very well-dressed and grown up, she thought. She couldn't deny her pride in "showing them off." More than that, a certain indescribable sense of contentment and peace that had nothing to do with material accomplishments dropped over her like a finely spun shawl. A keen awareness of her blessings filled her heart with humility and gratitude.

She hadn't noticed Craig in the sea of faces, though a few members of the film crew had taken seats in the back pew. Perhaps he wasn't coming tonight. She didn't plan on speaking to him again but thought it would nice to see him one last time, even from a distance—and for him to see her children.

Charlie was a deacon and still rushing about, finding latecomers a seat. As if he were still in the diner, she thought with a fond smile. In his best suit and tie, with a fresh haircut and a clean shave, he looked like a very different man than the guy behind the counter at the Clam Box.

The organist began a prelude, and Charlie slipped into the seat she had saved for him. He glanced over and smiled. "Is that a new dress? I like the color. It suits you."

Lucy was surprised he'd noticed but pleased by the compliment. "Zoey helped me pick it out."

Her daughter had refused to let Lucy leave the dark green satin dress at the store, insisting that the garment made Lucy look exactly like some redheaded actress. Lucy hadn't even recognized the name. But Zoey was so sweet, and definitely Lucy's biggest cheerleader. "If you don't buy this dress, I will. And I'll give it to you for Christmas."

Lucy had to take it. She couldn't let Zoey give her such an extravagant gift. She wouldn't feel right.

"She was right. You look very pretty."

Before she could thank him, a sharp note sounded the start of the opening hymn. Everyone stood up. Charlie squeezed her hand. He opened a hymnal and quickly found the page for "Hark! The Herald Angels Sing." She turned to share the book, and he slipped his arm around her shoulder.

The choir marched up the center aisle at a stately pace, their voices blending in beautiful harmonies. Reverend Ben followed at the very end. He still had a strong voice and sang in a deep baritone.

When the hymn was over, he greeted the worshippers, hands stretched wide, his eyes sparkling. "Welcome to our Christmas Eve service, church members and guests. Anyone and everyone who has gathered here tonight to share the good news."

The opening prayers were said, and Sophie Potter came up to read a scripture from the Old Testament. Lucy had always loved Sophie. How could anyone not? With Zoey dating Sophie's grandson James for so long now—and recently getting engaged—Lucy had begun to look upon Sophie, and her three daughters and son, as family. The Potters were a closely knit group, with good values. Lucy could see that in James and felt fortunate that her daughter had found such a fine young man and would soon be part of the Potter clan.

Sophie stepped up to the pulpit, her short, stout figure swathed in a flowered dress with black velvet trim, her white hair wound in a big bun at the back of her head. Reverend Ben smiled as she approached and adjusted the microphone for her.

She carefully put on a pair of glasses and gazed down at the Bible. Lucy usually enjoyed the New Testament scripture better than the Old Testament. She found it so much more accessible. Yet, the Old Testament was often so much more poetic. Sophie all but sang out the verses from Psalm 96.

"'Oh, sing to the Lord a new song! Sing to the Lord, all the earth. Sing to the Lord, bless His name.'"

It was a long passage that ended with powerful images. Sophie did them justice, reading in a clear, strong voice.

"'—Let the heavens rejoice, and let the earth be glad; Let the sea roar, and all its fullness; Let the field be joyful, and all that *is* in it. Then all the trees of the woods will rejoice before the Lord . . .'"

Lucy was sure she'd heard the words before. But tonight, she really pictured it, all of nature rejoicing at the news of the baby born in the manger. It was a beautiful notion.

Sophie removed her glasses, and with Tucker's help, she carefully stepped down from the pulpit and took her seat again.

Reverend Ben came up to take her place. He had been sitting beside his wife, Carolyn, in the first pew to the right of the pulpit, along with his daughter, Rachel, and her family, and his son, Mark, and his family.

"The scripture for tonight from the New Testament is from the Book of Luke, chapter two," he announced.

He stared down at the Bible with a solemn expression and pushed his glasses to the bridge of his nose.

"'Now there were in the same country shepherds living out in the fields, keeping watch over their flock by night,'" he began in an animated, storyteller's voice. "'And behold, an angel of the Lord stood before them, and the glory of the Lord shone around them, and they were greatly afraid. Then the angel said to them, "Do not be afraid, for behold, I bring you good tidings of great joy which will be to all people."'"

His quiet, steady tone rose with emotion. "'"For there is born to you this day in the city of David a Savior, who is Christ the Lord. And this *will be* the sign to you: You will find a Babe wrapped in swaddling cloths, lying in a manger."'"

He paused and gazed at the congregation for a moment. "'And suddenly there was with the angel a multitude of the heavenly host praising God,'" he reported, his voice filled with surprise. "'And saying: "Glory to God in the highest, and on earth, peace, goodwill toward men!"'"

Lucy found herself moved by the familiar words. The final message did sum up how she felt tonight—peaceful and filled with good intentions toward all. She knew that her talk with Craig wasn't the only reason, but it was certainly part of it. Ever since their meeting at the inn, she felt a burden had been lifted—one she hadn't even realized she'd been carrying.

Reverend Ben's gaze swept across the sanctuary. He smiled in his usual way, round cheeks hidden beneath his beard, which was mostly gray. "Well, it's finally here. Christmas Eve. The night we wait for, plan for, strategize and fret over for weeks. Even months. We have so many expectations about the holidays, don't we?

"We feel that way even if we consciously set out to keep it simple and not drive ourselves crazy hunting down the perfect gifts or decorating the most dazzling tree. And we all have memories of some past Christmas, mellowed over time, that raise the bar even higher. I don't know about you, but once that sense of expectation and wanting things to be just right gets a grip, it's hard for me to shake it.

"No matter how much I say, 'I don't need or want one thing this year,' I'm bound to describe a possible gift, or two, that I'd really, *really* love to find under the tree.

"Honestly, I not only describe it, I'm likely to email the precise information about where this particular item can be purchased. And a link to buy it online. Maybe even a coupon for the store as well?"

Muffled laughter rose, with everyone recognizing their own tendency to do the same. "Some say Christmas is a time for surprises," he continued. "But I don't know many people who like to be surprised that way. Who say, 'Oh, surprise me. Just get me anything.' Even if they aren't as fastidious and controlling as yours truly, I think they must be hoping that the gift giver knows what they want. Or has some idea?"

He paused again, his expression thoughtful. "Of course, there are always those gift givers who *completely* ignore your request and bestow something out of the blue. A gift that you were never expecting or never asked for. One that might end up in the attic or basement or donation bag? Or possibly regifted, as people say?"

He paused until more muffled laughter subsided. "God knows what we want and need. He knows the perfect gifts for us, better than we do. As the first and greatest Gift Giver of them all. You could say He's also the Supreme Surpriser—surely in the way He answers our prayers."

He looked down at the Bible again for a moment. "In tonight's Scripture passage, the angel told the shepherds—and I'm paraphrasing here—'Don't be afraid. I have good news. Your prayers have been answered. God has sent you a great gift. A savior. Your new king.'" He stopped a moment and looked out at them. "Can you imagine what the shepherds pictured at that moment? Who they pictured, I mean? A nobleman, for sure. Dressed in fancy robes, a big, jewel-studded crown on his head. A powerful man. Doubtlessly, one with an army at his command. But then the angel said, 'Look for a baby, who was just born in a manger, surrounded by animals and wrapped in rags.'"

He let out a long breath and smiled thoughtfully. "That is how the shepherds' prayer had been answered, how the gift they had asked for was delivered. Herein lies a powerful lesson at the heart of the Christmas story."

He paused and leaned forward. "God loves to surprise us, to confound our expectations. Not by ignoring our requests but by sending the gift in a way that we *never* imagined or expected. But a perfect way, we soon discover. A far better version of our prayer fulfilled than what we asked for.

"This child of lowly birth, who came into the world in such a humble way, marked a new day, a fresh start, for all of humanity. That's what God gives us on Christmas, a fresh start.

"A new heart to embrace the many blessings that arrive today, and every day. Often, in a way so unexpected, it's difficult to recognize. Just as Jesus was, the night of His birth. Unfortunately, we don't have angels hovering nearby to cue us in. Well, most of us don't," he added with a grin. "We must rely on our own hearts. A heart that is open and trusts the great Giver's plan for our life—that is the best way to accept His blessings.

"I pray that all the gifts you receive tonight and tomorrow, and all through the year to come, are perfect for you, in their way. May this Christmas mark a fresh start for all of humanity, leading us in a new and better direction. Merry Christmas."

Lucy knew the minister didn't mean gifts wrapped in paper and bows. He meant the kind that life delivers, out of the blue, like Craig's return to the village after all these years, and the chance she'd been offered to make amends.

The congregation was very quiet as Reverend Ben left the pulpit. The choir rose and began one of her favorite hymns, "O Come, All Ye Faithful."

Lucy leaned over and whispered to her husband, "That was a wonderful sermon, don't you think?"

Charlie nodded in reply and squeezed her hand. She could tell that he, too, had been moved by the minister's words.

When it came time to share blessings and concerns, Reverend Ben recognized a hand at the back of the sanctuary. Lucy turned to see Craig seated among his colleagues. She hadn't even noticed him slip into the sanctuary.

"Yes, Mr. Hamilton? Do you have a blessing to share with us tonight?"

"I do," he said, coming to his feet. "First, I'm thrilled to report that a very amazing Christmas gift for me and my wife arrived late last night. We were blessed with our first grandchild. A little girl, eight pounds, two ounces, named Nadia. She and her mother—our daughter, Kate—are doing very well and I can't wait to get home and hold her."

The congregation responded with a round of applause. "Congratulations," Reverend Ben said above the clapping. "That's wonderful news."

"I must add that I'm so grateful for all the wonderful cards and messages I received at the hospital. I'm sure those kind attentions helped me bounce back so quickly. Our entire crew wants to thank everyone in this church and in this town for making us feel so very welcome. I can easily remember why I loved it here so much," he added. "Maybe I'll come back someday."

Craig caught Lucy's gaze and held it. He smiled ever so slightly, but she knew his smile was for her alone. She felt as if he was trying to telegraph the message that he was also thankful for her letter and the way she had finally talked things out with him. She was thankful for that, too.

It wasn't the happy ending you might see in some romantic movie. But it was the perfect ending for them. Reverend Ben had been right about that.

A short time later, Lucy and Charlie made their way through the busy parking lot behind the church. Charlie held her arm as she wobbled on her dressy black heels. She wasn't used to wearing them, and the toe part pinched. It was amazing what women went through for a bit of glamour.

She dropped into the passenger seat with a sigh and slipped off the shoes for a few minutes' relief.

The Bates family was spending Christmas Eve with the Tulleys. Fran and Tucker's children, a daughter and son, were both married and had little ones of their own. And there were plenty of other Tulleys in town who might be there. Tucker had a large family, and few had left the area.

Tomorrow would be a quieter day, in their own home, celebrating and opening gifts with their children and Lucy's mother.

She was looking forward to that even more.

Charlie slid behind the wheel and shut his door. Lucy was so busy massaging her toes, she barely noticed that he hadn't started up the car.

"Why are you waiting? The kids are all going separately."

"I know. Good thing, too. No one else would fit in this car."

Which was true. The hatch and back seat were filled with gifts and containers of carefully wrapped food that they were bringing to the Tulleys' celebration.

"Since we're unlikely to have another minute on our own for the rest of the night, I think I should give you this now." Charlie opened the glove compartment and took out a large, square blue velvet box.

He held it out to her, watching her reaction. All she could say was, "What is this, Charlie? A gift? For me?"

"I was going to put it under the tree. But I want you to have it now, honey. Go ahead. Open it," he urged her.

Lucy took the box in her hand, feeling a little nervous. She never asked Charlie for jewelry, and he wasn't the sort of husband who came home with extravagant surprises. She could see that the gift meant a lot to him, and she hoped she liked it.

As she lifted the lid, her eyes grew wide at the sight of a beautiful necklace. The chain was made of woven threads of gold, with seed pearls set a few inches apart down the length of it. A dazzling, square-cut emerald in a simple gold setting hung from the center. It was one of the loveliest pieces of jewelry Lucy had ever seen. But this was not the first time she'd seen it. She'd met Zoey in Newburyport for lunch one day and they'd done some shopping together. Lucy had spotted the necklace in the window of a fancy jewelry shop and been mesmerized by the sight of it, which wasn't like her at all.

When Zoey had urged her to go inside and try it on, Lucy had laughed. "I wouldn't waste a salesperson's time like that, honey. I bet it costs a fortune. I'm never going to buy it."

But here it was, sitting right in her lap. It seemed like some sort of miracle.

"You like it, right?" Charlie asked, confused now about her reaction.

Lucy was so moved she could hardly speak. "I love it, Charlie. It's so beautiful. You didn't have to buy me such an expensive present, honestly. We can't afford this."

"Don't worry about that. The diner's done some good business this month with all the visitors in town. But that's not the point. I want you to have it. I really do."

When he'd asked her what she wanted for Christmas, she'd mentioned a bottle of her favorite perfume. Or a new winter parka. This gift was light-years beyond those modest requests.

"Are you sure? It seems awfully extravagant."

Charlie smiled. "Absolutely. I was looking for something special, and a little bird told me that you'd seen this in a store window. I think it was a Zoey bird."

Lucy wiped a tear from the corner of her eye. Drat—she almost never wore eye makeup, and now, when she finally put some on, it would be smeared to bits before she even got to the party.

He took her hand and squeezed it. "I know I'm not the easiest person to live with. Not by a long shot. Especially lately. Sometimes I don't know how you put up with me. And I know I don't say it nearly as much as I ought to, but finding you was the luckiest day of my life, Lucy. And it always will be. I don't know what I'd ever do without you. The wheels would fall off, honestly."

"Oh, Charlie. You know that's not true." Lucy was surprised by his words and warmed by the compliment. "Though I imagine Tucker would have his hands full."

They laughed again at the thought. "No one could ever replace you, Lucy." He took her hand and pressed it to his lips. "When I saw you in that pretty green dress, I thought you should wear this tonight, and enjoy it."

"I will." She opened the catch on the necklace and turned so that Charlie could fasten it. He squinted in the low light, but it was soon closed. She turned and checked her reflection in the rearview mirror.

"It's so lovely." She turned to him. "I'll cherish it always. And I'll pass it on to Zoey someday. Maybe she'll have a daughter who will wear it, too."

He grinned and snapped his fingers. "That little imp. That must have been her plan." He didn't mean it. He loved Zoey with all his heart and would do anything for her.

Lucy leaned over and kissed his cheek. He turned and hugged her tight, holding on longer than she expected. "Merry Christmas, honey."

"Merry Christmas," she said quietly.

He sat back and started the car. "I think I like giving you surprises. I ought to do it more often."

"That might take some getting used to," she admitted. "But you definitely hit this one out of the park."

He glanced at her and chuckled. She could tell that he was proud of her compliment. "I'm going to tell Tucker you said that."

Lucy smiled and glanced out her window. She looked forward to the party at Fran and Tucker's house. What other surprises might the night bring? Who could say?

"I DON'T MIND IF YOU GO WITHOUT ME, HONESTLY, LILLIAN. I'M JUST going to have a little soup and get back in bed."

Ezra had made it to the Christmas Eve church service, but when they returned home to pick up their presents and regroup before Emily arrived to take them to the Hardings' house, he'd settled in a heap in his favorite wingback chair.

"You don't want to go to the party?" Lillian couldn't quite believe it. Ezra loved parties. Especially this one. She was the one who detested the annual cattle call with Christmas decorations.

He shrugged and loosened his bow tie—a bad sign indeed. "I'd love to go. I just don't feel up to it. I don't want anyone to catch this cold. That would be very inconsiderate."

"It would be, if you were still contagious. You've been taking those pills that Dr. Harding gave you all week. I'm not sure it's an issue any longer."

Far be it from her to challenge him on the question. He was the doctor. Still, as sick as Ezra had been the past week, she felt sure that a cold bug was not the source of his ailments and low spirits. Not entirely. That scruffy lost dog was to blame.

"You go. Make my excuses. You need to give out our presents."

"I won't go out without you. They can come and just take the loot if they want it that much."

Lillian sat down on the couch, staking out her territory. She was testing him. Did he want to stay home so much that he'd deprive her of the gathering, too?

He leaned back and closed his eyes. "Suit yourself. But I don't want to spoil your Christmas Eve, Lily. I don't mean to," he mumbled, his words already thick with sleep.

She watched him for a moment; his breathing was deep but still raspy. She rose and covered him with an afghan; he didn't even notice. Perhaps it wasn't just a funk over the dog. This bug had knocked him off his feet.

What was the difference if she missed the Christmas party? No difference to her. Except there was nothing prepared for their dinner. Estrella always left something to heat up, but of course, there'd been no need of that today. Their housekeeper had left early to cook for her own family's Christmas party.

In the kitchen, Lillian pulled out a carton of eggs, opened it, and sniffed. It had been a while since she'd even made scrambled eggs and toast. But she could manage it tonight, with her back to the wall. There was still some chicken soup that Estrella had made for Ezra. He could have that, if he felt up to eating. She would urge it on him. He had to get his strength back.

The phone rang, and she found it on the counter. She could see from the screen that Emily was calling. "Mother? It's me. We're on our way. Are you two ready?"

"I was just about to call. We're not coming. Ezra doesn't feel up to it. He's already fallen asleep in his chair."

"Oh, that's too bad." Her daughter sounded sorry at the news. "Everyone will miss you."

"They'll miss Ezra, that's true," Lillian replied tartly. "Please relay our apologies to Molly and Matt. I'm sure they'll understand."

Matthew Harding had examined Ezra on Monday. The doctor knew the poor man's state. He wouldn't be insulted.

"I will. And I'll send over dinner. Maybe Dan or Sara will come by with it."

Lillian considered the offer. She was no fan of Molly's cooking, though the rest of the civilized world disagreed. Still, there had to be something among the many dishes set out tonight that would be better than scrambled eggs. Lillian found that if she carefully scraped off the gravy and sauces and avoided the spicy bits, she could usually sort out something edible. Like a scavenger hunt.

"All right. If you wish. We'll give out our gifts tomorrow, at Jessica's house. If Ezra is up to that visit. We'll see how it goes."

"Tell him we're sorry he feels so sick. Maybe a good night's sleep will do the trick."

"Perhaps," Lillian agreed. She said goodbye to her daughter and ended the call. As uncomfortable as she always felt at the noisy party, it did feel odd and unsettling to be home alone tonight. She hoped that they didn't miss Christmas Day dinner at Jessica's house tomorrow, too.

The infernal dog was to blame—for Ezra's horrific cold, and now for spoiling their Christmas as well.

LAUREN HAD ONLY BEEN TO LILLIAN WARWICK'S HOUSE ON PROVIdence Street once or twice. She had to drive slowly and watch the numbers. The big mansard-roofed Victorian loomed up out of the dark, a grand, three-story house, painted bluish gray and trimmed with white, the old-fashioned wooden shutters and front door a glossy black.

A pine wreath with a red bow hung from the door and a small tabletop Christmas tree was framed by a front window. The rest of the house was dark, and she wondered if Lillian and Ezra were asleep. Or perhaps they had both gone upstairs by now. Would they even hear her when she knocked?

Her mother had nominated her for the mission, since the car she'd been driving was the last in the driveaway. Emily had given her Lillian's cell phone number "just in case."

Lauren didn't mind taking a break from the party. She loved her family's annual celebration, but it did seem overwhelming this year, with everyone asking what she'd been up to and her having to explain how she didn't live in New York right now but planned to go back soon, or just being so vague that she was sure it seemed she was trying to hide something.

Her singleton status made her self-conscious, too. Her sister Jillian had invited her steady boyfriend for the first time, and Amanda was with her husband, Gabriel. All on her own this year, Lauren felt as if she stuck out like a skunk at a garden party. She knew it was silly but couldn't help the feeling, especially when relatives she didn't see often asked curiously after her long-gone boyfriend, Greg. She knew they meant well, but it felt like salt rubbed into the wound each time she had to admit the relationship was over.

Emily had told her to pull the car up to the side door; it was closest to the kitchen. Molly had sent a ton of food, enough to fill two cardboard boxes.

Lauren carried the first box to the door. To her surprise, a light within flashed on and Lillian appeared before Lauren had even knocked.

"My daughter told me to keep a lookout. You're Lauren, the oldest one, right?"

The oldest of her sisters, she meant, Lauren assumed. "That's right."

"You favor your mother," Lillian said.

Lauren wasn't sure if she meant that in a good way, considering the animosity between her mother and Lillian, but pretended to take the comment as a compliment.

"So I've been told. Here you are, special delivery. Merry Christmas," Lauren added.

The old woman eyed her suspiciously, as if she wondered why Lauren was being so nice. "Yes, Merry Christmas. Just bring that in the kitchen. Leave it on the counter. I'll sort it out."

Lauren did as she'd been asked. "How's Ezra? I heard he's sick."

"He needs some rest. He was not up to socializing in a huge crowd tonight."

Lauren sensed Lillian's disapproval of her mother's style of entertaining. If it was up to Lillian, families in the village would only host intimate dinner parties, with string quartets for entertainment.

"Give him our best. There's another box in the car. I'll bring it in."

"Another box of food? That's impossible. This offering will last at least a week." Lillian peered into the carton that was already on the countertop. "Even if I send some home with our housekeeper."

Lauren wasn't sure what to do. "You don't want the rest?"

Lillian shook her head. "At the risk of insulting anyone, certainly not. Waste not, want not. That's my motto."

Lauren suspected she had a few more, too, all equally rigid-sounding. "No one will be insulted. I'll bring it back."

"Please do. And please express our thanks to your mother for the gracious gesture. You really didn't need to interrupt your party for us."

Lauren headed for the door and pulled out her car keys. "It wasn't any trouble. It is Christmas."

"So I've heard," Lillian murmured as she followed. The old woman offered a crisp little wave and shut the door.

Lauren climbed into her car, suppressing a smile. Lillian Warwick was truly a one-of-a-kind personality. It was amazing to her how her aunt Jess and Jess's sister, Emily, had turned out so warm and easygoing.

She wasn't in any hurry to get back to the party and realized she shared that sentiment with Lillian tonight.

308

The gifts she'd bought and wrapped for Phoebe, Wilbur, and Cole were in a shopping bag in the back seat of the car, alongside the extra box of food, which was emitting a tempting aroma.

She'd spotted Cole and Phoebe in church and had wanted to wish them a merry Christmas. But at the end of the service, they'd been swept out of sight by the crowd and she'd been hurried outside by her family, who were all eager to get home and start their party.

Without giving the question too much thought—*Don't overthink things, Lauren*, a little voice reminded her—she headed toward Sawyer's Tree Farm instead of going back home. Maybe Cole and Phoebe would welcome her mother's special dishes and desserts. She was sure Wilbur, at least, would not refuse the offering.

Chapter Sixteen

*L*AUREN FELT A SUDDEN ATTACK OF NERVES AS SHE STOOD at the front door of Cole's cottage. Lights glowed behind the sitting room curtains, and she heard Christmas music—Burl Ives singing "Have a Holly Jolly Christmas." She felt as if she were intruding on their evening.

She would just hand him the box of food and the bag of the gifts and wish them a merry Christmas. She wouldn't even go in. Talk about departing from his family tradition; Cole might even be angry to see her there, interrupting this time with Phoebe.

But when he swung open the door and found her there, his expression immediately dispelled her panic. "Lauren, come in, come in," he said. "Phoebe was just talking about you."

Phoebe was kneeling on a kitchen chair; a big apron covered her fancy dress. She was up to her elbows in paste and glitter while Wilbur trotted about, a red satin bow fastened to his collar.

"We're making Christmas decorations. Our tree looks too bare," Phoebe explained.

"But it's a very pretty tree," Lauren said as she stepped into the small sitting room. The tree was in a stand near the sofa, opposite the small stone fireplace. A strand of colored lights had been wrapped around the branches, none too artfully, she noticed, and a few ornaments hung down here and there.

"We're just getting started. It will be perfect by the time Santa comes," Cole promised. He took the box of food from Lauren. "Let me help you with this. And please, take off your coat."

She did slip off her coat and scarf and tossed them on a chair. So much for dropping everything off and not even going inside. *But I don't need to stay long*, she reminded herself.

"That's some food from our family party. I had to make a delivery to Lillian and Ezra Elliot and thought you might like some, too. And these are just a few gifts," she added, offering him the shopping bag.

She followed him into the kitchen, where he started unpacking the box. "Wow, this looks great. Please thank your mom for us."

"I will. Her mission is to feed the world. She'll be thrilled to hear I reached this outpost."

He turned back to the box. "Smells great, too. I'm feeling hungry already."

"We need to finish the tree, Dad," Phoebe reminded him. She was trying to glue a nose on a cardboard reindeer's face, but the little pink pom-pom was stuck to her finger.

"Here, let me help you." Lauren removed the fuzzy ball from Phoebe's finger, then found it was stuck on her own. "How much glue did you put on this?"

"Too much," Phoebe admitted. Lauren laughed and stuck the pom-pom on her own nose. "How's that? Do I qualify to pull Santa's sleigh?"

Phoebe laughed. "You need antlers." She just happened to have a pair, made with pipe cleaners and decorated with gold glitter. She handed them over, and Lauren held them up on each side of her head. "How about now?"

"Perfect!" Phoebe declared. "Look, Dad."

Cole met her gaze and smiled. "She *is* perfect, now that you mention it."

Lauren glowed with the compliment but focused on helping Phoebe finish the many ornaments she had started. Working together, they completed enough to cover at least the front of the tree. There were others, the store-bought kind, wrapped in tissue paper inside many boxes scattered around the sitting room. Lauren let Phoebe and Cole hang them. Most seemed laden with sentimental value, and she didn't want to intrude.

Phoebe saw a dish of candy canes on the mantle and asked Cole if she could add them to the tree as a special touch.

"Just make sure you hang them high enough so they don't tempt Wilbur. Lauren will help you. And that dish of cookies for Santa better be in a safe place, too," he warned

"Wilbur has a sweet tooth," Phoebe whispered.

"I'm not surprised," Lauren whispered back. "Is it hard to live with a pig?"

"There are a few things we have to remember," Phoebe replied with a serious expression. "But we love him. Dad does, too." Lauren didn't doubt that.

Cole had been slipping in and out of the kitchen during the tree trimming and announced dinner was ready.

"Can you stay for a bite to eat?" he asked. "I bet your family is missing you already."

She suspected they might be but had texted her mother to say she'd made another stop. She checked her phone and saw just a question mark in answer.

Did she really want to return to the family party, or did she want to stay here? The answer was clear. If her parents and sisters didn't understand and got mad at her, so be it.

When she looked to the future, another chance to spend a special night like this with Cole and Phoebe seemed highly unlikely. Lauren knew for sure she couldn't pass up this one.

"I'd love to stay," she said finally. "There are so many people in our house right now, they'll hardly miss me. How can I help? Let me set the table or something."

Cole seemed pleased by her reply, and Phoebe was wildly delighted. With her help, the table was laid. Cole brought the many dishes over from the stovetop and oven, a combination of specialties sent by her mother—mixed greens with goat cheese; baked clams; stuffed mushroom; crab cakes; and beef tenderloin—and the entrée he'd prepared for himself and Phoebe, a tomato sauce and pasta bake that smelled wonderful.

Lauren sat across from Cole at the small table, with Phoebe between them and Wilbur roving around the kitchen, sniffing and snorting up any crumbs he could find.

At Cole's suggestion, they joined hands and he said a simple prayer. "Thank you, Lord, for this bountiful table, for all the gifts under the tree, and for our surprise guest. We're grateful for your many blessings on Christmas and always."

"And thank you for Wilbur," Phoebe shouted at the ceiling. Lauren met Cole's gaze and struggled not to laugh.

Dinner was not only delicious but the most fun she'd had in weeks. Phoebe was so excited about Santa coming, she could hardly eat or sit still in her seat.

"What did you ask Santa to bring you this year?" Lauren waited with interest for her answer.

"What didn't she ask for?" Cole cut in.

Phoebe answered the question. "A new LEGO set, and real boots to ride Buster. But the surprise I asked for most is a bike. A two-wheeler. A blue one with tassels on the handles and a bell. To warn everyone that I'm coming. And a basket in front. For Wilbur."

The vision made Lauren smile. "Good idea. But Wilbur will need a helmet, too, I guess."

Phoebe frowned. "I didn't think of that. Santa will remember, right?"

Cole glanced at Lauren. "If he doesn't, we'll figure it out. The thing is, honey, Wilbur is growing every day. You know how we talked about him going into the barn soon?"

Phoebe looked solemn and nodded. "I remember. But he has to get bigger, right?"

Wilbur seemed to know he was being discussed—or just knew the best time to beg at the table for scraps? He was sidled up to Phoebe, his head lifted against her leg and his nose just below the edge of the table as she stroked his silky head.

"I think he's just about there," Cole said quietly. "But we don't have to worry about that tonight. We'll figure it out after the holidays are over."

Lauren thought that was a good compromise. "Wilbur might like the barn. He'll make a lot of friends there. You're out at school all day. Maybe he gets lonely and wants someone to play with?"

Phoebe had been sneaking the pig a piece of pasta from her dish and looked up at Lauren. "I didn't think of that. I'll have to ask him."

Cole looked grateful for Lauren's suggestion. "Meanwhile, remember what I said about tonight?"

Phoebe's expression brightened. "Wilbur can pick the story?"

"That's right. Run up and get ready for bed. Then bring down some books he might like. You need to get to sleep, or Santa won't stop here tonight."

Phoebe didn't need to hear the instructions twice. She slipped off her chair and dashed out the kitchen door. Moments later, they heard her running up the staircase.

"It's so cute that she still believes in Santa," Lauren whispered to Cole.

He mocked a confused expression. "What do you mean, *still* believes? Is there some reason she shouldn't?"

She laughed at his reply, and his adorable expression made her heart do a backflip. She quickly rose and picked up dirty dishes to hide her reaction. They cleaned up the kitchen together, then set out cookies and cake on the table for dessert.

Phoebe came downstairs, wearing her pajamas, robe, and fuzzy slippers. Her little face had that freshly washed look. She dropped the picture books that were in her arms and made a beeline for the sweets. "Yum! Christmas cookies!"

"Just one to start, honey. And a glass of milk," Cole said. "You don't want a tummy ache."

Phoebe nodded, stuffing most of a large sugar-coated star into her mouth. "I made these with Christine and Jack Jr.," she said, talking through a mouthful of cookie. "Want to try one?"

Lauren knew she meant Christine Sawyer and her little boy. David and Christine lived just down the road from the tree farm.

"Yes, please. They look delicious." Lauren chose a Christmas tree with lopsided zigzags of colored icing. "Hmmm, these are good. Better than my mom's bakery." It was true, too. Because Phoebe had made them.

They were soon in the living room, sitting on the floor near the hearth, where orange flames flickered and danced. A real fireplace was more work than the gas kind her parents had in their family room, but Lauren loved the scent of the burning wood.

"Okay, let's see which book Wilbur wants to hear tonight." Phoebe spread out three books in the middle of their circle. All the stories seemed to include pigs, or at least farm animals. Lauren was not surprised. She was familiar with the titles, because of her little sister Betty, and impressed by the selection: *Click, Clack, Moo: Cows That Type*; *The Story of Peppa Pig*; and *The Three Little Wolves and the Big Bad Pig*, a reversal of the traditional big bad wolf story.

Phoebe put Wilbur in their midst. He sniffed each book, then started to chew the cover of the Peppa edition. "He wants Peppa again." Phoebe pulled him back, and he cuddled in her lap.

Cole picked up the winner and put the others aside. To Lauren's surprise, he held it out to her. "Would you like to read to us, Lauren? I'm beat from all the cooking."

She doubted that. Most of his culinary efforts had been heating the tins her mother had sent. But she was honored by the request. "I'd be happy to."

"Do you know who Peppa is?" Phoebe asked.

"Who doesn't know Peppa? She's my role model," Lauren stated. She caught Cole's grin but focused on starting the story. It was one of Phoebe's favorites and she asked to hear it a second time. Then she requested *Click, Clack, Moo*, and Cole took over.

Finally, it was time for Phoebe to head upstairs and get in bed. Her eyes were closing, and she rubbed them with her hands. "One more, please?"

"Tomorrow," Cole promised. "Maybe Santa will bring you some new books."

If the big guy fell short, Lauren had two picture books for Phoebe in her shopping bag of gifts.

"Time for bed. Say good night to Lauren," Cole reminded her.

"Good night, Lauren." Phoebe gave her a sweet hug. "I hope you had fun. Merry Christmas."

Lauren hugged her back. It was hard to let go. "I had the best Christmas Eve ever, Phoebe. I can't wait to hear if Santa delivers that blue bicycle. Let me know, okay?"

Phoebe stepped back and nodded, and Cole took her hand and led her to the stairs. Wilbur followed, trotting behind them as if he had a job to do.

Cole stopped and peered down at the pig, frowning.

"Can Wilbur sleep in my room tonight? Please? It's Christmas."

Cole looked doubtful, and Phoebe added, "He might scare Santa away if he's down here. He's a very good watch pig."

"A watch pig?" Cole echoed. He shook his head and laughed. "Okay, sweetie, but just for tonight. Because it's Christmas. Come on, Wilbur."

The pig did not need to be asked twice. He snorted and followed them at a fast clip for his stubby little legs.

Lauren waited in the living room as the muffled sounds of Phoebe brushing her teeth and being tucked in drifted down the stairs.

She found her shopping bag and set gifts for Cole and Phoebe under the tree. She felt self-conscious now about having bought gifts for them, though they were small items. It was unlikely Cole had gotten her anything, and he might feel awkward.

Then she wasn't sure what to do. She considered finding her coat and bag, so she'd look ready to go when Cole came down. Did he expect her to? She wasn't sure of that either.

Before she could decide, he appeared, smiling and shaking his head. "She fought it all the way but went out like a light as soon as her head hit the pillow."

He flopped onto one end of the couch, and she sat on the other side. *We'll just chat a minute or two. It would be rude to run off,* she told herself.

"All the excitement and anticipation tired her out, I guess," Lauren said.

"It's been building for weeks. But it's so nice to see her enjoy Christmas this year. The last two have been sort of grim," he admitted. "It sure helped to have you here."

Lauren felt the color rush to her cheeks. "It helped me, too. My annoying relatives were asking too many questions."

His expression was sympathetic. "About your plans?"

She nodded. "I know they were just trying to show interest, but it's hard to sound on top of your game when you're basically unemployed and recently dumped."

Cole's expression turned thoughtful. "Don't be so hard on yourself. You told me that you're taking a break. Recalibrating your course. I think that's wise. You'll end up in a happier place in the long run."

"I know. But I'm getting impatient to fill in the blanks. Maybe it's the New Year coming? It seems like the right time to know the answers. Does that make any sense?"

"Sure it does. Don't worry. You'll figure it out." He moved closer and put his arm around her. "You've just scored a big win for a client, on a case that's meaningful to you. That counts for a lot and could take you in a whole new direction."

Lauren rested her head on his shoulder. She didn't mean to unload about her problems on such a special night, but he was being so sweet, so comforting and encouraging. And she'd had no one to confide in and lay bare her vulnerability to this way. That was rare, too.

"Thanks for listening. I don't mean to bore you. But Maddie Belkin's situation did make me stop and think. I even applied for a position at a firm that specializes in defending women's rights."

He didn't answer right away. Then he said, "I had a feeling you'd say that sooner or later. Good for you. Find your bliss, as they say."

He was saying all the right things. Why did she feel a sudden tension between them? She lifted her head and tried to keep her voice light. "I might not even get it. I'm competing with people who are really experienced in this area."

"Don't count yourself out. Where's this job? In New York?"

She nodded and looked away, her gaze resting on the Christmas tree.

"So, you're still planning on going back?"

Lauren nodded again, not sure she trusted herself to speak. This was the part of the conversation she didn't want to have.

He kept his arm around her but pulled back a bit. "I never thought I'd being saying this to a woman again. Not for a long time. But I have a lot of feelings for you, Lauren. And now I don't know what to do about it. I know my wife never wanted me to be alone. And she wanted Phoebe to have a woman in her life. But if you're going back to New York, it's really hard to go forward. You and me, I mean. That is, if you feel the same?" he added quickly.

His expression was so hopeful and open, it filled her heart. She touched his cheek. "Since you asked, I do feel the same. I definitely do." Her quiet tone belied her high emotions.

He covered her hand with his own, then pressed her palm to his lips and sighed. "Where does that leave us, if you go back to New York? I don't see how it will work out. These long-distance things are so hard. And it's not just me," he added. "I have to think of Phoebe. I can't see her hurt and disappointed again by another loss. I see how great you are with her and how much she already loves you."

"I love her, too," Lauren admitted.

"That's just it. If you left tomorrow, it would be hard enough for her. What about two weeks or four weeks or ten weeks from now?" He shook his head with dismay. "I can't put her through that. She's made amazing progress here. Partly due to you, these last few weeks," he admitted. "I don't want to risk all that. I have to protect her."

"I understand. I wouldn't hurt her for the world. Or you," she added.

Her heart filled with a heavy sadness. She knew that what Cole said was true. Did it make any sense for them to get more involved than they were already if she was moving back to New York soon? It would be hard enough to leave Cole, no less Phoebe.

He didn't answer but met her gaze with a somber expression, as if he'd been holding out some slim hope that she'd change her mind and say that she would stay. But she couldn't do that. She'd been all through this with Joe. She couldn't stay here to be with him or to work at his firm. Was the answer to the question so different with Cole?

"I'm confused . . . I'm sorry," she said, suddenly feeling as if she might cry.

He rested his hand on her shoulder, then stroked her hair. "Hey, we don't have to talk about this now. I'm sorry for bringing it all up tonight. Everything was so perfect. What an idiot I am."

"Not at all. We needed to talk about it." She sat up and whisked her fingers under her eyes. "But we do have a little bit of Christmas Eve left," she reminded him. "So what about these presents, Santa? Is everything put together and wrapped?"

Cole grinned, looking grateful for the reminder. "Let's see . . . the toy store wrapped the LEGOs. And the boots are in a big bag with a bow on it. That will be fine."

"What about the two-wheeler with the tassels on the handles? And the bell and the basket for Wilbur? Does it need any putting together?"

He slapped his hand to his forehead. "The box is still in the barn.

Do you know anything about that stuff? I'm a disaster at following those diagrams."

Lauren just happened to be a whiz at putting together items that came in a million pieces with directions in four languages, amazing her many roommates over the years, and even her family.

"You're in luck. We reindeer hang around the workshop so much, we pick up a trick or two."

"I should have known." He smiled and gazed into her eyes, then leaned over and kissed her. The sensation was so sweet and full of longing, Lauren felt her breath stolen away. She never wanted it to end.

A snuffling, grunting sound broke the spell. She pulled back, and Cole did, too. Wilbur had wandered downstairs for a late-night snack and found the dish of cookies Phoebe had set out for Santa. He was on his hind legs, about to tip over a lamp table.

Cole jumped up and scooted him away. "Wilbur. That is not for you."

Lauren laughed at the sight. Whatever else she might say about this night, it had to be the most memorable Christmas Eve of her life.

CHAPTER SEVENTEEN

*L*ILLIAN HAD NOT SLEPT WELL. SHE BLAMED MOLLY WIL-
loughby's cooking, though she knew her tossing and turning and bad dreams had more to do with her worries about Ezra.
When she woke up, his side of the bed was empty, the covers tossed
aside.

She pulled on her robe and found her slippers, then headed downstairs. It was Christmas morning. She'd almost forgotten. He was
probably sitting by their tiny tree, waiting to unwrap the gifts they
exchanged. He was like a little boy about Christmas, though not this
year. She hoped that some of his good cheer had returned during the
night.

"Ezra? Merry Christmas," she called through the foyer when the
stair-chair came to a stop. She rose and made her way into the living
room. "Ezra? Are you down here?"

She did smell coffee. That was an encouraging sign. Was he possibly in the kitchen and didn't hear her? She hobbled through the
dining room, listening for morning sounds—the clatter of dishes and
cutlery. The swoosh of a newspaper page turning.

Nothing. A worrisome feeling began to take hold. In the kitchen, she found a cup, left half full on the counter.

And then she saw a note on the table. Ezra had remarkably legible handwriting for a doctor. Square, neat block letters. She picked up the sheet and read the short message.

Just had a promising call and "Left early, to find my dog," as Emily Dickinson nearly said. I believe I know where he is and hope to bring him home very soon.

—Ezra

Lily knew the verse well, about a morning walk to the sea. "I started Early—Took my Dog—" Clever, Ezra. High marks for that at least. She saw a local map on the table as well, one of the many he owned now, with all sorts of colored lines intersecting and various spots circled and dated. She sat and pushed it aside.

As sick as he'd been last night, he'd forced himself out into the cold for that dog. And on Christmas Day. He was lost to her. Totally and utterly lost.

She pulled her cell phone from the pocket of her robe and dialed Jessica. She imagined the family would be up and opening Christmas presents by now. She would be spoiling their morning. But what else could she do? Sit back and wait while Ezra froze to death? *If he hasn't already.*

Jessica came on the line quickly. "Merry Christmas, Mother. How's Ezra feeling? Well enough to come here later, I hope."

"You'll have to ask him yourself. If you can find him. He's disappeared again. Hunting for that dog. I'm not even sure when he left. There's a note on the table. It only says he got a call, and not even from whom, or where he was headed."

"Did he really go out already?" Even Jessica could not believe the extent of it, obviously.

Lillian detested redundant questions. "Would I be calling like this if he was here? I know it's Christmas morning and all that. But somebody needs to find him. You have multiple vehicles over there. And several able drivers." Lillian could tally up three—Sam's truck and a sporty car her grandson Darrell drove, and that ratty old van her daughter used to cart animals. All it was fit for, too. "I suggest an all-points alert, a real manhunt."

"Do you have any idea at all where he went, Mother? I wouldn't know where to start."

"How would I know?" Lillian snapped. "He's barely speaking to me lately, and I'm not a mind reader. Wherever stray dogs go," she offered, though if anyone knew where that was, the infernal creature would have been found weeks ago. "Wait . . . he left a map. He's been making calculations, like a treasure hunter," she murmured, looking over the squiggly lines through her reading glasses. "He's made a big X on Potter Orchard. I believe he's marked the date, too. Twelve twenty-five." Had she misread that chicken scratch just because she hoped it was true? "The orchard isn't far from you. It's as good a place as any to start."

"I'll leave right now. I'll let you know if I find him."

"*When* you find him, you mean," Lillian corrected her.

She could not tolerate any other outcome. "You realize this is all your fault, Jessica. You should have settled that dog with responsible owners who could have controlled him. Kept him contained."

"Teddy is not a criminal serving a life sentence. He's a dog," her daughter replied calmly. "I'd say if anyone's to blame, it's you, Mother. You could have simply agreed to keep him. You knew how much it meant to Ezra. Why was it so hard to bend a little and give that poor dog a home? And grant Ezra such a small request? He asks so little of you."

Her daughter's admonishment left her speechless. Finally, she replied, "Your opinion has been duly noted in the record." Then she hung up.

The stinging reproach echoed in her mind. It was actually a failure of her imagination. That was the problem. How could someone possibly care so much about a dog? She just didn't get it. If she had, it would never have come to this.

No help for that now. Life allowed for few, if any, do-overs. She'd learned that lesson long ago. She could only wait to see if her daughter found Ezra. Lost on Christmas morning, the same as that silly little hound.

Showered and dressed, Lillian roamed from room to room for what seemed like hours. She tried to read the newspapers. She tuned the radio to a program of famous choral groups singing Christmas music from the Baroque period, just as she and Ezra did every Christmas morning. But she quickly lost interest.

Finally, she heard activity at the side door. She hefted herself from an armchair and hobbled to the kitchen. She saw Ezra through the glass panes at the top of the door. Jessica stood behind him.

She felt weak with relief and also annoyed that no one had told her he was safe. "She found you. Thank heaven," Lillian greeted him.

"I wasn't lost. Not one bit. I was right about Teddy, too." He turned and looked back at the dog, who stood beside Jessica, secured to a leash. Lillian caught the creature's eye, and he wagged his tail furiously.

She looked away and tugged her cardigan around her. "Where was he?"

"At the orchard. It's deserted there this time of year, and he must have found a supply of food and water. Sophie Potter's dog was acting strangely the last few days, and she spotted a stray among the trees this morning."

Lillian had no great love for Sophie, though the rest of the congregation seemed to idolize the woman. She was so folksy and huggy, still cooking and baking things. At her age. It was ridiculous.

Sophie had been born on the orchard, and she ran it by herself, long after the death of her husband, Gus—an accomplishment Lillian *did* admire. Several years ago, she had sold the many acres to a young couple, all but a small plot where her house stood. With some outside help and visits from her family, she still lived there alone. With a dog, it appeared. That figured.

Lillian glanced at her daughter. "Are you coming in? You're letting all the heat out. I suppose you need to run home and prepare for your company?"

"I do. But we need to know what you've decided about Teddy."

"*I* need to know," Ezra clarified. His gaze was as stern as she'd ever seen it.

"Or what?" Lillian said, calling his bluff. Was Ezra going to leave her? Over this dog? The notion seemed crazy. Yet not beyond the range of possibility.

"Just tell me, Lillian. Yes or no. Will you agree to keep Teddy? He won't come in the house otherwise. Though I'm not sure I will either, without him."

Lillian felt as if she was riding in an elevator that suddenly skipped a few floors. She held on to the doorknob for support. Even Jessica seemed surprised by Ezra's ultimatum.

Lillian gathered her wits and raised her chin. If she was going down in defeat, she would do it with some dignity.

"I have given the matter more thought. If you must keep this animal, I relent. But there will be ground rules. And no exceptions. No licking, for one thing. Especially me."

"We can work on that. I've read a few training books. Jessica will help us sort it out."

Ezra's face glowed, as if someone had flipped a switch deep inside. Lillian stifled a sigh of relief. Not only had this confounded canine returned from out of the blue, but finally, so had her Ezra. *Welcome back*, she nearly said aloud. *How I've missed you.*

"Ground rules are not an unreasonable request," Ezra went on in a cheerful tone. "Mutually agreed upon," he clarified.

"Yes, yes. We'll bring in the finest legal minds to hammer it out. Whatever the cost."

"Very amusing, Lily. As usual." Ezra smiled, his reply without a trace of sarcasm.

He took the leash from Jessica and gazed at the dog. "Welcome home, my little friend. I bet you're ready for a splendid Christmas breakfast."

Lillian nearly groaned aloud. She rolled her eyes and shot Jessica a quelling stare. Jessica kissed her on the cheek quickly, then hurried off to her van.

Lillian couldn't really blame her daughter. Or even Ezra. This dog seemed fated to reside with them. Even she couldn't fight it anymore.

With his usual Christmas spirit, her husband headed for the living room to check the gifts under the tree. The dog trotted after him, tail wagging. She was about to remind Ezra of the rules, but she didn't have the heart, or the energy.

It appeared she would have to tolerate Teddy in the living room this morning. But only until she and Ezra were back to their usual routine, she promised herself. Though even she could not deny that all of her declarations and objections about this dog had so far been brushed to the wayside.

"What cannot be cured, must be endured," her mother used to say. In this case, fed, walked, and spoiled. All in all, it seemed a fair bargain for Ezra's return, she decided. The *real* Ezra. An unexpected but longed-for gift, delivered to her this morning.

CHAPTER EIGHTEEN

⌒⩗⌒

O N CHRISTMAS MORNING, LAUREN'S FAMILY WAS SO BUSY
tearing open presents—and squealing or shouting with
delight—that she was able to avoid most of the questions about why
she'd missed the Christmas Eve party. Most, but not all. Her sisters
Amanda and Jillian finally cornered her in her bedroom as she dressed
for the gathering at Jessica and Sam's house.

"So, it was that tall, dark, and cranky guy with the runaway animals? You said he was a jerk," Jillian reminded her.

Had she really said that about Cole? A handsome jerk, maybe. "He
was a pain when we first met. But once I got to know him . . ." She
paused. "I definitely had the wrong idea about him. Obviously, he's
not a jerk if I spent Christmas Eve with him and his little girl."

"This is the guy with the baby pig, right? Mom met him," Amanda
reported. "She definitely approves. And not just because he's such a
hunk."

Lauren felt herself blush, but she couldn't deny it. Cole was handsome in anyone's book.

"Wait a second." Jillian seemed confused. "He's a hunk with a baby pig? I totally get it now."

"And an adorable daughter." Amanda flopped onto Lauren's bed and paged through a magazine. "Mom said she's cute as a button."

"Her name is Phoebe, and she's cuter than an entire box of buttons." Lauren was brushing out her hair. She turned to Amanda. "What else did Mom say? She only met him for, like, thirty seconds."

Amanda peered at Jillian, and they shared a secret smile. Lauren guessed her romantic life been discussed at the party last night during her absence. She should have known that was going to happen. But it was still annoying.

"On second thought, I don't want to know."

"Amanda?" Gabriel, Amanda's husband, called from the hallway. "Did you see that new sweater you bought me? I wanted to wear it."

Amanda set the magazine aside and rose from the bed. "He thinks I have a tracking device for his belongings hidden in my body somewhere," she whispered with a grin.

"It's in a box on the dresser, Gabe," she called back as she left the room.

Jillian had been sitting in a chair and also came to her feet. She walked by Lauren and patted her shoulder. "I know we tease a lot, but we just want you to be happy, Lolo," she said, using the pet name she'd come up with when she was so little she couldn't pronounce the word "Lauren."

Lauren sighed. "I know. I'm trying to get there. But it's a little confusing right now."

She did want to talk to her sisters about her quandary—to stay here and see what might happen with her and Cole, or to find a new job in New York and go forward with her career. Why did she have to choose one or the other? It seemed so unfair.

"Hey, up there," her mother shouted from the foyer. "Time to head over to Aunt Jessica's. Your dad and I are leaving in five minutes. We have room in our car for two more."

"I'll ride with them," Jillian said. "How about you?"

"I think I'll take another car. I'm feeling a little tired. I might want to leave early." To come home and think. As if that was going to help anything.

A short time later, Lauren followed her family in a caravan to her aunt and uncle's house. The Queen Anne Victorian was beautifully decorated and looked like an image on a Christmas card, with its snow-covered, woodsy setting.

The gathering was much smaller, quieter, and calmer than last night's party, and Lauren felt much more relaxed, chatting with her cousins and even Ezra and Lillian.

Ezra had finally found his dog. Her aunt had told her the whole story, and Lauren was happy to see the pair united. He was so excited about being Teddy's official owner, he hadn't been able to leave the little hound home alone on Christmas Day. Even though her aunt had placed the dog with another, older couple in town a few weeks ago, they understood that Teddy would be much happier with Ezra and had even suggested that he keep him from now on. It seemed that they had many more pets—both dogs and cats—and would not miss one more. Of course, Jessica didn't mind Ezra bringing Teddy along. Her house was filled with furry creatures, so what did another four feet matter?

The dog lay at Ezra's side the whole night, looking very content. And so did Ezra. Though Lillian did not share the joy, Lauren noticed, her attitude a mixture of resignation and dismay. Resignation seemed to be winning out, however, which was probably a good thing for all.

Jessica always served a casual buffet with paper plates and plastic cutlery, a far cry from her mother's elaborate style. But there was still help needed in the kitchen after the meal. Lauren was loading the dishwasher with platters and glasses when her aunt came in to shoo her away.

"Oh, don't bother with that, honey. I'll take care of it later. There's a big Scrabble game shaping up out there. Don't you want to get in on it?"

"No one ever beats your mother," Lauren whispered. "She's the Venus Williams of Scrabble boards."

The comparison made Jessica laugh. "Don't I know it. Emily and I had to play in secret. She could spell rings around us."

"I don't doubt it," Lauren replied. "And I don't mind helping. It's a little easier than mucking out horse stalls."

Jess ran hot water into a pot to let it soak on the stove. "Yes, you've taken on some worse jobs around here. Speaking of horse stalls, how was your Christmas Eve with Cole and Phoebe?"

Lauren gave her a look and grinned. "There's a random jump in conversation."

Though not really, Lauren realized. She had spent an entire day with Cole here not long ago, and she knew Jessica was curious about the relationship, just like everyone else.

"I ended up there by accident. I had extra food after bringing some to your mom and Ezra. I only meant to stay for a few minutes, but we were having so much fun, it never seemed to be the right time to leave."

"That sounds like a lovely evening."

"It was." Aunt Jess wasn't like Lauren's mother. She wasn't the least bit pushy or nosy about personal matters, so Lauren thought she'd leave it at that.

"I could have invited them here today. There was plenty of food."

"I doubt they would have come. They had their own plans, and . . .

well, we had that talk that you don't like to have when you really like someone, but there are reasons why it might not work out."

"Oh, *that* talk." Jessica looked concerned. "Why won't it work out? You look so happy at the mere mention of his name."

Did she really? How corny was that? She was mortified.

Though she knew it was true.

"I have plans to move back to New York. I've been looking for a job there, and I have a big interview scheduled. I've already talked to a few people at this firm over the phone. This one is probably the last."

"Sounds exciting." Something in her aunt's tone belied her reply. "When is it?"

"Next Wednesday, the thirtieth. I'll drive down early in the morning. The interview isn't until four. I have plenty of time. I'm going to visit a college friend while I'm there, too. That will be fun."

Lauren was looking forward to seeing Shela Spinner. They'd roomed together for years, and Shela had also settled in New York after studying tax law.

"Will you stay down there for New Year's Eve?"

"I think so. Shela wants me to go to a party with her." Shela was unattached now, too, which would make it easy to stay over with her and hang out. Maybe even through the weekend.

"If you get this job, you'll move back to New York?"

"Yes, I think so. Cole understands. At least he says he does. He's very supportive about my work. But he doesn't see how we can go forward with me living down there. And there's Phoebe to think about. I'd never do anything to hurt her."

"Of course not," Jessica said sympathetically. "Now that you mention it, I had that same talk with your uncle. A few times."

Lauren was surprised to hear that. "You did? Gee, I thought it was love at first sight for you two."

"It was," her aunt replied. "Though it took me a while to realize that. I also had firmly set plans that I wanted to carry through on. I'd been living in Boston and had only come back to Cape Light temporarily, to help take care of my mother after her stroke. I never planned to stay here more than a few months. But I couldn't resist dating your uncle once he asked me out. When things started to get serious, I told him it wouldn't work out because I had to go back to my 'real life.'"

Lauren was surprised again. "How did he like that?"

Jessica laughed. "He didn't like it at all. But I'd never imagined marrying a guy like Sam. You know, the rough-and-ready type. The men I usually dated could barely change a light bulb, much less build a house. My mother didn't approve of him either. She made a real fuss. And coming back to live in the town I grew up in? That was last thing I wanted. It felt like . . . well, a failure."

Lauren felt exactly the same. At least, she had when Joe had courted her and asked her to join his law firm.

"What made you decide to stay?" Lauren was curious to hear Jessica's secret. She'd obviously made the right decision. She seemed so happy with her life.

Her aunt's expression turned thoughtful. "The situation seemed hopeless. We broke up, and even when I tried to make up, your uncle thought I wanted something more. 'A guy with a briefcase and a Mercedes,' I think he said. That was the kind of guy I'd been dating, and he was right, in a way. Your uncle was not what I had planned. He stood out like . . . a unicorn," she added with a laugh.

Lauren could identify with that, too.

"I thought we were through, and I accepted a job in Boston. I was all packed and ready to move away."

Lauren did recall the summer her aunt and uncle had been dating, though she had been far too young to understand what was going on between them. "I remember now. Your cat had kittens and you had to give them away before you left town. You talked my mom into taking two of them for me and Jill."

Her aunt laughed. "You talked your mom into that. We knew you were going to be a lawyer, even then. I was moving the next day, but a huge storm changed that plan. Power was down all over town and we all went to the Clam Box. The whole town was there."

"I remember that, too," Lauren said. "Digger ran in and said Uncle Sam had been in an accident?"

Her aunt nodded. "Sam had come out to this house, which was an unholy wreck back then, to make sure it hadn't blown away. His truck skidded on the way back to town and he drove into a tree. I rushed to the hospital, imagining the worst. Luckily, he wasn't seriously hurt. We both admitted that we'd been very stubborn and foolish. Worried about all the wrong things. We knew that we belonged together, no matter what. After that, everything fell into place perfectly."

"A happy ending, like in a romance novel," Lauren said.

"Just about. We were lucky. We got a second chance. It doesn't always work that way. Emily gave me good advice about Sam, too. She said, 'Love has no pride.' I think that's true," her aunt added in a wistful tone. "If you love someone, you owe it to yourself and to them to let them know. Even if it's hard or seems pointless to tell them. Love comes into our lives so rarely. It's a shame and a waste to let it go unacknowledged."

Lauren took the words to heart. Was she in danger of doing that? Was Cole the one for her? She hardly knew him. How could she be sure? But somehow, deep inside, she suspected that she did know the answers to those questions, and just wasn't willing to face them yet.

"That's a beautiful story and good advice, Aunt Jess. But my life is way more complicated. Maybe I'll get this job and my choice will be decided for me."

"Will it really, honey?" Her aunt held her gaze, her blue eyes bright and steady. "You said it yourself. It's more complicated than that."

Lauren didn't answer. She knew that was true. She would be fooling herself to deny it.

IN THE DAYS FOLLOWING CHRISTMAS, LAUREN SPENT TIME AT JOE'S firm, clearing up the details on the Dendur Software agreement and a few other loose ends from matters she'd handled. She had a few phone calls with Cole but didn't see him, even though he invited her to drop by while his sister and her family were visiting.

She had been surprised, all things considered, and was very tempted to accept. But then she thought better of it. What was the point of meeting his family? It might even feel awkward.

Every day she spent apart from Cole and Phoebe, it seemed more likely she would leave Cape Light, if not for the job she was trying for right now, then for some other job, and very soon.

The realization was painful. But it would hurt much more if things went further. Like meeting his family or spending more time with them while Phoebe was on her school vacation. She dreaded saying goodbye when the time came. To Phoebe especially. She wouldn't understand.

Don't kid yourself. Saying goodbye to Cole won't be any picnic either.

She pushed the thoughts aside as much as she could and focused on preparing for her interview. She set out for New York early Wednesday morning, with way too many clothes. Two spare interview outfits might be a little excessive, she realized as she hefted a heavy hanging bag to the car, along with a rolling suitcase and a briefcase.

But even if she had taken all the clothes in her closet, she would have still felt nervous, excited, and scared. On the drive down, her favorite psyching-up tunes filled the car from playlists prepared for the gym. She alternated those with podcasts that taught techniques to cultivate calm, focus, and listening skills.

Shela had left a key with her doorman, and Lauren was grateful for a place to change into her interview outfit and apply just the right amount of makeup.

After living in her parents' big house for the past few weeks, she was shocked by the apartment's tiny Manhattan dimensions, though she knew the rent for the one-bedroom in the East Side neighborhood, with a kitchen smaller than her mother's pantry, was astronomical.

There was an awesome view from the living room, of the East River and the RFK Bridge. And from the narrow terrace at the back of the apartment, even a bit of the George Washington Bridge could be seen, especially at night when the skyline was a mosaic of brilliant lights and shadows against the night sky. Even in the afternoon, when she stared out at it, she realized she was truly back, and all that it meant to her.

I can make it here, she coached herself. *I can and I will.*

SHE WAS INTERVIEWED AT A LONG TABLE IN A MEETING ROOM BY three high-level attorneys at the firm, two women and a man. She'd only met one of the women so far, during a video chat interview on her computer. Isabel Suarez was in her late forties or early fifties, Lauren guessed. Her personality was low-key but still projected strength and energy. Perhaps it was simply confidence, and being comfortable with herself, Lauren thought.

The conversation started off slowly. It was hard for Lauren to read their reactions to her answers. She tried very hard to listen and not make any dumb jokes or let her mouth run away with itself.

Sometimes, she failed. Especially when asked about the Belkin case, which she'd spoken about in prior interviews.

"Were you satisfied with the settlement offered by Dendur Software? Why not push for more? Or bring this case to court? It appears there were ample grounds for a favorable decision," the male attorney challenged her.

"That's a good question. I've asked myself the same thing," Lauren replied honestly. "Maybe because we were all so surprised by such a large offer coming in so quickly? My clients were pleased and didn't want to negotiate further or take it to court. I didn't advise them to do that either. Nor did the head of the firm I was working for," she added. "If I had it to do over, I probably would have handled it differently and looked for even more women who experienced the same treatment at Dendur. I have things to learn about this area of the law," she added. "But I feel I did some good for Madeleine Belkin and her colleagues. If given the chance, I know that I can be a strong advocate and find justice for many more women."

The trio interviewing her exchanged glances. Did they think she'd gone over the top with her *Ms. Smith Goes to Washington* moment? Lauren sure hoped not.

A few moments later, the meeting was ended and Lauren was shown to the lobby by Isabel, who would be her boss if she were hired there.

"Thank you so much for coming in today, Lauren. We didn't expect to keep you so long. We appreciate your time," Isabel said. They were the pat phrases that ended most meetings of this type, though delivered very warmly, Lauren thought. *Or am I grasping at straws here?*

"Thank you for meeting with me. I'm very interested in being part of this firm. I'd be happy to answer any other questions, or talk with you further, anytime."

Isabel smiled and nodded. "Thank you, Lauren. I think we'll be making a decision soon. I'll be in touch."

Isabel headed through the wooden doors to the office area. Lauren waited for the elevator to come. The bell pinged and the doors slid open. A young woman stepped out and walked to the reception desk, where Lauren heard her give her name.

"I have an appointment with Isabel Suarez, for an interview?" she told the young man behind the desk.

"Have a seat. I'll let her know you're here," he said.

Lauren stepped into the elevator and eyed her competition. She had felt good right after leaving the interview, but now, she wasn't so sure. What did Isabel mean by "soon"? Certainly not before the start of the new year, Lauren figured as the elevator descended. How many more promising young attorneys would they be meeting with?

She pushed through the building's revolving door and found herself on a noisy, crowded street. She'd forgotten what rush hour in Midtown was like. She quickly stepped back before she was knocked over by a stream of people leaving offices and heading for subways and buses. Cars honked and brakes screeched.

She wanted to call someone, vent about the meeting, and hear a reassuring voice say, "Don't worry, they'll pick you. If they don't, it's their loss and you'll find something even better."

Her sisters or her mother would certainly say all the right things. But she didn't want to call them. She wanted to call Cole.

She took a breath, put on her city face, and plunged into the crowd. She'd be meeting Shela soon at their favorite pub for drinks and dinner. A few other friends might join them. That would have to do for now.

*   *   *

LAUREN SLEPT THROUGH HER ALARM. SHE WOKE ON THE FOLDOUT couch in Shela's living room, feeling thirsty and confused. Her friend had left for work hours ago. She would be at the office until five, then come straight home. The plan was to hang out awhile doing hair and makeup and all that, then head to the New Year's Eve party around nine or even ten.

Which seemed very late to her for going anywhere these days. Last night Lauren realized she'd fallen out of shape for city socializing. The evening had turned into more drinks than dinner, and Lauren was feeling the effects this morning. At this rate, would she even make it to midnight to ring in the New Year?

She pushed the covers aside and sat up, then made herself a cup of coffee in Shela's tiny kitchen. She hoped a long shower and a workout in the building's fitness center would get her back on track. And maybe some shopping. Though it was hard to justify running up her credit cards when she didn't have much of a salary right now, and no job to dress up for.

But Shela had ordered her to run straight to Bloomingdale's today, to take advantage of the post-Christmas markdowns.

"That's what I would do. They're giving the clothes away. You won't believe it."

I didn't buy one thing for myself this Christmas, she rationalized. *And I'll have a job soon. I deserve a new pair of shoes at least?*

She weighed the pros and cons as she scanned the fridge for some breakfast. She saw a lime, a scallion, and a take-out container of something that looked like it belonged across town in the Museum of Natural History. Under a glass case.

Finally, a cup of yogurt. The obvious choice. She opened it and ate it, careful not to look at the expiration date. Then she took a shower and headed to the gym.

A few hours later, after a workout, a swim, and a soak in the hot tub, she was feeling mostly herself again. Lauren was back in the apartment, dressing for her quick and disciplined shopping trip, when her phone buzzed.

Isabel's name came up on the screen, and Lauren took a deep breath before answering. *She could be calling about anything,* Lauren reminded herself. *You may have missed a question on one of the ten thousand forms the human resources department sent you.*

But the senior attorney was not calling about that. The message was short and sweet. Very sweet. "We've made our decision, Lauren. A little sooner than expected. I'm happy to offer you the position," Isabel said.

"Really? That is such amazing news. Thank you." Lauren felt her knees go weak. Her possible future boss went on to describe the salary, starting date, and other necessary footnotes. Lauren barely heard a word.

"You should see an email by the end of the day confirming all the details. With the long weekend coming, we wanted to let you know today."

"I appreciate that. And I'm really very excited. And honored," Lauren said honestly. She swallowed hard, unsure if she should continue, though something urged her to say more. "I'm going to think about all this and get back to you right after the New Year. I hope that's okay."

"Of course. Take all the time you need." Lauren could tell from her tone that Isabel had expected Lauren to accept the job on the spot. But slowing things down to her own pace showed that she was a good attorney, didn't it? Though Lauren knew that wasn't the reason at all.

A short time later, Lauren was packed and heading down to a parking lot to pick up her car. She called Shela, feeling sorry to interrupt her work, but this time a text wouldn't do.

"Hey, what's up? Finding everything okay?"

"I'm good. But I need to get back home. I'm sorry to run out on you like this, but I can't stay for the party tonight."

"Is something wrong? I hope everything's all right with your family?"

"Everyone's fine. It's just me. There's something I need to do, and . . . it can't wait. I don't think I'd be much fun tonight anyway. I think my party meter hit the limit last night," she admitted with a laugh.

"I get it. No worries. It's about that guy with the pig, right?"

Lauren sighed. Was everyone in her life going to refer to Cole as "the guy with the pig" forever? Seemed so. "It is. And, you won't believe this, but I got that job. They called a little while ago and made an offer."

Shela squealed—worthy of any squeal of years past. Lauren pictured her bouncing in her leather desk chair. "Lauren, that is awesome! Why didn't you say that sooner? Now I really don't get why you're going back. Isn't this what you wanted?"

Lauren couldn't answer. The valet had brought her car, and she automatically exchanged the keys for a tip, then slipped behind the wheel.

"I thought I did. But now that I got it, I'm not sure, Shela. I'm not sure at all. Listen, I have to drive now. I'll call you later. Thanks for everything."

"It would have been fun to tear up the town with you, Willoughby, but I'll manage on my own." Lauren was sure her friend would, too. "You're a complete ninny, but I love you."

"Love you, too," Lauren replied, carefully easing out into traffic.

"I bet you never made it to Bloomie's, either," Shela scolded.

"Nope. But I downloaded the app. I'll catch up on the sales while I'm driving. I have plenty of time." Of course, she was teasing.

They laughed and said goodbye again, and Lauren was on her way to New England.

She was soon over the bridge and made good time through the Bronx. She had started out early enough to miss the worst traffic. With any luck, she would reach Cape Light by five or so, if she made the minimum of stops and pushed the speed limit.

The decision had been impulsive, but once the thought had come over her, she couldn't fight it. Maybe the only way to find out what she really wanted was to sort it out with Cole now that the choices were clearly set before her?

She wasn't really sure what she hoped to accomplish by going back. All she knew was that she had to see him. Not tomorrow, not two days from now. But as soon as possible.

What if he had plans tonight? A party somewhere. Or a date?

Lauren brushed the scenarios from her mind. She'd get there early enough to catch him before he went out. Or she'd just crash his date and spill her guts? In her usual fashion?

"Love has no pride," she recalled her aunt saying. It didn't seem to have any common sense either, she reflected. The wild ride seemed crazy. But totally compelling.

Her estimated time of arrival was very much on track, she noticed, as she passed the exits for Peabody and Salem. She felt bleary-eyed and hungry but pushed on. Only half an hour or slightly more to go, and it was just past three. She would have to stop somewhere and freshen up as much as possible before she went to see Cole, she decided. But not home. Too many questions. She'd face those soon enough.

Her phone buzzed, and she saw Joe's name and number on the

screen. He was probably calling with a question about one of the cases she'd been working on.

"Hey, Lauren, how's it going?" he greeted her. "I heard they welcomed you back to the city with a sign in Times Square."

She knew he was only teasing, but there was tiny note of derision in his voice as well. "That's right. Just in time for the big crowd there tonight to watch the ball drop."

"Seriously, how was the interview? Did it go well?"

"I had a good feeling about it, but I'm not sure what the results will be," she said as honestly as she could.

He didn't seem to notice she was in her car, and she decided not to tell him she was driving back. For a variety of reasons.

"I have some news for you. After that little piece in the *Globe* came out about Maddie's case, we've been flooded with inquiries." A business reporter from the *Boston Globe* who specialized in the tech industry had written an article about the claims against Dendur Software for discriminatory practices against women—and about the big settlement. It had appeared online, too, and had been picked up by other outlets that covered the industry.

"Potential clients, mainly women, who want to make similar claims against employers," Joe continued. "I never pictured myself as a defender of women's rights. But I'll sure feel a lot prouder about it than fighting for the rights of golf course sod."

Lauren laughed at his comparison. "I agree."

"My point is, any chance at all of you handling this area of the practice? Even for a few months more? I know it's not your specialty, but you certainly have a talent for it, and I'd pretty much leave you alone. Maybe the idea is a little tempting for you? You don't have to answer now," he quickly added. "I just wanted you to know what was going on. I'll need to refer some of these women to other firms. But I definitely need a new attorney to cover this territory. Maddie really wants me to."

Lauren was interested to hear that coda to his message. Her intuition had been on target about those two.

"I will think about it, Joe. I'll let you know soon."

"That sounds perfect. Enjoy your New York visit, Lauren. Happy New Year."

It had been enlightening and it was over, she nearly told him. But she stopped herself just in time. "Same to you, Joe. Give my best to Maddie."

"I will," he promised. She could tell he was smiling when he replied.

The call had surprised her. And confused her, offering even more possibilities. Was this one of those "jump off the cliff and wings will sprout" moments? Or was it the gift that arrives in a shape you didn't imagine, just like Reverend Ben talked about in his Christmas Eve sermon?

Half-dazed from the long drive, Lauren knew it was not the best time to figure it all out. All she knew for sure was that her future looked a lot different right now than it had twenty-four hours ago. Maybe she did have more choices than "stay for Cole" or "leave for her career."

When she reached the cottage, the sun had already slipped behind a fringe of trees just beyond the barn, tinting the horizon with a rosy glow. She saw the red truck parked nearby and a light on in the sitting room. She felt so nervous standing at the door, she nearly ran back to her car, but she finally forced herself to knock.

During the long drive back, she had practiced what she might say, but all her well-planned words flew out of her head as the door swung open and Cole stood there staring at her.

"Lauren, I thought you were in New York."

"I was."

"I thought you had that interview and you were going to stay a few days."

"I had the interview. But I came back."

"So I see."

She swallowed hard. He wasn't making this easy, was he?

"Can I talk to you? For just a minute or two?"

"Sure, come on in." He stepped aside and she entered. He still looked puzzled. "I was just about to pick up Phoebe. She's at a playdate."

Lauren rubbed her hands together, then put them down at her sides. "This won't take long."

He didn't invite her to sit down, and she felt awkward doing that without the offer. He stood at the door, his arms crossed over his chest. He wore a denim shirt with a black T-shirt underneath and looked very . . . woodsy. And very handsome. And very unlike all the men she'd seen in New York over the last two days.

"How did the interview go? Did you hear anything yet?"

"They made me an offer." She watched his reaction.

He nodded but didn't smile. "Good for you. When do you start?"

"I didn't accept it yet."

He looked surprised. "But you're planning to. I mean, that's what you came to tell me. You came to say goodbye, right?"

She shook her head, her words catching in her throat. "No. That's not why. I came because I had some time to think. Well, not like that exactly. I really didn't think very much at all. It's just when I heard that I got the job, it didn't seem to matter as much as I thought it would. I thought if they wanted me, I'd be jumping for joy and say yes on the spot. But I didn't. I just couldn't."

"Why not? I don't understand." He walked closer and stared down at her. She could have reached out and touched him, but she didn't dare. Not yet.

"It didn't feel right anymore. This thing that I really, *really* wanted—getting another big job and moving back to New York, showing myself and everyone else I wasn't a failure . . . I thought it would just drop into some empty spot in a big jigsaw puzzle that I call my life and make everything perfect and complete."

She looked up at him, struggling to put her complicated feelings and fuzzy insights into words. "But between the time I left New York and went back there, something changed. All the pieces on the table got moved around. This solution I was so sure about? It doesn't fit."

He tilted his dark head to one side, listening. "Why is that, do you think?"

"Because I met you. And Phoebe. You two mixed it all up." She sighed and met his dark gaze. "Thanks a lot, pal," she added, finally making him smile. "I don't know, maybe my imagination is too limited? Wasn't saving Wilbur something to be proud of? As big as any win in a law firm?"

"Phoebe and Wilbur would say so," he agreed quietly. A warm, familiar light had returned to his gaze, giving her courage to go on.

"The thing is, I thought the city was my world, the place where I belonged. But I don't think so anymore. Maybe my world is wherever you and Phoebe are. I know I won't be happy away from the two of you. No matter how many lawsuits I win or big settlements I negotiate. If I stay, will you give us one more chance?"

Cole looked shocked for a moment. Then his face lit up with pure joy. He stepped forward and took her in his arms, practically lifting her off her feet. She felt as if they were back on the pond, spinning together on the ice.

"Would I give you a chance? I've twisted my brain in knots trying to figure out how we could make this work. If you took that job, I thought Phoebe and I might move, too. To be near you. I drove my poor sister crazy when she was here, talking about you."

"You did?" Lauren was horrified. "Nothing like good advance press." She hoped Cole's sister didn't despise her now for torturing her poor brother.

"She was glad to hear that I met someone who could make me care so much again." He paused. "I'm just worried about you. Is this going to be enough? Are you going to regret turning down that offer?"

"Not for a minute. I was so dumb to think it was just a choice between here or the city. There are so many possibilities for me. I see that now. And a real relationship will always require give-and-take. And some risk. How can I ever feel shortchanged when I'll truly have it all? You, Phoebe . . . and an adorable pig?"

His wide smile and dark, shining eyes were all the answer she needed. Then he said, "Lauren Willoughby, you're the last thing I ever expected. But I love you. More than I can ever say."

Lauren felt as if she'd just been struck by lightning. In a good way, she decided. "Funny, I feel the same about you."

Before she could say more, Cole dipped his head down and kissed her long and hard.

"That's one way to shut me up," she whispered against his lips, then pulled him close again.

IT WAS ALMOST DINNERTIME ON THURSDAY. ESTRELLA HAD GONE home early but had left a platter of baked chicken with string beans and plain roasted potatoes in the refrigerator—Lillian's favorite meal. Ezra wasn't in the mood for it. He wanted something special for dinner. After all, it was New Year's Eve.

"New Year's Eve. Who cares? It's just another faux holiday. Cooked up by big business. So arbitrary. Many cultures celebrate the New Year on a completely different date," Lillian reminded her husband.

"I understand, dear. But I see no harm in it. I think it's good luck to ring in the new with a special meal and a toast or two," Ezra said. "I found a very fine bottle of wine in the rack, and we'll order Chinese food. And watch the festivities on TV?"

She sighed. "If you insist. I doubt I'll last until midnight."

"We'll see," he replied pleasantly as he set off to track down the wine.

Teddy followed him everywhere, shadowing his step as if he were a toy dog, pulled on a string. Lillian thought it was uncanny. It had been useless to try to put any limits on the dog's whereabouts in the house. If he was kept from Ezra, he peered at them from a distance, looking forlorn, and even whined a bit. Lillian couldn't bear the sound. And she didn't dare risk Ezra getting into another snit.

All she knew was that for the past week, ever since Ezra had found the mutt and brought him in, her husband had been more cheerful than . . . well, Mr. Rogers.

If Ezra wanted Chinese food for dinner and needed to watch some silly, simpering newscasters standing out in the cold all night in the middle of New York's theater district, what was it to her? She'd work on her crossword puzzle.

A few hours later, there they were, seated in the living room. Ezra had set up tray tables and portioned out the take-out food. Lillian didn't mind the soup, though she always left the wonton dumpling.

Teddy sat between them on a special couch cover Ezra had found in the pet shop in town. Who could imagine in their wildest dreams that she, of all people, would tolerate sharing her antique silk brocade sofa with a dog? She certainly would have bet the house against that.

She had to admit, the dog possessed remarkable self-control, especially tonight, with the exotic foods right under his snout.

He lay between them, like a stone lion, staring at the TV as if he actually understood what was on the screen.

It was fascinating to observe him. Though she'd never admit it to Ezra.

Ezra poured the wine and gave her a glass. "Here's to the New Year, Lily. Good health and many happy adventures for us all."

Lillian liked the health part, but the word "adventures" made her wary. She clinked her glass anyway.

She sipped her wine and gazed down at Teddy. "I suppose the dog was your adventure this year. Is that what you mean?"

"Maybe. An adventure with a happy ending," he noted. "And, in no small part, thanks to you."

"Me? What did I have to do with it? I thwarted your efforts at every step."

"Which made me all the more determined and helped me realize how much Teddy means to me. You relented in the end."

"So I did," she agreed, giving herself some credit. Though the alternative, Ezra's disaffection, had been too ghastly to consider.

"You know, Lily, Anatole France said, 'Until one has loved an animal, a part of one's soul remains unawakened.'" I think that goes double for dogs," Ezra reasoned. "I hope Teddy is growing on you, a little?"

"Not yet." She sighed, worn down by Ezra's relentless optimism. What did the man expect? She'd been subjected to this animal in the house, against her will, for only a week so far. But she patted the dog's head very lightly and quickly anyway. He panted in answer, as if to thank her.

"I suppose it's not entirely out of the question. At some point." She paused. "Can he eat some of this pork dumpling? Or it is too rich for him? It does seem a shame to waste perfectly good food."

Ezra's face broke into a wide smile. "I wouldn't feed him wonton dumplings every night. But in this case, I think giving him a bite or two is the perfect way to start the new year. For Teddy. And for you."

Ezra seemed to think that by this time next year that silly dog would be sitting on her lap and she'd be hand-feeding him tasty tidbits of who knew what sort of delicacies.

She held her tongue. From what she'd seen lately, stranger things could happen around here. She knew a lot at her age, though even she had to concede that she didn't know everything. Perhaps, overall, that was a good thing.

Lucy often met Reverend Ben at the homes of her patients who lived in the village. Especially those who had just been released from the hospital. On Saturday morning, she was leaving the house of a new patient, who lived near the harbor on Bayview Street, when she noticed Reverend Ben walking her way, his black Bible tucked under his arm.

"Good morning, Lucy," he said as they met on the sidewalk near her car. "I see we're involved in the changing of the guard again today. With the patient's medical needs attended to, it's my turn for the spiritual."

"Right on time, Reverend. As usual."

"How were your holidays? It was nice to see all of your children in church on Christmas Eve."

Lucy smiled. "We loved having them all at home, even for a few days. But I'm happy to be back at work again." New Year's Day had fallen on a Friday. School and work started again for most people on

Monday. But she'd been happy to get back to her normal schedule today. "I love the holidays, but I'm always glad when they're over."

"It's definitely my busy season. I'm glad when the merrymaking is over, too. We had the movie crew around this year. That made it feel even more hectic."

"It did," Lucy agreed, growing a bit quieter. "I liked your Christmas sermon, Reverend. It hit home with me. I had a surprise gift. Well, two, actually. A beautiful necklace that Charlie gave me." She shook her head, still amazed by the gift. "And the other was . . . oh, nothing you could lay a hand on, or even describe easily. But it was just as you said. Something I'd never imagined or asked for. But exactly what I needed, in a way." She paused. "I'm sorry, I'm rambling like a madwoman and not making any sense at all."

He shook his head, his blue eyes soft with kindness. "You're not rambling. And I understand."

She wasn't sure how much more to say, but she felt she owed him a tiny bit of clarity. Without going into any details.

"Someone wanted to apologize to me, for something that happened between us a long time ago. I wouldn't even hear them out at first. For a lot of reasons," she said quickly, knowing a big part of it was wanting to punish Craig. "When I finally did, I felt so much lighter. Older, too, putting away that chapter of my young life. But in a good way," she added. "It all came out of the blue. Nothing I ever asked for or thought I wanted. Or thought I needed. But it was the best Christmas gift I've gotten in long time . . . Except for the necklace from Charlie," she added. "That was remarkable, too."

Reverend Ben smiled and touched her hand. Something in his expression gave her the feeling that he knew who she was talking about. Was that even possible?

You're being paranoid. And silly. How could he possibly know, or even suspect?

"It sounds like you had a very interesting Christmas."

"I did, Reverend. I took a long look at my life and all the choices that got me here. I know now that even the most difficult times happened for a reason. And I wouldn't change a thing."

Reverend Ben smiled and gently touched her hand. "I'd say you're a very wise and fortunate woman for learning that. God bless you, Lucy. Now, and all through the new year."

Lucy thanked him and wished him the same, then went on with her day. Maybe it was just her imagination, but she did feel as if she was seeing the world differently now, her spirit free from shadows and full of light.

She had one person to thank for that. And God. In her heart, she thanked them both.